ON EARTH AS IT IS IN HEAVEN

Christine Kennevan

Pleasant Word
A Division of WINEPRESS PUBLISHING

Printed in the United States of America

Packaged by Pleasant Word, a division of WinePress Publishing, PO Box 428, Enumclaw, WA 98022. The views expressed or implied in this work do not necessarily reflect those of Pleasant Word, a division of WinePress Publishing. Ultimate design, content, and editorial accuracy of this work are the responsibilities of the author.

Unless otherwise noted, all Scriptures are taken from the King James Version of the Bible.

ISBN 1-57921-655-2
Library of Congress Catalog Card Number: 2003104049

Dedicated to my mother, the Proverbs 31 woman, who gave her daughters a road map to follow, a level to aspire to, and the confidence to know that in the end it will make a difference.

Table of Contents

Chapter 1

Did You Say Baby?

"Simon, who is that crying? Is that you?" Mrs. Kemp asked her son, the youngest of six Mennonite children. She turned to her husband, who was driving, and asked, "Would you slow down a little, or roll up your window? I cannot hear what is going on back there."

"A baby is in the back of the van, Mamma," Simon answered.

"What? What is in the back of the van?" she asked again, this time turning around in her seat.

"A baby."

"What! Did you say a baby!?" she exclaimed.

"Yah, a baby," Simon repeated, adding, "I think it is a baby girl."

The Kemps' Chevy van swerved to the side of the road. Simon grabbed his straw hat. Everyone braced themselves for a sudden stop. Mr. Kemp tried not to stop too quickly in case what he had heard was actually true. The wheels rumbled to a cautious stop on the gravel shoulder of the highway. He opened the door and swung his long legs out of the van, his mud-caked boots striking down hard on the gravel, crunching under his feet. He walked quickly to the back of the van, opened the heavy old van doors, and looked wide-eyed into the van. Mrs. Kemp turned to see her husband's face from the front seat. Mr. Kemp began to grin, "Well, would you look at that! It is a baby!" he said. "Ahh, and so small she is! Sara, come, see! Hurry!" Mrs. Kemp opened her door. She would have liked to move faster but Mrs. Kemp had an irresistible penchant for dumplings.

Mr. Kemp stood at the side of the road with his hands on his hips, looking like a misplaced pilgrim with his black felt hat, full beard, black pants and black jacket. He caught hold of his hat as a truck passed beside him on the road.

Six curious brothers and sisters peered over the back seat, all vying for a better position. They began to whisper, "Where did it come from?" "I wonder if it is lost." "It doesn't look like one of us." Lying on the floor was a tiny baby, no more than a few months old. She was wearing a homemade tie-dyed shirt, a cloth diaper, plastic pants with a small tear near the diaper pin, no shoes, no socks, and no blanket. She wore a beaded bracelet on her ankle. Pinned to her shirt was a pacifier tied to a piece of blue ribbon, decorated with a hand-painted peace sign and bobbing rhythmically in her mouth. The baby yawned, and the pacifier fell to the van floor beside her. Mr. Kemp picked it up to inspect it for dirt, blew on it, and put it back into the baby's mouth with his sun-weathered hand. Although he knew his touch was much too rough for such a little one, he couldn't resist brushing the baby's soft, white legs with the back of his hand then running his fingers through her dark curls.

Mrs. Kemp joined her husband at the back of the van. The wind blew back the brim of her green sunbonnet. Her freckles were more noticeable than usual after spending the afternoon in the hot sun at the fairgrounds. The cool September breeze was a pleasant reminder, however, that fall was on its way. "Oh my sweet Jesus in heaven, how did this happen? And so cute! Look at her, Pappa! Why didn't you children say something sooner? Her mamma is probably so worried and looking everywhere for her."

"I'm sorry, Mamma," said Simon, three years old. He sighed. It seemed everything was his fault lately.

Rachel, eight years old, spoke up, "It isn't your fault, Simon, her mamma's not looking for her."

"Now how do you know that?" asked Mrs. Kemp.

"Look, there is a note." Rachel pointed.

On the floor next to the baby was a note card with a picture of a stork carrying an infant in its beak. The card looked aged around the edges, as if it had belonged to someone's grandmother, as if it had been sitting in a drawer for quite some time. In big bold letters over the stork's head was written: CONGRATULATIONS.

Mr. Kemp smiled, "It seems we have won a prize." He opened the card and began to read: "My name is Vincent."

"It is a boy!" exclaimed Simon.

Mr. Kemp continued reading slowly, "I was born on April 14. I am five months old. My mommy can't take care of me anymore, so would you please take me? I won't cry much if you play this tape. Thank you."

"What tape? Does anybody see a tape?" asked Mr. Kemp.

Simon pointed, "Look, there is a lady's purse." It had slid underneath the back seat. Mr. Kemp used a tire iron to reach it. Everyone watched in suspense as Mr. Kemp caught the purse by the strap and lifted it out from under the seat. He flipped back the embossed leather flap and looked inside. There was a young lady's driver's license, an empty baby bottle, and a cassette tape.

Mr. Kemp inspected the tape and read, "Lou Rawls' Greatest Hits."

Then he looked at the picture on the license. He saw a young girl who didn't look old enough to have a baby. Her hair was blonde, long, and straight. "She looks like a townie," he said, passing the license to his wife.

"What kind of mother is this?" asked Mrs. Kemp. "She has given away her baby with no shoes, no diapers, no milk?" Mrs. Kemp frowned down at the picture.

"Maybe that is why she gave him to us," said Mr. Kemp. "All of those things cost money, Sara. Maybe she had no money, so she gave him to us," he suggested.

Mrs. Kemp looked up at her husband a little stunned. The reality of the situation was beginning to settle in. She saw that heavy-lidded smile in her husband's eyes. "You say that as if it is all settled and done," she said, feeling slightly panicked.

"Well Sara?" He waited.

She looked at him with frustration. She thought, the man is so naive. You would think we just found a stray animal, not a baby. And besides, I am not ready to take on more responsibility. Six children are already more than I can handle. In exasperation, she opened her mouth to answer him but then changed her mind. She shook her head with a sigh as she reached for the sleeping baby, muttering something under her breath.

"Can we keep him?" the children chimed in.

"He is not a puppy, he is a baby," she replied, steadfastly maintaining the voice of reason. "We'll take him to the police, and they will tell us what is to be done. They will turn him over to the right people, and our job will be finished." Mrs. Kemp lifted the limp, sleepy baby into her arms. His feet felt cold. "And no blanket," she muttered as she tried to shelter him from the wind. "You poor little angel baby," she said, nuzzling his soft cheek against hers.

On the way to the police station, the children began voicing their opinions as to why another baby in the family would be a good idea, while Mr. and Mrs. Kemp fell silent in the front seat. Mrs. Kemp knew what she should be doing. She should be asking God what she should do; but she already knew that what she wanted to do was not going to line up with what God wanted. Finally she prayed silently, "Lord, Jesus, why would you send this poor child to us? Already we have six children. How can we possibly take on another?" Then she said to herself, Oh this is foolishness. The police will find the mother, and that will be the end of it. Why am I upsetting myself for nothing?

Mr. Kemp suggested, "You know, Sara, Martin and Freida Mueller have been waiting for years and still they have no baby."

"Hmm," Sara nodded as she played with Vincent's soft, dark curls.

Although it seemed much too soon to be making arrangements for this little stranger, something was telling Sara this was not going to be temporary. She thought to herself, Martin and Freida, hmm, how nice. She heaved a sigh and began to relax.

The Kemps and the Muellers were Mennonites. They held certain things as sacred, as absolutes in life: close families, strong community ties, and above all, lives led according to the principles of God. They lived in Promise, Pennsylvania, a community populated almost exclusively by their growing sect of Mennonite families. Amazingly, everyone had managed to live a simple and peaceable life for hundreds of years. Church functions kept them in touch with one another. And all of their neighbors were lifelong friends.

Dealing with officials in the government was not easy for them. Simply riding into town, where life was so completely different, felt awkward; but talking to lawyers and signing contracts were completely foreign to them. Luckily, contracts and lawyers were, for the most part, unnecessary in Promise; a handshake between friends was usually all that was needed. And yet, here they were, pulling up in front of the police station in Carlisle, Pennsylvania. Soon they would find themselves across the desk from Officer Howard Grimes, the one and only officer on duty this Friday evening, and having in their possession someone else's baby.

"Name," he barked with authority.

"Sara and Will Kemp," said Mr. Kemp.

"Address."

"RR 5, Box 15, Promise, Pennsylvania," said Mr. Kemp nervously.

"Describe the incident."

"Well," said Mr. Kemp, "we were at de Carlisle County Fairgrounds," he stated, the words bouncing up and down with nearly every syllable like the sound of a handsaw moving across a log. "My wife wass selling her quilts and such, and I wass looking over de horses. We parked our van in de field along with all de other cars. We were there all day. Then this evening, we got into de van and wass driving home when we hear a baby crying. We pulled de car to de side of de road to see what wass going on, and there he wass! Bingo! A baby!" Mr. Kemp grinned a large undignified grin uncharacteristic of his Abraham Lincoln demeanor. Behind his beard, he was smiling a wide, friendly smile with gaps between each tooth.

"Look," said Mrs. Kemp, showing Officer Grimes the baby's face.

"You're telling me that's a boy?" asked Officer Grimes.

"Yah, his name iss Vincent," said Mrs. Kemp as she untied her green cotton bonnet and folded it on her knee. Quickly, self-consciously, she checked her white cotton voile prayer cap to see that it remained securely attached at the crown of her head. Her shiny auburn hair was pulled back in a bun and tucked modestly inside her prayer cap. She had never cut her hair as was the tradition in Promise.

"And he's not yours?" asked Officer Grimes.

"No, no," Sara insisted. "Here iss a note." She loosened her shawl and pulled the card out of her apron pocket.

Officer Grimes read the note, set it aside, and then surveyed the contents of the purse. Mr. and Mrs. Kemp waited nervously for him to finish his analysis. "Oh, yeah, I've seen this girl." He looked again at the photo license. He lowered his chin and tilted his head to the side. In a deep voice he said, "This is a fake I.D., ya know. That might be her picture, but that's not her real name," he said with a pride that comes from being able to recognize deception at a glance. He fiddled with the license, then used it to scratch his chin, searching his memory. The license scratched loudly against his whiskers, once, twice, three times. "Okay. Now I got it. Yeah, I remember her," he said with authority. "She's the girl we picked up for prostitution down at the truck stop, her and her buddies. She got sick as a dog in jail," he confided. "Turns out, she's a heroin junky. She probably whores so she can support her habit. 'Baby Bingo' here is better off without her, believe me. You nice folks don't really want me to go looking for her, do ya?"

The Kemps looked at each other, uncertain what to answer.

Officer Grimes put down the license and went back to eating his kielbasa and sauerkraut hoagie. He licked his fingers one at a time.

"Would de police really give a baby back to a heroin addict?" asked Mrs. Kemp.

Officer Grimes answered, his mouth still full, "They might, if she could stay off that junk for a few months. That's assuming she wants him back—and if they could find her." He gulped. "My personal opinion is she ain't around. She probably left town and couldn't be bothered dragging her kid around with her."

The Kemps looked at each other searching for what the other was thinking. The baby began to wake from his nap. He yawned a big, toothless yawn, spit his pacifier onto the floor, and nuzzled back into Mrs. Kemp's comfortable lap.

"Sara," Will asked, "what do you think?"

"Martin and Freida Mueller?" Sara suggested. "We could take care of him for a little while until we were sure that de baby could go with de Muellers permanently."

"Yah," Will agreed softly, nodding. "Martin and Freida then." He was a little disappointed at the thought of giving up the baby but relieved that at least they weren't leaving him at the police station.

Sara blinked when she saw Will's disappointment.

"Do this baby a favor and take her home with you," said Officer Grimes.

"Him," corrected Mr. Kemp.

"Him, her, whatever. If you don't take him, Children and Youth Service is so jammed up, I'll probably get stuck with this kid myself, and who knows for how long. I'm here by myself for the rest of the night." He leaned back in his desk chair and tugged on his belt buckle, John Wayne style. "For all I know, my compadres are going to bring in some ruthless killer for me to deal with tonight."

Sara and Will weren't certain whether he was joking, and therefore decided to sit quietly and listen.

"I can't be lookin' after a kid in the middle of something like that. Just take care of it temporarily, and in six months, if you want, we'll do an adoption."

"Are you sure?" asked Mrs. Kemp.

"In about six months?" repeated Mr. Kemp.

"If I say it, you can count on it, it's done. This is a clear-cut case of abandonment by an unfit mother, if I ever saw one, trust me. I'll take care of the paperwork, if you take care of the kid."

"Shouldn't we notify anyone else before we take him home?" asked Mrs. Kemp.

"I'll call 'em tonight, tomorrow, all weekend long," he complained. "But I can tell you this: they don't have enough foster mothers to go around. I've been this route before. If they don't call you by Monday, then they don't have nobody. In that case, I'll sign you up for temporary custody till the hearing."

"What about his health papers and his birth recording?" asked Mrs. Kemp.

Officer Grimes laughed out loud. Tiny chunks of kielbasa and sauerkraut were stuck in his teeth. "You don't think she had this kid in a hospital, do you? That baby's lucky his mamma didn't squat over the garbage can, just to save her the trouble of throwing him in. I'm telling you, this little girl is bad news. She's not your typical mamma. Oh no. She knows every four-letter word in the book, and she's not afraid to use 'em. Believe me, I should know. She used 'em all on me. She knows how to kick, bite, and scratch too, I might add. She's nothing but trash, filthy, stinking trash."

Mr. Kemp said shyly, "No one that God has made is trash, Mr. Grimes, no matter what sin they happen to get caught up in. 'It is not God's will that any should perish, but that all should come to de saving knowledge of de Lord.'"

"If you say so, preacher. My motto is: If it looks like trash, and it smells like trash, it's trash." He wadded up the paper from his sandwich, wiped his mouth with it, and lobbed it into the trash can. "Basket," he declared, satisfied.

Just then, Vincent looked up at Mrs. Kemp. His dark eyes were wide open. "Look Will, he iss awake." Vincent lifted his chin and cooed. It sounded soft and sweet, like a little bird.

"Cgggooo," he gurgled.

"Awww, did you hear that, Will?"

"Yah, I did, I diddy-did-did." Mr. Kemp tapped on Vincent's chin with his cracked, rough index finger. Vincent smiled back at him.

Sara laid him on the policeman's desk. They stared, smiled, and made faces at the baby. Even Officer Grimes joined in. The burly police officer began to talk in falsetto, "Look at the pretty, pretty little boy. Loo, loo, loo, loo." He began to tickle the bottom of Vincent's feet. "Looby, looby, looby."

It startled Vincent at first. He withdrew his foot, but then smiled at the police officer.

The Kemps smiled awkwardly at Officer Grimes, puzzled and surprised at the sudden change in his personality.

Officer Grimes cleared his throat, a little embarrassed, "I guess that settles it then. Don't worry, I got everything covered from this end."

"Yah, Mamma, I guess that settles it, like de man says."

"All right then," Sara answered. "My goodness, this iss going to be a wonderful surprise for Freida and Martin," she answered. She smiled at her husband, relieved.

The Kemps gathered up their belongings. Sara tied her bonnet and picked Vincent up from the desk, tucking him into her shawl. They walked back to their van even more excitedly than when they went in. They tried to digest the fact that Vincent's mother was a heroin addict with no family, prostituting for money, swearing and kicking her way through life, and that they were taking her baby home with them.

"It iss a terrifying world out there," said Sara. "We do not realize how fortunate we are."

Will agreed. "And a terrible shame about his mother, but how could we, in good conscience, let this little one be raised like that? It iss not his fault."

"I wass more concerned for his safety," Sara said. "He iss not crawling now, but what would happen to him if his mother wass doing her drugs, and de baby wass crawling around getting into one thing and then another? You cannot even look away from a baby before it finds some way of hurting himself. Remember when Rachel got lost at de rest area in Ohio? O my gosh and goodness, she disappeared so fast, like a rabbit, she wass." Sara smiled.

Will added, "I wass worried you wanted to leave Vincent there. I could not have done that, Sara. I wass praying that you would agree to take him with us. We could not throw him back into de world and hope for de best."

Sara patted the baby's chubby legs. "I know, Will. I wouldn't have felt right about it either. My goodness, feel the pork loins on this fellow. This is a hefty one." Then she said to Vincent, "We need to put a boy's shirt on you; this shirt makes you look like a little girly-girl, doesn't it, you poor thing. Yes it does, you little precious. We will get you a boy's shirt, that iss what we'll do." She took off the beaded ankle bracelet and put it in his mother's purse. "Will, did you notice on his shirt iss written scripture?"

"What do you mean, Sara?"

"See, look. On his shirt iss written, peace and love."

Mr. Kemp laughed, "Ah, yah, I see, but that iss not from de Bible. It iss something I have been seeing out in de world."

Embarrassed, Mrs. Kemp contended, "Corinthians 13:12 says, 'for now, these three remain: faith, hope and love. But de greatest of these iss love.'"NIV

"I do not think this little baby wass wearing scripture on his shirt, Sara, do you? But if that iss what his mother wass trying to say, at least she got de most important one right, love."

"Yah, at least she got de last one right."

Sara squeezed Vincent close to her, and love welled up in her heart. "Thank you, Lord Jesus, we will take good care of him for you. And, you won't have such a time convincing Freida like you did with me. She iss going to be so thankful, Lord, you brought him to her. I just know it."

As Will and Sara came out of the building, the children cheered at the sight of the baby still in their mother's arms.

"Settle down back there, and do not get ahead of de facts. He iss only staying for de weekend," she said as she got into the van. She pulled in her long black skirt and closed the door.

"Then what?" they asked.

"After de weekend iss up we will take him to a foster family's house, or give him to Freida and Martin Mueller to take care of for six months and maybe to adopt." They gasped and applauded. Mrs. Kemp interrupted, doing her best not to smile, "But do Not say anything to de Muellers until after de weekend is over, in case, maybe, Vincent's mamma changes her mind. We don't want to get de Muellers' hopes up and then have to disappoint them. Understand?"

Simon answered, "I want him to live with de Muellers. They would like that, and Vincent would be our neighbor, and I could teach him things."

"Well Simon," said Sara, "maybe that iss something you could pray about before you go to sleep." She placed Vincent over her shoulder, patting him on the back. He peered, bleary-eyed, at his newfound friends.

"Yah," Simon replied, determined.

"Awww, Mamma, look at him," said Rachael. "Let me hold him. Let me hold him."

"No, let me. Me first," another clambered.

By Sunday night the Kemps were exhausted, having had very little sleep for the past two nights. Mr. Kemp had driven twenty miles to buy a tape recorder at an all-night drug store, and had spent another half hour at home figuring out how to make it work. But, once that was accomplished, Vincent fell fast asleep almost instantly. The Kemps and their six children all dozed off to Lou Rawls crooning in the background. It was the very first time, ever, that any music—with the exception of hymns—had been played in the Kemps' home.

The children pulled their hand-stitched quilts up around their necks and fluffed their feather pillows. The last lamp was blown out, and the wooden beds stopped squeaking. Soon the old sleepy farmhouse was dark and silent—except for one sound. Lou Rawls' deep sexy voice crooned through the darkness: "You'll Never Find Another Love Like Mine."

Mr. Kemp lay next to Sara listening to the tape with amusement. He whispered, "At least there iss no baby crying, praise Jesus."

Sara whispered back, smiling, "Yah. Sing it, Lou."

The phone had remained conspicuously quiet all weekend.

2 Peter 3:9. The Lord is not slack in his promise, as some men count slackness, but is longsuffering to us-ward, not willing that any should perish, but that all should come to repentance.

Chapter 2

Condor

$\mathcal{B}$unny Muldare stared hopelessly out of the window at King's Korner Kafe in Carlisle, Pennsylvania. The cigarette Bunny held between her fingers shook, her nerves jangled, and her body ached. She was dismally aware that she wasn't going to be able to shoot up again until Danny Burns arrived with her fix, and the amount he was bringing was barely enough to get her through the day. She rubbed her forehead to help her think, but there was no thinking her way through this one. The truth was she had totally ruined her life, as well as her baby's life, all for the sake of heroin.

She was carefully avoiding eye contact with anyone. She was fairly certain no one would bother with her since she looked like "a damn derelict" as her mother put it; but if anyone asked, she was sure they would be so shocked by what they heard—they would run away. She was absolutely sure there would be no one with any pity. After all, it's not like she deserved it. There was no disputing she brought it all on herself. Then she thought, oh what do I care what they think. If I really gave a flip what these jerks think, I would have taken a bath five days ago. "I suck, they suck, everybody sucks," she mumbled aloud. She thought, never mind that I haven't eaten in two days, or however long it's been. But what does it matter? Nothing matters anymore.

Bunny reviewed what she had done to Vincent. She figured what she did to herself was her business, but Vincent was so innocent. How could she ever live with herself? If only she had a lot of money, she thought, she never would have given him to strangers. She reasoned, if she had given him to a social worker, or somebody like that, they would have made her go through some hellacious rehab withdrawal week. She envisioned an orderly from the mental hospital greeting her saying, "Welcome to the vacation from hell!" She thought, why should I go through all that misery so I can wake up to find out they took little Vinnie away from me anyway? Even if I could have gotten control over this thing, it's too late now. I'm never gonna know if he's all right, and I'm sure not ever gonna get him back, not in the shape I'm in. And it's not like I deserve him back. If it weren't for me, he wouldn't have had to go through withdrawal. That was awful, so, so, awful, and it was all my fault. She stared down into the ashtray. He never would have suffered like that if I wasn't too weak to control this damnable shit. "I wish somebody would just shoot me in the head," she mumbled. Bunny's body began to shake. She resisted the urge to curl up in a ball.

Two ladies passed by on their way to the cash register. One of them asked cautiously, "Did you say something, dear?"

"I said—shoot me in the head!"

Bunny looked up at them with contemptuous sickly sunken eyes. Her dirty blonde hair clung to the side of her head in tangled stringy clumps. She took a self-conscious drag on her cigarette and quickly exhaled, adding to the cloud of smoke that enveloped her. She stared into her ashtray.

The ladies hurried away without asking any more questions.

Bunny's problems began when she was sixteen. She prided herself in her good looks and unshakable self-confidence, or at least, how well she could appear to be self-confident. If only she had known then what she knew now: namely fearlessness can be a dangerous thing without wisdom to tame it.

When Bunny met Vinnie, he was twenty. He told her how much he loved her and how they were going to live together forever, and he meant it. As far as Bunny was concerned, Vinnie was perfect. To make a living, he and Bunny sold heroin, crack, weed, or whatever, as long as it made money. And it did—lots of money. Things were going so well it never occurred to her that he might someday be arrested, and she would find herself raising their baby on her own. But it happened. And now, not only was Vinnie gone, but all of their friends were gone as well; everyone scattered when they considered the prospect that Vinnie might name them when the DA offered him a plea bargain. However, since Vinnie shot a police officer, they neither offered him a plea bargain, nor were they ever going to release him from prison. He was going to be there for the rest of his life, probably for the next fifty years.

I have to face it, she thought. Heroin is all that's left for me. And nothing will ever bring Vinnie or the baby back. They're gone forever. Everybody's gone, everybody but Danny Burns, that is. Where is Burns!? He knows I'm counting on him. How long does he think I can sit here and wait?

Bunny took another drag on her cigarette and allowed the smoke to lull her into a daydream, a long welcome escape from the here and now. While the smoke whirled around her, she began to relive her trip to the abortion clinic.

About a year and a half ago, she was riding a bus on her way to the Condor Family Planning Center in Harrisburg, Pennsylvania. Bunny and her mother and brother lived in Carlisle, two exits away on the turnpike from Harrisburg, about thirty minutes away by bus. The smell of diesel was nauseating, and to make matters worse she was starting to be overdue for her fix. She thought to herself, it's a joke that they call it "family planning." The only people I know who go to Condor are getting abortions, not planning families. I just want to get rid of this alien freeloader that's taken up residence inside my body. Bunny saw her bus stop approaching and hurried to the front of the bus. She flipped her blonde hair over her shoulder and dropped the change into the box. She looked at the driver and caught him staring at her bare midriff. The change jangled down the box as the driver opened the door. Bunny hurried down the steps and onto the curb. A very short, elderly lady followed her off the bus.

"Hey Mabel, where's your pass?" called the driver.

The old lady's squeaky voice scolded, "You stinker, I showed it to you yesterday. You behave or I'm going to tell your mother."

The driver's belly jiggled with laughter as the bus rolled away.

"Hey sweetheart," the old lady called out. She shuffled down the sidewalk trying to catch up.

Bunny was surprised the old lady wasn't afraid of her since she put a lot of effort into dressing to make herself look unapproachable. Bunny wore a dozen necklaces around her neck and a different ring on every finger. She wore short shorts made from an old pair of jeans, a short tank top, orange. She wore dark eyeliner that encircled her eyes, making them appear even more sunken than they already were, and dark red lipstick. She had long, thin legs and long blonde hair that swung freely over her shoulders. She would have walked faster but one of her sandals came off. She stopped to put it back on.

"Look hon, I want to show you something." By then they were about ten feet from the front door of the clinic. She reached into her black leather handbag and pulled out a small jar. The label on the lid of the jar read: "8 WEEK FETUS." In it was a tiny plastic baby about two inches long, suspended in a jellylike liquid. It had toes and fingers and a little face with a mouth, nose, and ears. It appeared to be sleeping. "That's what a baby looks like at two months. How far along are you, dear?" she asked. She looked into Bunny's eyes without flinching. Her head tilted as she waited for an answer. She smelled like roses.

"I missed two periods plus a couple of weeks," said Bunny.

"Oh my," she said with excitement, handing the jar to Bunny, "Your baby is just about the same size. Take a look. Isn't that just amazing?" She smiled. Her perfectly aligned dentures gleamed in the sunshine.

Bunny held the jar up to her face for a better look. She tried to inspect the jostling baby as she walked, more slowly now, to the front door of the clinic. She reached for the brass doorknob and handed the jar back to the woman.

"Yeah, amazing. Look, lady, it's not like I planned this; it just happened. I don't have a choice."

"No dear, there's always a choice. There's adoption."

By then Bunny was inside the building and the door had shut behind her, but not before Bunny heard the old woman's answer. It echoed in her ears; there's adoption.

As she sat in the waiting room, the image of the baby in the jar kept haunting her like a bad dream. Bunny chewed at her nails and tried to dismiss it. The waiting room was overflowing with patients. Bunny kept her knees pulled together to avoid touching the girls on either side of her.

Finally the receptionist took her into one of the rooms where she waited for what seemed like an eternity. She studied the room. It appeared to have everything they would need for the abortion. There was a plate of stainless-steel instruments neatly organized on the counter next to the sink. The sink was tucked into the corner. It had a deep bowl with a faucet that stood up high. There was a table with a shelf for magazines underneath. There was an avocado-green electric clock on the pale blue walls. The room was quiet, so quiet she could hear the soft buzzing of the second hand as it droned on and on around the clock's face. There was a single picture placed high on the wall. Bunny jumped down from the operating table where she had been told to wait. She walked toward the picture for a better look. It was a picture of the ocean, and though the blue sky and gentle waves of the beach achieved a soothing affect, there were no birds, or people, or anything else living. Bunny sighed, dissatisfied, and hopped back up onto the examination table. She checked the clock and worried over the time, wondering how long it would be before she could get another fix.

When Bunny made the appointment, she was told that they were going to give her a drug to induce labor. Then she was to wait for a while until they returned to suction out the fetal tissue. The nurse told her there would be some cramping, but that the procedure would be relatively painless.

Bunny had been waiting close to fifteen long minutes when she began to hear someone crying in the next room.

She tiptoed into the hallway and looked through the crack of the door into the girl's room. What she saw was a nurse clasping a naked wet baby. It was about the size of a kitten. It was alive, wet, squirming, and in excruciating pain. The girl on the table screamed, "Is it alive? My God, it is! It's alive!"

Bunny crouched in the doorway to avoid being seen. The woman began to walk toward the door. Bunny was afraid she had been spotted. But then, suddenly, the nurse turned toward the sink to the left of the doorway. Bunny pressed her face against the door frame to get a better look. Its eyes were burned into the sockets like two lumps of coal. The skin looked red and badly burned. The head was writhing around as it cried in pain. The cry wasn't really a cry at all, but more like a squeal, as if it were burning. Just as the nurse was about to drop it in the sink, it slipped out of her hands and hit the tile floor, hard. Bunny gasped as she saw the baby dropping to the ground. First the body hit, then the head followed, bouncing off the floor like an apple. It slid and landed about five feet in front of Bunny.

"Did you drop it? It's alive!" the girl screamed as she tried to lift herself up from the table to see what the nurse was doing behind her.

The doctor pushed her back onto the table and held her feet in the stirrups. "Hold still, you're going to hurt yourself," he warned.

The nurse bent over and picked up the baby from the floor. Its arms and legs were still flailing, still struggling to live.

Bunny spun away from the door and leaned against the wall, breathless. She moved cautiously toward the door again. What she saw next was hard for her to take in. Could it really be happening? The nurse dunked the baby into the sink full of water, held him under, and waited—waited—

waited while the water bubbled and splashed, as the baby kicked wildly. After a few endless minutes the water was still. There was one last gurgle, and then the room fell silent. The nurse let go and the baby's body sank to the bottom of the water and then rolled over, ever so slowly, until it was face up, revealing the expression of an agonizing death.

Bunny watched, stunned. She had just witnessed her first birth, her first death, her first murder.

Dr. Kraus, who was attending to the afterbirth, glanced up at his nurse, interrupting the silence. "Terry?" The nurse held on to the side of the sink, motionless.

The girl cried from the table. "Oh baby, my poor baby." She knew there was nothing she could do to change it now. The baby was dead. She felt so guilty, so responsible for the murder of her baby. How could she let herself be talked into something so unspeakably horrid? "Oh, poor baby, poor little baby," she sobbed, over and over.

She began to thrash around on the table, crying while the doctor held on to her feet. "I need help over here," he demanded. "Terry, I can't hold her."

Just then, Bunny felt a sharp tap on her shoulder. She was so startled she almost choked. She spun around to see the receptionist glaring at her.

"What are you doing out here?" the receptionist asked. "You are supposed to be waiting in your room."

"Uh, I was just wondering if I could help."

"The doctor and nurse have everything under control," she said. "Now please, go back to your room and wait."

Bunny hurried back to her room, wide-eyed at what she had just seen. They just murdered that little baby! she said to herself. She jumped back up onto the examination table, where she remained in shock. She could still hear the girl sobbing, "Poor baby." Eventually the sobbing subsided as the sedative began to take effect, and there was nothing

but the eerie silence of death coming from the room next
door. Bunny was left alone in the silence.

A few minutes later the attending nurse rustled some
papers outside of Bunny's door. Bunny felt trapped. The
metal doorknob began to move, and then the door clicked
open suddenly. Bunny's heart raced. As the nurse approached her, Bunny could clearly see that she was not the
same cool and collected person who had led her to this room
not an hour ago. Her cheeks were flushed, and the veins in
her neck were bulging from stress. The nurse tried unsuc-
cessfully to smile.

"What was all the noise about?" asked Bunny, trying to
control her fear. She wondered what they would do if they
knew she saw it all.

"Oh, she was just a little further along than she wanted
to admit. That always makes things more difficult." The
nurse took a deep breath to collect herself. She shook her
curls behind her shoulders, clipboard in hand and asked,
"You won't have that problem though, dear. You did say
you've only missed two periods, right?"

"Yes," Bunny answered mechanically, breathlessly. She
knew she wasn't fooling anybody; it was obvious that she
was afraid.

"I need you to fill out these consent forms, then put on
this gown, and the doctor will be in to examine you."

The nurse handed her the clipboard, and with her other
hand, she held out a pen. Bunny reached for the forms,
trying not to touch the woman, but then, without notice,
the nurse held onto Bunny's bare arm and said, "There's
nothing to worry about. This will be over in a snap."

The word echoed through Bunny's mind: snap, snap,
snap.

Bunny was repulsed by her touch. She jerked her arm
away and took two short, deep breaths. She looked side-

ways at the sink next to her as if the nurse wouldn't notice her fear. This will be my baby's sink next, she thought.

"Just sit tight, hon. The doctor will be in before you know it."

The moment Bunny was alone, she began to gasp for air as her heart pounded in her chest. She began to look for a way to escape. She wasn't about to go through with it. The very thought of them touching her again was terrifying. She opened the door slightly and peeked to see if there was anyone there. She slid along the wall and turned to look in the room next door. The girl was gone. She wondered where she had gone so quickly. There was nothing she could do for her now; she had to get out of there. She listened and waited until everything was quiet. She raced through a maze of doors and hallways. She took a wrong turn and found herself trapped at the end of a hallway. She turned to go back where she had come from. Suddenly the receptionist appeared at the other end of the hall and walked slowly and deliberately toward Bunny. "Miss Muldare, you are very excited about nothing. Calm down. That's right. Let's go in here and sit down. That's it. I'll send the doctor in to talk to you. Be a good girl now. I know you are upset, but there's really no reason for it. Just sit calmly, and the doctor will be with you in just a moment."

The receptionist met the doctor and nurse at the end of the hall and began to explain what had happened. She explained, "I know the girl saw it all. What was going on in there anyway? When I tapped on her shoulder she looked like she about jumped out of her skin."

"Paula," explained the nurse, "it was a live birth. It was awful. And then I dropped it. She must have seen me drop it. It was just awful. For all I know she could have seen me at the sink. I don't know how that little guy survived all that."

"Oh my, this is not good," said the receptionist.

If Bunny was going to escape, she would have to get around the three by jumping onto the receptionist's desk, leaping over the counter leading to the waiting room, and running out the front door. Bunny started down the hallway and ducked into the receptionist's office. The receptionist saw her. She followed her into the reception area and caught Bunny by the back of her shirt just as she was climbing onto the desk. Dr. Kraus called to her. "Paula, no." She turned toward him as Bunny jumped up on the counter. A tray of utensils that the nurse had placed on the counter was under Bunny's foot and slid to the floor with a crash. Bunny's foot slipped out from under her. Her knee hit the counter, landing on a glass vial of blood and a hypodermic needle. The vial smashed, blood went everywhere, and the glass pierced her knee. She jumped to the floor and ran, limping, through the waiting room. She shoved aside two girls in the entry and ran outside.

The doctor explained, "Let her go. She'll be back when the shock wears off. She has no choice. She needs us."

"Yes, of course, I know you're right," replied the receptionist. "What else can she do?"

Paula turned her attention toward the nurse who was trying to smooth away the worry in her forehead. Paula and the doctor noticed her hands were trembling. She glanced up at them and confessed, "I'll never get used to that."

Dr. Krauss took a deep breath. "Come on girls, let's get back to work."

The nurse didn't move.

"Terry?" he urged.

She handed him the clipboard. She pursed her lips with determination and said, "I can't. I'm sorry."

"Sure, no problem. Take a minute. You'll be fine."

"No, I," she hesitated, "I mean I'm done."

In spite of the searing pain in Bunny's knee, she limped several blocks down the street until she came to a telephone booth, where she shut the door tightly behind her. She leaned against the wall and took some time to catch her breath. She fought with the inevitable, trying desperately to come up with another plan. Anything would be better than calling her mother, but she knew it was no use; there was nowhere else to turn. She pounded the wall in frustration, then took a deep breath, and began dialing—slowly. She waited.

"Hello."

"Mom?"

"Bunny?"

1 Corinthians 13:13. NIV And now these three remain: faith, hope, and love. But the greatest of these is love."

Chapter 3

Hello Mom, Hello Dad

"Hi Mom," Bunny mumbled.

Mrs. Muldare smoothed away a fingerprint on her gold-plated French phone. Dread set in at the sound of Bunny's voice.

"Mom, hang on a minute." Bunny supported her knee on the side of the phone booth, got a good angle on a piece of glass, flicked it out, and clinched her teeth in pain. She held her knee trying to recover.

"Hello, hello! What's going on!?" demanded Mrs. Muldare.

"Mom, can I come home?"

"What? Why do you want to come home all of a sudden?" asked her mother.

"I'm pregnant, I'm broke, and I'm feeling really sick. I know, I've screwed up everything, but I need help."

"I might have known it wasn't to tell me you had turned your life around. What might be the source of your affliction? Could it be that you have morning sickness, or you're going through withdrawal, or did you, perhaps, pick up some damnable venereal disease?"

There was a long pause. Bunny was trying not to let her mother hear her crying.

"I'm not sure, maybe all," she said concisely.

Mrs. Muldare closed her address book. She had been expecting a call from a friend, the mayor's wife. This call from Bunny was an unpleasant surprise. And now she was wishing she had never picked up the phone. As she so often explained to her friends, her daughter is a difficult child, no—impossible. She tightened the hairpins in her French roll and pulled off her earrings to brace herself for what was coming.

"The pregnancy part is easy Bunny. Get—an—abortion. And since you're so damned independent, it will be free. Also, while you're at the doctor, tell him you're on heroin, and he'll put you on a program to get you off that stuff once and for all."

"Mom, I'm not getting an abortion. I already went there once, and I'm not going back. The only difference between abortion and murder is, when you get an abortion, nobody can hear the baby scream. And they're real babies, not just things!"

"Is this your second abortion?"

"No, I went there today. It was horrible, and I'm not going back." She wiped her nose on her arm, resisting the temptation to sniff.

"That's ridiculous. What's to be scared of? You sit in the waiting room, you go in to the doctor, you come out, home free. People do it every day of the week with no problem. But not you, of course."

"No Mom, there was this g—"

"I am not going to listen to this nonsense, Bunny. How much do you think it's going to cost to raise a child? You don't think I'm going to raise it, do you? I have things to do."

No answer.

"And how are you supposed to take care of a child when you're on heroin? You don't even know what day it is half of the time. I can just see it now: you loitering on our street corner stoned out of your mind with a baby in your arms. You'd make a lousy mother, Bunny."

"At least you'd know where we were, Mother."

"Don't you dare use that tone with me. You are the one who insisted on running away and ruining your life, not me! Your brother doesn't act like this. He took advantage of the life your father and I provided for him; he graduated from college and works for a living. He married a nice girl from a good family and continues to live a respectable life. He has made me very proud."

"Yes I know. He's perfectly happy making you look good, Mother. And he's a doctor too; that must make you doubly proud. But have you ever considered that, just maybe, your children weren't put on this earth for you, but the other way around."

"Oh really. And just why were you put on this earth, Madame Bunny?"

The truth was Bunny hadn't the slightest idea. She only knew she was looking for acceptance, wherever she could find it.

"Mom, you didn't have anything to do with Vinnie getting arrested, did you?"

"Me? Now why would I want to stir up that hornet' s nest? I don't need any more enemies in this town, especially not from that unprincipled bunch."

"Well being a public servant and all, doesn't that make you just as unprincipled? Aren't you supposed to round up the bad guys. Where is your sense of civic duty? Are you scared, Mom?"

Bunny's mother was getting more perturbed.

"Mom, if you can just get past how much it's going to cost, and what the neighbors are going to think, I promise: I'll finish school, I'll get a real job, and before anything I'll go to rehab." Bunny whispered through her tears. "Mom, I'm living on the brink here." She began to cry in spite of herself.

"Oh please, stop being so dramatic. Tell me Bunny, what kinds of degrees are they giving out these days? You used to tell me a C stood for cute. Maybe you could get a degree in cute. On the other hand, I think you're probably better suited for professional parasite."

"Funny, Mom." Bunny had more to say, but she was getting too sick to let it out; the nausea was taking over.

"No Bunny. When you start acting like a human being, maybe you can be my daughter again. In the meantime, I guess you're just one of those people who have to learn things the hard way." After a short pause she asked, "Where are you living?"

"I got a room in downtown Carlisle."

"How are you paying the rent?"

"It's cheap. Ten dollars a week."

"Oh, that must be a charming place. What are you doing for money?"

"Waiting tables."

"You're not prostituting anymore, are you?"

"Not if I can help it. I'd rather die than let another one of those slime balls crawl all over me." She wiped her nose.

"And I would rather die than face the embarrassment of bailing you out of jail. I've got two words of advice for you, Bunny: abortion and rehab."

Bunny retorted as calmly as she could to avoid throwing up, "Ya know, Mom, I've got one word for you: NO!!!"

No one spoke.

"Hello," Bunny said.

"I'm here," her mother said, "though I don't know why."

"What's Daddy's number?"

"You don't think Prissy, or Peaches, or whatever her name is, wants to have anything to do with you, do you? Now there's a woman who deserves your father."

Bunny defended her father saying, "At least he loves me no matter what."

"Yes, very forgiving," she answered sarcastically. "Maybe he's so 'forgiving' because he too has plenty to be forgiven for. Go ahead and call him if that makes you happy, Bunny. God knows your father wouldn't want you to be unhappy."

"What's his number?"

"407-555-2443, and tell him his check is late." Click.

Bunny leaned her head against her hand waiting for courage to come. Since her father moved away, she always hesitated to call him even though he had told her many times to call him whenever she wanted. She thought he would probably still want to hear from her, but it felt uncomfortable to call, as if she were interrupting something, something unfamiliar. It was nothing like calling him at home. She gathered her courage, took a deep breath, and called him in spite of her feelings.

"Operator, I want to make a collect call."

"Your name?"

"Bunny Muldare."

"The number you are calling?"

"407-555-2443."

"One moment please."

It rang five times.

A young child's voice answered. "Hello."

Bunny asked, "Hello, is Mr. Muldare there, please."

"No, he hasn't come home from work yet."

Bunny could hear a woman's voice in the background. "Who is that, Danielle?"

"It's a lady. She wants to talk to Daddy."

"Let me talk to her."

Bunny hurriedly hung up the phone. She screamed into the air, "He's my Daddy!" She leaned into the phone and gave in to her tears. She repeated in despair, "My Daddy, not yours." She hated that woman, that total stranger who stole her father. And that little girl, who is she? she thought. Doesn't Daddy think about me anymore?" Bunny wondered why she was living; she hated her life.

Even if things were different, her mother was right—she was nothing but a parasite, a useless parasite with nothing to offer anyone but problems, expensive problems, and a history of stupid mistakes. She put her arm over her face and leaned on the phone. After a few minutes there was an irritating tap, tap, tap at the window. She lifted here head and glared at the person. Tap, tap, tap. It was the crazy old lady with the baby in the jar. The woman waved and smiled through the glass. Bunny tried to get out of the phone booth, but the old woman stood in the doorway.

"What!?" Bunny asked in exasperation.

"The Bible tells us that the sins of the parents will be visited on the children to the third and fourth generation."

"Oh that's real fair! They sin and I pay!" Bunny protested, resisting the urge to swear.

"It's not what God wants for your life. This is a warning to all parents to be watchful of what they do, because their sins will inevitably hurt their children. My question for you is this: Are you going to be strong enough to turn this downward cycle around, or will your child have to suffer as you have?"

"What do you think? Do I look strong? Do I look like Mother Teresa?" she answered. She wiped the mascara-streaked tears across her cheeks.

"With God's help, all things are possible."

"I doubt it. He never helped me before."

"Ask, and you will receive. Knock, and the door will be opened to you, dear."

"You are a real nutcase, a fruitcake! Please, lady, leave me . . ."

Huge waves of nausea began to overtake Bunny. She bolted past the woman without explanation in search of a restroom. She could only hope that she would make it that far. She rushed through the parking lot at the mini-mall, up the escalator, down the corridor into the ladies' room, into the first open stall. She flipped up the lid, and before she could wipe off the rim, she bent over the toilet and threw up. It was sour and burned the back of her throat. It had gone in her hair, on the back of her hand, and on the rim of the toilet. She tried to wipe it off with toilet paper, but it crumbled in her hand. She tried another piece, and it crumbled in her hair. It smelled as sour as it felt in the back of her throat. The frustration was too much. The tears were blinding. "Oh, God, if you're real, I need help."

She thought, there's no one to listen to me and my problems. She decided to grab her syringe for one last jolt. I'm gonna leave this world for good, she said to herself. My life is nothing but crap, and I've had it. Good-bye world, so sorry to leave you—as if anyone will miss me. Bunny filled her syringe, strapped up her arm, found a vein, and stuck in the needle. She liked her injections to work slowly, until they gripped every fiber of her body, until they smothered out all hints of the ugliness around her, leaving her all alone with her imagination. She searched quickly through her purse for whatever else she could find that might help her get it over with, once and for all. There were two tabs of acid she had been saving for Vinnie and herself, before he went to jail. She chewed them recklessly. What else was in there, she wondered. Why not, four aspirins, she said to herself. She was beginning to feel that old calm creeping over her. Her knees slid to the floor. She began to feel herself slipping painlessly away. She rested her head and hand on the rim of the toilet. She managed to get the aspirins up to her mouth and swallow.

Bunny could hear James Taylor over the PA system singing "You've Got a Friend." Bunny joined in, not realizing she was still in a public restroom. She sang, "You just call out my name and you know wherever I am . . ." She continued to sing along with her knight in shining armor. He was going to come and take her away. He was going to take care of her and her baby, and they were going to live happily ever after.

By the time the song was over, the floor had become white and puffy like marshmallow clouds. James Taylor said, "Hey, what's a girl like you doing in a place like this?" He put a pipe in his mouth and made his eyebrows go up and down like Groucho Marx.

"I'm checkin' out of this place." she said out loud with a false confidence. She flung her hair over her shoulder and played with her longest necklace.

"What about your baby? Is he checking out too?" he asked quietly.

Bunny panicked, "Oh my gosh! How could I do this? All I was thinking about was myself. It's too late. Isn't it? What am I gonna do now?"

"You must try to live, Bunny. Right now you're the only friend he's got. "If you die, your baby dies. Don't let that happen."

"I won't," said Bunny. "Not if I can help it. I hope it's not too late."

As she spoke, parts of his face were falling off like pieces of a jigsaw puzzle. He was transparent where the pieces were missing. Behind him, it looked like a beautiful sunset.

She began searching desperately for a way out of the stall. She was looking for a doorknob, but there wasn't one. She pushed on the walls hoping they would fall down. She tried banging on them, but no one came. She tried climbing over the walls only to find another stall on the other side. She fell back to the floor. It felt as if she were trapped in a foam coffin. If she didn't find her way out, she and the baby were going to die in the dark! "God, if you're there, I'm sorry God for being so stupid."

Her heart was pounding from struggling so hard, and it was beginning to hurt. She decided it might be best to lie still. She was afraid that if she continued to exert herself, she would have a heart attack. As she lay there, she tried to remember a time that was calming. She remembered when she was twelve and used to baby-sit for her neighbor's little boy. She loved that little boy. Like Bunny, he had blond hair and nearly invisible blond eyebrows. She would take the little boy for walks around the neighborhood and pretend he was hers. Every time Bunny would come for him, he would bounce up and down on his behind and stretch his arms out for her to pick him up. She loved it when he learned how to give her a kiss. He would hug and kiss her and then smooth her hair with his hands. He would knead her cheeks with his chubby, sticky little hands and say, "Aw, Bun-bun." It was the closest thing to love that Bunny ever knew.

"I love you too, little one. I'll get us out of here; just give me a little time to think."

"C'mon kid, you're holding up the line." A gruff voice startled Bunny.

"The line?" asked Bunny afraid she had done something wrong.

"Haven't you ever seen a toll bridge?"

"I need to get out of here." Bunny said. "Are you going to help me?"

"It'll cost you. Everything worthwhile does, you know."

"How much is it?" asked Bunny.

"Six hundred dollars," he said with a hideous grin, knowing full well she could never pay.

"Six hundred dollars!" Bunny said. "Just to get across a bridge?"

"Come now, it's not that much. Just about everybody can afford six hundred dollars. What's your problem?"

She looked through her purse. She knew there wasn't anything close to six hundred dollars in there. Embarrassed, she looked up at the toll booth operator. He was half goat, half troll.

He said, "You don't have it, do you, girly?"

"No, I'm sorry, I don't. But it's for my baby. Isn't there something else I can do for you instead of money?" She flicked her hair behind her shoulder. It was stiff and reeked of vomit.

"Hmmm," he grinned a bearded grin through greenish-yellow teeth and began to laugh a long, low evil chuckle. "A baby!" he said. "That means you would sacrifice anything, even yourself."

"Well yeah." She surprised herself with her answer. "He's only two inches long, and I'm the only friend he's got. I really don't care if I live, but he does," she smiled, complimenting herself for being so noble.

He answered, "See the knife in your purse? Cut the baby out, give it to me, and the next guy that comes along, I'll tell him the baby needs a ride. You'll probably die, but what the heck, it's for a good cause. After all, the baby was going to die for you just this afternoon."

"What do you know about that? Who told you?" He seemed to know everything about her.

He replied, "And just when you thought your dirty little secret was safe. You realize I'm not the only one who knows. Everybody knows," he said. "Now, do we have a deal?"

"I'm thinking."

"She's thinking," he mocked. "What's to think about? It's only fair. If it was good enough for him this afternoon, then it should be good enough for you tonight."

"Will it hurt?" she asked even though she already knew the answer. She was just buying time.

"A little, but there's really nothing to it. It's just a simple little procedure. People do it everyday. It's just zip, zip, zip, bingo, bango, bongo, we got a baby."

Bunny didn't move.

"Time's a-ticking," he reminded.

She withdrew the knife from her purse. I'll just look at it, she thought. Isn't this what I wanted? she asked herself. She turned the knife over in the palm of her hand. I never intended to kill the baby, just myself. If I can just go through with this, I get exactly what I want; baby lives, I die. Simple. "Okay, I'll do it," she blurted before she could change her mind. "Where do I cut?"

The goat man squealed like a girl, with delight, "Oh goody." Then with as much seriousness as he could muster, he explained, "You're going to have to make a cut completely surrounding the navel. Then you'll pull out the navel. The navel is attached to the umbilical cord. And the umbilical cord is attached to the baby."

"Whoa." She swooned just thinking about it. She loosened her grip on the knife.

"Do it. Go, go, go!"

He pressured her until she drew the knife across her stomach just above her navel.

"Deeper!" he shouted. "You don't want to have to do it twice." She tried again in another direction. The two-inch gash dripped blood down her stomach. Bunny shrieked in pain, but didn't dare stop.

"Is someone in here?" a lady called in a Spanish accent. "What you doing in there? Got to close up."

"Hurry up," the goat man urged.

"I'm trying, it hurts so bad," said Bunny out loud, crying in pain.

"I get help, okay? No worry. I be back," said the cleaning lady.

"They're coming. Hurry up," he said again.

"I can't. It hurts too bad," she said. "I got another gash started," she said. "She wiped the blood away to see where she had stopped. The loose flap of skin burned like fire when she touched it. It folded back across her navel. She threw her head back, clenched her teeth, and shrieked in pain.

"It was good enough for your baby wasn't it!" he yelled.

She quickly stabbed at herself the third time and screamed again.

Someone pounded on the bathroom stall.

"Oh well, too late," the goat man shrugged unsympathetically as if she had just lost a game of chance. "You lose."

"Is he going to die?" Bunny whined. "That's not fair."

The goat man whined, mocking, "That's not fair."

Pound, Pound, Pound. "Open the door!" a voice ordered.

Bunny reached for the doorknob, but it still had not appeared. The security guard unlocked it from the outside.

"Okay young lady, put down the knife," he demanded.

"NO!" insisted Bunny. "I have to get the baby out before he dies! The goat man told me!" Bunny scooted back sliding her sore knee through a puddle of blood on the floor. She positioned herself between the toilet and wall looking like a crazed animal. She raised the knife up in front of her. She warned him in a slow, determined voice, "Stay away from me."

As he stood studying her, the security guard realized he was looking at a young girl, not a young woman. This was someone's child, he thought. "Nobody's going to die, sweetheart. You don't need that knife."

"NO! You don't understand!" Bunny screamed, slashing out at the guard. Maria, the lady with a Spanish accent, jumped back and clutched her mouth.

Slowly, he bent down to Bunny's level on the floor. "I know the goat man, senorita," he reassured softly. "He's a liar," he whispered. As gently as he could, thinking of his own daughter, he said, "He just wants to hurt you. If you want to save your baby and yourself, you need to trust me. Can you do that?"

Bunny chewed on her filthy fingernails. The bathroom floor was disgustingly dirty. Her beautiful hair was stringy and smelly. She wiped the tears from her cheeks leaving dirty streaks from the bathroom floor across her face, her eyes bleary and red from the drugs. She remembered how mean and ugly the goat man laughed. She looked into the security guard's face as best she could through the drugs. He had on a light-blue shirt with a security patch on the sleeve. The silver badge on his chest made her more than just a little uneasy. But when she looked into his face, his cheeks were chubby to match his belly, and his eyes were

47

kind and concerned. He raised his bushy gray eyebrows at her and waited patiently for an answer.

She decided to take a chance and trust him. "Will you please call my daddy?" she asked in a childlike voice. She dragged her purse toward her across the bathroom floor. She dropped the knife as she pulled the number out of her purse.

Maria breathed deeply. "Thank you, Jesus," she whispered.

The guard looked at the number on the paper. "Does he live in Florida?" he asked.

"Yeah."

Fernando, the security guard, picked up the knife and syringe. "Where do you live?"

"On the corner of Hanover and Route 11, in Carlisle."

Fernando looked at Maria.

"We cover for you, Fernando," she said. "He's a good man," she told Bunny. "He take good care of you. Don't worry."

Fernando handed Maria the syringe and the knife. C'mon senorita, let's see if you can walk." As the two of them struggled to get through the mall, it was obvious they weren't going to make it to the parking lot. Maria managed to borrow an office chair from an office supply store for Bunny to sit in. She handed Fernando a box of tissues the store had given her for Bunny's stomach. Fernando wheeled Bunny to the curb and then hurried to get his car.

Maria joined Bunny at the curb. Maria said sweetly, "Don' worry, young lady. Fernando will get you a doctor. You be okay." Bunny stared blankly at Maria, lost in her own private world. Her mouth hung open slightly and her head bobbed as if she were a drunk on the verge of passing out. Maria was certain Bunny didn't know where she was or what was happening around her. Maria stood behind the chair holding up Bunny's head so that she wouldn't tumble out onto the concrete before Fernando came back with the car.

Fernando drove her to the hospital, where she was stitched up and given an antibiotic. The wound was ugly. She had sliced around her navel on three sides. "That belly button will never be the same," the doctor joked as he put the bandage over the whole swollen mess. "A shame really. It was kind of a nice one." Fernando grimaced just to look at it. "As far as the drugs go, the worst of it is over. We can keep her here overnight, or she can go home and sleep it off. She's lucky she vomited, or it could have been a lot worse." He didn't realize that Bunny had thrown up before she took the drugs.

Bunny raised her head from the gurney but gave up the attempt to explain.

"Did she try to say something?" asked Fernando.

"Yeah, kck," said the doctor, making a noise like a choking cat. He suddenly realized how insensitive he must have sounded but offered no apology.

"I guess I'll take her home," Fernando said as he looked at his watch.

"Give her this number. It's for a drug rehab program. You never know, this one might decide to kick the habit, especially when she wakes up to find out she ripped her bellybutton to shreds." Fernando was having a rough time with the doctor's sarcasm.

"I'm sorry for being so cynical," explained the doctor. "It's just that when you see this kind of thing day in and day out, you get fed up with it."

A nurse pulled Bunny's doctor away to handle another incoming emergency. She said, "Hurry, the boy is cyanotic." They ran down the hallway.

Fernando went out to the car and drove up to the entrance of the hospital. He lifted Bunny out of the wheelchair. She was no help at all; it was like lifting a one-hundred-and-twenty-pound bag of cement. He laid her in the back seat of his station wagon as best he could. He groaned as he tried to straighten his aching back. He was not a young man anymore. He drove her to the corner of Hanover and Route 11. After searching two corner buildings, he finally found himself in a doorway with rows of mailboxes in an enclosed corridor. The sign said, "RING FOR MANAGER." He pushed the button. It took forever for someone to answer.

"Who is it?" a sleepy man called into the speaker.

"I have brought Bunny Muldare home. Is this where she lives?" he said in his Cuban accent.

"Just a minute," the manager replied. He came down the steps and opened the door adjusting his bathrobe and smoothing through the few straggling hairs he had left on top of his head. Fernando looked down at the top of the man's head. He was short, so short that his bathrobe was dragging the ground.

"It's two o'clock in the morning," he complained, squinting against the light bulb in the corridor.

"I'm sorry to wake you up," said Fernando "She was hurt. I found her at the Shiffler Mini-Mall where I work, so I took her to the emergency room, and now I'm bringing her home."

"Where is she?"

"She's asleep in the car."

"Okay, bring her in. I'll open up for you."

Fernando carried her into the corridor. He followed the manager down the basement steps to a heavy metal door.

"My wife and I worry about this one," the manager said.

"The doctor said she will be all right, Fernando offered. He didn't want to betray Bunny by giving out more information than necessary.

"This time, but what about next time, and the next time, and on and on." He shook his head. "It's such a shame, a waste really. She can sing. Did you know that?"

"No, I didn't."

"And polite when she's not drunk, or high, or whatever it is she does. I've known this little girl since she could barely walk. We've had her for dinner a few times since she's been here. My wife just loves her, but we are at a loss for knowing how to help her."

They were in her room now. The manager was looking for an umbrella tied to a string hanging from the ceiling. The manager explained, feeling a little silly, "You pull on the umbrella, and it turns on the light."

Fernando wished he would hurry. He was about to drop Bunny.

"Ah-ha. There it is." Finally the light came on. Fernando realized they were standing in a boiler room. A muted blotchy red glow from the light swung back and forth on the walls to the rhythm of the swaying umbrella. It made the two of them dizzy, but they managed to lower her to the mattress on the floor in spite of it. She started to cry out in pain until Fernando supported her from underneath. Then she fell back to sleep as quickly as she had awoken.

The red ruffled umbrella sent out a glow that imitated candlelight. The mattress was covered with a red-and-pink, tie-dyed sheet. For a blanket, Bunny was using an old black fur coat she had bought at the Goodwill.

There looked to be an old metal sliding board ascending from the basement window to the floor.

"What is that?" asked Fernando.

"Oh, that's an old coal chute. Bunny sometimes uses it to get in, instead of buzzing me."

Fernando noticed she had hung the top sheet on the wall behind her bed, and there was a switch hanging from the wall beside it. Fernando turned it on. It backlit the tie-dyed sheet which read: Peace, Love, Peace Love. It looked as if it had been finger painted.

"That's probably something she'll never know in her lifetime," said the manager.

"You never know," said Fernando. "Nothing is impossible with God."

There was an awkward pause in the conversation.

Fernando noticed a white plastic bucket sitting in the middle of the floor, its lid covered with a red-and-purple silk scarf. Fernando lifted the lid. At the bottom of the bucket was a drain that led to the sewer. "How do you flush this thing?" Fernando asked, amused.

"Easy." The manager walked over to the washtub and turned on the water. "All the comforts of home for a mere ten dollars a week." They were chuckling at her ingenuity when suddenly something rattled the plastic bucket from the inside.

"A rat!" complained Mr. Gibbs. He clamped the pillow down on top of the lid. "He must not have liked it when I ran the water. Miserable little creature! Get out of here." He tapped on the side of the bucket while he held the pillow in place. "Get!"

Fernando quickly scratched a note on the back of her appointment card: "In case you don't remember what happened, you needed a guardian angel last night, and I guess I was it. You have a follow-up appointment. (See other side)." On the back of her drug rehab card he wrote, "There are people who care about you. Please take care of yourself and your baby. He's counting on you. You're the best friend he has. God bless you and yours, Fernando Verillo." He leaned both cards against the mirror on the night stand along with her medicine.

They covered her with her fur coat as she laid, sound asleep, as if nothing at all had happened that night.

"Well thank you, good sir, for bringing her back safely."

"Fernando's my name. What is yours?"

"Norm, Norman Gibbs."

The two strangers shook hands.

"Can I get you a glass of water or anything?"

"No, I really need to be going."

"Are you sure? You never know when you're entertaining angels unaware."

"No," he chuckled, "I have to get some sleep."

"Well she was lucky you were there for her."

Fernando said, "Sorry we had to disturb your sleep. Next time I'll have to send her down the coal chute." They both laughed.

Fernando started across the street. The manager called, "Let's hope there won't be a next time."

"A big Amen to that, brother," Fernando replied. He waved good-bye and smiled from across the street. He got into his car slowly, holding his hand to his aching back.

Neither Bunny nor Norm ever saw Fernando again. In fact, Bunny didn't remember much of anything about that night except what Mr. Gibbs told her. In the midst of her daydream, Bunny was subconsciously running her hand back and forth across her scarred navel when the bell over the door at King's Korner Kafe rang. It startled her out of her daydream. She looked up briefly to see if it was Danny. But she didn't know the man. She cradled her head in her hands as she wrestled with her pain. She knew it was just a matter of time before the manager threw her out of the restaurant, and she was beginning to think Danny wasn't going to make it. She felt a rapid tap, tap, tap on her shoulder.

Bunny responded, "All right, all right. I'm goin'."

"Miss Muldare, Miss Bonnie Muldare?"

"Yes?" Bunny answered, confused. A middle-aged man in a brown suit stood across the table. He raised his briefcase and placed it between them.

"I'm so glad I finally found you. I have something for you. May I sit down?"

"Uh, yeah, I guess."

Exodus 20:5. Thou shalt not bow down thyself to them, nor serve them: for I the Lord am a jealous God, visiting the iniquity of the fathers upon the children unto the third and fourth generation of them that hate me.

Chapter 4

All Things Are Possible

$\mathcal{T}$he Kemps lived two farms away from Freida and Martin Mueller. It was a handy three miles from mailbox to mailbox. Everyone living in Promise attempted to live as simply as possible, keeping frills to a minimum. Even so, as Sara traveled down Freida's gravel driveway in their horse-drawn buggy, she looked longingly at the perfectly kept yard. Freida's mailbox was freshly painted, and beautiful begonias overflowed the edges. The driveway was lined with tall cedars that looked as if they had been there forever. A covered bridge spanned the creek that bisected the Mueller's property. Sara looked down into the water as they approached the bridge. When they came out on the other side, her eyes followed the stream to the back of the house. In the evening when the windows were open, the gentle creek could be heard from inside. The tall cedars and covered bridge were especially beautiful after a heavy snowfall. There was no sign of snow today, however. The temperature teetered perfectly between summer and fall. Sara and Will parked their buggy alongside the other buggies then walked down the stone steps and winding pathway that led to the front door. It wasn't a big house, but cozy, and sturdy, made of stone. It was nestled against a hillside on the north that protected it from the winter winds. The smell of wood burning in the cookstove hovered around the old house and then drifted slowly through the boughs of the surrounding pines. The only sounds to be heard were the birds, the creek, and an occasional breeze passing through the trees. There was a bird calling "jiminy, jiminy."

Will called back. "Chiminy, chiminy."

"Jiminy, jiminy," it repeated. There was an indescribable peacefulness that always resided at the Muellers'. It was part of the reason why everyone loved coming to Freida's Bible study.

Usually Sara came to the Bible study without Will, but today, because of the baby, he decided to come along. They had purposely arrived fifteen minutes late so that they would be the last ones to arrive. Six Bible study regulars attended every Monday morning, but more often than not there were about eight ladies attending. Today there were nineteen! Freida was pleasantly surprised. She was the only one who didn't already know what Sara and Will were bringing. With Sara Kemp's six children having all been in church the day before, there wasn't even a slim chance that the secret would be safe until Monday morning. But somehow they had all succeeded. Neither Martin nor Freida had even a hint of what was about to happen on this very ordinary Monday morning.

The Kemps stood at the front door. Sara waited impatiently for Will to turn the crank on the door bell. "Come on, Will," Sara urged. "Ring de bell!"

"What bell?" he teased. He shut his eyes and pointed six inches to the left of the bell. "Here?" He pointed six inches to the right. "Here?"

Sara sighed and turned the crank herself. She tried to see who was inside by peering through the window in the front door, but the glass was too old and wavy to make out any faces.

"What do you suppose she iss baking?" asked Sara.

"Maybe cinnamon buns," guessed Will.

"Mmmmm," they both said.

"Maybe walnut streusel cakes," said Sara, knowing it was Will's favorite.

"Mmmmmm," they said at the same time, even more enthusiastically. It made them laugh.

Freida opened the door, "Hello Sister Sara. We've been waiting for you. Oh look, it iss Brother Will, this iss a surprise."

In the background Sister Martha whispered, "You have no idea." A few of the ladies stifled a chuckle.

"What do I smell? It smells so good," declared Sara as she slipped out of her shawl and bonnet.

"Walnut streusels."

Sara and Will looked at each other and exclaimed, "MMMM!" and started laughing again.

Freida took Sara's shawl and bonnet, along with Will's straw hat, and hung them on the iron hooks inside the door. Freida said, "Can you believe de crowd we have today? If we have any more visitors, I will be running out of hooks. I hope there will be enough cakes to go around. Oooh! What did you bring us in de picnic basket?" asked Freida.

"May we go in and sit down first?" suggested Sara, even though she was worried the blanket might pop up at any moment.

"Yah, surely." Freida clasped her hands around her mouth, megaphone style. "Everyone, everyone find a seat. Sister Sara and Brother Will brought something to show us." Freida wondered why today everybody was so cooperative. They never were before. Everyone immediately found a seat.

Will put the basket on an old trunk that served as a coffee table in front of the main couch.

When Freida sat down she noticed everyone had fastened their eyes on her instead of the basket. She began to wonder what on earth was going on. Just then the basket jerked a little. Then it jerked a little harder. "Whatever it iss, it iss alive," said Freida, laughing nervously, as did everyone else.

Out of the silence a wet gurgly sound started up. "Gggg," and a foot popped out from under the basket. Freida was so startled her chair rocked back. Luckily, Will was standing behind her and caught it before it tipped.

Mrs. Kemp pulled back the old patchwork blanket and said, "Peek-a-boo." Vincent smiled right on cue.

"Gggg," he continued. He tossed his pacifier out of the basket.

"Awww," the ladies all said in unison.

"Where did he come from?" asked Freida with curiosity.

"From God," Sister Tonya said. "Where else? He's our little angel baby."

"He iss beautiful isn't he, but who's baby iss it?"

"We don't know. Someone left him in our van," said Sara. "He iss surely a sweet one. Aren't you a little sweet, sweet, boy?" She lifted him out of the basket and nuzzled his soft neck.

Vincent began kicking with glee. He loved the attention.

"Left it in your van!?" Freida was shocked.

"With a note," added Sara. She handed the note to Freida.

She read: "My name is Vincent. I was born on April 14. I am five months old. My mommy can't take care of me anymore, so would you please take care of me? I won't cry too much if you play this tape."

"This iss de most incredible thing that ever happened to us," Freida said. "What iss on de tape recording?"

"Lou Rawls," Will interjected, handing the tape to Freida. "He has a soothing voice," Will explained, feeling a little defensive.

"You listened to it?" asked Freida curiously.

"Well, yah," answered Will, embarrassed. "Here iss his tape recorder."

Some of the ladies put their hands up to their mouths in an attempt to cover their amusement.

"Can I hold him?" Freida asked.

Sara passed Vincent over. Vincent reached out with his chubby little arms. He laid his head on Freida's shoulder like a rag doll. He was warm and soft. She looked at his face next to hers and said, "Look at that sweet little face. Are you keeping him?"

"Well no, not exactly. We were going to talk to you about that."

Freida looked around the room and realized they were all waiting for this moment. "But, did you report this to de police or someone?"

"Of course. It iss all taken care of," Sara explained. "De policeman in Carlisle told us we could take care of him for now, and then we could get de adoption finished in about six months."

"How can you be sure de mother does not want him back?" asked Freida.

Will blurted, "The policeman knows his mother. He said she iss a prostitute and a heroin addict. He said she probably dropped him off in our van so she could leave town without being bothered with a baby. He did not expect her to come back. He did not have anything kind to say about her, and wass calling her names. I told him not to call her trash, but he would not hear it."

Freida said, "You were going to talk to me about adopting him?" Freida struggled to contain her excitement in case it wasn't true.

Vincent began to squirm and fuss. "Not now boy, we almost got her," Will said as he reached in the basket for Vincent's bottle.

Freida turned him over to give him his bottle. Vincent looked up at her with contented curiosity. They both had dark hair and eyes. Freida had large friendly eyes and a bright smile that made people feel comfortable instantly. Her face was round and peach colored against her chestnut brown hair, which was pulled back in the traditional Mennonite bun and tucked into her prayer cap. As Vincent studied her face she said, "Well, I can not speak for Martin, but I think I am in love with this little boy." Freida's eyes had misted over. She looked up at the faces in the room.

The roomful of ladies began tapping their hands and feet quietly as they began whispering "Thank you, Lord." "Praise you, Jesus." "What a blessing."

"There iss not a dry eye in de house," Sister Claudia said.

Will's voice quivered and cracked like a schoolboy's. "I have already talked to Martin. He iss all for it, Freida. He will be home as soon as you can get rid of us."

Vincent continued to drink his bottle, oblivious to the fact that his life had just taken a tremendous turn for the better.

"Can you ladies pray over de prayer requests without me?" asked Freida, gently squeezing Vincent's bare leg. "I don't think I can get through them without crying."

"Go, go, take him somewhere. We can do this," Sister Claudia insisted.

"I am guessing we are crossing off your request for a baby?" Sister Sara asked.

Freida couldn't answer. She smiled through her tears and shook her head. Her prayer had been answered, without a doubt—God had done the impossible.

Once in the kitchen, she turned on his tape recorder, and the two of them began to dance. "You'll never find, as long as you live, someone who loves you tender like I do."

Vincent lay softly and relaxed in Freida's arms. "Thank you, Lord. Thank you, Lord Jesus, for answering my prayer." Freida said to Vincent, "You are my little angel baby sent from God."

Matthew 19:26. But Jesus beheld them, and said unto them, with men this is impossible; but with God all things are possible.

Chapter 5

Sunday Morning

Sunday morning came quickly for Freida and Martin.
The new parents didn't realize how much work an infant
could be. In Promise, Sunday morning was always an event,
taking considerable preparation. Each of the forty-three
households took the Lord's Day very seriously. They prepared their clothing and Sunday dinner on Saturday, so
that by Sunday morning they could step into their clothes
and go to church.

It made a parade from the past as they slowly clip-
clopped buggy by buggy toward the little white clapboard
chapel just north of the Pennsylvania turnpike. The families living south of the turnpike moved along Creek Road
across miles of woodland and manicured fields. The only
intrusion from the outside world came as they crossed the
overpass above the turnpike. The children leaned out of
the buggy windows, hanging onto their hats and bonnets,
to get a better look at the cars and trucks passing underneath them. After the excitement of whirling tires on pavement had passed below them, they would settle into the

gentler rhythmic clop, clop, clop, of horses' hooves once again. All back roads in Promise revealed the pathway that its members had taken for hundreds of years. No matter from what direction the buggies started, all paths led to the little white church on the hill they called "God's Acre." Many of them could have driven in their cars, but the buggy ride to church was all part of the tradition they had always enjoyed.

The buggies gathered in the field one by one, as families of two, five, and even ten children congregated inside the little church. There was a center aisle where the men and boys went to the right, and the women, girls, and small children went to the left. They slid along slick wooden pews that glowed with the wood polish and care they had received for more years than anyone present could remember. The older members of the congregation thought the church to be about two hundred and twenty-five years old, though there was no written record.

Freida and Martin walked the center aisle holding hands. Martin held Vincent in his right arm, tucked carefully under a blanket. As they came to the pew where they would be separated they looked sadly into each other's eyes. Martin passed Vincent to Freida, and she made her way to the end of the pew on the left side of the church. She took note that outside the window, next to her, a Carolina wren had her babies. She had been watching each Sunday to see whether the eggs had hatched. The sun was hitting the branches of the bush at the perfect angle so that Freida could count the babies. There were three.

"Good morning all my brothers and sisters in de Lord. What a beautiful morning, iss it not?" boomed Pastor Dunkin. His deep voice reflected off the white plaster walls and dark brown wooden floors. He rubbed his stomach and rocked back and forth as he waited for the congregation to respond. Pastor Dunkin was shaped like a big round candy apple with arms and legs. He loved farming, and his overalls were his attire of choice. However, today he conceded to his Sunday suit. He had parted his jet-black hair perfectly, brushed it to the side, and applied olive oil to hold it in place. His black beard was trimmed into a narrow band that edged his full face, and his expressive eyebrows were situated conspicuously between his wrinkled, sun-weathered forehead and dark brown eyes.

Freida found herself missing Martin more than usual. She leaned back in her seat, looking through a flurry of nodding prayer veils to find Martin. When she caught sight of him, he was already looking at her. It reminded her of when they were just sixteen, and she would catch him staring at her. This time however, twelve years later, he didn't look away. He was watching over her and the baby as best he could from a distance.

Martin was thinking how much he loved Freida. He appreciated how easily she stepped into the role of motherhood.

"De theme of this Sunday's message," said Pastor Dunkin, "iss, 'Study to Show Thyself Approved.' If you would, please turn in your Bibles to de book of Daniel, chapter nine."

The members began to flip through the pages until they found the chapter. The pastor spoke over the flipping pages, "As you know, I have just returned from our annual meeting in York. And while I wass on my way there, Brother Will and I were listening to de 'G' man. What iss his name?

"What's that?"

One of the deacons offered, "De 'I' man?"

"Heavens no. Not that slippery slope!"

"G. Gordon Liddy?"

"Yah. Thank you Brother Will."

Pastor Dunkin continued, "Mr. Liddy related this story. I thought you would enjoy hearing this. A Sunday school teacher wass teaching a group of five-year-olds. She asked one of them, 'Johnny, can you tell us what iss small, brown, furry, and eats nuts?' Johnny scratched his head and answered, 'Well, I know de answer iss Jesus, but it surely sounds like a squirrel to me.'" Pastor Dunkin raised his eyebrows at the congregation. They laughed. Martin's raucous laughter could be heard above everyone.

After a few moments they settled down, and Pastor Dunkin was able to resume. Smiling, he continued, "The point here iss this: the more we know God's word, the less we must guess what it iss we must do. God's word never fails. Amen?

For instance, most obviously, studying God's word will help us to understand, without a shadow of a doubt, what God's will iss concerning our own personal everyday lives. It may not tell us which shoe to put on first, but certainly it clears up, in innumerable ways, the so-called gray areas. How lucky we are. Amen?"

"Amen," echoed the congregation quietly.

"When it comes to de tiny details, I am not sure I could always remember things like which shoe to put on first. The Old Testament church had a much tougher time pleasing God than we. They had to remember this rule, and remember that rule, and generally to deal with de problem of too many rules. We New Testament believers are lucky. God could see that we have challenge enough just trying to deal with de larger issues of life, such as de kind of woman to marry, de way to handle our money, de way to treat our neighbors. In other words, what I am trying to say iss, God gives us His word, in as simple a way as possible, so that we can get through life without stepping into something we don't want to be stepping into, praise Jesus." Pastor Dunkin put his hands behind his back and stuck his chin out at a row of children. They smiled back at him.

"Secondly, and not as obviously, studying and understanding Old Testament prophecy, that has already proven itself by coming to pass, helps us to understand and interpret New Testament prophecy that iss still to be coming. And best of all it allows us to believe that what God says can be trusted. Today we are going to take a look at de triumphal entry of Jesus into Jerusalem, as wass predicted in de Old Testament, and wass described in de New Testament when He rode in on de donkey during Passover. We will discover that it came to pass to de exact day as predicted in de Old Testament book of Daniel. Does that not roll your socks down and make your hair stand on end. To de exact day it was predicted, and God told them about it hundreds of years before it happened! But why should we be so excited about a prediction that came true nearly two thousand years ago? What has God done for us lately, you may ask? What that means for us iss this: if He told us correctly to de day back then, He will be doing it exactly and correctly again, in de near future. Jesus will be coming back again, returning to us exactly as He hass prophesied it in the New and in de Old Testament. You wait and see. You can put it in de bank, because God's word says so! And further, if that iss true, we are all going to be seeing each other again on that great and glorious day when we will meet our Lord and savior up in de air. Brother Perl, you will be there. Sister Tonya, you will be there.

"We will be seeing him face to face, praise you, Jesus. And if that does not roll your stockings down and make your hair stand on end, then you must not be wearing any stockings, or maybe you don't have any hair." He stroked his thick black hair with pride.

Freida smiled as she rocked Vincent back and forth. She had heard her father use those old, worn-out lines all her life, but the church never seemed to tire of hearing them. She decided not to disturb Vincent by reaching for her Bible, so she depended on her memory. She could repeat, by heart, the passage her father now read: "Daniel 9:24: 'Seventy weeks are determined upon thy people and upon thy holy city, to finish the transgression, and to make an end of sins, and to make reconciliation for iniquity, and to bring in everlasting righteousness, and to seal up the vision and prophecy, and to anoint the most Holy.'" Pastor Dunkin pointed to the blackboard behind him where he had written in capital letters and began to read, "Know therefore and understand, that from the going forth of the commandment to restore and to rebuild Jerusalem, unto the Messiah the prince shall be seven weeks, and threescore and two weeks; the street shall be built again, and the wall, even in troublous times." He turned back to the Bible and continued the scripture, "And after threescore and two weeks shall Messiah be cut off, but not for himself . . ." Pastor Dunkin explained, "It goes on to prophesy about de end times, but we are not going to concentrate on that until next week. Today we are going to discover how long it took from de time de decree was given for Nehemiah to rebuild the wall surrounding Jerusalem, in Nehemiah, Chapter 2, until their Messiah, Luke 3. First we are going to study, according to de history books, how long that time period took and compare it to what de Bible predicted, and see if what de Bible says can be counted on. I don't think I will be spoiling the surprise if I tell you, yes, it can be counted on."

Freida looked down into Vincent's face. If she wasn't looking into the face of a miracle, then what was it? His ears were so small. They were no bigger than a quarter and yet they had every teeny twist and turn necessary for him to hear The sun came out from behind a cloud and shown down on the rim of his ear, making it pink as the light passed through. She studied the ring of golden fuzz that circled the edge of the rim. It was almost microscopic. His nose was also small. He had eyebrows, but they were nearly invisible, and his eyelashes curled up evenly on the ends in a perfect row. She stroked her finger across his soft cheek. "What a blessing he is Lord, thank you again," she prayed. Freida put her index finger into Vincent's hand as he slept. He squeezed her finger and held on tight. A peace enveloped her like a warm blanket, and love welled up within her heart. She was certain that God had blessed her with this precious little baby.

Freida had somehow lost track of the entire message, but she heard Pastor Dunkin's summation. "De allotted time for de Jewish people to expect their Messiah to come started from de time Nehemiah was given de command to restore Jerusalem (March 14, 445 B.C.) until he would be cut off or executed (April 6, A.D. 32) and it would take seven weeks, and three score and two weeks. How long is seven weeks and three score and two weeks? Raise your hand if you think that is seven weeks plus sixty plus two weeks." He worked out the problem on the black board. "Sixty-nine weeks, right?"

No one raised their hand. "Can one of you children tell me why it iss more than that? It iss a matter of weeks. Correct?" Pastor Dunkin saw Joel Hansfelter's hand go up.

"Yes, Joel."

"Because a week in de prophecy means to multiply by seven. It iss not really seven days."

"Right!" replied Pastor Dunkin. "Someone wass listening to de message."

Pastor Dunkin continued, "It iss seven times seven plus sixty-two times seven, which makes four hundred and eighty-three years. Since there are only three hundred and sixty days in a prophetic year that would be 483 years times 360 days, or 173,880 days from the time Nehemiah built de wall till Jesus marched into Jerusalem on His, now famous, donkey. De historic dates according to the Encyclopedia Britannica are March 14, 445 B.C. until April 6, A.D. 32. We see that when we translate those dates into de Julian, or Jewish, calendar those 173,880 days are precisely correct. It was exactly seven weeks, three score and two weeks from de time de decree to rebuild was given until Messiah declared, 'Oh Jerusalem, Jerusalem, if you only knew the things that belong to you on this your day.' The last week or heptad, of the seventy weeks in verse 24 we will discuss next week. To prepare yourself, read the rest of Daniel 9."

Pastor Dunkin ended with, "To conclude our message for today I would like to remind you, if you want to know if de answer iss Jesus or a squirrel, you must study God's word. Can you do that for me? I know you will."

After the parting prayer, everyone began to meander toward the large double front doors. The stiff long skirts swished past each other in the tight rows of pews. Freida gradually worked her way back to Martin. When she spotted him, she said to herself, he may not be the most handsome of the group, but he is certainly my favorite. Martin held his felt hat in his hands in front of him as he approached Freida. He turned to the side to survey which of his friends were nearby. His silhouette showed the crook in his long nose even from a distance. The crook in his Adam's apple matches de crook in his nose, Freida mused.

"Sister Freida!" someone called. "Let us see de sweet little boy we have been hearing about."

Freida smiled as she uncovered him. "This iss Vincent," she said.

The woman drew in an excited gasp. "Oh my goodness, look at you!"

"Hello Vincent," several more ladies joined in.

"What a cutie you are. Yah, you are," bubbled the on-lookers.

"How old iss he, Freida?"

"Five months."

Sara Kemp joined the group. When she saw Vincent, she said with a start, "My goodness, Vincent has new glasses!"

A myriad of feelings rushed through Freida. She was oddly ashamed that he wasn't perfect. She felt bad for Vincent, because the glasses hurt his ears and she had to keep putting them back on ever time he tried to pull them off. She felt uncomfortable that they were all looking at him with a combined curiosity and pity. And she felt angry toward his natural mother—if she hadn't used heroin while she was with child, his eyes would be perfectly fine.

The doctor told her that heroin manifests itself in a variety of ways. He also explained that Vincent could have other problems that hadn't surfaced yet, but by all appearances he looked very healthy. As Freida explained all this, she could see the unwelcome pity. It made her all the more determined to be a good mother to this little one who desperately needed her.

"How did they know what prescription to give him?" another lady asked with self-conscious curiosity.

"It iss all done by a machine. A shadow iss projected onto his iris, and as they flip through the different lenses, the shadow goes away when they get to de right one. I don't really understand it altogether."

"That iss something. I suppose it would be impossible to ask him, can you see this, can you see that?" The ladies laughed nervously.

"It iss a miracle, really, what they are able to do," said Freida.

"How did you know he needed them?"

"We noticed he liked to smell things. This iss kind of silly, but Martin and I noticed he would scoot along on his belly, until he got to our feet, and sniff them. I mean really sniff. I am guessing that iss how he was able to tell us apart."

Sara Kemp loved teasing her little brother, Martin. She joked, "My goodness, Martin and you look nothing alike. It would not take much looking to figure out whose feet were whose. I mean, look at de size of Martin's feet, not to mention de smell. That alone would be a dead giveaway. And what about de size of his Adam's apple! How could he not see that huge thing sticking out there like a grapefruit?" She looked at Martin excitedly, anticipating her brother's rebuttal.

"I wouldn't be so quick to talk about other people's big body parts, Sister Sara."

"Martin!" Freida elbowed him.

"What, Freida? I wass talking about Will. His Adam's apple iss bigger than mine. What did you think I wass talking about?"

Freida decided it was best to ignore him. She looked at Sara apologetically, shook her head, and rolled her eyes. Sara was giggling more than anyone. She knew perfectly well he was talking about her and not Will. Martin would always and forever be her favorite brother. But, of course, it would take nothing short of an impending avalanche for her to admit it.

"Anyway," Freida continued with a sigh, "I had a pile of towels and sheets and his blanket on de floor, folding them. He sniffed around in de pile until he found his blanket."

"I am guessing you are glad to be able to see. Aren't you? Yah, you are," said Sara, shaking Vincent's hand. "I think it makes him look all de more adorable. It makes his eyes look bigger."

Vincent smiled a toothless smile and turned his head shyly toward Freida's chest.

Freida continued, "One of his eyes kept crossing, and that iss what told me in de first place maybe something was not right."

Martin piped in, "We were thinking maybe you had been whacked in de head a few too many times." He made a face at Vincent, crossing his eyes as if he'd just been hit with a frying pan.

Vincent looked at Martin and burped in response. Martin laughed his raucous laugh.

"Martin, that is not funny," Freida scolded.

"Vincent," Martin said, "you did not get your feelings hurt now, did you? Come to your pappa, boy." He held the baby high in the air. Vincent's happy feet started kicking away as Martin began dancing with him while he sang in his best Lou Rawls voice, "You will never find, as long as you live, someone who loves you de way I do."

Two of the ladies looked puzzled. "Martin sings secular songs now? And in church?" they asked.

"We'll tell you all about it," explained the ladies from Bible study.

"De baby came with music," explained Sara Kemp.

They were still puzzled.

Sister Anna said, "Freida and Martin, de two of you look so very happy. I am overflowing with gladness God has blessed you this way." Everyone agreed. Freida looked a little choked up.

"It has been a blessing for certain," Martin agreed. "Well, we better be leaving ladies."

"If you need anything, Freida, don't be slow to ask."

"Thank you for offering. I will remember," she answered.

As they walked away Martin sang, "You will never find someone who loves . . ." He swung his big feet and long, bowed legs in front of him, taking about one step to every two of Freida's.

"Love you two," Sara called.

"Bye." Freida waved to them all.

Martin turned around, Vincent's cheek pressing against his. Vincent's round glasses and round pink cheeks contrasted with Martin's long thin nose and scruffy brown beard. Martin held up Vincent's arm and waved the baby's tiny hand at the ladies. "Bye-bye ladies," Martin called.

"Bye," they all responded together.

It was a beautiful September morning, perfect for the buggy ride home. Freida and Martin couldn't think of a time when they felt more in love. Freida put her arm around Martin's waist and held him close. The red and yellow maple leaves of autumn swirled around them as the buggy wheels began to turn.

Matthew 7:7. Ask, and it shall be given you; seek, and ye shall find; knock, and it shall be opened unto you.

Chapter 6

Miss Purdy

FIVE YEARS LATER: Age 5

*T*he Muellers and the Muellers' duck (Miss Purdy the Wonder Duck) were on their way to school for show-and-tell. "Now Vincent," said Freida as they bumped along squeezed together in the seat of their buggy, "when I talked to your teacher about bringing your duck to school, she said you could bring her, as long as you keep her in de cage. The only time you are to let Miss Purdy out iss during show-and-tell. Did you hear your mamma?"

"Yah, I heard, Mamma." His breath made steam when it hit the cold air. Vincent puffed out hard to make more steam. "Look Pappa, my breath iss smoking."

Martin said to Vincent, "You know son, it might get confusing today since you named your duck after your teacher."

"Yah, I know. It got me into trouble already." Vincent pushed up on his glasses with the back of his hand.

"Yah?" asked Martin.

"I showed Marshall one of her eggs, and he said, 'Where did you get that?' And I said, 'Miss Purdy laid it,' and then everybody started laughing, and she got mad."

"So," asked Martin, "I am guessing you got it straightened out?"

"Yah," he said, still unhappy about it happening in the first place. He loved his teacher. "Iss this enough food for her until she gets home?" He tugged on a little sack inside his pocket.

Freida felt his pocket before he had a chance to rip the bag. "Yah, yah, that iss plenty enough."

"I wouldn't want her to be hungry."

"That will be good enough." Freida reassured.

"Do you think she will forget what to do?"

"She will do wonderfully well as long as you are there beside her," Freida answered.

"I don't want them to laugh at her like they laughed at Miss Purdy," said Vincent.

"They might. But she iss a duck; she will not mind. You are going to have fun and so iss Miss Purdy. They are going to love her," Freida said.

"Yah, I am guessing they will love her too." Vincent sounded convinced.

"I love her." Vincent said a few minutes later.

"Yah," Martin said.

"So they will love her too, right?" asked Vincent.

"Yah," Martin replied turning to smile at Freida.

Vincent repeated with assurance, "They are going to love you, Miss Purdy." He nestled back into his seat.

It was nippy this morning, twenty degrees. It made the countryside look gray and stark. There was a layer of frost on the fields. The clapboard one-room schoolhouse was a welcome sight; the warm smoke from the heat stove rose from the chimney.

Martin tied up the buggy at the side of the building while Freida helped Vincent down. His felt hat almost blew off in the wind. He pushed it down tightly on his head. His hair was sandy brown in a bowl haircut. His ears poked out from underneath his hat. He wore gold wire- rim glasses that made his large brown eyes look even larger. He wore a black wool jacket, a dark blue broadcloth shirt, and a pair of black cotton pants with black suspenders, as did all the boys.

"C'mon Miss Purdy, time to do your tricks," he said.

Inside were forty noisy children of all ages from neighboring farms. They hung their hats and coats on wooden pegs just inside the front door. They each had their own wooden desk with a flip-top lid and iron legs. Some of the lids were being raised and lowered noisily by their owners as they prepared for the day. The blackboards were enormous, wrapping around three sides of the room. Miss Purdy kept three lessons going at the same time for different grade levels. The children's ages ranged from five to thirteen.

Behind Miss Purdy's desk, opposite the front door, there was a hallway that led to the restroom and kitchen. Behind the kitchen was a large covered porch that opened to a play yard with a dozen picnic tables and a baseball field. This area had been used since the 1800s for tug-a-war games, three legged races, picnics, and other social gatherings. Of the three schoolhouses built in Promise, this one had the best baseball field. The outfield was lined with apple trees. Raspberries and grapes grew on the fence bordering the play area. Beyond the fence at the edge of the property, there was a sharp drop off at the edge of the mountain overlooking the Susquehanna River. If the ball went over the fence, it was really over the fence, never to be seen again. Most times, the ball was stopped by the apple trees before it got that far. However, on that rare occasion when it went "clear to the river," as they said around Promise, it certainly added to the drama of the moment.

There was a ball that had been stuck on a precipice of the mountainside for at least ten years, and there were several men who liked to lay claim to it, Martin Mueller being one of them.

Vincent's teacher, Miss Purdy, seated Freida and Martin in very small chairs against the wall just inside the front door. These chairs were normally reserved for the smallest children who couldn't reach the wooden coat hooks. They were more like stools than chairs. Martin's knees were up to his chest, and Freida's skirt was draping the floor.

Miss Purdy said, "Everyone stand for the Lord's Prayer."

Martin rose from his seat towering over the crowd infront of him by several feet. He put his hat over his heart while Freida struggled with Miss Purdy's cage. A chorus of young voices began in a slow monotone, "Our father which art in heaven, hallowed be thy name. Thy kingdom come. Thy will be done in earth, as it iss in heaven. Give us this day our daily bread, and forgive us our debts as we forgive our debtors. And lead us not into temptation, but deliver us from evil: For thine iss de kingdom, and de power, and de glory, for ever. Amen."

Everyone quickly took their seats without a word.

Miss Purdy announced, "We are going to delay our current events this morning, because Vincent has something he would like to share with us. I think you will really enjoy this. Vincent?"

"Huh?"

"Vincent, honey, it iss your turn for show-and-tell," said Miss Purdy.

"Ah. Yah."

Miss Purdy wondered how he could look straight at her and not have the slightest idea what she was saying. He was concentrating on her glasses. They were similar to his own, though not nearly so thick. He wondered why she always wore them with a string attached around her neck. And why, he thought, did she always take them off and on? She was a small woman but not to be underestimated—a fact some of the children had learned the hard way. She could, if necessary, hit a student right in the head with an eraser from clear across the room, and she wasn't afraid to do it. Vincent wasn't afraid of her though; he knew what her rules were, and he was quite contented with them. The recent misunderstanding between him and Miss Purdy had upset them both, and Miss Purdy hoped this would smooth things over.

Vincent retrieved his duck from her cage. He struggled to heave her big white fluffy rear end up onto Miss Purdy's desk. Vincent and his teacher looked at each other. They both realized they were taking a risk leaving the duck on her desk for very long, but it was the only way everyone was going to be able to see her. Miss Purdy looked more nervous every time the duck wagged its tail. She wrapped one arm around her waist and pushed her glasses up. She reminded herself that this was her way of making up for what happened during the who-laid-the-egg ordeal.

"Hey, where did your front tooth go there, Vincent?" Miss Purdy asked.

"I swallowed it."

"Uh-oh," his teacher sympathized.

"I wass going to look for it, but I changed my mind."

"Did you say you swallowed it?" Suddenly it dawned on her. "Oh," she interrupted, "No need to explain, I think we get de idea. But that iss probably not a good idea," she suggested, hoping to discourage anything like this in the future.

"Yah, it iss a good idea. My mamma and pappa did that when my mamma lost de diamond out of her ring. It wass in de meatloaf and one of us ate it."

Miss Purdy glanced back at his parents. Jewelry wasn't worn by the people in Promise, not even wedding bands, and diamonds were nonexistent. Martin and Freida sat in their tiny chairs dumbfounded at what had just been revealed. Freida's mouth hung open. Martin stared motionless.

Miss Purdy searched her mind for a way to rescue them, but Vincent forged ahead.

He pushed up on his glasses. "My pappa won a diamond ring at de baseball game, and he gave it to my mamma. She wore it around, just at our house for my pappa for two days, but she lost it in de meatloaf. Diamonds are a lot of money, you know."

"Now how did your pappa win a diamond ring at a baseball game?" she asked. Miss Purdy was beginning to wonder if any of this was true.

Martin couldn't let Vincent look like he was making up a lie (though it was tempting under the circumstances). "All Stars," Martin admitted. "Our stadium ticket had de winning number on it. De local jeweler donated it, but I wass getting ready to sell it," he explained.

"Yah, and it wass worth $500!" Vincent said excitedly. But you see, they already ate de meatloaf, and when we looked at de ring on Mamma's hand, all that wass in there, where de diamond wass supposed to be, wass a chunk of hamburger meat!"

The children giggled.

"So Pappa told Mamma, since she wass so careless, she wass just going to have to go looking for it, and it did not matter who ate it since she cooked it." Vincent turned his little hands up at his sides and shrugged his shoulders as if to say, 'oh well, if you gotta, you gotta.'

"Oh my. Did she find it?"

"Well, she looked for one day but then she said, since my pappa loved it so much he would have to look for it his self. She left her poopski on de kitchen table."

Miss Purdy's mouth fell open.

"In, in a paper sack," Vincent explained.

By then the older children were beginning to glance back at the Muellers.

"Oh my goodness!" mumbled Freida. She looked down and started playing with her apron.

Miss Purdy asked, "Did they ever find de diamond?" hoping this would finally end his saga.

"Yah, after about a month." The children giggled again, louder this time. Vincent twirled his hair around his finger nervously. Freida smacked her knee and tsked.

"Or two days, or something like that," he corrected himself. Vincent didn't really know. His conception of time was still pretty sketchy.

Martin put his hat over his face, though it didn't cover up his stomach, revealing the fact that behind the hat he was roaring with laughter. Freida tried looking out the window. Her cheeks were turning red and blotchy.

Miss Purdy took a deep breath and said, "Well now, that iss not really what you were going to share with us today, iss it?"

"No."

The older children were snickering and snorting. Vincent stuck his finger in his ear and smiled self-consciously.

"What did you want to share with us today?"

"My duck. Her name iss Miss Purdy de Wonder Duck! Ta Daa!" he sang.

"She does tricks. Watch this." He took out a three- foot length of rope and asked his teacher to hold one end. Vincent took the other end and began to swing it around and around as Miss Purdy the duck maneuvered her huge feet and formidable rear end, slap, slap, slap, jumping to the rhythm of the rope. The children were fascinated. Vincent gave her some sunflower seeds from his tattered sack for her trouble. The children applauded.

"But that iss not all she can do. Are you ready to sing, Miss Purdy?" He began to sing, "How much iss that ducky in de window?"

"Quack, Quack," said Miss Purdy the duck.

"De one with de waggly tail."

"Quack, Quack."

"How much iss that ducky in de window?"

"Quack, Quack."

"I do hope that ducky's for sale."

"QUACK, QUACK, QUACK, QUACK, QUACK."

Vincent offered more sunflower seeds.

The children applauded as Miss Purdy the duck continued to quack, quack, quack and flap her wings.

Miss Purdy asked, "Where did you get your duck?" Mennonites are always interested in the breed and the breeder.

"Well, I found de egg at de creek. It wass big. My mamma said we could give it to Broody to sit on. That iss one of Mamma's chickens that likes to sit on eggs, alllllll day." He made a large gesture with his arm to indicate from sunup to sundown. "All kinds of eggs," he added excitedly.

Freida thought to herself, this sounds like a safe subject. Nevertheless, she couldn't help being a little nervous.

"She sat on it for lots of days, and it just hatched," he shrugged with delight. "Me and Miss Purdy, we started going to de creek together, and now we are friends."

"I am curious, Vincent. Why did you name your duck Miss Purdy?"

"Because I love her," he said, matter-of-factly.

His honesty embarrassed her, especially after the trouble they'd had over the egg. "Well thank you, Vincent. I love you too. We are very glad you brought Miss Purdy today. Aren't we children?"

"YAH!" they all agreed in unison.

Miss Purdy gave Vincent a hug and swallowed the lump in her throat.

Vincent thought his heart would burst with joy. Just then he noticed that Miss Purdy the duck had left her mark on the teacher's desk. He picked her up and did his best to use her rear end to wipe up the mess, followed by the seed sack. The rest, he managed to swipe clean with his sleeve. He whispered into Miss Purdy the Wonder Duck's ear, "Don't worry, I got it all cleaned up. You did a very good job." After he put her back in her cage, he gave her the rest of the seeds and put the dirty sack back in his pocket.

Freida and Martin walked out the door with as little fanfare as possible. Miss Purdy hurried to the door to thank them before they left. Freida put a fresh duck egg in Miss Purdy's hand and said, "Think of this as bribery."

"No need to worry, if anyone hears about this, it will not have come from me, Sister Freida."

Freida's forced smile suddenly vanished. Miss Purdy turned around to see what the problem was.

There were forty faces turned around in their desks looking at them.

"Thank you again." Miss Purdy called after them.

Matthew 6:12–13. And forgive us our debts, as we forgive our debtors. And lead us not into temptation but deliver us from evil: For thine is the kingdom, and the power, and the glory, for ever. Amen.

Chapter 7

Talent Night

TWO YEARS LATER: Vincent, Age 7

*F*reida's father approached the podium. "Good evening, brothers and sisters in de Lord." Pastor Dunkin thought the introduction would be enough to settle down the crowd, but there was still quite a bit of rustling in the congregation.

"Everyone has been looking forward to tonight, both de audience and de participants." He cleared his throat and waited, and waited. The rustling reluctantly settled.

"And as most of you know, de children have been working very hard to make children's night an enjoyable evening for us all. So, hold on to your suspenders—I know we are in for a most memorable evening." He gestured to Miss Purdy to come up.

Breathlessly Miss Purdy began, "Our first participant tonight will be Abigail Dietche. She will be playing de 'Twelve Days of Christmas' on de organ." As they were applauding, Miss Purdy raced back up to the podium; she had left her notes. She apologized and hurried back to her seat.

Vincent, Freida, and Vincent's closest friend, Marshall, were seated in the first row. Martin seated himself with the men, not out of necessity but because it was a habit. Marshall's parents didn't attend, but then they never attended any functions other than Sunday morning church.

One of the older women of Promise, Sister Ruth, approached Freida. She whispered, "Could you please watch my mother for me? They are asking for me behind de scenes. I am terribly sorry to ask of you like this." For years Ruth's mother had been the official piano teacher in Promise. Her mother had always been a straight-backed, humorless teacher, but she was very knowledgeable in her field. She had a music degree from Dickinson College. Even her name had a serious quality about it, Mother Christine Halt. Freida was more than a little anxious about it, since Mother Christine had suffered a stroke five years earlier and had never fully regained her senses. At first glance, she appeared to be perfectly normal, except for her speech. But then, since her stroke she very rarely spoke. It was the embarrassing behaviors that made it obvious that something in her brain had short circuited. Her daughter theorized that her stroke had given her mother a license to say and do whatever she wanted after all those years of repression. You never knew what embarrassing thing she was going to do next. She might sit quietly the entire evening, as dignified as ever, but there was always the other possibility that she would do something completely outrageous and, quite honestly, Freida didn't want to be held responsible for it.

"Of course, we would love to," said Freida.

Mother Christine was probably the oldest person living in Promise and certainly the oldest in this gathering. How could Freida say no? For one thing, Freida's father was the pastor, and for another, Freida could never say no to anything. "Don't worry, we will take good care of her." She tried to smile.

Vincent was thrilled, and so was Marshall. It wasn't everyday they could witness Mother Christine's antics firsthand. Freida sat Vincent next to Mother Christine, who was on the end of the row. Freida sat between Vincent and Marshall. She was sure the boys would act up during the program, but she wasn't sure about Mother Christine. So she took a chance and seated herself between the two boys. Eventually, though, the boys were lulled into comatose boredom as the "Twelve Days of Christmas" droned on. Vincent waved his head mechanically from side to side along with the countdown. "Seven swans a swimming, six geese a laying, five gold rings, four calling birds, three French hens, two turtle doves, and a partridge in a pear tree. On the eighth day of Christmas . . ." Vincent looked over at Marshall. Marshall looked over at Vincent putting both hands on his cheeks and pulled down in total frustration. They wondered if twelve would ever arrive. Marshall had a special talent for communicating by facial gestures. He had perfected his art in school. Vincent could tell what his best friend was thinking with a simple glance. Marshall's faces were continually getting Vincent into trouble, because, most of the time, the point of Marshall's faces were to make Vincent laugh.

As the twelfth day was wrapping up, Miss Purdy wasted no time. "Thank you Abigail," said Miss Purdy. Everyone applauded politely, everyone except Mother Christine. She stood up and applauded wildly as if she wanted another go-round. Freida grabbed the back of her skirt and sat her back down. Freida had the feeling it was going to be a long night.

"Next we have a testimony read by Joel Kessler. Come on Joel, sweetie, it iss your turn." Joel was six.

He cleared his throat, took a deep breath, and blew out. "This was in de *Christian Chronicles Magazine*," he began. "It iss called, 'Will Wonders Never Cease.'"

"A young boy's mother was warming milk on de stove. Before she left de room she said, 'Billy, don't go near this milk. It iss going to get very hot.'"

"After she left, de boy's kitten began to cry for de milk. De boy got up on a chair and poured some milk from de pot onto de floor. OOPS! He had poured too much. He put what was left back on de stove and began to pray. 'Please God, would you make some more milk before my mommy comes back? She is going to be terrible mad at me.' He opened his eyes and de milk began to boil over in de pan. 'Stop! That iss enough!' he exclaimed."

To Joel's delight everyone was laughing and applauding. He waved to his mother and grandmother before he made his exit. Joel hadn't understood the ending, but his mother had told him that everyone would like it. He was glad his mother had been right.

Freida looked over to find Vincent holding the entire contents of Mother Christine's purse. He and Mother Christine were sharing some dirty little M&M's from the bottom of her purse. She had pulled out a ball of rubber bands, about as big as a baseball, to show Vincent. He was impressed. Some of them she had wrapped in colored thread. Those were really quite pretty. They looked like Indian jewelry. She put about five of them on her wrist. Other ones were decorated with glitter, and the glitter was getting all over everything. Freida said in a loud whisper, "Vincent! Put everything back, Now!" Vincent gladly obeyed. He didn't want to stand up and sing with glitter all over himself anyway.

No sooner did they have everything back in her purse than Mother Christine pulled out a pair of little folding manicure scissors. Vincent was curious. So was Marshall. Freida allowed herself to become distracted by another testimony.

Mother Christine took off her shoe and raised her foot up to the edge of the pew. She stretched out the toe of her stocking and started hacking away at it with her manicure scissors. Vincent and Marshall looked at each other, trying not to draw attention.

She tucked the toe of her stocking into her purse. Then she started hacking away at her ancient toenails! When she was satisfied with the job she had done on one foot, she took off her other shoe to start on the other foot.

She raised her foot up to her seat, as she had done before, except this time her heel slipped off the slippery pew, and she accidentally let go of some gas. It was loud, loud enough that it startled Freida, who was seated two seats away. It startled Mother Christine as well. The unexpected seemed to have jarred her to her senses. She put her scissors back in her purse and slipped her shoes back on. "Oh d-dear," she said, looking down at Vincent.

The smell was creeping past Mother Christine toward Vincent. The longer it hung around the worse it got. Vincent had never smelled anything quite so rotten in his whole life.

"Oh dear," she repeated, this time with glitter on the end of her nose.

This was getting to be more than Vincent could handle. How could he keep a straight face when even Mother Christine was sitting there with a huge grin on her face?

By this time it had drifted over to Freida. It smelled like old broccoli or rotten cabbage. Vincent waited patiently for his mother's reaction. Freida sat stone faced. Marshall looked at Vincent. Vincent looked at Marshall. Marshall flared his nostrils and shot him a look of shock and horror. Once Marshall's look of shock wore off, he waved his hand infront of his nose and grinned, knowing full well that Vincent was helpless to resist his "faces." Vincent could do nothing but crumple to the floor in suppressed laughter. The harder he tried not to laugh the worse it got. He could hear his mother whispering angrily, "Vincent, Vincent, get up!" But there was nothing he could do. He also knew, if he didn't at least try to get up off the floor, his mother was going to kill him. Finally he managed to control himself enough, much to Marshall's disappointment, to be able to crawl back up into his seat with tears of laughter streaming down his face. Mother Christine, still smiling, made a paper fan out of her program and was fanning the stink toward the rows behind them. Vincent dared not look at Marshall.

Oh my gosh, Vincent thought, how am I supposed to sing after this? He pressed his fingers into his eyes, hoping the pain would distract him, but as soon as he remembered the look on Marshall's horrified face, he began to feel the giggles overwhelming him again. Freida pinched his arm and glared at him. He tried biting down on the inside of his cheeks.

Freida said, "This is no way to act in church."

"I can not help it," he pleaded, swiping away the tears on his cheeks. The look on his face, somewhere between pain and joy, told Freida that at least he was trying to recover. He knew it must have drifted farther back in the pews, because he could hear a couple of little girls giggling behind him. Do not look, he said to himself, or even listen. He covered his ears so he couldn't hear them, and swung his feet underneath him as a distraction.

Finally his thoughts began to wander, now that they weren't being held captive by the smell. He began to wonder what the parents were going to think of the song he wrote and his electric piano. He was doing something that had never been done before. He wasn't worried that they were going to banish him or anything like that. Everyone knew that he loved Jesus and that he would gladly recite the believer's oath any day of the week. He had convinced his mother it wasn't a sin to use different kinds of instruments in church by showing her that King David worshipped the Lord with just about everything—except a pipe organ. The way Vincent saw it, he could get the strings, the harp, the drums, or even the whole orchestra going, with just one little electric piano.

Anything new was scrutinized carefully by the Mennonites before they were willing to accept it, and for good reason. And in all other cases Vincent had understood and willingly conformed to the old ways. Even though the rest of the world called him old-fashioned, or backward, he'd rather be old-fashioned than be like the ones calling him names. He liked the fact that in Promise, nobody ever moved away. He liked that he knew everybody, and he knew that they could all be trusted. He remembered when his mamma had appendicitis, and every night someone different came to the house with dinner. But most of all, he realized that all their old-fashioned honesty and generosity was generated by Jesus who taught them how to live. He genuinely wanted to please God.

Still, there was something that would well up inside him. He liked God so much that he wanted to shout it from the rooftops. He wanted to be able to worship God better than he had ever worshipped him before, to play and sing from the bottom of his shoes to the top of his head, without holding anything back. He liked the old hymns; they had good words, but he couldn't get very excited about singing the same old hymns week after week. And he had trouble standing perfectly still.

Two years ago, he had traded a lady at the farmers' market three dozen eggs for her electric piano. She had asked him, "Do you have a tape recorder?"

He shook his head yes.

"Then plug it into the back of the piano, and you can record everything you play." She gave him a quick lesson. They put together "Jesus Loves Me" with violins and harpsichord in a waltz rhythm. He was sure this was going to be more fun than he had ever had. He couldn't wait to get home and try out some more songs.

"Thank you, ma'am."

"No problem, I hope you use it. Nobody ever played it at our house," she said.

"I am going to play with this every day," Vincent said excitedly. He waved good-bye.

"Wait," she said. "Here's the instruction booklet."

Vincent ran back for it with the piano tucked under his arm. "Thank you," he said, even though he was too young to read it.

After he got the piano home, he tried out everything the lady had told him. She had explained that he could record up to ten different instruments on top of each other. So he would start with the violins playing the melody, and then pick a rhythm, such as calypso, bluegrass, or whatever, to go with the melody. Then after he listened to the melody and the rhythm together, he would continue to add a horn here, a flute there, until it sounded like the whole orchestra. Once the music was taped, and he was ready to sing, all he had to do during his performance was bang on the keyboard any old way, and it looked like he was really doing something. He set the keyboard to play only drums while he sang, and the tape recorder did the rest. By listening to Lou Rawls, he was able hear how all the instruments blended together. Freida promised to stop fretting over his new hobby, as long as he dedicated his music to the Lord. Martin didn't say much about it either, although he was concerned that he might be allowing too much of the world's influence into his home. However, one morning Vincent caught his father whistling to his jazzed-up version of "Power in the Blood" during a milking session. He had a pretty good rhythm section going as the milk hit the bucket, thought Vincent.

"Marshall Mueller."

The name startled Vincent out of his daydream.

"What are you going to be doing for us tonight?" asked Miss Purdy.

"I have some bloopers I want to read."

Miss Purdy knew what Marshall would be doing, but she wanted Marshall to have the opportunity to give a correct and ready answer for the crowd. She knew Marshall had a very difficult time getting up before a group. "May I present to you Marshall Mueller and his bloopers," said Miss Purdy, bowing to Marshall.

He was very self-conscious. He took every available moment to lick his upper lip, causing his long skinny nose to bob up and down. He had a long narrow face and a long neck and big hands and feet just like Vincent's father. Marshall planted his feet in one spot and stayed there without budging. He took a crumpled piece of paper out of his pocket and, licking his upper lip, began to read in a monotone, "There will be a self-esteem seminar beginning on Monday night. Please use the back door."

Everyone chuckled. Marshall licked his lips as though he had just pitched a strike and had two more to go. There was a long pause. "Is that it?" asked Miss Purdy.

"Uh, I got one more." Then came another long pause. Vincent started making faces at him and sticking out his tongue. Freida leaned forward to encourage him to begin.

"The choir will begin practicing this Wednesday night for the Christmas program. If you enjoy sinning, please attend." This time everyone laughed a little more enthusiastically. Marshall grinned his horsy grin and accidentally snorted. That would have embarrassed him enough to quit, but he was sort of enjoying the laughs.

"Are you finished?" asked Miss Purdy.

"Um, can I do one more?"

"Of course," Miss Purdy answered. "Please do."

Marshall rushed through the last joke like a race horse at the finish line, "There will be a meeting of Overeaters Anonymous on Thursday night. Please use de double doors at de side of de building."

Everyone laughed again. Marshall smiled, took a quick bow and ran back to his seat. Vincent gave him a thumbs up.

Miss Purdy announced, "Next, Rebecca Perl will be playing the 'Twelve Days of Christmas' on de flute."

Vincent complained, "Not again."

Marshall rolled his head around in protest.

Freida knocked both of them in the side.

Becky repeated, "I will be playing de 'Twelve Days of Christmas.'" The original plan was that Becky and her classmate, Abigail, would be doing a duet. But when they got together they realized they had each learned it in a different key. Vincent marveled at how Becky was able to wrap those enormous buckteeth of hers around the flute and actually make it work.

By the time Becky was up to the "five gold rings," Vincent was lulled back into worrying about his song. Part of the problem was that he had made it up himself. The words went: "We've got the power of the Lord." Vincent was afraid no one would hear the next line; "We've got the power of love." Vincent worried, what if they might think I wrote some stupid kind of song like "Here I come to save the day. I am mighty man! I have de power!"

It was supposed to be a song about how everybody loved one another. He tried as often as he could to wear his favorite T-shirt to the market because it said, "By this all men will know that you are my disciples, if you love one another." For the most part, everybody in Promise did love one another. The few times there had been a disagreement among the brethren, everyone agreed it was the worst thing that could happen. It was worse than fire, flood, or famine. Everybody would get together and try to smooth things over until finally the parties gave in. Usually they ended up not caring whether they agreed or not, they would just give in. Vincent had learned when he and Marshall ended up in an argument, it was worse being mad at each other than giving up.

"We got de power of de Lord," he whispered to himself. "We got de power of love. We, we, we, we got de power of de Lord. We're gonna take that power and spread it all over de world."

The part about taking it around the world was another problem. The people of Promise were always worried about mixing too much with the world, the reason being that the world might cause them to start living in sin and turn away from God. Vincent never worried about the world being able to influence him like that. He was certain that he could share with the world the special love he had in his heart without letting the world change him. Of course, no one was going to let him test out his theory, especially not at seven years old. It was a real issue with himself and everybody he knew, although some were less serious about it than others. But Vincent was absolutely convinced that he loved God so much that nothing could ever take him away. And besides, he said to himself, I do not want to be taken away; I am happy where I am. He certainly wasn't jealous of what he saw of the world at the flea market. He felt sorry for them.

Suddenly he heard Miss Purdy rattle him out of his thoughts. "Vincent Mueller will now sing and accompany himself on de piano. He will be singing a song he wrote himself. It will surely roll down your stockings and make your hair stand on end." Miss Purdy chuckled. "Come on up, Vincent honey, let us hear you!" Miss Purdy was aware of the pressure he was under.

He prayed to himself as he walked to the platform. "Holy Lord, God, I hope you know that everything I worked on for tonight wass because you are de best, and you deserve de best I can do. I hope everybody understands. If it iss not right, I will find out, and I will never do it again. But I hope they like it. And I hope you like it too. Amen."

Vincent started out with a loud driving drum solo intro-duction that was programmed into the piano when he got it. It certainly got things started. Boom chicka, boom chicka, boom chicka, boom chicka . . . There were children sitting together who started swaying back and forth to the beat. Miss Purdy motioned for him to sing real loud so every-body could hear, and did he ever.

"We, we've got de power of de Lord." His body moved to the beat.

"We've got de power of love," chicka boom chicka boom chicka boom chicka.

"We, We, We, We got de power of de Lord," he belted.

"We're gonna take that power and Sprrrread it all over de world," he growled.

"Take it to de East, take it to de West,
Take it to old Cairo, and take it to Tibet.
Take it to St. Petersburg, take it to Beijing.

But take it, take it, take it, that's de most important thing!!! Cause,

We got de power of de Lord.

We got de power of love.

We, we, we, we got de power of de Lord.

We're gonna take that power and sprrrread it all over de world."

By this time Mother Christine was doing a combination tap dance/belly dance in the aisle. Freida tried to stop her, but it was no use; she wouldn't hear of it. When Vincent got to the part "take it take it take it," Pastor Dunkin, in the interest of acting as Vincent's grandfather, started to stand in protest. He was sitting in the back row. Anticipating a reaction like this, Vincent's grandmother had been standing directly behind him. She put her hands on his shoulder. When he tried to stand up she gently pinned him to the pew. She leaned over to him and whispered in his ear, "There iss wisdom in de counsel of many. Why not take some time with this and do not just react." He sat still. He had no choice.

On the last line Vincent dragged out the ending, stretching it out for all it was worth. He sang, "ALL OVERRRRRRR"

Mother Christine started swinging her purse round and round as if she were winding up for a pitch. Vincent saw her and imitated what she was doing. "This woooooooooooorld." Round and round their arms swung.

There was a full-orchestra finish. "Ooooooo yah." Vincent went down on one knee, Al Jolson style, as the saxophone finished it out.

The applause began to swell and Vincent listened with an excited smile. But then, inexplicably the applause stopped. Vincent wasn't sure why. His smile turned to concern. Miss Purdy rushed to rescue Vincent. As he was leaving the platform in disgrace and disappointment, she caught him by the sleeve, she put one arm around his shoulder and said, "This might be an excellent time to remind you that the children have been collecting 'Pennies for Pedro. ' The money will be used to minister to the children living in the garbage dumps of Mexico City. The collection barrel is inside the front door."

Vincent waited patiently for her to finish as the lump arose in his throat. He reflected on what just happened. He was pretty sure God was pleased. He knew Marshall liked it. His mother liked it. Miss Purdy liked it. And Mother Christine really liked it. The children seemed to like it, but with the rented spotlight shining in his eyes, it was hard to see past the third row. The sound of the clapping echoed in his ears, as did the crushing silence. He returned to his seat confused and disheartened.

Freida took his hand. "Look at me, Vincent." She turned his face toward hers. "You did a wonderful job. I am so very proud of you. No one could ask for a better son than you. You were de best one so far." She kissed him and gave him a squeeze.

Mother Christine stuck a gold star on the back of his hand.

"Thank you," said Vincent.

She concentrated as hard as she could on forming the words and finally managed to say through her stroke-stricken tongue, "Very g-good job, Vin-cent."

He smiled.

By Sunday the pastor had his answer. The "Pennies for Pedro" barrel was overflowing. They put a footlocker beside the barrel, and when the footlocker filled to overflowing, all Pastor Dunkin could say as he passed by was, "Praise de Lord." It wasn't that he could be swayed by pressure from the congregation. His dilemma was that he couldn't find a definitive scripture in the Bible that proved Vincent had done anything wrong. There was one thing Pastor Dunkin was certain about, concerning Vincent; namely, God had a plan for his life. And the best thing he could do for him as his pastor was to help him find his way.

Psalm 13:6. I will sing unto the Lord, because he hath dealt bountifully with me.

Chapter 8

School's Out

Age 8

Marshall arrived on horseback outside Vincent's barn. He cupped his hands over his mouth and called loud and long, "VINCENT." There was no answer, so he tried again. "Brother Vincent."

A disheveled head of light brown hair with pieces of straw in it peeked out from around the open barn door. "Aren't you finished yet?" asked Marshall.

"Almost," Vincent said, pushing up his sweaty glasses with his wrist. Big gardening gloves dangled from his hands.

"You want some help?"

"Sure. I got to put new straw down for de chickens, and then I am finished."

Marshall said, "If you scoop de stinky straw into de wheelbarrow, I will take it to de garden."

"Sounds good." Vincent had already started scooping it out of the nesting boxes and into the wheelbarrow.

"Marshall said, "You want to go up to de baseball field and practice? I brought my bat, if you want to use it."

"Ah, Yah, we're playing de bulldogs. I would love to hit it clear to de river on them," said Vincent.

"Yah, and me."

"I'll ask Mamma."

Vincent returned in a few minutes with his glove and ball. "You think I can ride with you. Petey has a sore hoof."

"How did that happen?" asked Marshall. "Petey, let me see your hoof." Marshall lifted his hoof to take a better look.

"Aw, he stumbled yesterday, and I did not know it till this morning, but he got a stone under his shoe. I got it out but he iss still not putting his foot down, so I must give him some time to get better. I would have put some liniment on it," Vincent explained, "but I couldn't find it. I don't know what Pappa did with it. Do you have any?"

"Yah, but I can not ask my pappa for any; he will just say no."

"Oh, sorry. I forgot. I shouldn't have asked," said Vincent.

"We will look at him again tonight," assured Marshall, rubbing the horse's neck.

"Did you put down the new straw?" asked Vincent.

"Yah," answered Marshall, pulling himself up onto his horse.

Vincent said, "Okay girls, you are back in business." He fanned his straw hat around, scattering the chickens. Marshall grabbed Vincent's hand and pulled him up behind him. Vincent held on to the back of Marshall's shirttail, and they were off.

When they arrived at the schoolyard, there was another horse tied beside the well. "Oh no. Guess who it is," said Vincent.

"Oh no," complained Marshall, "Bucky, I mean Sister Becky Perl."

"Hi boys," she said in a mocking tone. She got a drink from the pump and wrapped the hose back around the handle.

"What are you doing here?" asked Marshall.

"Picking raspberries. You have a problem with that, Marshall Mueller?"

"We are practicing for de game, and girls are not allowed, so just run off and pick your berries," said Marshall.

"You don't need to worry about me. Why would I want to bother myself with you two?"

"Good," they both declared.

Vincent batted and Marshall pitched for awhile, then they traded places. Vincent threw his best fastball. Marshall cracked it a good one. It continued to roll to the fence right next to Becky and her berries.

"Oh darn," said Marshall.

"You go get it," said Vincent.

"C'mon, Vincent, you go get it."

"We'll flip for it," said Vincent.

"Got any money?" asked Marshall.

"No, you?"

"Me? This iss Marshall. Remember?" Marshall turned his pants pockets inside out. "At least come with me; must I go by myself?"

"I guess not," Vincent complained.

"If I did not know better," Becky teased, "I would say you boys were following me."

Vincent retorted, "Do not kid yourself, Miss Becky, the boring, bucktooth, bug-eyed Brahma bull." He added, "With a bugger on her nose."

"You don't know anything, Vincent Mueller. You're not even a real Mennonite. You are only adopted."

Becky's comment didn't disturb Vincent in the least. "So what. My mamma and pappa had a choice. They could have given me back whenever they wanted. But you, your mamma and pappa took one look at you and wished they could put you back, but they had to keep you whether they wanted to or not."

Marshall looked over the fence, spying one of the famous home runs. "Vincent, come here. I'm going after that ball."

"No you are not!" warned Vincent.

"It will be easy," he said. "Look, there iss a ledge two-feet wide practically the whole way." It was about twenty feet below them. To get to it he was going to have to traverse a ledge about fifty feet long. "What could be so hard about that?"

"It might not look so bad from here, but what happens if you should slip or something like that?" reminded Vincent.

"When wass de last time I slipped? I can't even remember."

"Marshall, please, do not try it. Take a look at how far down that cliff drops." They leaned over the fence to take a long look. Vincent could only hope it would convince him not to try. The river was so far below, it looked more like a piece of thread on a green carpet. At the top of the mountain were large craggy rocks and gravel. A strong breeze blew past them, reinforcing what Vincent was trying to tell him.

"No, I have already made up my mind. It looks too easy to pass up." Before Vincent could grab him, Marshall was over the fence and down the hill. Vincent leaned as far as he could over the fence to watch Marshall's progress. Marshall walked along just fine at first, but then he began to hesitate and lean cautiously against the hill. He managed to climb over a large rock and slide to the other side. It must have been the sliding that scared him.

"VINCENT!" Marshall shrieked.

Becky said, "What's going on?"

Vincent ran along the fence until he could see Marshall directly under him. Everything seemed to be clear going ahead of him. "What iss de matter?" Vincent asked.

"I don't know. I can not move."

"What?"

"I can not move!" He sounded like he was going to cry. His body was pressed against the hillside, and his hands were glued to the rocks behind him.

"Don't look down," suggested Vincent. "Then come back up. And whatever you do, do not try to go any further."

"NO!" Marshall screamed, more terrified than before. In slow motion he admitted, "I am too afraid to move."

Vincent and Becky tried to talk Marshall back up the hillside for probably twenty minutes, but it seemed the more time that went by, the more frozen he became. The main problem was that he didn't want to climb up and over the rock again. Vincent finally decided, if I can help him back over the rock, he will be able to walk the rest of it.

"Are you looking down?" Becky asked with genuine concern.

"NO! Don't even say that. I have my eyes closed so I don't have to look."

Vincent said, "I am going to go get him."

It was against Becky's better judgment, but she convinced herself that since Vincent was a boy, everything would be all right.

Vincent tied his shoes extra tight. He told Becky to stand by. He checked out his pathway down, and headed off. It was really not so bad. Marshall was right. He was even considering going after the baseball himself. He reached the rock on the other side of Marshall, who was absolutely frozen in place. He looked like a frightened cat with its claws dug into the mountain.

"Marshall, this iss easy. You have got yourself all worked up over nothing. Give me your hand."

Marshall crept his hand slowly across the rock. His hand was ice cold.

Vincent said to him, "Now, all I want you to do iss turn sideways and lift your leg up onto de rock."

Surprisingly Marshall again obeyed. He spun one leg over and smacked himself against the rock like a magnet. Now they were facing each other and looked into each other's face. Marshall looked really funny. Vincent had never seen him like this. He turned away so his friend wouldn't see him laughing. Marshall's eyes were opened so wide it looked like they could pop right out of his head.

Just then, the gravel under Vincent's feet began to shift. "Marshall! Hang on to me. I am going to fall!" Marshall squeezed Vincent's hand as tight as he could. Marshall's hands were much bigger than Vincent's, but they were clammy. He could feel himself start to lose his grip. The ground under Vincent continued to fall away. He could see straight below him about halfway down the mountain. "Don't drop me. Please don't drop me." Vincent was too scared to cry.

His body was hanging suspended in midair. The only thing keeping him up was Marshall's slippery hand. As his body swung from side to side in the wind, it was twisting his wrist unbearably, but he didn't dare do anything about it. It could mean his life.

"Jesus, save me," Vincent cried out in desperation.

"Help us, Jesus," repeated Marshall at the top of his lungs.

Just then Vincent could feel Marshall's hand slipping away. His fingertips left Marshall's, and in an instant he was sailing through the air helplessly. The jagged rocks were speeding toward him. Vincent screamed uncontrollably. He began rolling through brush until he reached another landing. Into the air, he went sailing. He was freefalling until a dead tree branch jabbed him in the back. It hit him in the ear and caught him by his suspenders. He hung, caught on a branch, his arms and legs swinging hundreds of feet above the river. He caught his glasses as they were sliding off the tip of his nose. He secured them tightly around his ears. Marshall was screaming wildly above him. Maybe he wasn't too far away, thought Vincent.

Vincent tried to look up, but he didn't know how securely he was attached to the branch. He decided to stay put and see what he could hear from above. He could hear Becky yelling something, but he couldn't make it out, because Marshall continued to scream. Marshall was certain Vincent had fallen all the way to the river since Vincent's hat had blown off and sailed below Marshall like a paper airplane.

"Marshall," called Vincent. "Marshall," Vincent called even louder. "Marshall!!!" Finally, Vincent was able to get Marshall's attention. Marshall stopped screaming. Vincent looked at the base of the branch he was attached to. It must be a sapling, he thought. The roots were exposed. He realized that what had been upright a few minutes ago was now beginning to lean. He didn't know how long this grace period was going to last.

Becky went to the well for her horse. She appeared just above Marshall. She tied the rope to the saddle horn. She tied a loop at the other end and threw it over the hillside in front of Marshall. "Marshall, listen to me," she said.

"Yah?" Marshall replied.

"See if Vincent can reach de rope."

Marshall mustered up his nerve and lifted his head slightly away from the hillside. He stretched his face long, as if to get his nose out of the way. He leaned forward just a little farther, and he could see the top of Vincent's head swaying in the wind.

He snapped his head back again and started breathing deep to chase away the fear.

Marshall called tentatively, "Vincent, can you reach de rope?"

Vincent didn't see any rope in front of him, so he yelled back, "No."

"No, he can't," repeated Marshall.

Becky ran back for the garden hose. She tied the rope and the hose together. She put a loop at the end of the hose and threw the rope and hose over the hill again. "Now can you reach it?" she asked.

Vincent could see the rope to his right. It was long enough, but it was too far over. "Tell her to move it to the left."

Marshall said without looking, "Move it to de left."

Vincent's sapling was now perpendicular to the mountainside. Becky took firm control of her horse. "Over this way girl, a little more," she urged.

"That iss enough," called Vincent.

"That iss enough," repeated Marshall.

"I need more rope," yelled Vincent.

"He iss needing more rope," called Marshall.

She moved her horse as close as possible to the fence turning her to the side. "Iss that enough?"

"No." It might have been before, but he kept getting lower as the sapling continued to bend over. He could hear the roots snapping as they let go one by one from between the rocks.

She took the rope off the saddle horn and tied it to the stirrup. "That iss all I have," she called.

"That iss all she has," called Marshall.

Vincent took the chance while he still had one, and kicked himself forward. He reached for it, but it just brushed his fingertips. "Marshall, get it swinging toward me, and then I will grab it."

Marshall wrapped himself around the rock. He could just barely grab it. He began to swing it slowly. It was working.

"A little more," Vincent yelled anxiously.

"I got it!" Vincent yelled again.

"He got it!" Marshall repeated with excitement.

Becky sighed with relief.

Vincent looped the rope through his shoe. The slip knot gripped tightly around his foot.

"Tell her to back me up—slowly."

"Back her up slow."

"Back up, girl," Becky said. Her horse seemed to sense the seriousness of the situation and cautiously obeyed.

The branch that he was connected to began to lift up. When it was completely upright, the roots let go of the hillside and the whole thing went tumbling down, end over end.

"Vincent!" Marshall yelled.

"Yah, I am still here."

Becky continued to back up. She checked to make sure there was steady pressure on the rope. Finally Marshall could see the top of Vincent's head and then his body. Vincent gave him a quick wave, but concentrated on where he was going.

"Keep on going Becky. He is up here by me." She knew when she started to see the end of the garden hose he was getting closer. Vincent's hand gripped for the bottom of the fence. When he pulled himself through the fence, Becky ran up to him and hugged him. He clung to Becky as the two of them began to cry.

Becky said, "I am so glad you are alive. I thought you were going to die."

"If it wasn't for you, I never would have made it. I was so scared. I didn't want to die. Thank you," he said between sobs.

Marshall's shadow suddenly appeared over the two of them. "Hi," he said.

"How did you get back up?" Becky accused, wiping the tears from her face.

"I wass so glad to see Vincent climb through de fence, I wanted to get back up, and I was not afraid anymore."

Vincent looked at Becky. All Vincent needed to say was, "Get de rope."

He chased Marshall back to the schoolhouse and trapped him on the back porch. He backed Marshall up to the porch post and held his hands behind his back. Becky wound her rope around Marshall, then ran over to the spigot and hooked up the hose. Marshall knew what was coming next. "No, No!" he screamed. Don't do it. Don't do it. I am begging, no, NO!" he laughed.

Vincent started priming the pump with a grin while Becky held the hose over Marshall's head. Once the water was flowing, Becky hosed Marshall down top to bottom. She was scolding, "Are you ever going to do that again?"

"No!" he sputtered between laughter and screams. The water was ice cold.

"Say it again."

"NO! I promise."

Vincent thought, I want a turn at him. "Give me de hose," he said, grabbing it away from Becky. He rammed it right down Marshall's pants. "How do you like that, de scardy cat iss wetting his pants."

"Aaaaaaagh!" Marshall screamed, begging for mercy, the icy water running down his pant leg.

A man on a horse came around the side of the building. It startled everyone.

Vincent gasped and said, "It iss Bishop Perl!"

"Grandpappa!" said Becky, embarrassed by how it looked.

"What do you two think you are doing to this poor boy?"

They were pondering where a good place to begin might be. They were all fully aware that going over the fence was strictly forbidden. Vincent made a nervous attempt at taking a drink from the hose just as the water pressure was dying down. He stuck his finger into the end of the hose and said, "Surely iss hot out here." He licked his finger.

Bishop Perl looked at Marshall, his hair dripping down onto his face, into his eyes, and off the end of his nose.

"Untie him, immediately!" Bishop Perl said.

They did.

Bishop Perl ordered, "Vincent, Becky, stand against that pole. We are going to tie you up and see how you like it."

Bishop Pearl grunted and huffed as he wound the rope around the guilty parties, all the while quoting scriptures like, 'do unto others,' and 'reap what you sow.'

"Here you are, Marshall," said Bishop Perl overflowing with sympathy as he handed him the hose. "Now, you do to them what they think iss so very amusing. Go ahead, son, hose those bad children down."

The three of them were all screaming, sputtering, and laughing at the same time. Marshall especially enjoyed getting Becky in the face until her pigtails were flapping. They all went home soaked from head to toe. When Becky got home, late and soaking wet, she had no choice but to explain to her mother everything that had happened, and eventually the real truth got back to Bishop Perl. At the ball game the following week against the dreaded Bulldogs, Bishop Perl made a very serious announcement about the dangers of going near the fence. He told everyone all about how bravely Becky had saved Vincent and Marshall. Becky and her horse were lauded as the local heroes of the day. As for the baseball game; Promise lost, Vincent struck out, and Marshall didn't get to play. His mother wouldn't let him; he caught a cold.

Isaiah 12:2–3. Behold, God is my salvation; I will trust, and not be afraid: for the Lord Jehovah is my strength and my song; he also is become my salvation. Therefore with joy shall ye draw water out of the wells of salvation.

Chapter 9

Bishop Perl

"Hello. Bishop Perl, I'm Michelle Calazeri, child advocate for the Pennsylvania Children and Youth Services."

"Yah?" Bishop Perl stood tall and wide in his front door. He looked down at the small young woman with the large briefcase and khaki raincoat. Her darting, insecure eyes betrayed her conspicuously loud voice. Bishop Perl had never had a townsperson at his door before. "Iss there a problem?" he asked.

"We are looking for a child who was kidnapped from the Carlisle County Fairgrounds about seven years ago. He would be eight years old now, and his birth name is Vincent Muldare. This is a picture of his mother."

She handed him a folded black-and-white copy of a copy. When Bishop Perl unfolded it, he discovered it was a picture of a girl about sixteen with long blonde hair and bangle earrings.

Miss Calazeri continued, "There may be a resemblance, but we're not certain of that. She put together a campaign to find her son right after it happened, but with no success.

Do you think you might be able to give us any information?"

It is Vincent's mother, thought Bishop Perl. A terrible dread came over him. The position he held in the community burdened him with the responsibility of being the bearer of all bad tidings. This was not going to be easy. The picture was undeniably Vincent's mother, and Bishop Perl knew it. But how could he possibly lie and send the woman on her way? Bishop Perl bought himself time to think and possibly get more information. He handed the picture back and asked, "You are looking for a child here? Why would he be here?"

"Your people go to the fair every summer, don't you?"

"Yah, we do."

"Miss Muldare had her baby in a stroller at the Carlisle County Fairgrounds. When she had her back turned, someone took the baby out of the stroller."

"Maybe de people who found him thought de child wass abandoned," he replied.

Miss Calazeri thought it was odd that he would automatically start making a case for the kidnappers. She answered, "Even if we were to give the kidnappers the benefit of the doubt, Mr. Perl, they never contacted the authorities about it. If it weren't intentional, they would have contacted someone, wouldn't you think?" she said suspiciously.

Bishop Perl didn't answer.

She continued, "There was no police report filed, nor was the state ever contacted; and that being the case, our agency can only assume the perpetrators meant to keep their dirty, little deed a secret. This was clearly a kidnapping, Mr. Perl, and that is how the state police see it as well."

"What would happen if de child wass found among us?" he asked cautiously.

The question startled her. She had come to Promise on a long shot, but now it was evident this old man knew something. "It's a felony to steal a child, Mr. Perl, and anyone who knowingly conceals information can be charged with felony conspiracy. In other words, you could all go to jail," she warned.

"But what if I discovered something and de child wass returned, what would happen then? I don't know anything yet; I must ask our people." Bishop Perl knew he had just told a flat out lie, and there was no way of rationalizing it. The fact that he could go to jail for it hadn't fully occurred to him, not yet.

She studied his face and had her answer. "It wouldn't be up to me. It would be up to a judge. I can tell you this; it would go much better for everyone if they cooperated fully with the authorities. As for the kidnapping parents, they disregarded the rules regarding the discovery of a lost child, and since his mother wants the full extent of the law to be applied, quite simply, they'll go to jail. You better believe the chances of them keeping the child are nonexistent."

"God help us." Bishop Perl exhaled with a quiet groan. He sought comfort by gazing out at the old maple tree in his front yard.

"Bishop Perl, is there something you want to tell me?"

"Do you have a number where I can reach you?" he asked.

"Yes, I do, as a matter of fact." She flipped open her purse and handed him her business card.

He reached for the card. His old wrinkled hand was trembling.

"Today is Friday. I'll give you till Monday, Mr. Perl. I know in the end you will do the right thing. I hope to hear from you before the agency pursues this further. And they will pursue this; you can count on it," she warned. He watched as she got back into her car. She rolled down her window as she studied his worried face. "I'll be talking to you," she said, leaving Bishop Perl holding her card and the picture of Vincent's mother.

As she drove down the road, she tried to contain her excitement; she was certain she had found the kidnappers. Suddenly it occurred to her, "Oh no, I never should have told them there was no chance of keeping the child, and worse than that, I should never have said somebody was going to jail. What if they decide to run? And like a dummy, I gave them till Monday. There's probably nothing to worry about," she reassured herself. "Where would they go? This place is all they have ever known. They can't all get up and leave, and it would be too risky to hide the kid." After a few minutes she had almost convinced herself there was nothing to worry about. She thought, if the police tell us it's too risky to wait till Monday, Mr. Perl will just have to deal with it, that's all. Wait till I tell them at the office. They're not going to believe this. And after all this time, who would have thought that I would actually find him! This is so incredibly cool!"

"Oh, kripe! I forgot to turn it off." She pulled a pocket-sized tape recorder from her raincoat then began rewinding in search of the part where Bishop Perl sounded like he knew where the boy was.

"Matthew, who was that?" asked Mrs. Perl as she scuttled down the hallway toward him, her white hair frizzing out from under her prayer cap. She wiped her hands on her apron. A faint smell of peaches wafted up from her hands.

Bishop Perl handed her the card as he began to explain, "De police think Vincent wass stolen, and Freida and Martin may go to jail for it. That iss what his birth mother wants them to do." His favorite easy chair creaked as he slumped down into the sagging leather seat. He said, "We could all have big troubles, Mamma." He took off his glasses and wiped his face. "I wish I had more time to pray about this. Oh, my sweet Jesus." He heaved a heavy sigh.

Mrs. Perl asked, "Did you say they are going to come back to us on Monday?"

"Yah, Mamma. And I don't see how we can hide this. All she needs do iss go to de school and look at de attendance roll. How many Vincents are there in this world? And how many children look so much like his mamma? I am afraid this can only turn out badly for us. De question iss, how can we keep Freida and Martin from going to jail?"

"It wass de Kemps who found Vincent, wass it not?" Mrs. Perl recalled. She placed the business card carefully under the candle holder on Bishop Perl's side table.

"Yah, it wass."

"Maybe you could gather de four of them together, de Muellers and de Kemps, before Vincent comes home from school. At least de Kemps could tell this girl on Monday that Vincent wass found in their car, and this wass all a mistake. It seems to me, Sister Sara told Sister Freida she would get some adoption papers in de mail. But I don't know, that wass such a long time ago. I know Sister Sara talked to someone though," she said, wringing her hands. "I think it was a policeman. No, I am sure of it. It was a policeman, in Carlisle."

"That iss not what de police are saying. They say no one told them anything about it."

"Oh my," said Mrs. Perl. "This does look bad."

Bishop Perl pried himself up out of his chair. "I best start now if we are going to accomplish anything before Vincent comes home. Lord, help us, I am not looking forward to this," he groaned.

"I know dear, this iss not going to be easy." Mrs. Perl patted Bishop Perl on the back and put her arm around his waist as they hobbled slowly down the hallway. "That poor boy iss about to lose his home, his family, his entire way of life.

Bishop Perl added, "An eight-year-old iss much too young to deal with de ways of de world."

"Iss there something I can do? Shall I call de women to prayer?" asked Mrs. Perl.

"No, we must not start an uproar. De next thing they will be thinking iss we are all going to jail. Let me try to get this straightened out first with de Kemps."

"Iss Gabrielle still in de barn?" he asked.

"Yah, my dear heart. I will pack you a dinner,"

Bishop Perl pulled his suspenders up onto his shoulders. "Thank you, Mamma, I will get my satchel." He kissed her cheek and headed out to the barn. He always carried his leather satchel with the long wide strap; his Bible and notes fit perfectly inside. He had been carrying the same leather satchel for over forty years.

He saddled Gabrielle and rode him back to the house. Gabrielle used to be a tall black handsome horse, but now he was old and slow, not that the bishop minded. His saddle creaked as they walked. Mrs. Perl waited at the front door. She lifted his lunch bag into the air. "Thank you, Mamma." He put his lunch into the satchel and strapped it on across his chest. In his younger days he would have bent over to kiss her, not anymore. They settled for looking into each other's eyes and took comfort. "I will be back before supper," he sighed. He turned Gabrielle around to go, clicking his heels into her sides. Gabrielle obliged by walking slightly faster. The bishop was especially glad Gabrielle was in no hurry this morning, since he was in no hurry to break everyone's heart.

Several hours later as he crested the top of the hill to the Kemps farm, Bishop saw Will Kemp in the valley below loading pumpkins into his hay wagon for market.

Bishop cupped his weathered hands around his mouth. "WIL-BUR KEMP," he called. The sun was behind him, creating a silhouette bigger than life. The shadow that he and Gabrielle cast was at least four times their size. Will looked up and knew immediately who it was.

"Whoa," he called to his horses and laid the reins aside. "How are you doing there, Bishop?"

Bishop didn't answer, but wound his way down the hillside.

Will met him at the bottom. He was already concerned since Bishop Perl hadn't answered. And why had he come all this way. It must be something important, he thought.

"Brother Will, iss Sister Sara at home?"

"What iss de matter, iss? . . ."

"No, no. Everyone iss fine, but I need to talk to you and Sister Sara about Vincent, about how you came to bring him to Promise. I'm sorry to interrupt what you are doing, but this can not wait."

"Not to worry, Bishop. De wagon iss almost full. I can carry de pumpkins I have back to de barn, and de rest can wait until tomorrow."

Bishop Perl said, "Gabrielle can follow along behind us. That way I can ride up in front with you. We can talk on de way home."

They strolled slowly back to Will's farm as Bishop explained.

When they told Sara, she was inconsolable. She felt as if she had set Freida up for heartbreak. She kept saying, "It iss all my fault. If I had only reminded Freida about those silly adoption papers, this never would have happened."

Will reminded her, "If Sister Freida had tried to file papers back then, they would have arrested her then. His mother was claiming we kidnapped the boy since de beginning, remember. At least we can be thankful that Vincent has de Lord's word in his heart, a blessing he would not have if he had not been raised in Promise."

"How could this be happening?" Sara asked. "We were only trying to do de right thing, and now look at what hass happened. Lord, help us all."

Martin and Freida were waiting for them on the front porch. They didn't know why they were getting company in the middle of the day. They only knew that it was important. Martin imagined that Will might have a disagreement to discuss, and he was bringing Bishop Perl to be the mediator. Freida asked, "Will iss not upset with us, iss he? Sara never mentioned anything to me about it."

Freida made sandwiches and iced tea. Once they had arrived, she seated everyone around the wicker table on the porch. Bishop Perl procrastinated by insisting on dividing his lunch five ways. Eventually the small talk ran out, and it was getting extremely awkward; no one knew where to start. Will and Sara played with their food, hoping Bishop Perl would begin.

Finally Bishop blurted, "Remember de day de Kemps brought Vincent to de Bible study?"

"Yah," Freida and Martin replied nervously.

"Sara mentioned that you should fill out some papers for de adoption after six months."

"I don't remember anything like that," Freida said.

"I told you, Sister Freida," Sara blurted, and then just as quickly retreated, adding, "But I should have reminded you; you were too full of emotions to try to remember something like that. Who could expect you to remember?" Sara grabbed Freida's hand in apology.

"No, Sister Sara. You said it would all be taken care of," Freida replied. "But what does it matter, what iss this all about?"

Bishop revealed slowly with dread, "De mother has been looking for him, and she wants him back."

Freida pulled her hand away from Sara's. It was as if a bomb hit. Freida and Martin looked into each face, checking to see if perhaps they hadn't heard correctly. Each pained face stared back at them, motionless, wishing it weren't true. Finally Freida stood up. She leaned into the Kemps and the Bishop like a mother bear protecting her cub, "Well, she can not have him back. It iss too late!" She threw down her napkin and stomped her foot down on the old wooden porch. "That woman waited too long to change her mind now. This iss his home!"

Martin shouted, "She threw him in a stranger's car and walked away! What kind of mother would do such a thing? Why didn't she put him up for adoption instead of throwing him away like a piece of garbage in de garbage can? Iss she not so busy with her sexual escapades now, so she has changed her mind? Now maybe she thinks it iss time to be a mamma again! I agree with Freida. It iss too late!"

Bishop answered, "She says he wass in a baby buggy, in de parking lot, and someone took him when she was not looking."

Freida and Martin looked at Sara and Will for reassurance. Sara was still thinking about the adoption papers. Freida asked, "Well that iss just nonsense. Am I right?"

Will said, "Of course it iss. She iss lying. With our own eyes we saw him in de back of our van, and then we went right away to de police. It wass de policeman himself who told us about her. He knew she wass a prostitute and a drug addict; soon he will be telling de others, and we will explain she made it all up and be on our way."

Bishop Perl asked, "It iss not possible that perhaps de kidnappers changed their mind and put him into your van?"

Sara reminded, "But what about de note. How would de kidnappers know Vincent liked that tape? No, she did it. She gave him away."

"Yah," said Bishop Perl. "On Monday we will explain to them everything."

"But what becomes of Vincent!" said Martin. "Will they take him away from us after all these years and give him back to her, a stranger?"

Freida said, "Yah, are we expected to drop him off and say, 'Sorry we didn't mean to take your boy, and leave him there'?" said Freida. "Leave him in de care of a woman like that?"

Bishop Perl explained, "Well, that iss de hard part. She had a certain amount of time to change her mind, and she did what she wass supposed to do. I am guessing they were searching, but nobody wass able to find him for her. There iss no use arguing whether she has de right; she iss his mamma."

Freida exclaimed, "She has rights? A woman who tosses him away at birth, changes her mind, and then lies about him being kidnapped? De woman with a baby and no husband, who iss doing her drugs, no home, no family, making a baby with no way to take care of him, she has rights? Well you tell them this: Vincent has rights too! We can not just toss him into de lions' den. We must protect him! Hide him! I will move away if I have to!"

"Freida, you can not mean that," said Sara. "You are not being sensible."

"Well what else am I supposed to do? He iss my child. I must protect him!" Freida was on the verge of tears.

Martin looked to the bishop for answers. When he didn't offer any suggestions, Martin said, "We must fight for

Vincent. It iss not as if we can just hand him over. That iss not right."

Bishop said, "There iss something I have to explain to de two of you. They are already saying we took de child without telling de police. That iss kidnapping. If we don't cooperate with everything they tell us, it makes us look guilty. Normally, I would say that de community will be behind you, no matter what. There iss a problem though." He cleared his throat. The lie he had told to Miss Calazeri came to mind. He continued, "If de community does not cooperate with de authorities, if we do not tell them everything we know, we can all be put in jail for conspiracy to commit a felony. Then where would de rest of our children go? Shall we let them all be sent away to be raised by de world, while we all go to prison? It would only be a matter of time before de police could find one among us who could not bear to go to jail and leave our own children behind. De weak ones would give you away, and then de police would come and get you anyway. Iss that what you want? We must let de courts decide what to do. Maybe they will decide his mother iss not fit, and Vincent can return to us. Yah? That would be good, yah Freida? Martin?" he pleaded.

Freida laid her head on the table and started crying. Martin put his arm around her, but there was no consoling her.

Sara added, "Freida, they would not give Vincent back to a woman like that. Don't worry."

Freida raised her head and shouted through her tears, "No one said she wass an unfit mother while they were looking for Vincent. Why would they say she is unfit now? Then Sister Sara started crying to see her friend and her brother so upset. Freida laid her head back down on the table.

"Brother Martin, Sister Freida," said Bishop Perl, "no one wants you to lose Vincent. We do not want to lose him either. We will find a lawyer, and he will probably prove his birth mother iss unfit, and life will go on as it has. De authorities do not know de whole story. They only know bits and pieces. We must trust that God will help us through this. We can not allow life's situations to rule over our emotions. We must give God a chance to work. Maybe God is testing our faith. Let's show him we trust him in this situation, too. Nothing is impossible for God. Monday morning we will meet again, we will call a lawyer, we will find that missing copy of de police record, and we will call Children's Services, and maybe this will all be settled in no time at all."

Freida pleaded as she wiped her tears, "Mary and Joseph ran to Egypt when Jesus wass born, did they not?"

Bishop Perl said, "Freida, dear one, I did not hear about any angels coming to you in de middle of the night to warn you about this."

"But what if we can not prove her unfit?" Freida asked, burying her face in her apron.

"We will take it one step at a time. Do not get ahead of de facts. There iss enough to worry about only for today," he said.

Freida and Martin were too upset to continue being hospitable. Freida went inside the house, and Martin followed to comfort her. There were muffled cries coming from the kitchen that were unbearable for Sara to listen to. She did her best to tidy the dishes and set them inside the screen door. She heard Freida say, "Do you think I care about going to prison. I would gladly go to prison if it would save Vincent from being raised by his mother."

Bishop Perl said, "I don't think there iss anything else we can do here. I am going home to make some phone calls."

The Kemps and Bishop Perl began the ride home in silence, feeling terrible about leaving the couple in such a state. The October sky was thick with the clouds of winter approaching. Four birds of prey stoically braved the storm clouds above them as they circled high above. Bishop Perl finally broke the miserable long silence. "How could this be happening? What iss to come of our little Vincent?"

Will shared what he had been thinking. "There iss a scripture that says, 'Know therefore that the Lord thy God, he is God, the faithful God, which keepeth covenant and mercy with them that love him and keep his commandments to a thousand generations.'" That must be true for Vincent too, yah?"

Bishop Perl replied, "That iss true, but God has only promised to be with us in our trials. He never claimed that de trials would not be there; quite de opposite, in fact. I am afraid Vincent iss coming into de trial of his life. My heart hurts for him."

Will said, "God must have a plan in mind for Vincent. He must. Maybe, even if he iss sent back into de world for now, maybe he will return to us after he iss grown."

"Perhaps," Bishop Perl answered, unable to muster any confidence. "Perhaps. He iss so very young."

Deuteronomy 7:9. Know therefore that the Lord thy God, he is God, the faithful God, which keepeth covenant and mercy with them that love him and keep his commandments to a thousand generations.

Chapter 10

Kidnapped

"Good morning, church!" Pastor Dunkin boomed enthusiastically.

"Good morning, Pastor Dunkin," repeated the congregation with equal exuberance.

"De theme of today's message iss: 'Without faith it iss impossible to please God.' All of us old Bible thumpers know that verse. Right? It has become a cliché. We have heard it all our lives. But de question iss, do we live it?"

"I don't think there iss a person in this room who does not want to please God. If there iss someone here who does not want to please God, would you please stand? Ah, I see Mother Perl iss standing."

Everyone turned around to see. She was seated in her usual seat turning red and waving away Pastor Dunkin's attention. She tried to hide behind her Bible.

"I am sorry, Mother Perl, you are just so much fun to tease. Of course we all want to please God. Do we not? He iss our provider, our heavenly father, our bright and morning star. He iss our all in all. Amen?"

"Amen," they all agreed reverently.

"Let us test our faith for a moment, shall we, with another scripture. Let us find out if we are pleasing God with our faith—or not." He read, "All things work together for good to those who love God, and who are the called according to His purpose. That wass Romans 8:8, of course. Iss there anyone here who hass not heard of that scripture? As I thought, everyone knows that one."

"Now let me ask you a question. Do you always trust God to work things out for you, or do you, from time to time, begin to wonder if God knows what he iss doing? We sometimes do not have the patience to wait for God to work. At other times it iss difficult to trust God when we see that sometimes he allows suffering, even death. At other times it looks as if de good guys do not always win. These things begin to eat away at our faith. If we allow it, they can steal our peace.

Vincent began to wonder why his parents had spent so much time in prayer this weekend. It wasn't unusual for them to pray, or even pray a lot, but this time they didn't seem to be coming out of it for the better. They both looked very tired and were being unusually quiet.

"Let us examine de word 'faith' in several contexts this morning."

Suddenly the roar of engines was heard ascending the hill. Then automobile tires came screeching to a halt outside. Everyone listened as car doors opened and shut. It sounded like rifles were being cocked. Pastor Dunkin motioned for everyone to stay still.

As the noise settled, a voice over a megaphone called out, "No one make a move or we'll shoot. Do not try to escape; we have the building surrounded. We have come for Vincent Muldare and his kidnappers. We know he's in there, so come out with your hands up." No one moved, including Vincent and his parents.

Pastor Dunkin projected his voice as loudly as he could, "This iss de pastor. May I have a moment with de police-man in charge?" He waited.

A voice came over the megaphone again. "Pastor, come to the front door slowly and open the door with your hands up. You may walk two steps and then get down on your knees."

Freida managed to grab Vincent's clenched fist. Pastor Dunkin passed by his daughter on the way out. His eyes darted in her direction with concern. As soon as he left, the congregation listened. There was a clamoring outside the front door of the church. It sounded as if army boots rushed up the wooden porch steps and then clamored back down again.

They dragged Pastor Dunkin by the arms down the front steps and threw him face down into the dirt. Three rifles were pointed at him within inches of his body, and there was a foot in his back.

"Pastor," said the man in charge, "we know that the kidnapped boy is in there. We intend to take him with us this morning no matter what, so you might as well give him up without giving us any trouble."

"Yah, uh, uh, yes, sir. May I talk to de congregation?" asked Pastor Dunkin, gasping for air, "You will have de people you came for. I give you my word," he gasped.

"Back off men." The foot lifted from his back. Pastor stood up and resisted the urge to brush himself off for fear of being shot. His freshly starched white shirt was stained with dirt and grass down the front and on both elbows. His suspenders had come loose on one side, and pieces of grass stuck out from his beard. He didn't dare raise his arms to fix his hair and beard. He looked out at the sea of police cars. There must have been twenty. For every car there were two police officers with guns pointed directly at him. There were guns pointing through every window in the church, as well.

"You have five minutes," the chief ordered. "I hate to think what could happen here if you don't deliver."

"Yah, I understand. God help us all." He took one step toward the church and stopped. Without turning around he said, "May we stand in place to speak to one another?"

"No sudden movements. Stand up slow, and do not let them turn around."

Pastor understood and shook his head in agreement. He carefully walked up the steps with his hands up.

The chief ordered, "Bring out the people we want one at a time."

He said nothing but moved slowly and deliberately toward the podium. He began, "Do not move from your seats. If you have something to say, you may stand slowly; but do not turn around; you must face me at all times. Children, that includes you. Do not move, do not turn around, stay where you are. Now, can someone please tell me what this iss all about?"

Bishop Perl stood up slowly. "Vincent Mueller has a problem with Children and Youth Services. His birth mother hass accused us of stealing him out of de parking lot. Vincent, Martin, and Freida must appear before a judge to plead for custody and to free themselves of kidnapping charges. We were told we have until Monday to clear this up, but it appears they have changed their minds."

"Thank you, Bishop. It seems we can do nothing today but cooperate with de police. Iss there anyone here opposed to letting Vincent go with de police?"

No one moved. "Freida, Martin, you must remain looking forward while I go with Vincent outside. Do you promise to do that?"

Freida reluctantly let go of Vincent's hand and nodded.
The people sitting behind Freida watched as her shoulders
shook with grief. Martin nodded from across the room.
Vincent felt betrayed. He protested, "I can not go out there
Grandpappa; they are going to shoot me!"

Pastor approached Vincent, who was sitting in the first
row. He knelt next to Vincent and held his hand. "They
promised me that no one will get hurt, not you, not your
mamma and pappa, not anyone. All we have to do iss cooperate. They did not hurt Grandpappa, did they Vincent?"

"No, well, not too much." He looked down at the floor
asking, "But will somebody come and get me later, or am I
going away forever?" When he looked up tears were brimming over in his eyes. His chin began to quiver. It was breaking Pastor Dunkin's heart.

"Did you listen to Bishop Perl?"

"Yah," Vincent's voice quivered.

"Bishop Perl will get everything straightened out tomorrow morning. I will come and get you myself. Would that
be all right?"

"Yah." Vincent stood to leave. His muscles ached with
fright. He covered the front of his pants with his Bible. Freida
noticed he had wet his pants.

She prayed, "Lord, how can this be your will? Set your
angels around and about him, Lord. Protect him from these
men and their guns. He iss just a little boy. Keep him calm
so he will not try to run, Lord. He needs your peace and
your protection. Lord, this iss my baby. You gave him to
me. I need you. Protect him, Jesus. Protect him, Jesus. Protect him." Her shoulders began to shake harder as she tried
to control her sobbing.

The pastor took Vincent's hand as they walked slowly
out of the church. Not a man, woman, or child turned to
see him go. Vincent and Martin locked eyes as long as pos-

sible. His sad and frightened face caused Martin to start crying. With tears streaming down his face he mouthed the words, "Love you. Be brave."

The front doors creaked as Pastor Dunkin slowly opened them. The sunlight streamed in and then disappeared as he closed the door behind them. The congregation sat listening, waiting.

Boom! There was a gunshot. Boom! And then another! The congregation screamed but dared not move. Mothers grabbed their children and held them in close to them. Freida's shrieks echoed through the church. She resigned herself to a whimper. One of the bullets went through the door and lodged in the back of the pew where Bishop Perl was sitting. He turned his head slightly in Mrs. Perl's direction and reassured her. The sunlight shined through the bullet hole in the door like a flashlight. It streamed to the front of the church where it landed on the front of the podium.

Pastor Dunkin and Vincent fell to the floor of the front porch looking at each other.

"Vincent!" Pastor whispered, "Are you hurt?"

"No. Are you?" Vincent whispered, frightened out of his tears.

"No," he whispered. "Do not move until they tell us to."

"Yah," Vincent obeyed.

The chief yelled to the pastor, "Are you hit?"

Pastor Dunkin yelled back. "No, sir."

The chief swore a string of profanities, smacked his hat against is leg and demanded, "Who fired that shot?"

"Brady Grimes, sir," said the man who fired the second shot.

Brady was grimacing in pain. "I shot myself in the foot." he grunted.

"You idiot! Well you scared the hell out of all of us! You realize that, don't you? I hope you shot your foot off! Go sit in your car!"

There was a hole at the tip of Officer Brady's boot, as well as the hole in the front door of the church.

After everyone composed themselves, Vincent was lead by an untidy woman, the emergency care worker, to her car. And Pastor Dunkin was allowed to return to the podium.

Pastor Dunkin explained, "Vincent iss sitting in the back seat of a woman's car. He iss being very brave." Everyone sighed with relief. "Freida, Brother Martin, you must go with the sheriff. He will be holding you until de custody hearing, probably forty eight hours. That iss all I know. Maybe we can come for you sooner than that."

Martin stood slowly. "Will you be calling, for us, a lawyer?"

"Yah, of course, Brother Martin," said Pastor Dunkin. "We will do everything possible to get this over with as quickly as possible. You can count on it."

"Amen," said all the deacons in quiet agreement.

The chief yelled into his megaphone, "Let's go. Hurry up in there, Pastor."

Pastor Dunkin led them out one at a time. Martin was handcuffed first and pushed into the police car. He searched the parking lot for Vincent. He was in an old maroon Pontiac station wagon. The woman had dyed black hair and wore a bright pink coat. Martin hoped to get Vincent's attention, but he never looked over. He looked straight ahead and never moved.

Freida was brought out next. She was having trouble keeping her balance. She leaned against her father as they walked the center aisle to the back of the church. He tried to reassure her everything would be all right. "Do not worry my sweetheart. We are going to straighten this out in de morning. Vincent will be well taken care of until then. You'll see, this iss only for a short while."

"Why iss this happening, Pappa?"

"I do not know, sweetheart. Only God knows. He will take care of everything, you will see."

Freida and her father opened the door and walked out onto the porch. Freida looked out at the sea of policemen with their rifles pointed straight at them. Her knees buckled under her. The blood went out of her head and into her feet. Her tongue became numb and Pastor Dunkin had to hold on to her so that she didn't collapse. "Freida, Freida," he warned. "You must stand up." Her head tipped forward and she regained her footing.

The chief, concerned, hurried onto the porch and took Freida's other arm. He and the pastor carried her to the police car. She was handcuffed and placed inside the car along with Martin.

The chief said to Pastor Dunkin, "Sorry, Pastor. I didn't mean to swear like that back there. And also, I'm sorry about disrupting your Sunday service, but we had to do what we had to do. I hope you understand it's not the way I would have handled this if I thought there was another way. We couldn't take the chance that these people would take off with the kid, and we knew if there was one place we could find you all together, it would be on Sunday morning. Try to remember, these people have brought all this trouble on themselves and their neighbors."

Pastor replied, "That iss my daughter."

The chief nodded and looked at the ground.

"Martin," whispered Freida. "Where iss Vincent?"

Martin tipped his head toward Vincent.

Freida looked in Vincent's direction. Vincent continued to look straight ahead.

Freida attempted to explain to the policeman, "You must understand, that woman Vincent iss with, she gave her baby away; we did not steal him."

The policeman answered gruffly, "That woman isn't his mother. Funny, you didn't even know that, seeing as how she gave her baby to you and all," he said.

Freida tried again. "I did not steal him; he wass given to me."

Martin frowned at Freida. He thought he heard an edge to her voice.

"Sure he was. And that's why you can't tell the emergency care worker from his mother. Oh well, you'll get to meet her face to face soon enough," he said smugly.

Martin put his foot on top of Freida's to keep her quiet. He looked into her eyes, wishing he could hold her hand. Her face was pale with worry.

Freida reminded herself, at least Vincent is not with his other mamma.

They continued to watch Vincent as they were driven away. They couldn't understand why he wouldn't look at them. Maybe he couldn't bear seeing his parents taken away in a police car. Maybe he thought it would embarrass them.

Maybe he was still looking forward so that no one would get shot. Maybe he was angry, because he thought they were guilty. Maybe he felt betrayed.

It was unbearable being separated when they were all going through so much. All they could do was pace and worry, alone. Freida was taken to the women's prison in Harrisburg, while Martin was taken to the men's prison. Vincent was taken to the emergency care worker's home, somewhere in the Harrisburg area, but no one was sure where. Miss Purdy and Pastor Dunkin tried everything they could think of to reach Vincent, but Children and Youth Services had been instructed not to give out any information until after the hearing. Pastor Dunkin regretted giving Vincent his word and then not being able to follow through. The congregation committed themselves to constant prayer for their friends. Groups met at the church in shifts to kneel at the altar for them day and night.

> Hebrews 11:6. But without faith it is impossible to please him: for he that cometh to God must believe that he is, and that he is a rewarder of them that diligently seek him.

Chapter 11

As Filthy Rags

Wednesday Morning:

*F*reida waited anxiously for Martin to arrive in the court-room; he and the judge were the only two who hadn't yet arrived. Frieda sat to the left of the judge's podium with her lawyer, Mr. Jeremiah Kurly, whom she had only just met. To her right were Bunny and her lawyer, Mr. Marcus. Freida studied Bunny carefully. Bunny's hair was shoulder length, straight, turned under slightly at the ends. She wore a pale peach wool jacket and matching skirt with a white silk blouse, bone-colored heels, and gold hoop earrings and bracelet. She appeared comfortable in her clothing, though uncomfortably aware that Freida was watching her.

Vincent and the social worker sat directly behind Bunny. She turned around, smiled at Vincent, and whispered, "Hi, Vinnie. I'm your mother." Vincent shrank back in his seat avoiding her eyes.

Next to Vincent sat Bunny's boyfriend, Michael. He was a tall, slim young man, a boy, thought Freida, a boy with piercing, unfriendly eyes. His white shirt was new, and he wore a red-and-black striped tie that he tugged at in frustration.

Behind Vincent sat Marshall. Freida saw that when Marshall arrived, he squeezed Vincent gently at the back of the neck. Vincent turned around in his chair, excited to see his best friend again. The foster mother whispered to him to turn around. Vincent turned around as he was told, but not before he got a good second look.

Freida was instructed by the guard not to talk to anyone but her lawyer or her husband. When she entered the court room she was in handcuffs and prison clothes. Her prayer bonnet and hair band were gone and her long hair hung straight down over her shoulders. Freida held her arms close to her side; she was freezing, as she had been since she arrived at the prison. The shirt they gave her was short-sleeved and much too big. Her cell was cold and the drafts seemed to whip right through. She had asked for a sweater; so far they hadn't been able to come up with one. However, there was a gray wool blanket on the bed that she was using to keep warm, but this morning she had to leave it behind in her cell. She nodded to Bishop and Mrs. Perl, the Kemps, her mother and father, Freida's sisters, and Martin's family. She took comfort in knowing that she could count on each one of them to have spent time in prayer for her and her family. She looked again at her little boy, still dressed in his Sunday clothes, sitting among strangers, and who seemed to be searching for someone, probably Martin, thought Freida.

As Bunny looked around at the crowd her perception was much different. She was reminded of a movie she had seen on PBS about the Salem witch trials with their black dresses, shawls, and prayer bonnets, and men with beards in old-fashioned suits. She had seen the Mennonites often enough passing through town, but never had she been in such close proximity to so many at once. It was as if she were in a foreign country.

The newspaper headlines had read "Amish Kidnap Muldare Child." It had created enough public curiosity to catapult the news story into national prominence. The families had been besieged by reporters since Sunday and were grateful the cameras were not allowed inside the courtroom.

The side door swung open. Martin finally appeared in the doorway accompanied by a prison guard. He, like Freida, was handcuffed and in prison clothes. As he got closer, Freida could see he had a cut over his eye and his lip was swollen.

Vincent stiffened with excitement. "Pappa!" he whispered. "Pappa!" he repeated louder this time, smiling and waving.

"Shush," warned the social worker. She gave him a tap on the arm.

Martin looked over immediately. He nodded to Vincent. Vincent's smile vanished when he saw his father's face. He adjusted his glasses to get a better look. Martin's lip was split and bruised. The chains strapped to his ankles dragged across the wooden floor convincing the onlookers that he truly was a criminal. His face was pasty white and filled with insecurity. It hurt Vincent to see his father looking so defeated. He could usually count on his father to cheer him up, but today it was obvious his father needed him. Vincent wanted to run over to his father and sit with him. The social worker, reading his thoughts, shook her head, no. Vincent folded his arms in front of him in frustration.

"What happened to your face?" Freida asked. She touched his puffy lip. He winced.

"De guard did not like when I asked him not to use de Lord's name for a swear word. He showed me all of his other fancy words, and then he told me what he thought of me. I do not think he likes me. What do you think?" Martin smiled with his eyes.

"The Lord will repay," said Freida.

"No, he wass right in a way," said Martin.

"What are you saying? Have you seen your lip?"

"I know, sweet one. I can not see it, but I can surely feel it. It wass his ring that got my lip. But, it says in God's word that my righteousness iss as filthy rags. I started thinking about it and then I realized—why should I expect him to understand anything about de goodness of our Jesus. I should have been telling him how much Jesus loves him instead of making demands. I must have sounded like I wass in love with my own righteousness, like I wass better than him. But let's talk about something else, Freida." Martin grabbed her hand desperate for human contact. "I am so glad to see you again. How I have missed you, my sweet one. Your hands are cold. Let me warm them up."

"All rise, the honorable James Lenhart is now presiding," the bailiff announced. The smell of musk enveloped the courtroom, and it nauseated Freida, as if she didn't already have a nervous stomach.

Everyone stood noisily. Freida was surprised at how small the courtroom was; the people were elbow to elbow. She thought, this is no bigger than my living room. It seems to me that such a serious matter should be given a larger room. And there is no jury. Everything hinges on this one man, she thought, indignant, "Mr. Musk"!

All the civility had drained out of Freida after Sunday morning. Her confidence in people was nonexistent. She was left with a bitter cynicism she had never known before. Freida noticed she wasn't the only woman with this bad attitude. It was the prevailing attitude throughout the prison. Fortunately, there hadn't been any fights breaking out yet, only harsh words. Freida had to admit the harsh words were flowing easily for her, and she was getting pretty good at it. This morning she had determined to steep quietly in her disdain, primarily because her lawyer had instructed her to keep quiet during the trial.

Freida's stomach tightened as the judge scanned his papers and asked, "Miss Calazeri, briefly explain why we are here today, and tell us what Children and Youth's recommendation is?"

Freida leaned forward to see a young woman seated next to Bunny. The woman said, "This is a custody hearing between Miss Muldare, the natural mother, and Mr. and Mrs. Mueller, the alleged kidnappers. The Muellers are here to contest the suitability of Miss Muldare to raise her son, Vincent. It is their contention that the boy should stay with them, even though Miss Muldare is the natural mother and has been searching for him since he was a baby."

The judge cleared his throat. "Yes, yes. So, this is the preliminary custody hearing?"

"Yes, Your Honor," she said.

Judge Lenhart asked, "What has the agency determined about Miss Muldare?"

"We have done an in-home evaluation, and that went well. Then we did a search in the files for any complaints against Miss Muldare, and there were none."

"So, your recommendation is that the child should be returned to his natural mother?" asked the judge.

"Yes, sir."

"Well, Mr. Marcus, would you please call your first witness. And let's keep the dramatics to a minimum. I realize the news people would love to keep this case going, but let's see how quickly we can bring it to a conclusion.

"Yes, Your Honor," the lawyers agreed.

"Miss Muldare, take the stand, please," said Bunny's lawyer. Her heels clicked quickly and confidently across the tile floor. The bailiff asked her to place her hand on the Bible. "Do you swear to tell the truth, the whole truth, and nothing but the truth, so help you God?"

"I do," she replied.

Freida leaned toward Martin and whispered, "That iss like asking de fox if he iss going to steal de chicken."

"Please be seated," the bailiff said.

Her lawyer continued, "Miss Muldare, will you please tell the court what happened the day your baby disappeared?"

"Yes. Vinnie and I went to the county fair. He was just a little baby a few months old. We were waiting in the parking lot for our ride home." She wrapped her hair behind her ear.

Bunny continued, "Vinnie was in the stroller. When I saw the guy who was going to give us a ride, I started waving my arms and running toward him. As soon as I got his attention, which only took a minute, I ran back to the stroller; but when I got there it was empty. She put a lace handkerchief up to her nose. "I looked everywhere. I was frantic. But after a while people were all starting to leave and it was getting dark, so I finally had to give up. It was just awful."

"Thank you, Miss Muldare."

The Muellers' lawyer approached Bunny. It was difficult for him to refrain from launching right into her and ripping her testimony to shreds. Patience, he told himself. Mr. Kurly asked, "Miss Muldare, would you say that you're a good mother?"

"Yes." Bunny began to twist the hanky around her index finger.

"Did you have a hard time buying diapers?"

"Well yes, but I had a few cloth diapers, you know, for when I ran out."

"And what about formula?"

"Yes, but I got free formula from WIC, it's a government thing. But sometimes I ran out and I had to buy it myself. I always took very good care of my baby."

"According to the Carlisle police, you were arrested for prostitution when you were only sixteen years old, and during that arrest it was discovered that you were also a drug addict."

"Objection, Your Honor. Miss Muldare was never officially charged in that regard. I move to strike that from the record."

Judge Lenhart said, "Mr. Marcus, how can I make a determination if we can't bring up Miss Muldare's past. It will be up to you to disprove it. Proceed, counselor.

Martin and Freida's lawyer continued, "Did you nurse while you were addicted to drugs?"

"I did the very best I could," she blurted. "It wasn't easy. But if I ran out of formula, I had to do something. So I nursed, but only if I had no other choice."

"So you were at least concerned that your drug habit would be passed to your son. Very commendable Miss Muldare," he said sarcastically. "You must have had a lot on your mind being so young with so much responsibility and no one to help. Yes?"

"Yes," she agreed.

"So unbearable that you might wonder if your baby would be better off without you?"

She managed to dodge the question. "I was all he had. We were managing"

"Would a good mother give her baby away?"

"Oh no! That would be a terrible thing to do."

He leaned toward her and looked into her face. "And a terrible thing to admit to, if a mother had done such a thing. Right?" He turned toward the courtroom for reinforcement on the Mennonites' faces.

"I loved my baby. I could never do such a terrible thing."

"Probably if a mother had done such a terrible thing, she should never be able to have that baby back. Right?"

"Probably not." Bunny looked down at her lap.

"Thank you, Miss Muldare. That's all, Your Honor." Mr. Kurley sat down next to Martin.

It was Bunny's lawyer's turn. He called Martin to the stand. Martin hobbled to the witness stand. He hadn't mentioned to Freida that he had been kicked in the kidneys. He remained handcuffed and chained at the ankles. Martin looked over at Vincent. His glance was supposed to tell Vincent he was going to do his best to do battle for him. He tried to hide his own anxiety.

Vincent bit his bottom lip and smiled. He thought he would use a trick he learned in school. It's called the "how to talk to your friends without really talking trick." He put one hand discreetly under his chin and waved his fingers at Martin, so no one would notice. He grinned without letting any teeth show.

Martin saw him wave. It gave him renewed courage to do his best for Vincent. He prayed, "Lord Jesus, help me to say the right thing. Praise you, Jesus."

"Do you swear to tell the truth, the whole truth, and nothing but the truth, so help you God?"

"Yah, I do."

Mr. Marcus said, "So, Mr. Mueller, you are Amish?"

"No."

"No?" Bunny's lawyer asked.

"No. We are Mennonites."

"There's a difference?"

As Filthy Rags

"De Amish are more serious about keeping to de old ways; we Mennonites use cars, electricity, things like that, if we choose to. But de Amish and de Mennonites both agree that too much attention to worldly possessions can interfere with our walk with God. De Amish and Mennonite ways of life iss most similar in that our communities live according to de laws of God."

"What was that?" asked Bunny's lawyer.

Martin repeated carefully, "We are most alike because our communities live according to de laws of God."

"According to the Bible you mean," he qualified.

"Yah."

"That all sounds very noble, Mr. Mueller. But now that we all know you are so 'holy,' does that put you above our laws?"

"No, at least not usually. Most of de laws were written with God's law in mind, at least up until recently." Martin remained calm.

"You and your wife have never conceived?"

"No."

"Are you unable to conceive?"

"I am guessing not."

"Would you say you have been good parents for Vincent Muldare?"

"We do our godly best."

"Are you better than say, a prostitute?"

"Yah."

"Better than say, a single mother?"

"Yah."

"Better than someone who has no money?"

"Yah."

"Better than someone who does not share your beliefs?" he charged.

Martin paused. "Yah," he said cautiously but with conviction.

Martin's lawyer was leaning back in his chair and rocking. He puckered his lips and nervously tapped his thumbs together.

"Well," Martin began to clarify, "if you think God thinks I am better just because I am lucky enough to know His word, that is not de way it iss. I thought you were asking me if a child iss better off being raised by a mother—and a father. Also, I am not—"

"Just answer yes or no, Mr. Mueller. Are you better than someone who does not share your beliefs!"

Judge Lenhart said, "Oh Marcus. Stop playing Perry Mason and let the man finish his thought."

"I am not so wonderful and good that I could steal other people's babies, so that they could be with me instead. That would not be right. God loves everybody de same. 'There iss none righteous before him', the Bible says. Jesus died for all. 'He came for de sinner not de right—'"

"Okay, okay. Spare us the sermon, if you don't mind, preacher. So your position is: you would not and did not steal this child from his mother."

"Yah, our neighbor gave him to us," Martin answered.

"Someone gave him to you?" The lawyer chuckled, surprised.

Bunny sat up in her seat. She thought it was going to be her word against the Muellers'.

Bunny's lawyer asked with a sneer, "And who was that, Mr. Mueller?"

"De Kemps." He pointed in their direction.

"Did you know anything about this?" the judge asked Bunny's lawyer.

"No, Your Honor."

Both lawyers approached the bench. The Muellers' lawyer retorted, "If Miss Muldare had told you the truth, you would have already known about the Kemps. If she concealed it from you, that's not my fault."

Bunny's lawyer replied, "How could she possibly know all of the circumstances regarding the kidnapping? If she had a description, she would have given it to the police. You should have disclosed this before hand, and you know it."

"Shall we proceed?" Judge Lenhart looked at Bunny's attorney. He hoped this wouldn't hold up the proceedings. They were making progress, and who knew when another day could be set aside. He added, "This should have been disclosed ahead of time, but it is just a custody hearing, not a trial. We need to get this child out of state custody and back into his home."

"Go ahead and call them up," said Bunny's lawyer in disgust. He was certain it would be a slam dunk to prove the Kemps were attempting to protect the Muellers by providing an alibi.

Surprisingly the Muellers' lawyer said, "I'd rather call the mother's landlord. You do know about him, don't you?"

"Yes, go ahead," he said, obviously irritated.

"Norman Gibbs, please take the stand."

"Do you swear to tell the truth, the whole truth, and nothing but the truth so help you God?

"I do," said Bunny's landlord.

"Take your seat."

Mr. Gibbs hopped up the step and brushed his hair to the side. He pushed himself up into the chair like a normal-sized person would lift himself out of a swimming pool. He folded his small hands and rested them on the railing in front of him. His stature gave him an air of child-like innocence. Freida was curious. She didn't know anything about this man. Why was he of any value to their case, she wondered.

Mr. Kurley asked, "Mr. Gibbs, how long have you known Bonnie Muldare?"

"I guess about twenty years."

"Does she live in your building?"

"Um, I am the manager, not the landlord, but yes."

"I see. Was she living in the building when Vincent was born?"

"Yes."

"Do you remember the day that Vincent was allegedly taken?"

"No. I found out later."

"How much later?" asked the Muellers' lawyer.

"About two weeks, I think."

"Did something unusual happen between the time the baby was taken and the time you heard about it that made you suspicious?"

"Yes. Bunny lived in the boiler room when she had the baby. She didn't have much, but she always paid me the ten dollars right on time. She loved that baby. She made him a nightgown out of an old orange sheet. It made him look like a girl. But at that age, who cares? He was so cute, I called him pumpkin. She called him angel baby."

The Muellers were beginning to think this man was there in Bunny's favor, not theirs.

"Can you just tell us about the incident?"

"Well, my wife said she was going to the basement to check on Bunny and the baby. She hadn't heard the baby cry for quite a few days. We worried all the time because of Bunny's drug problem."

"Objection Your Honor."

"Objection overruled."

Norman Gibbs continued, "Sometimes Bunny didn't know if it was day or night. She knew she wasn't going to be able to take care of him for much longer; she had to choose between the drugs and the baby."

"Object . . .," said Mr. Marcus.

"Overruled. Give it a break, Marcus."

"She asked my wife and me if we could take him, but my wife and me couldn't take care of a baby; we are seventy years old. Well anyway, my wife goes down to check on them, and Bunny says the baby is visiting her mother. So then, a few days later Bunny comes up to pay her rent, and she says to me she wants to move upstairs as soon as an apartment opens up. I ask her how she's going to afford it, and she says, 'My dad died in a car accident and gave me some money in his will.' Then she says, 'As soon as I get Vinnie back, we want to move up here.'

"'Where did Vinnie go?' I said.

"'Didn't you hear? Somebody took him,' she says. 'But the police are going to get him back.'

Mr. Gibbs continued, "After that she just seemed like she didn't want to talk about it anymore. She wasn't sad at all, she just acted like she would rather talk about something else. It just didn't smell right. The girl had just lost her dad and somebody stole her baby all in the same week, and she's making plans for the future. It seems like she would have been at least a little bit upset. When I told my wife, she said Vinnie was at her grandmother's, and she didn't know anything about the baby being stolen. My wife said that didn't sound right to her either."

"The conversation your wife had with Miss Muldare during which your wife was told the baby was visiting with his grandmother, was that before or after the baby was taken?"

"We're not sure. I asked my wife the same thing, but she couldn't remember. Another odd thing was that Bunny's mother, the grandmother, never wanted anything to do with Bunny's baby before. Why the change in her mother's attitude all of a sudden, you know?"

"Thank you, Mr. Gibbs," said the Muellers' lawyer.

Bunny's lawyer remained in his seat, tapping on his lower lip with his pen. As he posed his question, he appeared unshaken by Mr. Gibb's testimony. He stood calmly and began to pace in front of the courtroom. "Mr. Gibbs, you aren't really sure if the baby was given away, kidnapped, visiting his grandmother's, or what, are you?"

"No, not really."

"So all this talk is just supposition, isn't it?"

"I guess so."

"And in that case, it would have been better not to say anything at all, isn't that right?"

"Well, but if she gave that baby away, and then changed her mind because she got some money, then she should have just said so and not lied about kidnapp—."

"Thank you, Mr. Gibbs," he boomed over the witness. "That's all we need from you for now."

Mr. Gibbs could see Bunny's face turning red. He knew she was ashamed of herself, first for giving Vinnie away, and second for lying about it. It wasn't going well, she thought. And who were those people over there, the Kemps? She was glad Mrs. Gibbs wasn't there.

Mr. Gibbs wasn't the only one who saw Bunny's face turning red. Vincent saw it, too. This was the first time in his life he'd ever seen his birth mother. How could she do this to his parents? he thought. This woman has no conscience, she has no heart, he thought. Until now, he had been studying with curiosity the back of her neck and her shoulders. Suddenly that delicate neck and narrow shoulders were sickening to him. He didn't care that she was a heroin addict, or that she had given him to strangers, or anything else. But how could she be so selfish, he thought, to lie about his parents and let them go to jail? All she had to do was tell the truth, but all she cared about was what she wanted, and it didn't matter what happened to anybody else. She didn't want me back, he thought; she doesn't even know me. She just wanted her baby back, and she didn't care who she hurt to get it.

Vincent looked at Freida, who was also watching Bunny. Freida realized for the first time that if Bunny's father had died a few weeks earlier, Bunny would never have given Vincent away. Mr. Gibbs was the first person who had ever said Bunny loved her baby. Freida thought, surely the good Lord would not have set me up for heartbreak. The timing of her father' s death was no accident. God wanted Martin and me to raise Vincent. Otherwise, he would have taken Bunny's father before she gave her baby away. She will never get away with this, not in a million years.

"I want to sit with my mamma," Vincent said to the social worker.

"I know you do, but we'll just have to wait and see what happens," she said.

Freida heard Vincent. She looked at him and tried to comfort him with a smile.

"I have nothing further, Your Honor," said the Muellers' attorney.

"Go ahead then, Mr. Marcus," said the judge.

"I'd like to call Mr. Wilbur Kemp to the stand," said Bunny's attorney.

"Do you swear to tell the truth, the whole truth, and nothing but the truth, so help you God?"

"Yah."

Sara Kemp noticed as he took the stand that her husband still had his milking pants on. He had mud on both cuffs, and he must have put one knee in the dirt, because there was a big brown muddy spot on one knee. Even his hands were dirty when he was asked to swear on the Bible.

"Mr. Kemp. It seems that you would like to take some credit for having stolen this child away from his mother."

"I just want to explain what really happened," said Mr. Kemp, as calmly as possible.

"You would say and do just about anything to free your friends, isn't that right?"

"No. That would be lying."

"Ah, well tell us Mr. Kemp, how did you come upon this child, and how did you arrive at the conclusion that you should give it to your neighbors?" he said sarcastically.

"Plain and simple. We were driving home from de Carlisle County Fair, and de baby started crying in de back of our van. We opened up de back doors, and bingo, a baby."

"And so you decided to take it home to your neighbors? Look mother, a baby, let's take it home to our neighbors," he mocked. He expected a chuckle from the courtroom once they could see the absurdity of it. There was only silence.

The judge interrupted, "You'll restrain yourself, Mr. Marcus."

"Yes, Your Honor."

"First we went to de Carlisle police, and de policeman there said he would take care of de papers, if we took de baby home. De policeman wass supposed to write some kind of a police record about it, but I do not think they ever found it." Mr. Kemp looked toward the Muellers' lawyer for confirmation.

He shook his head no.

Mr. Kemp said, "I know he wass writing something about us on a paper, but I am guessing it wass lost or thrown into de trash."

"How convenient for your story, Mr. Kemp. I can hear it now, 'we'll just tell them they lost the police report.' You got together with your friends and cooked up this huge story so your friends would have an alibi, didn't you Mr. Kemp?"

Mr. Kemp tried to say no, but was interrupted by Bunny's lawyer. "What really happened was: Mr. and Mrs. Mueller saw an opportunity for a baby of their own; they figured the baby was better off with them—and so they took it. They looked around the parking lot, saw Miss Muldare running the other way, and they took the baby out of the stroller and put it into their car. They drove away, thinking no one would ever bother them about it ever again. Isn't that right, Mr. Kemp? Basically, Mr. Kemp, the only thing your scheming has accomplished is to get yourself indicted for conspiring with the kidnappers. Isn't that the real truth, Mr. Kemp?"

"Not exactly." Mr. Kemp scratched his beard and then gave a thumbs up to his children.

Suddenly six teenagers stood on cue.

"Well," said Judge Lenhart, "who is this now?"

"We were in de van too, Judge," they said with excitement. Bunny spun around in her seat, as did the rest of the courtroom. There was one child not standing. That was because Sara had just become pregnant with her when they found Vincent.

"My," said the judge, "I've never seen so many bright shining young people all at once." It made them smile all the more. It was finally their appointed time to save the day.

"But Judge, this trial is a travesty of the American justice system!"

The judge answered calmly, "Let me remind you, Marcus, I am the one to decide that. I'm still the judge, after all."

The judge turned his attention back to the children, "We can't put you all on the stand at once. Why don't you stay there, where you are, and we'll bring the Bible to you."

"Do you promise to tell the truth, the whole truth, and nothing but the truth so help you God?"

"Yah!" they exclaimed loudly and in unison. One of the girls giggled at how loud it was.

"You can turn down the volume," said the judge.

"I must object, Your Honor," protested Mr. Marcus.

"Oh sit down, Marcus. I want to hear this," said the judge.

The children remembered every detail. They corroborated everything: the fake ID, the purse, the note. Simon said, "I found him first."

Pauline said, "We told our mamma that we should surely keep him, especially since his mother wass a drug addict." She chuckled nervously trying to gain the judge's approval.

Mrs. Kemp turned toward her daughter, "Pshh," she scolded. There was something in Pauline's tone that brought Mrs. Kemp's disapproval. It sounded prideful, and certainly had no consideration of the scripture: "But now ye rejoice in your boastings: all such rejoicing is evil."

Sara added humbly, trying to redeem herself, "But then our pappa said since de Muellers did not have any children, maybe we could give Vincent to them." Pauline knew immediately why her mother had shushed her. She glanced at Bunny apologetically.

"I found de purse," said Simon.

"I found de note," said Rachael. "It said, 'My name iss Vincent. My mommy can't take care of me. Would you please take me? And if you don't want me to cry, play this tape.'"

"What tape?" asked the judge, curious.

"A Lou Rawls tape," said Martin with excitement.

"Mr. Mueller, it's not your turn," said the judge.

"Sorry," said Martin, realizing he had just made another mistake.

"Lou Rawls' Greatest Hits," said Rachael.

"It worked too." They all chimed in. "We played it, and he wiggled around for a few minutes and then he listened for a little while longer, and then he was out for de night," said the oldest Kemp boy. At least, I did not hear him wake up." He looked at his mother for confirmation.

"We never heard that kind of music before," they explained, wide eyed.

They continued relentlessly, until every detail was described, rapid-fire. "We would have told you all this before de police had to come and take de Muellers to jail, but it happened so fast we did not have a chance."

"Can Vincent come home now?" asked the Kemps youngest.

The judge said, "Let's talk to Miss Muldare for a moment. Thank you, children."

The judge called the two lawyers into his chamber. He said, "We must remember this is not a kidnapping trial; it is a custody hearing, and though we have leveled the playing field, we have not established custody. When am I going to hear whether this Miss Muldare meets the requirements for maintaining her parental rights?"

"But Judge," said the Muellers' lawyer, "what she did was perjury."

"I'm aware of that, Mr. Kurly, but how old was she when she made up that whopper?"

"Seventeen," he admitted.

The judge said, "I'm not in the habit of stripping away parental rights every time someone tells a lie—a lie to get their child back. I'd have everybody's kids."

"But she still hasn't come forward with the truth voluntarily, and the Muellers spent the last three days in jail because of her lies."

The judge said, "From what the children said, the Muellers were in jail before anyone knew what was happening, and that would include Miss Muldare. Besides, if the Muellers want to file a civil suit, that's their business, not ours.

"But . . .," said the Muellers' lawyer.

The judge interrupted, directing his comment to Mr. Marcus saying, "I realize this is a high profile case for the two of you, however gentlemen, we have a lot of other cases besides this one. And quite frankly, you may care about the publicity, but I am too old to be ambitious. I'd like to speed up this determination by asking Miss Muldare a few questions myself. And remember, this hearing is about ruling within the confines of the law, and that is all. When we return to the courtroom there will be no showboating, or so help me, you'll pay for it."

"Yes, Your Honor," they agreed.

The judge re-entered the courtroom. He instructed Bunny to come to the witness stand. She dreaded going to the stand. Her heels clicked across the floor much more self consciously than before.

"Miss Muldare," said the judge, "the children have testified that you are the mother according to the 'fake ID' found in the purse."

"I am the mother," she said emphatically.

"Then you are also the mother that has an unseemly job?"

"I work for AAA as a secretary for an auto insurance underwriter."

"They pay you pretty well at AAA?"

"No, not really," she complained. "I get by, but I know for a fact that the men there make a lot more than I do."

"How long have you worked there?"

"Four years."

The judge made a note. "You have proof of that?"

"Yes, my lawyer can show you my rent receipts, my W2s, even my diploma."

"You must have gotten some education somewhere along the way then?"

Mr. Marcus handed the judge a folder containing the proof he requested.

"I have a business degree from Community College."

"Your landlord said that you have a drug problem. What kind of drug problem is that?"

"Heroin, crack, marijuana, cigarettes, but heroin was the main problem."

"Was?" he asked.

"I went to drug rehab. As long as I stayed off drugs they paid for my school."

"They? Who sponsors that program?"

"I don't really know."

"You should find out, Miss Muldare, and thank them. Did you come into a sizable inheritance?"

"It seemed like it, at first, but it ran out, or just about. But I have a car and furniture, and an apartment, and Vinnie will have his own bedroom."

"Wouldn't it have been more prudent to give the baby to Social Services than putting him in a stranger's car?"

"If I took the baby to them, they would take him away, they would know I was on heroin, and then they would make me go through withdrawal. I didn't think I was ready for that. Even if I did get straight, they might not let me keep him anyway, because I didn't have a job, or a husband, or anything. I figured, what was the point? I figured I would find the baby a home myself, since I was probably going to lose him anyway, and not have to face my drug problem until I was ready. I didn't want anybody to force me. I had to be ready myself. When you have to walk through the fires of hell, you don't want anybody rushing you, you know?"

"What about your family?"

"My mom was divorced, and my dad lived in Florida."

"Does your mother live in Florida?"

"No, she lives in Carlisle. Maureen Muldare."

"Oh, I've heard of her," replied the judge.

Bunny couldn't be sure if that was good or bad. "We both live in Carlisle, but I couldn't go home. She didn't want me to have the baby in the first place. She said it would cost her too much money. She told me to get an abortion and go to rehab and that would solve my problems. I went to the abortion clinic once, before she ever suggested it, but it was so terrible I ran out of there and never went back."

"I see," he said. He twirled the hair of his eyebrows as he reviewed his notes. Everyone waited anxiously until the judge was finished making notes.

Finally he said, "From what the children have testified, you were not taking good care of the baby. Vincent had to get medical attention for his eyesight because of your drug abuse, he was not given any food, and he had no shoes, no blanket, nothing but the shirt on his back. If you weren't a good mother then, I have no reason to believe you would do any better today."

"That was because of the heroin. It was all I could concentrate on. It took all my money, my mind, my health, Vinnie's father, everything. But it seemed like once I was addicted, it was all I could do to get from one day to the next without getting so sick I wanted to die."

"Can you tell us about that?" asked the judge.

"I can take pain pretty well, usually. But when heroin first starts out, you have to kind of keep the beast at bay, and the only way to do that is to take more horse. Then it takes over until you'll do anything to get more."

The judge said, "So you thought you could keep up with the heroin when your father sent you your inheritance."

"Not really. I saw a way out that I never saw before. At least I could get a real apartment and pay for groceries and stuff. I could get Vinnie back. I still knew I had to get off 'H.'"

"You said it's not so bad if you have money," said the judge.

"Not so bad, meaning, you can stay out of jail for robbery, but the addiction is still eating up your insides. I still have dreams that I'm back on it, but as long as I have Vinnie to live for, I'm going to keep on saying no. I have the upper hand on the beast now, and that's the way I'm going to keep it."

"How can we be sure of that?"

"It's worked so far; I've been clean for about eight years. I don't see any reason why I would go back to it now." She sounded resolute.

"What makes you think you are any more deserving of this child today than you were back then? Yes, Miss Muldare, you went to school, and got a job like any normal person is expected to do. But while you were getting an education and getting a job, your son was establishing roots in his current home. He has a home now, and is doing just fine where he is. Why should we upset him and his household? I agree that a mother has first rights to her children, but in this case the two of you no longer have a relationship. If he passed you on the street, he wouldn't even know who you are.

"He might not know who I am, but I would recognize him anywhere. I knew every hair and freckle. I'm the one who knew what music he liked. That's because I was his mother, his real mother, and I've been trying to find him ever since I g-gave him up. Most of the inheritance money went to pay for ads in the paper, posters, private investigators, and a child-find organization. He was my one and only reason strong enough to get me through the hell of heroin addiction. He was my reason for going to school, for getting a job, and all the rest. I never gave up completely on finding him someday, and I wanted to be ready. The only thing that stopped my search was that I ran out of money. And yeah, it took me over eight years to find him, but that doesn't change the fact that he was my baby then, and he's my baby now, and I love him so much. Ever since I put him in that van, I've felt like half a person. My heart was broken when I turned my back on him, but I knew I had to do it for his sake." She pulled the lace hanky from her pocket again and covered her face. Freida looked at her in disgust.

The judge asked Bunny's lawyer, "What was the date of the police report that Miss Muldare filed concerning her lost child?"

Mr. Marcus answered, "September 15th." He handed the report to the judge.

"And the day the Kemps discovered the child?"

"September 10th," said Mr. Drummond.

"Thank you," said the judge, and noted it in his records.

"I see." He cleared his throat, "It appears to me that you made up a whopper of a story about these innocent people, who took in your child, loved him with all their hearts, and gave him a good home. And yet, you would let them go to jail, so that, essentially, you could steal him back from them eight years later. It appears to me, Miss Muldare, you are the one who belongs in jail. At the very least, you need to move on, and let this one go. No one asked you to have an illegitimate child, or any of the other problems you brought on yourself; you did that on your own. This courtroom is about accountability."

Bunny started to explain through her tears, "I never wanted anybody to go to jail. I didn't even know they found Vinnie until Monday morning, and they were already in jail by then. I never knew who had him, or how well he was being taken care of. For all I knew, he was living with a wicked stepmother. I didn't know. All I could think about since Monday morning was that I was finally going to get my baby back. That lie, about him being taken, happened so long ago I barely remember doing it."

"I'm sorry I told that lie back then. Now it's coming back to haunt me. And I know saying I'm sorry seems pretty lame, but I've tried so hard to do everything I'm supposed to. I could have just kept on doing heroin until I dropped, but I didn't. I kept on sticking it out until I conquered it. I did it because I loved my baby. Love kept me motivated. He was the best thing that ever happened to me. It just took me a little time to get it together. Nobody knows better than me that Vinnie had it bad in the beginning, and it was all my fault. But is there no such thing in this world as a second chance? I've worked so very hard to stay straight. Heroin ruined my life back then. Is it going to keep on ruining it forever? I'll be a good mother from now on. I promise. You can check on me everyday if you want to."

Bunny broke down and wept uncontrollably. The judge left Bunny on the stand for about five minutes without saying anything. He stared at the ceiling, he pulled up his socks, he rubbed his chin. He stared at a blank wall, tapping his pen on his desk pad. He finally got up and went into his office, returning ten minutes later. When he sat back down at his chair he said to the lawyers, "If you boys don't have anything else, I think I'm ready to make my determination."

The Muellers' lawyer stared into the judge's face and swallowed. He knew it could go either way. Vincent took a deep breath and stretched until he shivered. Freida could feel the knot in her stomach get even tighter. Pastor Dunkin took Mother Dunkin's hand and squeezed. Every eye was on the judge.

"Miss Muldare, for the record, I agree with Mr. Mueller that Vincent is better off with a two-parent family."

"I have a boyfriend," she reminded.

He tossed his glasses onto his desk and rubbed his eyes in frustration. He stalled for a time in order to collect himself. Once he had mustered some patience, he began again. "While we are on the subject of boyfriends, Miss Muldare, I suggest that the next time you engage in an activity that could, even remotely, result in making another baby, you make absolutely sure; that whoever it is says 'I do' with a ring and a contract—first," he wagged his finger at her, "no ring, no wedding, no baby. That way, if you make an innocent mistake like picking the wrong guy, and he doesn't hold up his end, at least if you're married to him you have legal recourse. The courts can chase him around and try to make a man out of him," he explained. He rolled his eyes and sighed. "Otherwise we'll be seeing you in court all over again with yet another mess. Do we understand each other?"

"Yes."

Bunny's boyfriend squirmed in his seat.

"To continue," he sighed, "After the disclosures that were made today, I am going to suggest the charges of kidnapping against Mr. and Mrs. Mueller be dismissed and that they be released from prison before the day is out."

Martin breathed a huge sigh.

"Bailiff," said the judge, "Would you find the guards who accompanied these unfortunate people over here, and tell them to take off these handcuffs and chains?"

"You, Miss Muldare, have done these people a great disservice. I'm not sure that you wouldn't have let these poor people rot in jail forever. Lying under oath is a serious offense. We'll leave that verdict for God to decide; the purpose of this meeting does not entail resolving that issue. It's worth considering, Miss Muldare, that the Muellers are entitled to sue the pants off you, as well they should."

Martin interrupted, "That will not be necessary, Judge."

The judge peered sadly at Martin over his glasses. Martin feared by the expression on the judge's face that there was bad news coming.

Vincent listened intently as his entire future hung in the balance. Freida turned her attention away from the judge and began watching Vincent.

"However," he said, "I must admit you have gotten your life together. I see hundreds of heroin addicts come through this courtroom and quite frankly, you are the only one I've seen who actually recovered. You probably saved this boy's life by giving him away when you did. And I must admit, that single act of heroism took an honorable amount of selflessness. And to sacrifice the tenderness he must have given you, for the sake of his safety and security, is commendable. Had you kept him much longer, he probably would have crawled right out into traffic. For that act of heroism, I congratulate you.

"My displeasure comes in telling the Muellers that you, Miss Muldare, have met the legal requirements needed to reclaim your son." The courtroom gasped. Freida put her hand to her mouth. The judge looked sadly at Freida. "Had the adoption gone through years ago, and before Miss

Muldare was able to get her life in order, this would have ended quite differently for all of you, but unfortunately, it did not. Therefore, custody is hereby granted to the natural mother, Miss Bonnie Louise Muldare." The gavel went down like a guillotine.

Freida tried to get to Vincent, but the bailiff held her back. She struggled against him with all of her might, but he refused let her go. Martin sat helpless with his face in his hands. Vincent threw his head back on the seat.

Marshall jumped over the back of the chair and cradled Vincent's face. "I will come and see you, brother. We will play together again, I promise. You'll always be my best friend. You'll see. I will come and see you. It will be just like always. I will never forget you. Are you listening to me, Vincent? Just shake your head yes."

Vincent was wailing deep long sobs that echoed throughout the courtroom and into the hall. He tried to shake his head yes, but really he knew he would be forgotten eventually. He didn't even like these strangers, and he was never going to go home again. No more Mother Freida, no more Father Martin, his grandmammas and grandpappas, Miss Purdy, his animals, his school, his church, all gone. "All gone!" he wailed. "No more!" he cried again, even louder.

Freida blasted Bunny from across the courtroom, "Is this what you wanted!?" She shouted. "Is this what you have been waiting for!? Listen to your boy. You are selfish. Selfish! Listen to what you have done to him!"

There was noise and confusion all throughout the courtroom. Vincent's relatives tried to say good-bye to him, but Michael, Bunny's boyfriend, snatched him up and carried him away. As Michael walked passed Freida and Martin, Vincent tried to squirm away, "Let me go, let me go! I want my mamma, I want my pappa!" he kept screaming. Michael held on tightly in spite of Vincent's flailing arms and legs.

Michael said, "Pipe down, you're going with us, whether you like it or not."

Bunny tiptoed behind him, none the happier for her victory, still holding her handkerchief to her face.

As Bunny and her boyfriend passed in front of Freida, she screamed, "God will punish you for this! I hope you burn in hell for this!" Freida was out of control. Her face was bright red, the veins in her neck and temples bulging as she screamed. The bailiff continued to hold her arms tightly behind her back. "I hate you for this! I hate you, and my son hates you!" As Vincent left the room Freida started screaming uncontrollably. "No. No. No! You can not do this. No!"

Martin grabbed both her shoulders and forced her to look him in the eyes, "Freida Dunkin Mueller! Listen to me! God has a plan. Look at me! All things happen for de good to those who are called. We were called to be Vincent's parents. Remember? Show me your faith, Freida!"

"No! They can not do this!" Freida continued to scream.

Martin shook her shoulders. "Show me your faith, Freida!"

"This can not be happening. This can not possibly be God's will." Her knees buckled and she fell into Martin's chest. "Martin how can we live with this?" she sobbed. "I can not bear it." She sobbed into Martin's chest. Martin signaled the bailiff that he would handle it. The bailiff left them alone.

"We can, and we will! We must trust God," he said. "We must," he whispered. He wrapped his arms around her and let her cry.

All of the Kemp children were upset. Mr. and Mrs. Kemp wished they hadn't agreed to let the children testify. Marshall Mueller was in the worst shape. As Vincent was being carried out kicking and screaming Marshall stumbled along behind Michael holding on to his shirt. After about ten minutes of weeping, they were told they would all have to leave the room, but to leave meant that it was all over, and that was much too difficult to face.

Why God? was the huge unanswered question they were left with, as they moved reluctantly toward the door, overcome by emotion.

There were reporters and cameras outside the courthouse waiting to pounce.

"How did you answer the charges of kidnapping?" they yelled toward Martin and Freida.

"No one wass kidnapped," Bishop Perl replied as the crowd pressed in. "He wass lent to us by God for a short time. We can only pray that what he has learned with us will carry him through life."

"Some call that brainwashing. How do you respond?"

Bishop Perl patted his brown leather satchel containing his Bible, looked into the camera and answered, "Better to be washed in de holy word of God than awash in this world with no direction."

"Who is he going to live with?"

"His natural mother," said Bishop Perl. His voice cracked and his eyebrows furled as he choked back the tears. The camera zoomed in on his face.

"How did the boy respond to the verdict?" a reporter asked.

Bishop Perl couldn't answer. He could only shake his head no.

Mrs. Perl answered, trying not to cry herself, "He wass very distraught."

The camera panned to Marshall who was hanging onto his mother's skirt, hiding his tears.

"What is your name young man?" asked a reporter.

"Marshall," he answered meekly.

"How did you feel when you heard the boy was going back with his mother?"

Marshall fell apart all over again. He put his face back into his mother's dress and hung on.

"No more questions," said Bishop Perl.

Another reporter called after them. "What about the kidnappers?"

As they worked their way back to the bus terminal the cameras continued to flash.

Matthew 9:13. But go ye and learn what that meaneth, I will have mercy, and not sacrifice: for I am not come to call the righteous, but sinners to repentance.

Chapter 12

Love thy Neighbor

*I*t had been three weeks since Vincent came to live with Bunny and Michael, and during that time, he had not spoken once—not to anyone. Marshall had tried to call Vincent, but Bunny answered the phone and told him, "Vincent is not allowed to continue with his old friendships. He has to get used to his new home. Don't ever call again." With that, she hung up the phone. A few days later Pastor Dunkin invited Bunny and Vincent to come to church, but Bunny declined. "If God saw me coming through the church doors, you can be sure you'd have to put out the fire," she said laughing nervously. "God doesn't want anything to do with the likes of me, and to be perfectly honest, the feeling's mutual." It was clear that she didn't want Vincent to have anything more to do with Promise, and that Vincent had no choice but to try to move on, so far without success.

It was Tuesday. Bunny was at work. She had dropped Vincent off at the schoolyard as usual, but today, as soon as she was out of sight, he walked back home. He didn't have the courage to face another day at school.

Each day seemed harder to bear than the day before. On Friday of the previous week, the children were having recess in the gymnasium. It was raining outside. Two boys saw Vincent standing against the wall by himself, not far from the fire alarm, and began to whisper to each other. Vincent watched them cautiously.

"Hey Vinnie, if you stand right here, we'll throw baseball with you."

Vincent didn't answer, but didn't refuse either. They walked over to the baseball that was lying in the corner, and on their way toward Vincent, they passed the fire alarm. One boy hid the other while he used the baseball to break the glass. They handed Vincent the ball just as the alarm began to sound. "Stay there Vinnie, don't move," they warned.

The teacher shouted, "Everyone freeze!" Vincent had never heard of a fire alarm. It was like everything else in his new surroundings, strange and unfamiliar. She walked over to the broken alarm, and coolly reset it. She spun around toward the class to study each face staring back at her. Since Vincent was the closest to the alarm with a baseball in his hand, she said to him, "Did you set off the fire alarm, young man?" Vincent couldn't speak. His eyes got bigger for fear of what would happen next, which made him look even guiltier. "Answer me. I know you can talk. Did—you—do-this?" Vincent stood frozen in place. He dropped the baseball on the wooden gym floor. Bang. It rolled out into the center of the floor. She was satisfied she had her answer. She grabbed him by the elbow and escorted him to the principal's office where he was placed with his face to the wall for the rest of the afternoon. The two boys had been taunting him with their accomplishment ever since. Anyone who dared to make friends with Vincent would have to endure the rejection of everyone else, and so far no one had tried. He was an outcast, he knew it, and it seemed to suit everyone just fine.

He bounced an old tennis ball against the wall in the hallway of the apartment building. It helped him to keep his anger from turning to tears. Bump, bump, bump. The tennis ball made a constant unrelenting rhythm. Vincent repeated the taunt he had heard at school to each bump of the ball: bug-eyed Bible boy, bug-eyed Bible boy, bug-eyed Bible boy. I will never go back to school again, never, never, ever, he thought.

What Vincent had learned about Michael, the man who was supposed to be his replacement father, was that he was not a nice person. He was attending college and wanted to be an airplane pilot, but in the meantime he had a job at night parking trucks for the post office. The model airplanes that Michael had built hung from the ceiling of Vincent's bedroom, looming over his head as a reminder of the man who was more like a boy, a boy who had no interest in being his father, and didn't mind letting it show. Vincent had concluded that Michael would rather have Bunny all to himself, and Vincent was in the way, not that Vincent cared whether he was accepted by Michael. Michael wasn't his father; he already had a father. Vincent tried not to dwell on the fact that he and Michael might have to tolerate each other for the rest of their lives. And, though tolerating Michael was trying, it was nothing compared to the agony of losing his pappa.

Bunny continually doted over Vincent. She had taken him shopping for some "normal clothes," but Vincent couldn't bring himself to wear them. It felt as if he were wearing a costume. She begged him to talk to her, but he couldn't. All he wanted was to go back home, but he was trapped, trapped by circumstances, and trapped inside himself. The things that he was feeling were so devastating he was unable to give voice to them. It was no use trying to speak; he couldn't. So he just kept to himself, where he could exist in his own private exile, a place where he didn't have to say anything to anybody. He placed the blame on one person, that Miss Muldare, the liar. Bang, went the ball against the wall. The liar. Bang went the ball, louder this time. The drug addict. Bang. The real kidnapper. Bang.

Mr. Gibbs opened his door at the opposite end of the hallway. "Vinnie, is that you making all that noise?"

Vincent started for his apartment door to go inside. Simultaneously, Mrs. Gibbs was coming up the steps. She had a bag of groceries in her arms.

Mr. Gibbs said, "Margaret, this is Vinnie."

Vincent turned toward the woman. Vincent made an effort to speak, but in the trying, it made him start to cry. He put the back of his hand up to his mouth to try to hide his face. He wrapped the other arm around his waist to close himself in. He was embarrassed to be so vulnerable around a total stranger. He wanted to run and hide.

Mrs. Gibbs could see he was in emotional trouble, and she had the good sense not to press.

"Hello there, Vinnie," she said cheerfully. "I knew you when you were just a little bitty baby. You certainly have grown since then. I never knew you would become such a handsome young man."

Vincent turned to escape into his apartment, but Mr. Gibbs called him into service. "Vinnie, would you help Mrs. Gibbs with her bag? She's been carrying that bundle of groceries for a few blocks."

Vincent didn't feel he had the right to refuse helping an older lady. He took the bag without looking at her; maybe she hadn't noticed he was crying. The two walked together down the hallway, with Mrs. Gibbs doing all the talking. She told him about how cute he was as a baby, and how they all loved playing with him. "We don't see many babies around here anymore," she said, "I think they must have gone out of fashion or something. And your mother! If you think she's pretty now, you should have seen her then! My, my, she turned every head on the street. Just gorgeous, but then, she's still gorgeous, isn't she?"

Vincent was not impressed with how she looked or anything else about her, and when he reached their apartment door he tried to hand off the groceries to Mr. Gibbs, but Mr. Gibbs asked, "Could you put them on the table over there, son? My back isn't doing so well today."

Vincent obliged, but it didn't change the fact that he wanted to escape. Vincent smelled something baking. It smelled like stuffed pork chops, he thought.

"Norm, did you remember to check the pork chops?"

"Yes, yes, I did. I just turned them down," he said as he shut the front door.

"Vinnie," said Mrs. Gibbs, unloading the fresh produce from her bag, "would you like to have some lunch with us?"

Vincent didn't answer. Mrs. Gibbs took note that he wasn't crying or running away. "I'll take that as a yes," she said, smiling.

Mr. Gibbs spotted Vincent looking longingly at the oranges Mrs. Gibbs had placed in the wooden bowl in front of them. Mr. Gibbs took two oranges. He put one in front of Vinnie and said, "Have a seat and try one of these oranges. They're terrific this time of year. These come all the way from Jerusalem. Can you believe it? What a lucky couple of guys we are to live in the United States." Mr. Gibbs picked up the orange and began to peel it with his hands. The juice dripped onto the avocado-green plastic placemat. "Someone picked this orange in Israel, you know, all the way on the other side of the world. And just think, all we have to do to get one is walk a few blocks down the street to the fruit market and, alacazam, we have the most wonderful oranges in all of God's creation. That just amazes me," he said adding, "I'd love to go to Jerusalem someday and pick those oranges myself. Have you ever been to Jerusalem?"

Vincent stopped peeling his orange long enough to shake his head no, but he didn't look up.

"It's a shame really. Here we are living in a world that a guy can travel anywhere he wants, and we don't even take the opportunity to go see where Jesus lived. I'm going to go there before I die," he said. "Will you go with me, Mother?"

"I'll go," she said. "How about you, Vinnie, would you like to see Jerusalem some day?"

He had a big bite of the most delicious orange he had ever eaten. It began to drip down his chin. He shook his head yes.

"Didn't I tell you these are good oranges?" asked Mr. Gibbs. "I wouldn't lie to ya. You can always count on old Mr. Gibbs."

Vincent hadn't forgotten the testimony that Mr. Gibbs gave about Bunny telling a lie to get Vincent back.

Mr. Gibbs must have read Vincent's face. "I've known your mother since she was just a little girl. Her mother, I guess that would be your grandmother, only lives a few miles from here. Your grandmother used to bring Bunny's brother, Richard, to the baseball games and she would bring Bunny with her. Bunny was probably about five years old back then, when she started coming to Richard's games. I think Bunny would rather have been playing baseball herself, but Mrs. Muldare, classy woman, anyway, she always brought Bunny dressed to the nines in fancy little party dresses. She was definitely the best-dressed little girl in the bunch. Nobody could outdo Mrs. Muldare."

Mrs. Gibbs put a plate of stuffed pork chops and mashed potatoes in front of Vinnie and Mr. Gibbs. "Would you like water, milk, juice?" she offered.

"Milk, please." Vincent startled himself when he realized he had just spoken. His eyes opened wide, and he started to get a little panicky, and wanted to run.

"I knew you would say that," said Mr. Gibbs. "Growing boys always drink a lot of milk. Am I right? Do you drink a lot of milk?"

Vincent went back to a safer shake of the head.

"Where do you get your milk, Vinnie?" asked Mr. Gibbs.

Mrs. Gibbs realized Vincent hadn't picked up his fork to begin eating. "You ask too many questions, Norm. Let the boy eat."

Vincent bowed his head, and waited.

"Oh, yes, the prayer," said Mr. Gibbs. He cleared his throat. "Bless these thy gifts which we are about to receive, and bless them to our bodies. In the name of the Father, Son, and Holy Ghost. Amen."

Mr. and Mrs. Gibbs made the sign of the cross and began to pick up their forks and knives, noisily slicing away at their pork chops. Vincent took a long sniff of the stuffing before he put it in his mouth. It smelled like Freida's pork chops, he thought. Vincent chewed slowly and reveled in the delicious meal. He hesitated, and then found the courage to say, "From our cows."

Mr. Gibbs looked puzzled.

Mrs. Gibbs rushed in, "Oh, you have your own cows do you? That must be wonderful to be able to have your own milk right there on the farm, so fresh and all."

Vincent shook his head in agreement. Vincent wasn't looking quite so uncomfortable. "What flavor is it?" asked Mr. Gibbs.

Vincent looked confused.

"Chocolate, strawberry, vanilla?"

"Oh, Norm, don't be so silly."

Vincent tipped his head and smiled. "Guernsey," said Vincent.

"Ah, Guernsey," said Mr. Gibbs disguising the fact that he wouldn't know a Guernsey from a longhorn steer. "You ask most boys your age where milk comes from and they'll tell you, 'Duh, it comes from the grocery store.'"

Vincent laughed, trying not to make any noise.

"Vinnie, can you tell the difference between Guernsey milk and other milk?"

"Yah," said Vincent, "Guernsey iss de best." It seemed surprising to him that he was getting his voice back. He considered telling Mr. Gibbs that he could tell if the cows had been eating wild onions, but then decided to keep quiet. It was nice to finally have someone to talk to, he thought. There was a second round of mashed potatoes and fresh rolls. They ate until everyone was pleasantly full.

Mr. Gibbs opened his mouth wide and let out the longest, loudest burp Vincent had ever heard. He laughed out loud this time. Mr. Gibbs patted his round belly and smiled, "Thank you, mother. That was tres delicio-so."

"Norman, mind your manners," she chuckled. She was glad he liked it so much and especially glad that Vincent was beginning to warm up to them.

Mr. Gibbs said, "That's how they say thank you in China. I was just being polite, Mother, Chinese style. Did you know, Vinnie, that in China everybody sits around burping like that, and if you don't burp after the meal is over, the cook gets insulted?"

Vincent shook his head no.

"Me and my bowling buddies went to this Chinese restaurant one time for a banquet. There was about twenty of us. Anyway, after the meal we all had our turn at seeing who could belch the loudest. The cook was very pleased. Every time someone belched he would take another bow. Yep, that was one happy Chinaman. It was a great time. I had no idea men could belch that loud. We had the whole restaurant rolling in the aisles. Old Calvin Cooper took the prize. It wasn't the loudest, but it was definitely the longest. It started out real slow, and just when you thought he was done, he'd start up again, sometimes long, sometimes little shorter, er, er. Like that. It must have gone on for at least a full minute, maybe even two. From that day on he was given the job of doing the official bowling league after-dinner belch. He loved to do it, too. Those were the days. I miss those guys. They're mostly dead now. I loved those guys." Mr. Gibbs fell into a daydream, and then began to yawn. "Mother, Vincent, will you excuse me? I need to go catch up on my beauty rest." He gave a girly grin and patted himself on the cheeks.

"Go ahead, dear. Maybe I can talk Vinnie into helping me with the dishes."

"Yah," said Vinnie quietly. He knew he had the rest of the afternoon to himself. Bunny wouldn't be home until after five. These were nice people, and Vincent liked the way it felt in their home.

Mother Gibbs had a concerned look on her face that lasted all the way through the dishes. She hoped that given a chance, Vinnie would open up to her. She waited patiently through the dishes. She seated herself in her lounge chair, where she was joined by her tabby cat. Finally Vincent spoke. "I don't like my new mamma."

"You don't?" she said as though she were surprised.

"No," he said.

"Well, I guess that's understandable."

"She doesn't seem like my real mamma," he explained.

"She's the real thing all right. I bet she remembers every freckle you were born with."

"I don't remember her."

"I see. That doesn't help matters, does it?" she said, as she peered compassionately over her reading glasses. Vincent noticed her eyes were misted over, but he wasn't sure if they were like that all the time. Her eyelids sagged on the bottom, showing her age. Mrs. Gibbs had on a bulky brown knit cardigan with a stretch polyester shirt underneath. Her matching brown polyester pants exposed her bare swollen ankles and black shoes that were run over at the heels. Vincent noticed that Mrs. Gibbs fingers were gnarled and wrinkled, but still quick with the yarn. He thought, she must use her hands a lot. Her cheeks were lightly powdered, soft and full. When she tucked her chin to look at Vincent over her bifocals, it made her double chin look even chubbier.

She leaned toward the windowsill, picked some leaves from a plant, and folded it into the ball of yarn she had started. This was the windowsill Mrs. Gibbs and her cat enjoyed every afternoon. It was the perfect place for a nap, according to the cat.

"What iss that you are picking?" asked Vinnie, curiously.

"That's catnip. It keeps kitty young. You'll see, she'll be chasing around here after this ball of yarn in a few minutes, having just the best time."

There was a pause and then Vincent said, "Mrs. Muldare used to be a heroin addict."

"Yes, she was."

"That iss why she gave me away, so she could use her drugs," he added.

"That's sort of the way it was, but not exactly," said Mrs. Gibbs with reservation.

"If she didn't like her drugs more than me, she would have picked me instead of her drugs."

"Vinnie, she loved you more than anything, and she hated being an addict. She tried with all her might to stop, mainly because she didn't want to give you up, but she was already in over her head and couldn't stop."

"She stopped," he accused.

"It was a very hard thing to do. We need to give her some credit; she bravely fought her way through something that most people are never able to do. She asked me to help her through it several times before she finally succeeded, and I saw with my own eyes what that drug addiction did to your mother. Heroin addiction is a terrible thing. Do you know what made the difference for her in being able to succeed?"

Vincent shook his head. "What?"

"Her love for you. She did it for you, Vinnie," said Mrs. Gibbs softly. She looked in his eyes biting her lower lip.

"She didn't do it soon enough. Why did she give me away since she loved me so much?"

Mrs. Gibbs looked out the window and sighed deeply before she began to explain. "It was because of me, Vinnie. I talked her into giving you away, because I didn't think she would ever be able to give it up. She came to me a few days after you were gone saying she had to get you back; her father had left her money. If it weren't for me convincing her it was the best thing, she never would have gone through with it. I felt just awful about it, because she did everything to try and find you and get you back, and if it weren't for me, she never would have lost you in the first place. I asked God many times how I could have misunderstood so badly and messed everything up. I was just sure that's what God wanted. I never would have thought she could get over her drug problem. Who knows, maybe if she had never missed you so much after you were gone, and she could keep on getting by with the money her father left her, she might still be trying to keep up with that heroin. I know the police would have never helped her out if she showed up for a meeting high and out of her right mind. We'll never understand why some things happen the way they do. But I do know one thing: if God is on a mission, nothing is going to stop it. Maybe he's got a plan and he's working it out."

"Why did she throw me away, instead of giving me to an orphanage or something like that?"

"I suggested that, but she didn't want anything to do with the government, police, or anything like that. She thought when they asked her why she was giving you away, they'd put her in jail, or worse, a mental hospital, and that they'd keep you even if she did recover, and they'd put you in a hospital where nobody would pay any attention to you. She thought it might be better to find a nice home for you, herself. That's when I suggested she go to the farm show and look for a nice family there. She took my advice, and at least that part turned out well."

"Yah," said Vincent.

"It took a lot of courage to give you away. It took her several weeks and several buckets of tears to convince herself it would be for the best. Know this though, she did it so you could have a chance at a decent life. She knew there wasn't much hope for you as long as she was a heroin addict."

"I wish she would have just left me there forever. She never asked me what I want."

"Ya know, Vinnie, I think everything important that happens to us, happens for a reason, especially if we love God. I bet he has a special reason for you and your mom getting back together again. I had given up on that ever happening, but fate has brought you back together. I believe in God, not chance. How about you?"

"I have never been this unhappy before," he replied, "not in my whole life." The tears began to well up and his chin quivered, but he was determined not to cry. "Is that what God wants too?"

"Come here dumplin'," she said. She held out her big, friendly, old arms to coax him in for a hug.

Vincent couldn't help himself. He collapsed into tears in old Mrs. Gibbs' lap.

"I just want to go home, can't you tell her again to let me go. Please tell her to let me go home. I want to go home."

Mrs. Gibbs rubbed Vincent's hair and tried to comfort him. "I know you do, sweetheart. I know you do. I know you do. Just lean on old Mrs. Gibbs. It's all right."

After a time she said, "Vinnie, I have known your mother since she was a little girl. I've known her parents longer than that. We are talking about people who never taught their children the word of God. But you and I, we are very lucky. God has shielded us from so much, compared to the temptations that people like your mother have to face. Tell me something, Vinnie. What is the most important thing that God wants us to do?"

"To love God with all our heart, with all our mind, and with all our soul."

"That's the easy part," she said. "What's the next most important thing?"

"To love each other."

"That's right. But that's the hard part, isn't it?"

Vincent nodded. "I don't love my mother, I don't even like her. But I can't just pretend like I do. That is not really loving somebody, is it?"

"Something you don't know about your mother is that she is capable of more love, and is willing to sacrifice more of herself for the sake of the people she loves, than most people who claim they are the holiest thing God ever put on this earth. When I saw your mother in such bad shape downstairs she was curled up in a ball. She was shaking all over. It was all she could do to keep from screaming herself hoarse. She didn't go through all that misery for herself; it was for you."

"What was the matter with her?"

"She told me months before that she was going to get off of the heroin so she could keep on being your mother. After that, I saw her get real sick about three times, and it was the third time I saw her like that, I could see she was in serious trouble."

"What did you do?"

"Well, first I took you to the drug store and we bought some formula. That formula is more expensive than her heroin, by the way. You drank two bottles of formula straight down. I didn't think that little stomach could hold that much. But, unfortunately she ended up giving in to it again. She felt so bad about it. All she could say was 'I'm sorry, I'm sorry, I'm not strong enough to beat it.' I asked her what she was going to do about this. I said, 'You can't keep going like this,' and she said she didn't know what to do, that she couldn't do it all by herself. That's when I offered to help her.

"We tried a couple of more times to get her straightened out, and then the last time was when she agreed to give you away. It hurt your mother so much, Vinnie, to have to give you up. She just didn't think she had a choice.

"Now, while you were in court, I know you heard a lot of things about what happened, but do you want to know what really happened?" asked Mrs. Gibbs.

"Yah," he answered sadly.

She continued her story. "I told Norman, 'I'm getting worried about Vinnie. Bunny has tried so hard, but I just know she's not going to make it. I need to go down to see if the baby is doing okay.' So I went downstairs. I could hear you crying from outside the door. I knocked but there was no answer, so I let myself in. When I looked inside the lights were out. I turned on the lights and opened the curtain. I went to the basket where you were sleeping, and picked you up. You would not be consoled. My goodness, you had a set of lungs! I told your mother you were going to be an opera singer with lungs like that."

"I still have a good set of lungs," said Vincent.

Mrs. Gibbs smiled down at Vincent. She continued, "Well, then I asked Bunny where the formula was. She didn't answer me. I bent down next to her but she still didn't answer. I shook her and she stirred slightly. I noticed she had messed the bed, and when I put my hand on her shoulder, she was shivering uncontrollably. I tried covering her with her fur coat, but it didn't help. The shaking got worse and she started to go into a convulsion. Her teeth rattled and she started to grunt in pain. I cradled your mother's head. Finally the convulsion passed but then she was fully conscious, and she tried to speak, but her muscles were cramping, and it hurt so much she could only groan. I told her I was taking her to the emergency room. She wouldn't hear of it. Then she started bleeding from her eyes. I told her I was afraid she would die if we didn't do something.

"She said, 'No. No doctors. No police. I can do this. They will take Vinnie. No.' And then she curled up in a ball and continued to lay there and suffer. So I scooped you up, and we went to the drugstore to get you some formula. I felt bad about leaving her there all alone. I didn't know what else to do.

"When we came back, Robert, a homeless man in the neighborhood, was leaving Bunny's room. I knew whoever was supplying your mother with her drugs had sent Robert over to give Bunny her fix. We hurried in, and I saw her with the spoon on the bed getting ready to give herself a shot. I screamed at her, 'What are you doing!' She said, 'I have to Mrs. Gibbs, I'm sorry.' I tried to stop her. We even tussled over the syringe with you in my arms. I told her, 'If you do this I am going to give Vinnie away, and you can do the explaining. You can't keep doing this to him.' I kept holding on to the needle and she kept trying to push it in. It was about an inch from her arm, when she stopped struggling against me. She didn't put down the needle, but she didn't try to use it either. We sat there staring at each other. 'It's Vinnie or this needle, which do you want?' I asked her.

"She thought about what she was doing, she looked at you for awhile. We locked eyes until finally she put the syringe down. I put all that drug junk into my purse, made you a bottle, and changed your diaper. You were soaked all the way through. We were a mess; you were crying, I was crying, Bunny was shaking and crying. I sat with you and your mother the rest of the day. We got your mom cleaned up. We got you back to sleep. She started to have a few moments when she could hold you, so I put you in her arms. She loved you so much Vinnie. Your mom was just very sick. That night I took all of her drug things with me and threw them in the garbage. I don't know who came to visit her that night, but by morning she had somehow gotten high again. Whoever was giving her that stuff probably came back for their money. I know Mr. Gibbs didn't let them in, so they must have come in through the window. All I know is; when I got downstairs, Bunny was sitting with her head in her arms crying and all she kept saying was, 'I'm sorry. I just can't help myself. It's too hard.'"

Vincent asked, "Do you think she went out the window herself?"

"She was still very sick when I left to go to bed. I don't think she had the strength to walk anywhere, let alone climb the coal chute and squeeze through the window. But anything's possible, I guess.

"I was angry at first, and I told her so, but she felt so bad about it. I insisted that she give you away. Now remember, this was after I saw her try to stop time after time, and it wasn't working. And it seemed like every time she tried, you had to suffer right along with her. She wanted Norman and me to take care of you, but we knew we were too old to take care of an infant. After many tears and much convincing, Bunny and I finally agreed that we would take you to the county fair. If we took you to the police, they would have started asking questions about the mother, and she would have been forced right back into withdrawal, and she wasn't ready for that. After I saw what she had to go through, I understood why. She didn't want to go through that much suffering so soon, and especially not by someone else forcing her. A few days later, I put you and Bunny in the back seat of my car, and we drove to the fairgrounds. I watched to see where the Amish people were parking. I had decided beforehand, that if we were going to give you to strangers, we should give you to one of them, since I knew they would give you a good, Godly home. There were a few cars and buggies in that area. I couldn't be sure that the van belonged to an Amish family, but I had seen them using vans like that before. I noticed they could put lots of people in one van. We waited till the sun started going down, so you wouldn't be too hot in there. We watched some other Amish families leave the fairground from that area of the parking lot, just as I thought. I pulled up behind the van, and checked to see if the doors were locked. They were. But then I checked the back doors and they opened. I looked around to see if anyone was watching. Then I hurried and put the baby basket with the note I had written, and the bottle and the tape into the back. Unfortunately I forgot to bring your formula. You had finished your bottle before we put you in the van. I had to hope for the best that they would think to get you something to eat before you got too hungry. I put the driver's license in the purse so you would know what your mother looked like. It wasn't that she didn't love you, Vinnie. I thought maybe the picture would help you to know that. Once I had everything in place that you would need, I told Bunny, 'It's time.'

"She got out of the car with you. She was holding on to you and bawling her head off. She was saying to you, 'I love you my sweetie, but I have to do this. Please forgive me. I love you, I love you, please forgive me.'

"I had to pry you away from her; she wouldn't let go. I'll never forget that image of her with her little hands pressed against the glass trying to see through her tears for just one last look at you. I would have given her more time, but we had to hurry before someone saw us."

Mrs. Gibbs pulled a Kleenex out of the box that was sitting in the windowsill. She wiped the tears away from underneath her glasses. "I was so sure I was doing the right thing. I never would have hurt Bunny that much if I thought she could have recovered like she did."

"Anyway," she sniffed, "like I said, we had to hurry, and I don't know that any amount of time would have been enough for her; she would have stayed there looking at you forever. I helped her back to the car. She lay back down in the back seat and cried her eyes out. We didn't stay to see what happened to the van. To tell you the truth, I was afraid we would be found out. I drove Bunny to the river, and we stayed there and stared into the water until dark." Mrs. Gibbs whispered, choking back the tears. "Then we went home."

"I'm sorry it's turned out like this for you, Vinnie. I feel like this is my fault. Don't blame it all on your mother. She tried, she really did. You'll see. Your mother hasn't always used good judgment in the past, but she has a good heart. You'll see. You just need to give her a chance."

Vincent didn't say anything for a while. He and Mrs. Gibbs just sat and rocked. Vincent thought about what Mrs. Gibbs had said.

"I think I'm going to go home now," he said.

"Do you mind if I say one more thing before you go?"

"I don't mind," he shrugged.

"Maybe you could start asking God why he would send you here; maybe he needs you here for some special reason. If not, well, then when he hears you praying, he'll find a way to send you back home. It's worth considering, don't you think?" she said tearfully.

"Yah," said Vincent softly. He knew she was right. "I will try," he promised.

As he was going out the door he called, "You make good pork chops. It wass so good it wass even as good as my mamma makes, I mean, my old mamma makes."

"That's quite a compliment. Thank you, sweetheart. You come and see me and Mr. Gibbs whenever you want. We're always here."

He smiled and nodded, closed the door behind him, and felt in his pocket for his key.

Matthew 22:36–40. Master, which is the great commandment in the law? Jesus said unto him, Thou shalt love the Lord thy God with all thy heart, and with all thy soul, and with all thy mind. This is the first and great commandment. And the second is like unto it, Thou shalt love thy neighbor as thyself. On these two commandments hang all the law and the prophets.

Chapter 13

Jump in

Six weeks after the trial:

"Vinnie, honey, it's time for dinner," called Bunny.

"I'm coming," he complained.

"Oh, no," he moaned to himself, "hot dogs again." He missed Freida's cooking. It wasn't that Bunny wasn't trying, but how could she compete with his mother, who spent most of her life in the kitchen. And it wasn't just her lack of experience; the food itself was like it was old and leftover. The milk tasted like it had powdered milk in it, and it was kind of watery. The eggs weren't any better. They were deflated and tasteless even though the carton said "Farm Fresh." His only defense was to put ketchup on them. Hmm, he thought, these hot dogs have biscuits around them. That is different."

Bunny chirped proudly, "Hey there, guy, all we need is some silverware and napkins, and we'll be ready."

Vincent mechanically put the silverware around the three plates.

Michael arrived at the dinner table as unenthusiastically as Vincent. He would much rather have taken his dinner into the bedroom and continued studying. "Aw, man, hot dogs again," he complained.

"Give me some money, Michael, and I'll buy you a steak!" complained Bunny. "Otherwise you get a hot dog."

"You got a deal. I can't choke down another damn hot dog."

At least Michael and I are thinking alike for tonight, thought Vincent.

Michael pulled his chair out flipped it backwards and sat with his legs straddling either side of the seat. He began to stir his baked beans. "I might look for another job," he said.

"Why?" Bunny asked, concerned.

"Because this guy keeps getting on the CB every stinking night of the week and dragging me into a fight and then calling me Foghorn Leghorn. I hate that f—"

"Michael!"

Vincent said, "When my pappa and I went to the farmers' market, a man used to try to get an argument going with Pappa all the time. I asked him: 'Why do you never say something back to him?' and Pappa says: 'Because when you get in a fight with a pig, you grunt and snort, and get yourself all upset; and then, three hours later, you figure it out: the pig iss having fun.'"

Bunny laughed, which irritated Michael. Michael didn't say anything. It was too hard for him to admit that the kid was right.

Michael continued stirring his dinner, "Ya know, the thing about the Amish—"

"We are Mennonite."

"Whatever. They live in our country like a bunch of hermits, but then when the country goes to war, they want everybody else to do their fighting for them. It seems to me, they're just sucking off of everybody else. They're just a bunch of parasites who are too chicken to fight."

"We are farmers. Where do you think this milk comes from?" Since Vincent had gotten his voice back he had discovered over the past several weeks, that as long as Bunny was around, he could be bold about voicing his opinions to Michael. She was always there to come to his defense. He had taken Mrs. Gibbs' advice and tried to look for the good in Bunny.

"What, you think we wouldn't have any milk if it weren't for the Amish?" sniped Michael.

Vincent turned the carton around. "Not this milk, you wouldn't." He pointed to the name of the dairy and the address: Schuster Farms, Plainfield, PA.

"You want to know something, Bunny?" asked Vincent.

"What, Vinnie?"

"If we go to de farmers' market on Saturday, de Kemerers have really good milk. De cream floats right to de top and it iss kind of sweet. You would like it." He held his glass up to his nose, "This tastes like they mix powdered milk with it, or maybe water. I don't know, maybe it iss de carton. I am used to always drinking it in a pitcher."

Michael mumbled something to Bunny. She didn't respond.

"Well maybe sometime, Vinnie," she said. "Did your family go there every Saturday?"

"Well it depended on what wass ready for market. We grew corn and tomatoes in summer. In spring I used to sell my eggs. Pappa would take out his share for chicken feed, and I got to keep de rest, except I put some in de Sunday offering. I made about four dollars a week. That iss how I got my piano."

"Is your new piano as good as you expected, Vinnie?"

"Yah, I like it, except Michael says it iss too loud."

Bunny reminded Vincent in a soft voice, "Vinnie, remember Michael is going to be your father now."

Vincent said nothing. Neither did Michael. They just looked at each other. It looked like they were once again on the same wavelength, but this time, it was better to go unsaid.

"You put your own money in the church offering?" she asked.

Michael interjected, "I'd never throw my money away like that. All those guys want is money. They just keep getting richer and richer, and the suckers that give it to them just keep on givin'."

"My Grandpappa Dunkin iss de pastor, and he saves up de money till somebody needs it. Like, there wass one time my Grandmamma Mueller, she wass burning leaves and stuff like that in de front yard, and there wass a rock that exploded and hit her right in de eye. It wass very bad. De doctors tried to fix it but, it wass too bad burned. De church paid for her operation; she got a glass eye. It iss funny to watch people who don't know her. They don't know which eye to look in. They start on one eye, and it starts going out to de side; and then they start looking in de other eye. Just when they think they have it figured out, she looks de other way. It makes them crazy. Sometimes I think she does it on purpose. I always ask her, 'look over here, look over there' ' cause I like to watch her eyes go around in opposite directions."

"Vinnie!" Bunny said with her napkin up to her mouth so he wouldn't see her smiling.

He crossed his eyes and rolled them around. "It iss sort of like an iguana," he said, sticking his tongue out.

"That's not nice to make fun of your Grandmother."

"You think I am bad. You should hear my pappa and his brothers when they get together."

"Your poor Grandmother," said Bunny.

"Oh, she likes it." He squinted one eye and stuck a crooked finger in the air. "She always says: 'You are not too old to smack.' And then if they keep it up, she starts to chasing them around de house dragging her bad leg around. They love to be bad and get her going. She iss real funny.

"This one time, we were at my grandmamma's, I think it wass Easter, and we were eating dinner. Pappa starts out: 'Ya know, my chicken iss not done in de middle.' Everybody else says: 'Mine is done.' So my grandmamma gets up real nice and gets him another piece. She says, 'Sorry, Martin.' Then he eats some mashed potatoes and says: 'My potatoes are a little lumpy, Mamma.' Now she is getting irritated with him, so she says: 'Iss anybody else's potatoes lumpy?' 'No,' they all say. 'Real good dinner, Mother Mueller.' She says to him: 'Eat them lumpy, Martin! Or I will give you a lump on your head.' Then we get to dessert. Pappa says: 'I hate to say this Mamma, but your peach pie isn't quite as good as Mother Dunkin's.' That iss her lifelong rival at the county fair every year. Mother Dunkin iss my other grandmamma, and she cooks verrry good," Vincent exclaimed. "So, my grandmamma stands up and slams her fists down on de table. She's pretty short. 'Okay,' she says, 'That iss it, Martin!' She and my pappa start running up de steps. I run up de back steps, and right into my pappa. He falls down in a heap on the landing. Here comes my grandmamma right behind him smacking her cane on de balusters. He starts to get up and she jumps right on his stomach. She straddles him and sticks de bend in her cane under his Adam's apple. My pappa has got this big giant A dam's apple," Vincent explained, his eyes sparkling with excitement and putting his hands up like he was holding a cantaloupe.

"Why doesn't your dad just shove her off?" asked Michael.

The question took Vincent by surprise. "My pappa would never hurt my grandmamma!" Vincent was too far into his story to stop now. He continued, directing his story to Bunny. "Like I said, my pappa has got this big Adam's apple; and when he laughs, he sounds like 'Huck, yuck, yuck,' and his Adam's apple bounces up and down when he laughs. 'Huck, yuck, yuck.' Like that."

Bunny laughed.

"So Grandmamma got him on de ground with her cane in his Adam's apple, and says to him: 'Are you sorry you said that?' And real high, he squeaks out: 'Yes.' She says: 'Do you want to talk like this de rest of your life?' He squeaks: 'No.' She says: 'Then don't you ever say that again.' He says: 'I promise,' only he starts laughing and it sounds just like um, like that little girl mouse on TV."

"Minnie Mouse?"

"Yah, Minnie Mouse, like, Ha ha, ha ha ha." You shoulda heard it. And then my grandmamma gets up and pokes her cane right into his stomach. He screams and holds on to it so it won't poke into him too bad. At de bottom of de stairs everybody's whistling and applauding for my grandmamma. She straightens up her cap, real dignified like, and says: 'Now, let us have our dessert, shall we.' I love my Grandmamma Mueller. My Grandmamma Mueller never tries to be fancy like that. Like if we were eating this for dinner, she wouldn't bother with de knife or de spoon. She would say, 'What do you need it for? I will just have to wash more dishes. But what she cares about iss if every-body iss there to eat it on time, and if it tastes good."

"How does your dad make any money growing corn and tomatoes?" asked Michael.

"We grow mostly corn for feed. It gets turned into chicken feed and cattle feed. We have some milk cows too, but my pappa says he would rather work a team of horses and feed everybody else's cows, than to milk a whole barn full of his own cows. It iss kind of stinky and boring he says. We have de big horses with de hairy legs."

"Clydesdales?" asked Michael.

"Yah, well, draft horses. How did you know what they were called?"

"The Budweiser horses. Yeah, those are bad-ass horses."

"Budweiser?" said Vincent.

"Beer," said Michael.

"Ah, Budweiser," said Vincent.

"Do they actually teach you that God made all the animals at the same time, like poof, here's a cow?" asked Michael.

"Yah," said Vincent.

"Haven't they ever heard of the theory of evolution?"

"Yah."

"Well how can they argue with scientific fact?"

"Fact? It's just something a man made up. He wass only guessing, and everybody believed him because he wass in college."

"If every science class in America accepts evolution as a fact then that's the way it is. Period. I suppose you're going to say they are all wrong?"

"This iss what Miss Purdy says; that Darwin made up his theory because of how some animals look different when they don't breed on the same farm, and because of how you can make different flowers when you cross them together.

But any farmer knows you can cross corn with corn, and you can cross daffodils with daffodils, but you can not cross corn with daffodils; and you surely can forget about crossing pigs with chickens. It will never happen, not even if you wait a million, zillion years."

"If it's soooo dumb, then why is it that every museum around the entire planet has pictures of how the ape man developed into a human being?" asked Michael.

Bunny completely missed what Michael said, and amused herself with the thought of pigs mating with chickens. "Yeah," said Bunny, "the chickens run too fast."

"Yah," added Vincent. "The chickens might be dumb, but they are not that dumb!"

Then Vincent asked, "Ever seen flying pigs?" He and Bunny laughed.

"Not yet," laughed Bunny. "When pigs fly," she joked.

Vincent said, "I wonder what would happen if you crossed a man with a zucchini?"

Bunny blurted, "Don't answer that, Michael."

"You didn't answer my question," said Michael.

"What?" asked Vincent.

"Why is it that every museum around the planet has pictures of ape man and how he developed into a man?"

"I am guessing because they have not figured it out yet, or else they want to feel important. Maybe it iss just an honest mistake. Somebody had to prove de world wass not flat, and that wass only a few hundred years ago."

Bunny added, "1492."

"That's a myth," said Michael.

"No it's not, I learned it in school!" insisted Bunny. "Christopher Columbus proved that the world was round!"

"Myth," repeated Michael.

Vincent said, "So it must be that everything you learned in school iss not so true after all. When you go to de museum ask de owner where iss de proof. Every time there iss another scientist who tells everybody he found de missing link it turns out to be an orangutan or a pig, or something like that. None of it hass ever turned out true. I can get a list for you."

Vincent left the table and zipped into his room before Michael had a chance to turn him down.

Michael said, "This kid is too much. It's like he's from another planet or something. I don't know how long I can stomach him, Bunny."

"You'll see. He'll grow on you. Do it for me, Michael. Bunny stared into his eyes. At least he's talking now."

Vincent returned from his room with a booklet which he pulled proudly from his Bible. He began to read, "De case of His-par-o pith-i-ca . . . Here, you read it." He handed the paper to Bunny.

"'Evolutions Bloopers and Blunders,' by Dr. D. James Kennedy. Clarence Darrow, an atheist and evolutionist, said to William Jennings Bryan, during the famous Scopes Trial, 'Did you know that in your home state of Oklahoma lived a whole race of men who lived over a million years ago?' Bryan said he didn't realize anything of the sort, and didn't believe it either. And so, Darrow brought Dr. Harry Fairfield Osburn of the American Museum of Natural History, the most re-spected paleontologist in America at the time. He testified that just three years prior, in 1922, a whole race of men had been discovered that lived a million years ago. Bryan was dumbfounded. Then from that, the information was pub-lished all over the world. This evidence was discovered by a man named Harold Cook. And so the finding was Chris-tened, 'his-par-o pith-i-ca Harold Cook-ee-i, meaning West-ern Apeman. They found that the evidence consisted of one single solitary tooth. And then sometime later in the same area they found another identical tooth. But this tooth was connected to a jaw, and the jaw was connected to a skeleton. And the skeleton belonged to a pig, an extinct pig. And as Dr. Duane Gish has said, 'It was neither a man-like ape nor an ape-like man, but an extinct pig. This is a case in which a scientist made a man out of a pig, and the pig made a monkey out of a scientist.'"

Bunny laughed and searched for more cases. "There's a lot more cases here, Michael."

Vincent said, excitedly, "If the museum owner tried to get me to believe he had something, I would not believe him. Not anymore. But as long as he could keep the story going, it would be a good way for him to sell tickets, don't you think? Hey!" Vincent's eyes got real big as he stuck his index finger up in the air. "That just gave me a great idea. I saved a big tooth at home. It iss pretty big. It iss a horse tooth, but we don't have to tell them that."

"Vincent." Bunny said, surprised.

"I am only kidding."

Bunny scanned the page. "We've got, um, a slew to choose from. There's Ontogeny Recapitulates Phylogeny, and the development of the fetus. There's Eoanthropus Dawsonii, or Dawn-Man, the missing link. Archeopterics, the flying reptile. How about this? Listen to this one Michael: 'Sir Fred Hoyle of Cambridge examined impressions of a purported fossil of a flying reptile with feathered wings, and discovered someone had impressed the casting with chicken feathers. Thus the fossil was coined 'The Pilkdown Chicken' by Sir Fred Hoyle."

Michael had heard enough and conceded round one, but was ready for round two. "And for another thing, don't you think it's pretty arrogant to think that the Bible is the only true religious book? What about all the other religions around the world that have been getting along fine without the Bible? How do you know its sooo right? How do you know that Mohammed wasn't the messiah, and all you Amish guys will be sitting around with egg on your face?"

"Well, because."

"Because what?" Michael retorted angrily.

"It iss kind of hard to explain with only a few words."

"See, I knew it. I gotcha buddy."

Michael's emotional pitch was starting to worry Vincent. "Should I answer?" he asked Bunny.

Bunny was reading the rest of the article. She read out loud, "Aldous Huxley, author of The Brave New World, and leading evolutionist and atheist is quoted, 'I had motives for not wanting the world to have meaning. Consequently, I assumed that it had none, and was able, without difficulty, to find satisfying reasons for this assumption. For myself and for most of my contemporaries the philosophy of meaninglessness—'

"Godlessness, I guess he means," Bunny inserted. She resumed, "'For myself and for most of my contemporaries the philosophy of meaninglessness was essentially an instrument of liberation. The liberation we desired was simultaneous—'"

"Orgasm," Michael joked.

"Shut up, Michael," said Bunny. "Was simultaneous liberation from: a political and economic system (Capitalism), and liberation from a certain system of morality. We objected to the morality because it interfered with our sexual freedom.'"

"Giving God the thumbs up for intruding in your life would definitely put the brakes on your sex life," said Michael.

"It depends on what you're doing," said Bunny. "I'm sorry Vinnie, what was it you asked me?"

"Don't ask," said Michael. "I told him all the Amish guys will be sitting around with egg on their faces when

Mohammed meets them in heaven."

"He asked me how I know if Jesus iss de real messiah. I can tell you how. Should I?" Vincent turned quickly toward Michael, who was still clearly irritated.

"I want to hear. Michael, if you don't want to hear it, just ignore it." Bunny said.

"Well because the Old Testament, that iss de first half of de Bible, it had prophets to tell us about what de messiah was going to be like: where he was born, where he would die, how he would die, who his relatives would be, lots of things like that. All de prophets wrote about those things hundreds of years before he was even born. All de Jews were waiting for their messiah so long, they were getting tired of waiting. There iss about a hundred and thirty predictions like that. You want me to read them to you?"

"A hundred and thirty scriptures? Are you kidding? No thanks," said Michael.

"Well can you just give us an example?" asked Bunny.

"Okay, um. It iss hard to pick just one." He scrunched up his face and tapped his cheek. "I know, Isaiah, Isaiah fifty-three. I used to know this by heart. Okay: 'Who hath believed our report? And to whom iss de arm of de Lord revealed?' Wait a minute," said Vincent. "I must look in my Bible."

When he found the place he said, "Now you must see, when you read this, for it to make any sense, you must already know that in de New Testament, when Jesus died, everybody hated him, at least de priests who didn't want to lose their importance hated him, and so they put him to death. They only pretended he wass bad and told de government guys from Rome that he wass bad and deserved to be killed.

"So this iss what it says in de Old Testament: 'He iss despised and rejected of men; a man of sorrows, and acquainted with grief; and we hid as it were our faces from him; he wass despised, and we esteemed him not. Surely he hass borne our sorrows, yet we did esteem him stricken, smitten of God, and afflicted. But he wass wounded for our transgressions, he wass bruised for our in-i-qui-ties; the chastisement of our peace wass upon him; and with his stripes we are healed.'"

Vincent interjected, "See, de stripes means when they whipped him forty times on his back until it wass bleeding and almost killed him, that iss before he was put on de cross. Since you know he did not deserve it, it makes you sad to hear about it, and it makes you feel sorry, and it makes you not try to be so tough. You see? And we know it was really him, who he said he wass, because de predictions in Isaiah came true. Did that make sense?"

"Hm," said Bunny. She wasn't sure she understood. She looked at the words herself and read. Really she didn't care if she understood or not, as long as she could bring Vinnie out, and he was certainly out, maybe "out there," but out nevertheless.

Vincent explained, "De marks that de whip left on his back, de forty lashes, those stripes make us not feel so big after all. If you feel sorry, then you might want to ask Jesus if you can belong to him. That iss why he did it, for us, for anybody who would change their minds about him and not want to hate him."

"Do you want me to keep on going?"

Michael said, "Does it predict Jesus as the messiah, or not?"

"Yah."

"Go ahead, Vinnie, honey. Keep reading," said Bunny, handing the Bible back to Vincent.

"All we like sheep have gone astray; we have turned every one to his own way; and de Lord hath laid on himself de in-i-qui-ty of us all. He wass oppressed, and he wass afflicted, yet he opened not his mouth: he iss brought as a lamb to de slaughter, and as a sheep before de shearers iss dumb, so he openeth not his mouth." Vincent looked up, satisfied. "See, I told you."

Bunny said, "How do you know that it's Jesus?"

"Well, listen to de New Testament about when he had to go in front of de head priests to see if he deserved to die." He flipped back to Matthew twenty-seven in the New Testament. "Okay, ready! 'And when he wass accused of de chief priests and elders, he answered nothing. Then said Pilate unto him, "Hearest thou not how many things they witness against thee?"'"

"In other words," said Vincent, "Don't you hear all de stuff they said you did?"

"Anyway," he continued, "'And Jesus answered him not a word; and it made de governor marvel greatly.'"

"I'd hardly call that proof," said Michael. "He's God because he's speechless."

"There's more," Vincent suggested.

"Just one more," said Bunny.

"Old Testament, Psalm twenty-two. This iss what he said just before he died on de cross." Vincent cleared his throat and read with authority: "'My God, my God, why hast thou forsaken me? Why art thou so far from helping me, and from de words of my roaring?'"

"I don't get it," said Bunny. "Isn't that just more of the same cross stuff? I think I'd be screaming the same thing at that moment. Anybody would."

"Well yah, but it iss his exact words. Listen to what it says in de New Testament, Matthew twenty-seven."

"Oh come on," said Michael, "how do you know they didn't change stuff around to fit the Old Testament after he died? Don't you think Jesus read the Old Testament and knew what he was supposed to say? Even if they didn't make stuff fit, and change stuff around on purpose, which they obviously did, other stuff gets changed in translation, like: for all we know what God really said was screw your neighbor before he screws you."

"Michael." He's just a kid. Watch your language.

"Oh this whole thing gets me so irritated. Who knows what the thing really said. It's thousands of years old. They didn't even have a printing press till the eighteen hundreds. I suppose the people were following these prophets around with stone tablets and writing it all down?"

"Fourteen hundreds," said Vincent. "The first book ever printed wass de Bible, by Johann Gutenberg, and de monks were very glad. Up until then, they had to write everything out in ink, on a piece of paper, by hand; and if they made one eensie teensie mistake, they had to write de whoooole page over again!"

"My point exactly, bucko. So how do you know they didn't keep screwing it up and hoping nobody would notice?"

"Well because, for one thing, de last page of de book says if anybody changes anything, they are in big trouble, like huge trouble. Also, they still have some very old copies of de Bible called de Dead Sea Scrolls. They are from about A.D. 300 or something like that, and they are written in Jesus' Hebrew. They found out, once they had them all pieced back together, and translated, they say de same thing our new Bibles say. It says so in de encyclopedia, you can read it yourself."

"Pretty amazing," said Bunny.

"Yah, and this boy, a shepherd boy, goes into this cave and finds these scrolls in a bunch of old jars about fifty years ago, like maybe around de 1940s, and now they got them all put together again. I guess God did that so de people

would know de Bible still says de same thing as always."
Vincent beamed with excitement.

"You know what?" Michael stormed, "We got it figured
out just fine without God and all his thou-shalt-nots. Nobody needs to be told right from wrong. You're just a bunch
of self-righteous, Bible thumping browbeaters, feeling all
superior about everybody else's sins. You make me sick."

Vincent replied, exasperated, "What about de mission-
aries who got eaten by de cannibals? De cannibals didn't
have it figured out just fine. What about de people that killed
their little babies to keep their gods happy? They do not
have it figured out so good, do they? Everybody needs to
know what God says, or they'll get all mixed up."

"The missionary shouldn't have poked his nose in where
it didn't belong. And if you know what's good for you, you'll
forget all this crap and enter the real world! Bunny, I've
been patient up to now; but I'm not living with this Bible
thumper forever." He glared at both of them as if just saying it was going to make them obey. The longer they stared
stubbornly at him, the redder he got.

Michael looked so angry they weren't sure what he was
going to do next. He stood up. The table tipped over and
the dishes clattered to the ground. He grabbed Vincent's
Bible and started for the door.

Bunny ran after him, "Where are you going with that?"
she shouted.

"I'm putting this thing in the trash where it belongs."

"No you're not!" Bunny said. She tried to pull it out of
his hand, but Michael held on tightly. Then suddenly he let
go of it, sending Bunny falling backwards onto the floor.
She hit her head on the corner of the coffee table.

"You should not have done that!" Vincent protested.
He knelt by his mother to see if she was all right. She lay on
the floor rubbing her head.

Michael picked up the Bible and went out the door.

"It's okay Vinnie, honey, I'm all right. He's not usually like this. I don't know what's the matter with him."

"He still should not have done that," Vincent repeated, helping his Mother to her feet.

"You're right, he shouldn't have done that." She wobbled to the bathroom to see if her head was bleeding.

Vincent went to his bedroom window and looked down. He watched as Michael pitched his Bible into the trash bin, got into his car, and drove away. Vincent knew what he had to do. He waited until it started getting dark. Bunny was taking a bath. He put his shoes on, slipped on his coat, and tiptoed to the door. He had his hand on the doorknob.

"Vincent!" He jumped. His mother stood at the bathroom door in her bathrobe and towel. "Where are you going?"

He didn't answer. He didn't know what to say.

"You're planning to run away, aren't you?"

"No, I wass going to go get my Bible out of de trash," he explained nervously.

He wondered how much trouble he was in.

"Oh," she sighed in relief. "How do you know it's in there?"

"I watched Michael throw it in there from my window."

"Wait up. I'll go with you." She put on her house shoes and slipped her coat over her bathrobe. "We'll need a flashlight, ya know."

"Do we have one?" Vincent asked.

She reached on top of the refrigerator, "Here, one flashlight," she said. "Slip the cord over your head so you don't drop it."

The two headed out to the trash bin. Vincent said, "I am glad it iss dark."

"Why?" asked Bunny.

Vincent said nothing, but pointed at her feet and smiled.

His mother looked a little strange with her plaid coat pulled tightly over her bathrobe, striped towel turban on her head, and puppy dog slippers on her feet. It was a little nippy for wet hair on this cool November evening, but Bunny didn't mind. She was doing something for Vinnie.

Bunny laughed, "Maybe if we hang around this trash bin long enough, somebody will come by and give us a free Thanksgiving turkey."

"You look like you could use a free turkey," he smiled. Bunny tightened her towel in preparation for jumping in the trash bin. Vincent tried hopping up from the front, but it was too high.

"No," Bunny said, "See, you put your foot on the side over here. See where it sticks out."

"Yah?" Vincent said as he stuck his foot up on the side of the bin.

"Okay," she said. "Now hold onto the side and lift yourself up." She looked up at the windows above them to see if anyone was watching.

"Now what?" he asked.

"Jump in," she said.

He took a look at the loose garbage with his flashlight and decided to ease in one foot at a time. "Ahh, there iss nothing like slipping into a nice warm pile of garbage," he chuckled. "Ugh, something slimy just went up my pant leg."

Bunny said, "Something slimy. I don't like how that sounds. What was it?"

"Just a banana peel," said Vincent. He held it up to the light for her to see.

"Give me a little light, Vinnie."

He shined the light in her direction. She hopped up and over like a pro. He said, "You have done this before."

"Well, yeah. We'll just call those the lean years," she admitted dodging the question. "I don't see your Bible. Are you sure he threw it in here?"

"Yah, I saw him."

"We probably made it sink when we got in," she said. They started a process of throwing the big bags on the ground, but every time they took a step their feet sank in deeper. "Something really stinks in here," said Bunny.

"Everything stinks in here," said Vincent, laughing, now up to his hips in garbage.

"Hi, Miss Bunny."

"Oh, hi Robert."

"Robert, this is Vinnie, my son."

"Hi Binnie. Pleased to meet you Binnie." A big black man with a tattered tousle cap smiled up at Vincent with a nearly toothless grin. He only had one tooth, a huge white tooth front and center. He was retarded. He scratched his head through his tousle cap.

"Hi," answered Vincent with curiosity.

Bunny explained, "I caught Robert going to the bathroom in my window well when I lived in the basement. I might have been able to live with it if it had stayed on the outside, but it started dripping down my wall into my bedroom! Unfortunately, I got a little angry, and I told him I would break every bone in his body if he ever did that again. He felt so bad."

"Yeah, Binnie, I felt sooo bad. I didn't know a pretty lady lived there."

"He felt sooo bad that he went to the thrift store and bought me a beautiful pair of earrings. Isn't that right, Robert?"

He shook his head yes. "Now we friends, right Miss Bunny?"

"Right, Robert." Bunny smiled at Vincent as if to say, lucky me. "You go along now Robert. We have important matters to take care of here."

"Okay, we friends, we friends," he kept repeating as he walked away. "I love you, Miss Bunny," he yelled across the parking lot.

"I love you too, Robert," she answered quietly, a little embarrassed.

"Do you see it yet, Vinnie?" she asked.

"I think it was right here." He stuck his arm down between two bags. You try it, Bunny. Your arms are longer."

Bunny reached down in, deep. A look of horror struck her face. "Get out!" she screamed.

"What?" Vincent froze in fear.

"Get out!" she yelled again.

They both scrambled out of there. They slogged their legs through the heavy plastic bags, until they reached the edge of the bin and exited to the ground at top speed.

"What wass it?" asked Vincent, breathless.

"I think it's a rat. It's gray and furry." Bunny's eyes were wide open.

"Did it bite you?" he asked.

She shined the flashlight on her hand to see. "I guess not."

"Did it move?" asked Vincent.

A horrid thought went through her head. She smelled her hand and grimaced, "Oh, I'm gonna puke. Uck. It was dead. Really dead."

"Oh my goodness," Vincent smiled, trying not to laugh. Bunny asked, "Ya wanta smell it?"

"No! no, no, no," answered Vincent, laughing.

"How bad do you want this Bible? We could buy you a new one," she offered as she dangled her hand out from her side.

"My teacher, Miss Purdy, gave me that one. I had everything taken away from me when de police came except my Bible and de clothes I wass wearing. I don't want to lose my Bible too."

Bunny couldn't stand the disappointment on his face. "Let's do this, you hand me the bags and I'll put them on the ground till we find it," suggested Bunny. "But first let me get that rat out of there." She shined the light, tracing the tops of the bags until it reached a mound of gray fur. It was barely detectable. The fur was striped.

"Vinnie, guess what."

"What?" He tried to see over the edge.

"It's a dead cat."

"A cat?"

"Yeah. Ugh, yuck." She started to gag. "Why don't we put it in a bag?" she said.

"Here's a stick." He handed it to Bunny.

She got back in the bin with the stick. She picked it up once, dropped it. Picked it up again, dropped it. "Oh for Pete's sake!" she complained.

"Bunny! Look!" Vincent shouted.

Bunny just about jumped out of her skin. Vincent shined the light on a broken coffeepot.

"Wow," she said. "I'm glad you saw that; I could have cut my leg off."

"No, underneath it."

"Oh, there it is!" she exclaimed. She held her breath, reached over the dead cat, tossed the broken coffeepot aside, and held the Bible in the air like the Statue of Liberty. "Ta Dum!" she sang triumphantly.

"Yea!" he exclaimed, applauding.

Bunny reveled in the pride of their accomplishment for about one second and then choked, "Now let's get out of here, quick."

Vincent turned to run then stopped short when Bunny said, "Oh, wait. Throw the stuff back in." They threw the bags back into the bin double time and hurried up the steps, down the hall, and closed the door breathlessly behind them.

"Whew, I'm out of shape," she panted.

"Oh my gosh and goodness, that was really stinky!" laughed Vincent.

"That had to be the stinkiest bin I ever dived into," Bunny joked.

Vincent laughed even harder.

"Uh, Bunny, you got spaghetti on your forehead."

She felt around for it. She popped it in her mouth.

"Oh, yuck! You ate it!" said Vincent, thoroughly disgusted.

"Mm, good sauce."

"I can not believe it. You ate it!" he exclaimed again. "That iss really sick-en-ing." Vincent gritted his teeth.

"Oh Vinnie, look." She opened her sleeve. To Vincent's relief, there was the spaghetti, stuck to her arm.

Bunny laughed long and loud, a sound Vincent had never heard from her before. He liked it.

"Oh my," she sighed. "That was fun. But we better start all over again on the baths," she said. "Michael will come home, and we don't want to have to explain why we smell like garbage on dead cat."

"Yah. Me first," said Vincent.

"No, me first."

They both raced to the bathroom door. Neither would let the other get through the door.

"We'll flip," said Bunny.

Bunny pulled a quarter from her purse and threw it in the air. "Heads!" Vincent yelled as it sailed into the air. Bunny tried to catch it but missed. It rolled onto the floor and underneath the armchair.

"I'll get it." Vincent scrambled for the quarter.

"No you won't. Mitts off till we can both see how it landed. Bunny scooted the chair back so they could both take a look. They crouched down onto the floor on their hands and knees, both hoping to be the first to see.

"Ah, darn it, it's heads, you stinkpot," she said.

"Ha!" Vincent looked up into Bunny's face, flashing the quarter in victory.

They smiled at each other.

"Thanks, Mom," said Vincent. He had never called her that before but decided to take a chance.

"Anything for you, Vinnie," she said softly. Vincent knew she meant it.

Then her voice changed back to playful. "Now get a bath—and hurry up!"

By the time Vincent reached the bathroom door, Bunny was already digging the bleach bottle out from underneath the kitchen sink. She poured it straight out of the bottle and drenched her hand with it.

"Ahhhh," she sighed. "So this is motherhood."

She ran the water over her bleached hand. "I like it."

Isaiah 53:6. All we like sheep have gone astray; we have turned every one to his own way, and the Lord hath laid on him the iniquity of us all.

Chapter 14

Meanwhile in Promise

"Good morning, church."

"Good morning, Pastor Dunkin."

"I want to thank you all from de bottom of my heart for all of your prayers and for de concern you have shown for Vincent, Freida, and Martin. Please continue to pray for our Vincent. Even though he iss not here this morning as we would all like, there iss one thing we can be sure of; God's hand iss on that young man's life."

"Amen," they agreed.

Pastor Dunkin's voice quivered, "We will continue to pray for him and trust that God's plan will be worked out in Vincent's life. Yah?"

"Amen," they promised.

Freida looked at Martin to see what his reaction was, but she couldn't see him very well from where she was sitting. She wrapped her arms tightly around her sides, and squirmed tightly into her seat.

Pastor Dunkin began his message, "We have been talking about how much faith we think we have until it iss put to de test. And, if you remember, we have looked at some examples of people with faith in de Bible. Who were they, children?"

Rachel Kemp raised her hand.

Pastor Dunkin nodded his head at her.

"Shadrach, Meshach, and Abednego?" offered Rachel Kemp.

"Yah, that iss right," said Pastor Dunkin, "in de fiery furnace. Anyone else?"

"Daniel in de lions' den," said Rebecca Perl.

"Abraham," said Abigail Dietche.

"That iss right," said Pastor Dunkin. "Abraham wass willing to sacrifice his son just because God said so. That took some faith, yah? We could go on and on, could we not?" Pastor Dunkin put his index finger up in the air for emphasis, "The common thread we can recognize, among all these men, iss that they trusted God to come through for them, in de midst of de impossible. They might have to wait on God to move, like Mary and Joseph, who waited thirty years for Jesus to begin his ministry. And what about Moses, he waited forty years in de desert looking for de promised land with all those people grumbling at his back complaining, 'He does not know what he iss doing. We must be crazy for letting him talk us into this.' The man of faith might wait a lifetime for his moment, like Noah. The people were saying, 'Hey, crazy old man, I don't see rain clouds. That iss a mighty big boat you are building, crazy man.' But when God told Noah it wass going to rain, Noah believed God, no ifs, ands or buts, no matter what his friends around him were saying about him. This week we need to ask ourselves: Do we have de faith to believe, when we walk humbly before God, that he iss working out everything for our good? I wish our Vincent were here this morning to hear this. I am sure he iss wondering if God forgot about him."

Pastor looked in Freida's direction, but she looked away, avoiding his attention.

Pastor cleared his throat and resumed, "Turn to Mark, chapter 4, verses 37 to 40. 'There arose a great storm of wind, and the waves beat into the ship, so that it was now full. And he (Jesus) was in the hinder part of the ship, asleep on a pillow: and they awoke him, and said unto him, Master, carest thou not that we perish? And he arose, and rebuked the wind, and said unto the sea, "Peace, be still." And the wind ceased, and there was a great calm. And he said unto them, "Why are ye so fearful? How is it that ye have no faith?"'"

Freida felt as if a volcano of emotion was about to explode inside her if she had to sit through much more.

She prayed, "Lord God, I came this morning to worship you, but I can not hide that I am angry. I am so angry that, if I don't leave, I am going to start crying right here. I know I am supposed to be showing my faith, but de truth iss, I don't have any faith left. And why should I?"

The longer she tried to keep her emotions in check, the harder it became. She had to get out of there and quickly. She rose from her seat to exit, deciding to make her excuses later. She locked eyes with Martin as she passed, certain that he would follow her, but he didn't. If Martin didn't come out after her, she decided; he will have to find his own way home. She was not going back in to get him.

She pulled herself up into their buggy. She waited for the front doors to open. She couldn't wait any longer. "Giddy-up Zach. Go!" she commanded. She smacked Zach in the back with the reins, hard. It startled him. He hurried out of the parking lot.

She said to herself, what right did he have to talk about faith—today of all days? It iss a little late for faith now. I tried that before. "Hear me, Jesus, I had enough faith to go to jail without complaining to you, did I not? I sat quietly in de courtroom while they discussed giving Vincent away to that liar! Just exactly when did I fail you in my faith? And just exactly how did you come through for me? You gave me this second-rate body, this infertile, barren body. But that was not so bad, because you found a child for Martin and me. But what, in this world, did we do to you, so awful, that you would take him away from us now!? Now that we have given Vincent our hearts? Now that we have invested all these years in caring for him? I guess I should have faith to wait until we all get to heaven; I can't wait forever. I want a life of more than wishing. And what about Vincent? Why should he be ripped from everyone he has come to love, only to be thrown to de lions? What chance does he have being thrown into a heathen world—at only eight years old. If that iss your plan, I think you need to go back to de thinking table. Oh yah, I could put on some kind of phony faith act for my father's sake, but you know all my secret thoughts, and we both know you have put more on me than I can bear, and that I will never recover. You have broken my heart, you have broken my trust, and you have broken my spirit. Just write me off, because I am done with you, and I am done with your phony baloney church. I used to think you were a loving God, but not anymore!"

The buggy wheels clattered down the old gravel road at top speed. The bend in the road seemed to arrive well before Freida expected. Where am I, she asked herself. Oh, no! This is much too fast for this bend! Her buggy suddenly demanded all of her attention. Freida knew she was going dangerously fast. Luckily, she didn't follow her first instinct to pull tight on the reigns like a driver would slam on the brakes. If she slowed Zach down, he would break stride. He could jerk and upset the carriage just as the bend was at its sharpest. She leaned her body to the left as far as she could. She could only hope that the wheels would stay on the ground. She could feel the left side of the buggy lift as the road bent to the right. The buggy was riding on two rims now. Her seat was lifting under her. She knew she was getting close to a hole somewhere in the bend of the road, but she was traveling too fast to see it. If we can just stay upright for five seconds, we'll be home free, she thought. The trees raced by in a blur. Freida worried about the weight on the wheels. The entire weight of the buggy was pushing down on the outsides of two rims. Zach knew they were in serious trouble. There was a drop on the right side of the road in which Zach could only see the tops of the trees. On the other was a sharp ditch, then a field. He leaned against the curve and against the leaning buggy, but it was too heavy. He struggled to keep his legs from being pulled out from underneath him. His hips strained against the weight. The end of the curve was in sight. "Jesus, help!" screamed Freida.

There was a crack and then a bang—all four wheels were airborne. A large rock in the road hit the undercarriage. They had run over it with their right wheels and it had jerked the buggy into the air and slightly to the left. Then, when it hit the undercarriage as all four wheels were airborne, it tipped the entire buggy far enough left to cause them to land upright, crashing down hard on the gravel.

"Oh my gosh, ho down there, Zach. Good boy," Freida said breathlessly. They clip-clopped to a stop. The silence was wonderful. She stayed still for a moment, putting her face in her hands. She got out of the buggy to look at the undercarriage. There was a dent in one of the floor boards, but the axle and rims seemed to be all right. She stood beside Zach by the side of the road, until he stopped panting. "I'm sorry Zach, it wass all my fault. You did good." She tried to calm him by rubbing his neck, but he was still terribly rattled. He was soaking wet and couldn't hold still from all the excitement. Finally, after Zach stopped twitching and jerking his head, they walked slowly home side by side with Freida's emotions shifting from guilt over Zach and the buggy, to anger at God for not answering her prayers, to despair at being unable to bring Vincent home.

Pastor Dunkin finished with: "So you see, de secret to finding de peace of God, in de midst of de storm, can be found by examining our faith. Can you calmly walk through your fiery furnace? Try repeating these two scriptures when you find you are sitting in de lions' den: First, we know all things work together for de good to those who are chosen according to his purpose in Christ Jesus. It says so right here, Romans 8:28. And, second, since we also know all good things come to those who wait upon de Lord, we will wait, and we will rest, and we will find peace. All we really need to understand in any situation iss that God loves us, and he has everything under control. Can you say that? God loves us and has everything under control."

"God loves us and has everything under control," they repeated, some more convinced than others.

"Is everything under control if your life is not governed by de Lord?"

No one answered.

"De answer iss no. It depends on whether you are working with God on one day, or getting in his way on de next day. But in de end, with your cooperation or without, he will do his work.

"Iss everything under control when you do not take de time to talk to God about your concerns? God's plan will go forward without your prayers, but you will not know peace in de midst of it.

"I have a peaceful scripture for you, if you are willing to wait. I know it iss getting late. Shall I read it to you?"

"Yah," they said, searching for their own measure of peace after everything that had happened.

"This iss Isaiah 30:15 to 21. 'In repentance and rest is your salvation, in quietness and trust is your strength, but you would have none of it. You said, No, we will flee on horses. Therefore you will flee! You said, We will ride off on swift horses. Therefore your pursuers will be swift! A thousand will flee at the threat of one; at the threat of five you will all flee away, till you are left like a flagstaff on a mountaintop, like a banner on a hill. Yet the Lord longs to be gracious to you; he rises to show you compassion. For the Lord is a God of justice. Blessed are all who wait for him! O people of Zion, who live in Jerusalem, you will weep no more. How gracious he will be when you cry for help! As soon as he hears, he will answer you. Although the Lord gives you the bread of adversity and the water of affliction, your teachers will be hidden no more; with your own eyes you will see them. Whether you turn to the right or to the left, your ears will hear a voice behind you, saying, This is the way; walk in it.'

"So, what iss our part of de bargain if this peace iss to belong to us? We will live according to God's laws, and we will wait upon him. God will take care of de rest. Not a bad deal. I am so glad that He iss God, and I am just one of his simpleton lackeys. All right, well, may de Lord bless you and keep you. May de Lord make his face to shine upon you, and give you—what?"

"Peace," they answered.

"Have a good and 'peaceful' week everyone," said Pastor Dunkin.

Martin went immediately after the service to find Freida. He discovered the buggy was no longer where they parked it. He could only hope that Freida went home.

"Freida!" Martin yelled as he burst through the front door.

"I am in here," she called from behind the closed bedroom door.

Martin stood at the bottom of the steps and called up to Freida, "Your mamma and pappa are here. They brought me home. Do you want to say hello before they leave."

She didn't answer.

Pastor Dunkin took hold of the old stair railing, saying, "Let me try to talk to her." Freida listened with dread as they walked up the wooden staircase.

"Freida?" Her father tapped on the door. "I know you are upset, and you don't want to talk to anyone; but just try to remember one thing for me."

She still didn't answer.

"Jesus loves you."

Freida swung open the door in a torrent. "Oh really!" Freida stormed. She choked out, "He hass got a strange way of showing it. Do not tell me, Pappa, that this makes any sense! Vincent does not deserve this! Martin does not deserve this, and neither do I!"

Her mother put her arm around her and led her back to the edge of the bed. "Sometimes we do not always understand what God iss doing, dear one," she explained.

Her father added, "She iss right, Freida. Maybe Jesus wants Vincent to take his message to de world, maybe with his music."

Freida stood up, "Pappa, he iss only eight years old. He has to be reminded to brush his teeth, and you are expecting him to save de world? De heathens will eat him before breakfast!"

"Remember de scripture, 'Train up a child in de way he should go, and when he iss old he will not turn from it.'"

Freida said nothing. She knew her faith in God was shattered, but should she destroy everyone else's faith as well? She thought, whatever gives you comfort. She turned her face away so as not to let him read her thoughts.

Her father supposed he had said what he came to say. He stood looking at Freida wishing he could help her.

"Thank you for bringing Martin home, Pappa, but I really need to be left alone for a while."

Maybe she is right, thought her father. She needs time to think.

Freida's mother tugged on Pastor Dunkin's sleeve. "I think Martin can handle this."

Freida said, "And, Mamma, would you cancel Bible study for me tomorrow? I am not up to it."

"Surely, dear one. Talk to you tomorrow," said Mother Dunkin as she kissed her daughter on the cheek.

Martin walked with Pastor Dunkin and Mother Dunkin to the front door.

Pastor Dunkin said, "Take care of my baby, Martin. She iss going to need a lot of love."

Mother Dunkin added, "And Martin, she probably does not want to hear any suggestions about how to get over this. Just let her grieve for a while. Hold her and listen. Then when she iss finished, hold her and listen again." Her eyes were brimming with care and concern.

"Thank you, Mother Dunkin. I will do my best."

"The two of you need each other right now," she said. "Take de time to get as close as you can. You need Freida, and Freida needs you."

Pastor Dunkin agreed. "One last thing," he said. "You are not alone in this. De church held a prayer vigil for de three of you on de Sunday when this all started. It lasted well into de night. Everyone iss very concerned, and I am sure they will continue to pray. But somehow, I must tell you, in de midst of all de excitement of that Sunday, I had an unusual peace. Why would a man who had rifles pointed at him feel calm?"

Martin looked at the Pastor without answering.

Pastor Dunkin said, "Why are you looking at me like a cow at a new gate?"

"I thought maybe it was a trick question," he answered, confused.

"What are you talking about, brother Martin?"

"Well your message today was that we can always be peaceful, if we remember that God iss in control. So we do not need to worry and be afraid."

Pastor Dunkin was thoroughly amused. He said, "At least I know you were listening."

"I am confused," said Martin. He smiled a crooked smile.

"Just because I preach it, does not mean fear can not sneak up on me and scare the bajeebers out of me. Believe me, when de police grabbed my arms and dragged me down de steps and into de mud, it was like a quick trip down de silo. I wass not expecting to ever get up again. Especially I wass not expecting it when de rifles went off and Vincent and I hit de floor. De message today was more about keeping de concerns of life from wearing on us and beginning to consume us. It can be devastating if you let your faith slip. We don't need to let that happen if we trust God."

"So when did you feel peaceful, like you said?" asked Martin.

"The only thing I know iss that when I wass standing at de podium addressing de church after de police were driving away, a calmness settled over me from nowhere and for no logical reason. It must have been a supernatural peace. I do not know how everything will all turn out, but one thing

I do know: God iss in control. We must trust him. We have nothing to fear."

"Thank you again." Martin heaved a sigh of relief.

Mother Dunkin gave Martin a hug. "We will be talking to you later, Martin. Go to Freida, dear, she needs you."

She and Pastor Dunkin started up the stone walkway to their buggy.

"God bless you." Martin called, waving to them from the doorway.

Martin returned to the bedroom where he found Freida with her head buried in her pillow, sobbing uncontrollably. She overheard what they had said. It felt like she was the weakling who needed to be coddled, the only weakling that couldn't manage her emotions. He put his hand on her back to let her know he was there. He waited quietly, as Freida's mother had suggested, until Freida was ready to talk.

Finally Freida said, "Martin, I am so worried. We do not know anything about these people. We do not know what these people will do to him. He iss so very helpless, and we are helpless to do anything about it." She started crying all over again.

"I know, Freida. I am feeling the same way. This iss the hardest thing we have ever gone through. I must trust that God will protect him." He would have liked to say, let's trust that God will bring him home, but he didn't want to give Freida any false hopes. He started to get up.

"Where are you going?"

"I wass going to put together a package of Vincent's things for him. Shall I stay here with you?"

"But, we don't know where he lives," Freida reminded.

"Maybe Children and Youth Services will send it to him. And maybe you would want to write him a note? Yah? It iss worth trying, for Vincent's sake."

Freida looked into Martin's face. She realized that Martin was hurting just as she was, but he wasn't asking anything for himself. She realized Martin was putting her ahead of his own feelings of despair.

"I love you Martin."

"I love you too."

Freida pulled Martin toward her. "Ow, ow, ow," he said.

"I'm sorry. I didn't mean to hurt you. Let me see your bruise." He turned to show her. "Iss it getting any better?" she asked.

"Some," he said. "My kidneys are working better. It iss just sore. Ow."

"I am so sorry, my dear husband. I would like to drag that guard behind de buggy for hurting you. How could he do such a thing to you?

Martin leaned over carefully, kissed her on the forehead, and went into Vincent's room. He had been avoiding Vincent's room until today. There was a dirty T-shirt tossed in the corner. He picked it up and put his face into the little shirt. He could smell Vincent, and suddenly his feelings overwhelmed him. How he missed his Vincent. He kept the shirt up to his face and cried quietly so Freida wouldn't hear him. "God, I want to lean on your love, and to find your peace, but it iss draining through me like a sieve. All I feel iss grief. Lord, help us get through this. Help Vincent. He iss just a little boy. He iss my little boy, and I miss him so much." Martin groaned a long sorrowful groan that came from deep within his spirit. "Give me strength, by your spirit, to live by your will, not my own. Thank you for your spirit. Stay close during this time. How we need your love to comfort us. Thank you that you are with me in the good and the bad. Praise you, Lord Jesus."

Freida raised herself up to find a paper and pen. She was so exhausted it felt as if she were the one who had been beaten up. She found an old school tablet and a pencil in a kitchen drawer. She sat at the table and began to pour out her heart. She took a deep, exhausted breath and began.

"Dear Vincent. Hello, my little man. We are missing you so much. I hope this is not the last time I will be able to talk to you, but it might be. So I want you to know I will be thinking of you everyday, and so will your pappa. If you are having a bad day, and you think nobody cares, think of me, Vincent, and know that I will be thinking of you. If you are sick, just know that I would be there, if only I could. If you need encouragement, try to remember everything we have told you. Most of all, never think that nobody loves you, because I would give anything on this earth to be able to see you, hold you, talk to you just one more time. How can we be only a few miles apart, and yet seem so far away? I miss your sunny smile in the morning. I miss you at the dinner table. I miss your clothes swinging on the clothesline. If you could pile up my hugs to you from the farthest, farthest, farthest star away in heaven to where you are right now, I love you and miss you even more than that. See the circle I drew on this page? If you need a mamma kiss, you can put that spot right up to your cheeks, or your forehead, or your eyes, or your fingers, wherever you need a kiss, because I gave that spot a mamma kiss, and it is loaded with love just for you. I will always love you forever and ever. I will never ever forget my precious little boy. XOXO Mamma."

Isaiah 30:15. In returning and rest shall ye be saved; in quietness and in confidence shall be your strength: and ye would not.

Chapter 15

Party Line

$\mathcal{M}$other Dunkin waited until after dinner to call the Bible study regulars—for the sixth week in a row. She hoped by seven o'clock everyone would have had their Sunday visiting out of the way. She picked up the old telephone and rang for Sister Anna, the community operator.

Sister Anna picked up at the other end. There was a clatter as if the phone dropped to the ground, and a baby was crying in the background.

"Hello," called Mother Dunkin. "Hello, anybody there?"

"Hello!" said Sister Anna. The baby continued to cry in the background.

"Hello, Sister Anna? This is Mother Dunkin. How is everything with you?"

"Fine, but I think Ruthy iss teething. Sorry I dropped de phone. I had it on my shoulder when she grabbed it."

"No problem. I hope she iss all right."

"She will be fine. She iss just terribly cranky, and now I am getting cranky too." Anna yelled for her husband, "Luther, would you hold de baby for me? Thank you my

219

sweet husband." She handed the baby to her husband. "Ah," Anna sighed with relief. "My ears can not take anymore screaming. What can I do for you, Mother Dunkin?"

"I am sorry to say, but Freida must cancel Bible study again. She has asked me to cancel for her five times already, and I have been calling everyone, one at a time, as you know. Do you think we could ring all de regulars at de same time, so that I can talk to them all in one call?"

"Yah, good idea, Mother Dunkin. We should have done this all along. How iss Freida doing?"

"Not well. This has been very hard for her to deal with."

"I can only imagine. Tell Freida for me that I am praying for her family, and tell her I miss her very much."

"Yah, thank you, Anna. I am sure she iss missing you too."

"Do you have a list of the regulars, Mother Dunkin?"

"I think I can do this by heart," she answered. "Let me see. There iss Mother Perl, Mother Mueller, Sister Mary Amman, Sister Esther Amman, and Sister Elizabeth Fyfe. There iss me and Freida, and Sister Sara Kemp."

Anna plugged everyone in from her switchboard and their phones began to ring. A multitude of hellos came in like popping popcorn. After the voices died down, Sister Anna said, "We have a ladies' announcement. Are there any children on de phone?"

"Yah, yah," two little girls giggled.

"Yah," answered a big gruff voice.

"Who was that!?" asked Sister Anna.

The gruff voice answered doing his best to sound like a woman, "It iss only me. Don't you know who this iss?"

The little girls giggled again. "Would you girls go get your mamma, please. Thank you."

"And Brother Daniel, will you please get your wife. This iss for ladies only."

"I am very hurt," he answered.

"And we do not care," said Sister Anna. "Would you please get your wife?"

"Yes ma'am," he said.

"What iss this all about?" someone asked as they waited.

"Mother Dunkin?" Sister Anna called.

"Yah, Freida iss still not doing very well. Worrying about Vincent still has her so very upset."

"Hello."

"Hello."

"Hello."

"That iss everybody," Sister Anna announced.

"De reason I called wass to let you know that Sister Freida iss canceling Bible study again.

"Aw, such a shame. It iss hard to accept, yah?" someone asked.

"She hass not been in church lately, has she?"

"I am afraid not," answered Mother Dunkin, sounding a little helpless.

"What iss de matter with her? Does she not know that all she needs iss to put her faith to work, and Vincent will come back home? Why iss she letting herself get so depressed?" asked Sister Mary.

Mother Dunkin answered, "Well you do know, it iss much more likely that she will never see Vincent again, and she iss doing her best to deal with it."

"Well, I still think she should put her mind to it and pray that de boy come back home. Do you not remember what Pastor Dunkin said: 'We need to have faith,'" she retorted.

"But wait a minute," explained Mother Dunkin, "he did not say you could make a wish list for God, and all we need do iss ask, and it will be done. Prayer iss not a wish list. Let me say it this way: Would all ladies over sixty please answer this question? Are we all going to get old and ugly some day?"

"Yah," chuckled Mother Mueller.

"I am seconding that," said Mother Perl.

Mother Dunkin said, "I have hoped, and prayed, and tried to convince myself otherwise; but no matter what kind of proclamations I make in my prayers, I just keep getting older."

"And uglier," said Mother Mueller.

Mother Dunkin replied, "I will speak for myself, Mother Mueller, thank you very much,"

"I did not mean you, Mother Dunkin," chuckled Mother Mueller. "I meant me. My face looks like it hass been hit with de old and ugly stick. I understand what you are trying to say though. It does not mean God does not hear our prayers, if things are not working out the way we want. God's plan iss many times different from ours, and I know that from experience. I would not have planned for my husband to die, but that iss de way it iss, and no amount of praying will bring him back. I think I am probably stronger for it. But, until I get to heaven, I will not really understand why Philip had to die."

Mother Dunkin said, "We all prayed for Vincent to return, but he didn't. So now we must pray for his safety, and for Freida to believe that God will protect him. What my husband really said in his message was: to find de peace that you are looking for, examine your faith. That iss, we must believe that de word of God iss true, that God loves us, that he hears our prayers, and that he iss working in our behalf. You see, Sister Mary, God iss in control; we are not. We need to have faith, that iss all. And it iss good that Jesus iss in control. We must always believe God iss good, and he knows best. In that truth lies peace."

"Maybe she should never have taken de baby in de first place," Sister Mary said.

"Why iss that?" asked Sister Sara Kemp with irritation.

"Well because, we are not to mix with de world. We are to stay separate. His parents were certainly polluted by de world, so certainly their child iss also of de world."

Sara Kemp said, "You sound like you think we are de superior race, or something. We are only very lucky sinners like de rest of de world. God's truth iss for everybody, de Jews, de Greeks, de bond, de free. Remember? Not just us."

She went on, "It iss not as if Vincent wass a hardened criminal we were hiring to be our new teacher; that would be different. But when Vincent came to us he wass only an innocent little tiny baby, abandoned—or so we thought." Sara's resolve trailed off, mired in her own guilt once again.

"Well maybe she should have waited to hear from God before she jumped at an opportunity for a baby of her own," said Sister Elizabeth.

Mother Dunkin said, in her daughter's defense, "Any one of us would have taken in a little baby that had no home, eventually. It iss de right thing to do."

Sister Sara Kemp said, "I would have taken Vincent if no one else had. He wass such a sweet little guy. He still iss. De only difference between us and Freida iss that she did it wholeheartedly. De Lord did not need to talk her into it; she wanted to do it. De word says de church iss to take care of de orphans and de widows. Why would Freida have reason to hesitate? De answer iss already in God's word, plain and simple."

"Are you sure there iss not sin in their lives?" asked Sister Elizabeth.

"Who's life, Martin and Freida's? Why would you ask such a thing?" asked Mother Dunkin.

"Because it says in de word, if a husband and wife are not getting along, God will not hear their prayers."

"I know that iss not de case," said Mother Mueller. "Do not waste your brain on that thought. You know what this sounds like to me? This sounds like we are all looking for some reason why God would allow this terrible thing to happen. It iss such a terrible tragedy, so terrible that it iss hard for us to make any sense of it. It really challenges our faith when something so awful happens. We cannot understand how a loving God could allow this to happen, especially to such nice people. So we start looking for something or someone to blame."

"If anyone iss to blame, it iss me," said Sara Kemp. Her voice trembled. "If it wass not for me, none of this would have happened."

Mother Mueller insisted, "Sara, stop it now. Do not blame yourself. You only did what you thought wass right. You could not predict what wass going to happen."

Sara didn't answer.

"Look," said Mother Dunkin.

Click.

"Sister Kemp?"

"Yah?"

"I thought you hung up," said Mother Dunkin.

"No, it was not me."

"Uh oh," said Sister Anna.

"What, Anna?" asked Mother Perl.

"I just realized, I plugged Sister Freida in. I am thinking she heard de whole thing." Anna's stomach went into a knot.

"Sister Anna! Why did you not tell us?" demanded Sister Elizabeth.

"I'm sorry!"

"Wait until I get hold of you," Sister Mary said.

"Listen to me, I must go over to Freida's," said Mother Dunkin. "Let me just say this. God iss up to something in little Vincent's life. We must believe God knows what iss best. If it iss hard for us, imagine what it iss like for Freida. And now, de poor thing, she has to deal with our putting de blame on her. If there iss one thing Freida needs right now, it iss her friends, not criticism. Please, just pray for peace for Freida. And for Vincent, pray for safety, and that he keeps God's word in his heart. It may be a long time before he iss in church again. I must go."

Sister Anna asked, "What are you going to say to Freida, Mother Dunkin?"

Mother Dunkin paused to consider and then said, "I am going to tell her not to worry what other people say or think. In de end, it iss God who will be sorting it all out."

No one spoke.

"I must go now," repeated Mother Dunkin. "Bye."

1 Corinthians 13:2. And though I have the gift of prophecy, and understand all mysteries, and all knowledge; and though I have faith, so that I can move mountains, and have not charity, I am nothing.

Chapter 16

He Leadeth Me Beside Still Water

*V*incent and Bunny were beginning to develop a genuinely affectionate relationship. Not so, Vincent and Michael. They were able to avoid each other most of the time, but today it was Saturday morning, Bunny was working overtime, and the two of them were stuck with each other. In the past several weeks Vincent realized that his best defense against Michael was to avoid him altogether. And if he had to sit in the same room with Michael, it was best not to speak.

Vincent was in his bedroom, setting up dominoes from his window to his dresser when suddenly his elbow bumped the dresser, setting in motion a clattering chain reaction. He tried to stop it but the noise continued until the last three dominoes dumped bang, bang, bang, into a metal garbage can.

"Hey!" Michael yelled sharply from his bedroom. "I'm trying to study in here. Keep it quiet."

"Oh for Pete's sake," Vincent rolled his head around and sighed. "Study time." Michael's concentration wasn't the best. Vincent knew that if it wasn't as quiet as a tomb,

Michael couldn't think. What Vincent really wanted to do this morning was play his mom's "Dizzy Gullespie" tape. He was hoping he might someday play his keyboard like him, and he was hoping to start on his goal today, but there was a problem. If he used the earphones with his keyboard, Michael wouldn't be bothered by the music, but the tapping on the keys, with or without music, still bothered him. Maybe he could clear out his mom's shoes from his closet, squeeze his keyboard and himself in there and shut the door. He'd need the flashlight, he thought. That is it. I must get the flashlight.

"Vincent, what are you doing?" Michael called.

"Getting de flashlight."

"Do you know where it is?"

"No." Vincent learned it was better not to know where something was, than to be grilled about knowing too much. Michael was very territorial with his things.

Michael sighed, "It's on top of the refrigerator, but don't break it."

Vincent got a chair and pulled it beside the refrigerator.

Michael droned, "Vincent, be quiet."

Vincent reached for the flashlight, grasping it tightly over his head and hanging on so as not to drop it as he made his way back onto the floor. He decided to leave the chair at the refrigerator to keep it from making any more noise. Then he got a glass of milk to take back with him so he wouldn't have to make another trip which would disturb Michael again. He tiptoed past Michael's door with flashlight and milk in hand.

"Where are you going with that milk?"

Vincent pointed toward his room; the milk shook.

"No, you are not! Food belongs in the kitchen!"

Vincent turned around without a word and went back to the kitchen.

"Did you put the chair back?"

"I didn't want to make noise," said Vincent.

"Am I supposed to put it back!?" he roared.

It might have bothered Vincent that he had just been yelled at, but he had learned that no matter what, he was always going to be guilty of one crime or another. But it didn't really matter to Vincent that he couldn't please Michael. He didn't need Michael's approval; he already had a father. Michael was just a nuisance. Vincent continued on his way to the kitchen, dragged the chair to the table, and drank his milk. He looked at the clock. It was only 10:00 A.M. His mother wasn't coming home for another six hours. He drank his milk slowly, just to pass the time. The tedium was killing him. He decided he would once again tiptoe past Michael's door. He crept carefully, step by step. He avoided making any floor boards creak. Even if one sounded like it might creak, he stopped and altered his course.

"How long are you going to use that flashlight?"

Vincent jumped. "I don't know," he said.

"Just use it for a minute and then turn it off. Otherwise you'll use up the batteries."

"Okay." He decided to wear the flashlight around his neck and only turn it on if he really needed it. He knew it wasn't really necessary to leave it on while he was playing, since he could play his keyboard without looking. He closed his bedroom door and began to pull out his mother's shoes, laundry basket, and miscellaneous boxes.

Michael burst through the door. "What are you doing now?"

"I am putting my keyboard in de closet so you can't hear it," Vincent explained.

"And you think I can't hear shoes, and boxes, and every other damn thing hitting the floor?"

Vincent was out of ideas, and patience. "Why don't you get a pair of earplugs?" He snapped.

"Why don't you shut up, runt?"

Vincent replied, "If you had some brains in your head, maybe de sound would not rattle around so much in there."

"Okay, that's it. Michael grabbed a badminton net from the closet. Vincent began to run around the living room. They circled the armchair and around an end table until Vincent tripped on the lamp cord. The lamp crashed to the floor. Michael paused. He had him cornered. Vincent fell back on the couch, when suddenly the phone began to ring.

"Don't answer that. Remember, you have to hang up eventually, and then you'll have to deal with me again."

The phone rang again. They faced off. It rang again. Vincent asked, "If I do not answer it, will you leave me alone?"

"Deal," Michael said.

After six rings it stopped. Michael gestured for Vincent to go back to his room. Michael followed. Vincent didn't trust that Michael was really finished with him. He could feel Michael walking behind him; it felt like he was being stalked by a wild animal. He wasn't sure which would be smarter, to run or walk. He reached his room and turned to shut the door. He saw the look in Michael's eyes; they were filled with hate. His teeth were clenched and he was ready to strike. Vincent rushed to shut his door, but it wouldn't shut. Michael had stopped it with his foot. He tried stepping on Michael's foot, but he wouldn't budge. Vincent leaned his whole body against the door. He could feel his feet sliding on the carpet as the door opened wider and wider. Michael made his way inside. Vincent ran two steps from the door, and Michael knocked him down. His teeth knocked together as his chin hit the floor; he bit his tongue. He tried to scramble to his feet, but the net fell over him with a swack. Michael began rolling Vincent over and over in the net, squeezing him tighter and tighter until he was completely enveloped. All he could move were his toes and his fingers. His glasses were on sideways and getting ready to break. Michael breathed his smoke-and-coffee breath into Vincent's face. "What are you going to do now, runt?" asked Michael satisfied that he had so thoroughly dominated Vincent.

The weight of Michael's chest on Vincent's was making it difficult to breathe. "What are you going to do to me?" groaned Vincent.

Michael put Vincent's glasses back on him and patted his cheek. "There you go, little buddy. Let's see, what else can I do for you? Oh, I know! You wanted to go in the closet, didn't you? Vincent's eyes got wide. Michael stood up, towering over Vincent. Michael picked Vincent up by the ropes and tossed him into the closet. His head slammed into the wall then hit the floor. Michael hissed with laughter. "There. Serves you right, you little weirdo."

Vincent's head was reeling in pain.

"Aw, did I hurt you? I'm so sorry." He kicked Vincent's legs until they cleared the closet door.

Vincent stared up at Michael helplessly. "Michael!" Vincent pleaded, "I can not move. Please, you must let me go!"

"Who says?" Michael grinned. "And, if you can't keep your mouth shut, we can fix that too. Now who's stupid, my little friend? Maybe next time you'll remember to keep that smart mouth of yours shut!" He squeezed Vincent's lips together and gave them a final yank.

"I won't make anymore noise, I promise. Please, let me out of here. Please, Michael! I'll be perfectly quiet! No! Don't shut—"

The closet door slammed shut. Vincent began to struggle against the ropes, but it was no use; the harder he struggled the tighter they held him. He laid there trying to catch his breath. He was beginning to panic; he couldn't move his arms. He thought, if only I could get something loose, it would feel a little better. Nothing worked. He was wrapped tight as tight could be. It was even getting hard for him to breathe. Emotion seized him when he realized he could be there for hours. He began to struggle wildly all over again.

"Michael! Michael! Come back!" he screamed. He banged his feet against the closet door.

Michael opened the door with a piece of duct tape in his hand. "You can't say I didn't warn you," he said, slapping the tape over Vincent's mouth.

Vincent knew he was defeated. It was awful, like being buried alive. He wondered if this was what claustrophobia felt like. There was one thing he knew; he never wanted this to happen again. His muscles ached to be able to move. The more he tried, the greater the need. He flopped around in the dark like a fish till his strength had completely drained out of him. He tried to think how he could get out of this. Maybe the neighbors would hear him if he tapped on the floor with his foot, but that would just make Michael mad again. Maybe if I pretend that I like this, he thought. Yah, I am floating in the ocean on a raft. I am wrapped in a fishing net. I need the net. He struggled against his emotions. He tried to get control over his crying. I am floating in the sea, floating, floating. He took several deep breaths. I do not want to move or I will lose my raft from under me. The net is keeping the raft safely underneath me. The ocean is so relaxing under me. I must not loosen my arms and legs though, or I will lose my balance. I will just float, float, until I float ashore. Ah, he said to himself, I will be floating ashore by mid-afternoon. Yah, I am safe as long as I hold still. Thank heaven for these ropes to hold my raft safely underneath me.

Reality gripped Vincent again, and he began to cry. Try again, use your imagination, said a voice within him. He recited the twenty-third psalm, "The Lord iss my shepherd; I shall not want. He maketh me to lie down in green pastures: He leadeth me beside still waters. He restoreth my soul." His muscles eventually stopped rebelling against the ropes. Vincent began to hum softly to the rocking of the waves "Jesus loves me this I know, for the Bible tells me so." Finally he relaxed enough to drift off to sleep on his imaginary raft in the sea.

Some time later, the closet door suddenly swung open. The light flashed in his eyes. "You got mail." Michael dropped a package on top of Vincent's aching head.

"If you promise to be perfectly quiet, I'll take the tape off your mouth." It wasn't mercy that motivated Michael. His only concern was that the tape might leave marks, and he would have to explain it. He peeled the tape away carefully. He inspected Vincent's mouth and head, closed the door, and left.

The light shown through the door in narrow beams between the slats. Vincent tried to adjust the box on his stomach so that he could see the return address. His glasses were turned sideways but he could see out of one eye. He closed the other eye and leaned slightly toward the light. The box tumbled off his stomach and wedged against the door with no hope of reading it now. He thought he saw the word Promise. Even if he hadn't seen it, he was already convinced it was true. He thought about his pappa, and how much fun they had together. Nobody else's pappa could make bailing hay seem like play, he thought. Marshall used to come over to work on our farm, because it was so much fun. Then he thought, if Pappa knew what was going on, he would come and rescue me. My pappa would bust the door down if he had to. It gave Vincent confidence just thinking about it. He leaned his head as close as he could toward the box. It certainly smelled like home. He thought he smelled leather. He rocked and rocked until he got the box to lie tightly against his chest. It was almost like being able to hold it. He knew if Bunny had been there when the package arrived, she probably wouldn't have let him have it. "God bless my mamma and pappa," Vincent prayed. "And thank you for this package." He tucked his chin down every few minutes, so he could smell it again. It kept him content for about two more hours.

The closet door opened, flooding the closet with light. Vincent squinted. Michael finally released him without saying a word.

"I'm sorry, Michael," Vincent said. He genuinely meant it. He had been humbled into total submission and would do anything to appease his captor.

"Don't tell your mother about this."

"I won't, I promise. I will do anything you say."

"Good."

Before his mother returned home, they put the closet back together again, including the badminton net, which was neatly put back on the shelf.

Vincent opened his package. He tried not to allow the horror of the afternoon interfere with the joy of the moment. He wiped his nose and proceeded to inspect it thoroughly before he opened it. The box was wrapped in brown paper from an old grocery sack. He knew his mother had wrapped it; his father would never have been so neat with the tape. His father addressed it, though, with a black magic marker. When he wrote the word "Vincent," he turned the V into branches of a tree with leaves on top. The leaves looked like musical notes. There was a rainbow drawn reaching from Promise down to Carlisle. Vincent knew his parents were still praying for him. It meant a lot, especially this afternoon. Vincent sniffed involuntarily from his long cry. He opened the lid of the shoe box. Inside, wrapped in newspaper, was his baseball glove. His pappa had freshly oiled it with mink oil. Underneath the glove was his autograph book that all his classmates had signed at the end of last year. He particularly liked Becky's comments: "You might be short, and you might be ugly, but you're not always that bad, sometimes. I'm only saying this because I have to. Sincerely yours, Becky Perl."

"She loves me," Vincent whispered out loud and smiled.

They sent his favorite T-shirt. It was perfect. It had holes and stains everywhere. On the back it said, "You will know them by the love they have one for another." It had two bears roasting marshmallows under a cherry tree. There were birds and squirrels playing in the tree. And there was a cat and dog wearing paper hats sitting on the ground sharing a bowl of milk with spoons. He put it on. Freida had washed it and hung it on the line outside. He loved that outdoor smell. He was surprised to find that it fit tighter than before. It barely covered his bellybutton. He didn't care. He was keeping it on anyway.

Martin enclosed a cartoon he had drawn of Freida and himself. He had copied the famous painting of the farmer and his wife, *American Gothic,* except he replaced the faces with Freida's and his own and made a few artfully considered adjustments. He blacked out Freida's two front teeth, and made swirly lines wafting up from his armpits.

Vincent's favorite thing of all was the letter from his mamma. Oh how he needed to hear her say she loved him. He read the words over and over again. She said: "How can we be only a few miles apart and yet seem so far away? I miss your sunny smile in the morning . . . I miss your clothes swinging on the clothesline." He kept reading it and reading it, eking out every bit of love that he could. How he wished everybody would just let him go home. "Jesus, let me go home soon," he prayed. "I can not do this anymore." He read again. "I will never ever forget my little boy." When Bunny finally arrived home she looked exhausted. Vincent doubted there would be any dinner tonight, not real dinner anyway. She flopped onto Vincent's bed wearing her coat and flinging her purse into her lap. She asked cheerfully, "Michael said you got a package today, is that right?"

He could tell she wasn't at all pleased with Michael for giving it to him, but it was too late to take it away now; the damage had already been done.

"Yah, do you want to see what they sent?" he asked. Vincent hopped down and pulled the package out from under the bed. He decided at the last moment to leave the picture and the letter underneath his bed, for safekeeping.

As he began to open the box, Bunny noticed his cheeks were flushed. She felt his cheeks and forehead, checking for a temperature. He didn't feel hot, she thought, but sensed something wasn't right. His joy seemed subdued for some reason.

"Hey, how do you like that? That's my old Lou Rawls tape. You used to love that tape."

"I still love that tape," he replied.

"Ugh, my goodness," said Bunny. She held Vincent's elbow up to the light. "How did you get that burn on your arm?"

Vincent half opened his mouth, but nothing came out. The pause was awkward. Vincent wasn't a seasoned liar and he was afraid if he said anything it was going to sound insincere.

Michael appeared in the doorway and said, "Vinnie and I were wrestling on the carpet. We were just horsing around. Oh yeah, and we knocked over a lamp. Sorry."

Bunny spun around to face Michael. She burned holes through him with her stare. She knew perfectly well Michael had not had a kind word for Vincent since he moved in. Now she was supposed to believe they were horsing around!? She turned back to Vincent. He had planted his most angelic smile across his face, and shook his head in agreement. He hoped that pleased Michael. Boy, did he hope.

Bunny said nothing, but got up and passed by Michael with an icy-cold stare.

"It's just a brush burn!" Michael protested. He would have been better off saying nothing.

Vincent awoke that night to an argument between Bunny and Michael. Vincent caught the gist of it. Michael told Bunny he didn't do anything. Then Bunny told Michael she knew he did, and if he ever laid a hand on Vincent again, there would be serious consequences. Michael laughed at Bunny and said, "Ugh, serious consequences," and then made some joke about her beating him up. That's when Vincent could hear it perfectly. Bunny said quite clearly, "You have to fall asleep sometime tough guy, and I'll—be—waiting! In fact, I am so angry, if I were you I'd sleep with one eye open!" That was the last thing that was said.

Psalm 23: 1–3. The Lord is my shepherd; I shall not want. He maketh me to lie down in green pastures: he leadeth me beside still waters. He restoreth my soul.

Chapter 17

O Little Town

$\mathscr{B}$unny tiptoed down the hall toward Vincent's room. She noticed a dim light coming from under the doorway, and it sounded as if he might be crying. As she got closer she could hear him whispering. A crinkling page turned in the darkness.

"Be merciful unto me, O God," he whispered. "Be merciful unto me, for my soul trusteth in thee: yea, in the shadow of thy wings will I make my refuge, until these cal-am-e-ties be over-past. I will cry unto God Most High, unto God, that performeth all things for me. He shall send from heaven and save me from the reproach of him that would swallow me up, Selah. God shall send forth his mercy and his truth." Vincent took a long, labored breath. "Jesus you must help me," he cried. Then he continued, "My soul is among lions; and I lie even among them that are set on fire, even the sons of men, whose teeth are spears and arrows, and their tongue a sharp sword."

Vincent flopped himself down and cried quietly into his pillow so no one could hear. Bunny walked quietly into the room and knelt by his bed. She stroked his hair. It startled him; he didn't realize anyone was there.

"Vinnie, are you crying?"

"A little," he admitted, wiping his tears on his pillow-case.

"Do you cry yourself to sleep every night?"

Vincent didn't answer. He didn't want to hurt her feelings.

"What can I do?"

Still no answer. Instead, he buried his face again in his pillow.

"Do you want me to read to you?"

Vincent shook his head yes, and tried hard to stop crying.

He rolled over long enough to point to the place where he left off, and Bunny began, "Be exalted, O God, above the nations; let your glory be over all the earth. They have prepared a net for my steps; my soul is bowed down."

Vincent's chin began to quiver. It was always harder to hold in his feelings when he was talking to God, since it brought his problems to the surface. He didn't think he was going to be able to contain his feelings for very long.

"They have digged a pit before me into the midst whereof they are fallen themselves."

By then Vincent was ready to burst. He gave into it and started crying again. He wished Bunny were not there to see.

Bunny knew this was her fault. She knew what Vinnie wanted to say when he buried his head was send me home. But she was also certain that she didn't want to open the door to that conversation. She sat quietly until Vincent finally said, "Nobody likes me, especially Michael."

"Nobody at school likes you?" she asked, surprised.

It was getting even harder to talk. He choked out, "De children do not like me."

"How could they not like you? You're so much fun, and such a good guy."

"They say I am weird. Mostly my clothes are weird and I talk weird. They even call me 'de weirdo', or 'bug-eyed Bible boy.'"

"Ya know, Vinnie, we bought those new school clothes for you," she suggested, "Maybe you should start wearing them instead of your old clothes."

Vincent reached up to his bed post and grabbed his black felt wool hat. He pulled it into his side, tucked it underneath him, and with indignation said, "How would you like it if I made you wear my mamma's clothes?"

Bunny had no doubt she didn't want to wear Amish clothes. "Hmm, I see what you mean. Still, they shouldn't call you weird; they don't know how special you are. You sing and you play keyboard. Maybe you could take your keyboard to school and sing them a song."

"They would not like what I sing. All I know iss church music."

"You know Lou Rawls," Bunny suggested. She started on a low note, "You'll never find—"

"Mom, I am not Lou Rawls, and neither are you," he laughed through his tears. "I would sound stupid."

"Sing me something, then," she urged.

"Like what?"

Bunny considered, "I guess it'll be a church song, right?"

"Do you know any church songs?" he asked.

"The only church songs I know are Christmas Carols. Uh, well, I know 'O Little Town of Bethlehem.'"

"Will you sing with me?" asked Vincent.

"Okay, I guess."

They began a little roughly at first: "O little town of Bethlehem, how still we see thee lie. Above the deep and dreamless sleep the silent stars go by. Yet in thy dark streets shineth the everlasting light. The hopes and fears of all the years are met in thee tonight."

Bunny clapped. "That was terrific."

Vincent felt a little better. "There is more. Do you want to hear the rest?"

"Sure."

"For Christ is born of Mary; and gathered all above, while mortals sleep the angels keep their watch of wondering love. O morning stars together proclaim the holy birth, and praises sing to God the King, and peace to men on earth.

"How silently, how silently, the wondrous gift is given! So God imparts to human hearts the blessings of His heav'n. No ear may hear His coming; but in this world of sin, where meek souls will receive Him still, the dear Christ enters in.

"O holy Child of Bethlehem, descend to us we pray; cast out our sin and enter in, be born in us today. We hear the Christmas angels the great glad tidings tell, o come to us, abide with us, our Lord Emmanuel."

"Wow! I never realized what a beautiful song that is, maybe because I never heard you sing it. How do you know all the verses?"

"Because my mamma sings it all de time, even in de middle of summer. She hangs out de clothes, de sun iss beating down, de fireworks are going off in de middle of July, and she iss singing: 'O little town of Bethlehem.'" He laughed.

Vincent's Bible lay open beside him. Bunny asked, "How do you understand the Bible? It doesn't make much sense to me, or rather, I should say, it makes no sense to me."

Vincent answered, "Grandpappa Dunkin says, 'How do you eat an elephant? One bite at a time.'" They both laughed.

"I never heard that before. That's funny," she said.

"That iss an old joke where I come from. Try this," he said. He shut his Bible and closed his eyes, then he let it fall open. He started reading the first thing he saw. "My grace is sufficient for thee: for my strength is made perfect in weakness. Most gladly therefore will I rather glory in my in-firm-i-ties."

Bunny asked, "Does that mean anything to you?"

"Yah, I know what he means," said Vincent. "I am weak, but He iss strong, and that iss good. He can do his work better that way. Now you try it. See what He says to you."

She read what her eyes landed on: "'And all the bread of their provision was dry and moldy.' Ugh, that was lovely. What could that be about?"

Vincent crunched up his face and thought. "Um, maybe they were garbage bin diving?" He shrugged his shoulders, "I don't know. Try it again."

She let the book fall open again. "'Be ye not unequally yoked with an unbeliever.' Do you get that?" she asked.

"Yah, it means that Christians should marry Christians."

"Oh, I guess that makes sense. A lot less problems that way."

"Yah," Vincent nodded emphatically.

Bunny said, "There was a lady, one time, who said to me that if parents sin, then God will punish their kids. But she said I can turn it around for my kids."

"What? That does not sound right," said Vincent.

"Yeah, let me think what she said." Bunny did her best to come up with a direct quote. "'The sins of the father will be transferred to the children three or four times.' Or something like that."

Vincent rifled through the pages until he came to the ten commandments. "Exodus 20:4–6," he said. "You read it. See if that is it."

"Thou shalt not make unto thee any graven image, or any likeness of anything that is in heaven above, or that is in the earth beneath, or that is in the water under the earth." Vincent said, "You know, like, you are not supposed to worship other stuff besides God, like a statue of some guy, or de biggest diamond in de world, or something you hang around your neck; that kind of stuff. Ya know de people that were traveling around in de desert with Moses?"

Bunny nodded.

"They built a golden cow out of all their jewelry and started worshipping it. Seems kind of dumb to me. Doesn't it to you? What iss so special about a cow? I love you, O great and mighty moo-cow. You are de wisest of all cows, oh my moo-cow. No one can eat grass and spit it up again like you, almighty one," Vincent said mockingly.

Bunny was glad to see Vinnie smiling and joking again. "I think I'd be tempted to tease it to see what would happen," said Bunny, "like, make faces at it when no one was looking." She stuck her tongue out and crossed her eyes.

"I would throw snowballs at it, even if they were looking." Vincent pretended to throw a snowball, complete with sound effects. "Poosh! Ugh, got it right in de butt."

They laughed. He threw another one, "Ugh, right in de ear. Look, it iss dripping down on his neck, and he iss just standing there like a big dope."

"Should I keep reading?" she laughed.

"Yah."

"'Thou shalt not bow down thyself to them, nor serve them: for I the Lord thy God am a jealous God, visiting the iniquity of the fathers upon the children unto the third and fourth generation of them that hate me.'"

"Keep going," said Vincent.

"'And showing mercy unto thousands of them that love me, and keep my commandments.'

Bunny protested, "Yeah, see. I told that woman, that's not fair. Why should I be punished for what my parents did? That's not right."

Vincent explained, "First of all, God does not like it when anything bad happens to any of us. He likes everybody de same. That iss why he wrote de book and made up all de rules in de first place, to keep us from hurting each other. See, God starts out, at de beginning of de book, real strict like your teacher does at de beginning of de school year. She comes in and makes ugly faces and acts real mean for a while at de beginning and makes everybody follow de rules. Like, she will say with a real mean face, 'There shall be no talking while de teacher is talking!!'"

"Heil, Hitler," Bunny saluted.

"Yah, like that. Then if you talk out, she beans you one, or makes you do extra work, or something like that. Well you see, God starts out setting down de rules, because all de people were acting like bad kids. You know how when de kids are good until de teacher leaves de room? That iss how de people were acting. That iss de part that you are reading in de book. He iss telling them de rules, and he scares de bajeepers out of them so they will behave. So, you are understanding that, so far?"

"Yeah, but I still don't think he should punish their kids to make a point."

"But, but, wait. In de middle of de book he gets a little easier. Everybody knew de rules by heart, and mostly they were using them to live by. In fact, de priests were so strict and bossy, they started making rules on top of rules, like do not put de whole mint leaf into your teacup. You must rip exactly one tenth of it off and give it to de priest, because that iss de rules and we priests are de bosses for God. They got so full of themselves, they were starting to drive de people crazy, nuts, and nervous with all their rules. So de next thing

God did wass show them he loved them by dying on de cross. It iss not like he had to let de people torture him to death on de cross. He could have called up a giant dragon and had them all eaten for lunch. But he did not do that. He volunteered. He allowed them to hurt him bad, real bad, and to put him to death, because he wanted them to see just how rotten they could be. And he wanted them to understand how much he wanted them to listen. He loved them, that iss why. They figured it out after he was already dead that he was de real Messiah they were waiting for. There wass more and more miracles to prove it, even after he was already dead. He was hoping that after they figured it out, then maybe they would choose to listen to him just because they loved him too, not because they had to."

"Listen to what? That he's the great and wonderful Oz."

"No, silly. Listen to how to be."

"So, how are you supposed to be?"

"The same way he always wanted them to be. He wants you to treat people de way you would want to be treated. De most important thing iss to love other people as much as you love yourself."

"That's it!" she complained.

"It iss not so easy," said Vincent. "He wants you to be nice to your parents, and to be fair with people in your business. And he wants you to take care of people that can not take care of themselves. He doesn't want you to lie to people, especially about people to other people, or cheat people. That kind of stuff."

"Hmm."

"And then he says at de end of de book that everybody who sticks with Him will have a mansion waiting for him in heaven. And by then, all your neighbors will have practiced a long time on how to get along on earth like it iss in heaven. That iss what makes heaven, heaven."

"What happens if a person just decided he wants to hook up and be Jesus' friend and then the next day he gets run over by a train?"

"It does not matter how long you were one of his friends, only that you meant it. If you are his friend, he will be your friend for life—if that iss what you want. You don't have to earn badges or sell cookies or anything. It iss free from de start."

Vincent continued, "See, he iss not trying to punish de kids, he iss trying to get de people to love each other, and if you follow de rules, then everybody gets along, and de kids have better parents, and de kids grow up being better parents, and that iss good for de grandchildren, and on and on. See? But, if everybody only talks ugly all de time, or runs off and leaves de kids for somebody else, and never teaches them how God wants them to be, it only turns into a bigger and bigger mess. See, God loves us, and he does not want a big mess, especially for de little kids. He said de parents sins will get passed on to de kids, but he also said, 'Let de little children come unto me, for such as these are de kingdom of heaven.' He likes kids. Do you understand it now?"

"Sounds good, but I'm not ready to join the covent."

"Well, at least for your question, de answer iss: He tries to be tough at first, and then when that iss not working out, he puts himself through torture just to show them how much he iss willing to sacrifice for them and how ugly they can be. After that, if you would still rather fight, and lie, and cheat, then it iss your choice. But Jesus does not want you coming up to heaven and making more trouble for all de other saints."

"I'm always nice to people," said Bunny.

"You were not very nice to my mamma and pappa," reminded Vincent.

"I guess I wasn't. But I had a good reason for it. I did it to get you back. And besides it was a long time ago."

"I almost wass shot! And so wass my grandpappa! I have never been shot at before! See, if you were living God's way, you would not have tried to get me back by lying. You are just kind of making up what you think iss right as you go along. You can not make up your own rules as you go along. If you would have studied God's book, then you would know you should not have done that, no matter even if you did not get me back."

"I guess not. Do you forgive me?"

"You must ask God first to forgive you. Maybe you could tell Him you are sorry, and then ask Him to put His spirit in you to help you be good.

"Does that really make it easier?"

"Well of course, silly! Who could be good without Him giving you the want to? Everybody does bad stuff, but some of us feel bad when we talk to God about it. But if we only keep on doing bad stuff, that iss not good. That means you do not really want to be like Him. If you only want to be bad, you don't really want to belong to Him. But that iss what you pick, not God. See?"

"You sure are smart for such a little boy."

"About de Bible, you mean? Everybody knows that stuff. That iss only de teenie-weenie peanut version of de Bible."

"I don't even know the teeny-weenie peanut version," admitted Bunny.

"You would know it if your grandpappa wass Pastor Dunkin, and your teacher wass Miss Purdy, and your mamma wass de pastor's daughter. If I didn't understand at least that much by now, I probably could not spell my own name, and you would probably be helping me hold my pencil. My grandpappa says," Vincent lowered his voice to sound like his grandfather, "'We teach you de Bible so you can get through life without steppin' in something. Now, if you do not want to listen, that iss your problem, but you will be scraping off your own shoes.' One time I wass always being mean to a girl I did not like. Then, one day, I almost fell off a cliff, and guess who saved me!"

"The little girl?" asked Bunny.

"Yah," Vincent admitted, "de last person in de world I would pick to save me. It iss still embarrassing. And then her grandpappa told everybody all about it at de baseball game!"

Bunny laughed. She asked, "Hey, you want to do something fun after school tomorrow?"

"What?"

"Walk down to my office, and I'll take you to the music store. It's pretty close to where I work. You can stay there till I get off, and I'll come pick you up. We can buy you something before we go home. That way you can avoid mean old Michael."

"I wouldn't even know what to buy, because I wouldn't know what I wass looking at."

"No, they have headphones and you could listen to whatever you want. Then if you find something you really like, we'll buy it. They have gospel, R&B, classical, whatever you want."

"R&B?"

"You'll see. The lady who works there is real nice. She'll let you listen as much as you want."

"You mean it iss like a music library?"

"Yeah, sort of. Ya wanta go?"

"Yah!"

"Okay, we'll do that then. But, it's getting late. You better get some sleep. Oh, and make sure you hide that Bible good. I don't want to go diggin' in the trash again. The neighbors will start talking about us." Bunny blew Vincent a kiss as she left. "Night, night." Vincent felt much better.

Bunny paused outside Vincent's door and listened. He prayed, "You really must work your way into my mom's heart. You could really make her into something good. Forgive all her sins, Jesus, 'cause she really doesn't know too much. I'll try to teach her. Amen."

The following day after school, Vincent went to the music store. After a couple of hours, Bunny came to pick him up. The lady behind the counter put her index finger up to her lips. "Shh," she smiled and pointed in the direction of the soundproof listening booth. He had his eyes shut and he was hopping up and down and shaking his head. It looked like he was doing an Indian rain dance. She looked back at the cashier and smiled. The cashier explained, "He's been doing that for about an hour now."

Bunny made arrangements for Vincent to come in every day after school. In return, Vincent became their best customer. By the time Vincent had spent several months going to the music store, he had evolved into Carlisle's gospel music aficionado.

2 Corinthians 12:8–9. For this thing I besought the Lord thrice, that it might depart from me. And he said unto me, My grace is sufficient for thee: for my strength is made perfect in weakness. Most gladly therefore will I rather glory in my infirmities, that the power of Christ may rest upon me.

Chapter 18

How Long, Lord

One Year Later, Nine Years Old

Bunny was in the middle of her normal morning routine, rushing to get ready for work, and getting Vincent ready for the day. She was finally ready when she began to head for the front door. Vincent followed her into the hallway and shut the door behind him.

"I don't want to stay with Michael," begged Vincent. "Can't I go to de music store?"

"No, Vinnie," insisted Bunny. "Sandy isn't there today. Now try to get along with Michael. I know it's not easy, but try your best."

Vincent complained, "I do try to get along, but he does not like me, and there iss nothing I can do."

Bunny finished smoothing down his shirt and brushed his hair to the side. "Michael is a big help to us. By this time next year you can tell people your dad is an airplane pilot. You'll like that, won't you?"

"I have a dad, and he iss a farmer."

"Vinnie," Bunny warned, "we've talked about this. He is not your father anymore."

"Neither iss Michael. He only wants you, not me."

"That's not true; if it weren't for him, we'd be living in the boiler room."

"I would not care. I would rather live in de basement with de cobwebs than in a castle with cranky old Michael."

"Yeah, you say that now. What do you do when you see your first rat?"

"Uh, throw it in de garbage bin?" Vincent grinned.

Bunny said, "Funny, very funny."

Bunny took one last look at Vincent, and turned to go. "Now you be nice," she called back. "I'll be back before you know it."

Michael and a friend of his from school had gone into the bedroom shortly after Bunny left. Vincent waited almost an hour for Michael to come out. There was no milk in the refrigerator, and Michael had promised Bunny he would go to the store.

Vinnie took a chance and called outside the locked door, "Michael."

No answer.

"Miiiiichael," he called through the keyhole.

"Get away from the door," Michael warned.

"But there iss no milk, and it iss eleven o'clock. If you give me some money I will get it myself."

"I said, get away from the door!"

Vincent lay down outside the door for another hour. The sense of belonging he had known while he lived with his Mennonite family was a distant memory. It was getting more and more difficult to remember what it was like to feel accepted by the group. And while insults used to roll off his back when he lived in Promise, where he knew he had friends and a supportive family, now the stares and insults could penetrate with just a look. Each new insult dug into his spirit before the last insult was able to heal. Vincent felt fortunate on days when the children were polite.

His mother was the only person he could turn to for support, but she was alienated from the community as well, not only for her own behavior during her heroin years, but also because of Mrs. Muldare's reputation. Her mother had worked her way into local politics and had no use for anyone without money and influence. Her name was continually popping up on the news concerning one political scandal after another. Bunny never knew whether to believe what she heard, so she chose to ignore it altogether.

Michael barely tolerated Vincent, though Bunny kept Michael's temper at bay, most of the time. She was able to tolerate Michael's surly behavior toward Vincent, because she had come to expect conflicts in a home. Her mother had treated her and her father with the same contempt, while her father saved his frustration for her brother.

Vincent talked to Bunny about going to Sunday school, but so far he hadn't been able to convince her. "Maybe we can find some friends there," he would tell her.

She would always resist by saying, "No one wants someone with my history in their church. We would be sitting by ourselves."

He would tell her, "De church iss full of people that mess up, all de time. That iss mostly why they need to go to church."

Bunny was not convinced. "I know, I know, the story of the rabbi and the tax collector. And God blessed the tax collector but not the rabbi, because the tax collector knew he was a sinner, and the rabbi didn't. You already told me."

Vincent lay outside the door praying, "Jesus, I know you still hear my prayers; I can feel you waking up inside me when I call to you. But why don't you ever answer me? I don't want to hurt my mom's feelings, and I know I already asked a zillion times, but there must be a way you could figure out for me to get back home. I just want to go home where people like me. I miss Mamma and Pappa. Michael does not want to be my pappa, and he never will. And Mom does not want to go to church. I am wasting your time being here."

Michael knew Vincent was still outside the door, and that, in itself, was enough to enrage him. But when he heard Vincent sniffling, he swung open the door and screamed, "What do I have to do to get rid of you, you little freak!?"

Vincent mustered the courage to say, "Well, somebody hass to be my pappa."

Michael spied his freshly painted picture of a woman, riding naked on horseback, tilting precariously against the wall. "You touched that, didn't you?"

"No."

"You touched that, didn't you!?" he repeated even louder.

Vincent said nothing.

"Yes you did, you little liar. I warned you; never, never touch my paintings! He began to chase Vincent into the living room. Vincent had not forgotten the badminton net. He grabbed for the front door, flew down the steps, and out to the sidewalk. Michael was right behind him all the way. When Vincent reached the street, he darted between two cars. He felt Michael at his back. He heard a loud horn from a huge truck and the squeal of brakes. There were people shouting and screaming on the sidewalk who could already see the inevitable. They were shouting, "Get up!" "Hurry up!" "Run!" By the time Vincent had time to turn back, he felt the bumper ram his hip. It tossed him into the air. His arms and legs were flailing, and he was grabbing at thin air as he was thrown mercilessly onto the back of a parked car. His body slid onto the hot trunk until his head hit the back window. Vincent could hear the voices and screams begin to fade, as the light grew dim around him. He grabbed for the trunk to hold him, then he could feel his grip weakening until he lost consciousness. The people who had seen were now frozen in silence and disbelief. The truck engine growled in the background. As Vincent's blood puddled on the trunk underneath him, his body slid slowly to the ground in a crumpled heap, leaving a streak of blood behind him.

Michael stared from the curb at what had just taken place. He knew he was to blame. He was joined by his friend, Perry.

Michael said, "Vinnie's been hit. Call an ambulance."

"Oh my God!" Perry ran upstairs for the phone.

The truck driver pulled on his airbrakes, slowly opened his door, and climbed down from his truck. The roar of his motor was silent now, and in its place the crowd recovering from the shock of it, began talking and explaining what they had seen, some shouting, some gasping. The driver's face went pale and his knees were weak. He walked reluctantly, toward the body. He was sure that the child was dead, and like it or not, he was going to have to look at what he had done. Traffic backed up, horns blasted, and a crowd grew larger on the sidewalk.

"Don't touch him till the ambulance gets here," shouted Michael.

Michael and the driver looked down over Vincent's little body as it lay lifeless in front of them. His leg was twisted and contorted from his hip; his foot was turned in the wrong direction. The side of his face had hit the window, hard, leaving his jaw turned out to one side. The side of his face was smashed and bloody where it hit the glass. His glasses were shattered and mangled. His ear was torn halfway off, and was bleeding badly. It was unclear what happened to his torso, as it was turned toward the ground and he was lying on top of his hands.

"He's breathing," someone in the crowd shouted.

His cotton shirt was twisted tightly against his back. His rib cage moved up and down ever so slightly as he struggled to stay alive.

Vincent thought he heard voices. He tried to lift his head; it bobbed twice, his raw face smacking against the gravel in the road. Then he slipped back into unconsciousness.

The truck driver was so stunned he couldn't speak. His heart sank as he wondered if that was the little boy's last breath. A police officer appeared and began to ask the driver questions, but he was unable to do much more than stammer and point at the body. He couldn't even tell the officer who he was.

Michael explained, "He ran right out in front of the truck. That's all I know. I caught up to him just before he ran into the road. I tried to grab him, but it was too late."

Within a few minutes the rumor reached the pharmacy where Bunny was shopping during lunch.

The cashier asked, "What are all the sirens doing out there, anybody know?"

One of the customers answered, "It's about three blocks up. There was a little boy got hit by a truck."

Bunny spun around instantly, "Was he wearing a white cotton shirt and suspenders?"

"I don't know for sure," said the woman. "I think it might have been white."

Bunny dropped her purchases on the floor and ran out the door. She ran as fast as she could up the hill to her apartment. She knew it must be Vinnie. She began to question why she ever thought she could take care of him by herself. She remembered Vinnie's face looking up at hers before she left for work. He had begged her not to leave him with Michael, but she refused to listen. Flashing lights were everywhere. She weaved her way through the maze of people and cars. She arrived just as his body was being lifted onto a stretcher. An EMT had gently secured a surgical collar around Vincent's neck, and another EMT held a pressure bandage to Vincent's ear.

"Get back! I'm his mother!" Bunny screamed frantically, as she thrashed her way through the crowd.

"Do you want to ride with him?" asked the ambulance driver.

"Yes," she answered. "How bad is he?"

"He's alive, but critical. There could be internal injuries; we don't know yet. We're especially concerned about head trauma."

Bunny put her hand to her mouth. She looked down at his distorted bloody face. It could be the last time she would see him alive. "Vincent, baby, Mom's here. Don't worry. Mom's here."

The attendant helped Bunny into the back of the ambulance. He seated her next to Vincent, saying, "Pray we make it to the hospital, ma'am."

That's what she did; that's what they all did—the truck driver, the policeman, the TV news crew, the witnesses, the ambulance crew, the onlookers. They all prayed, in their own way, that Vincent would live. The doors of the ambulance slammed shut, making everything seem so final. As it began to roll away, the neighbors wondered if they would ever see the little boy from Amish country again.

Michael and his friend went back up the steps to the apartment. They seated themselves on the couch where the window directly behind them gave them a view of the street below. They watched as the owner of the car looked in horror at the streak of blood and listened distractedly as the police relayed to him what had happened. The truck driver sat on the curb in shock. People continued to point and wave their arms as they gave their rendition of what they had seen. Another policeman was in the street directing traffic and urging them to keep it moving.

Michael said, "He never should have run from me like that. How was I supposed to know he'd be dumb enough to run in front of a semi? By the way, if anybody asks, you never heard me yelling at him, and you never saw me chasing him," Michael warned.

"You want me to lie?" asked Perry.

"Tell them you don't know anything. I don't want you giving them any ideas that this was my fault. You say one incriminating thing, and the next thing you know they're going to try to say I pushed him."

"Who's they," Perry asked.

"The insurance company, the police, who knows."

"It is true, I didn't see you push or anything, Michael. It's not like you wanted this to happen. It just happened."

"That's right, it's not like I planned this out. It just happened." Michael sneered a smile that didn't escape Perry. It was disturbing.

Michael thought to himself, some days are just luckier than others.

Michael and Perry turned their attention back to the window as a tow truck came for the tractor trailer. The policeman took the driver to the station. Everyone else tried to go back to what they had been doing before the accident, but there was a shared painful awareness of how fragile life is. "He's so young," said Perry. "Time is a strange thing. You get up in the morning and it's like every other morning, and then all of a sudden without any warning, something like this happens that's so final. You can't change it, you can't fix it, and it will be that way forever. It's too sudden to deal with, but there it is, and then the rest of the world goes back to doing what it was doing, like it's just another day. The sun keeps on shining and the earth keeps moving along like nothing ever happened. Meanwhile Bunny's life may be changed forever while the rest of the world will go on, life as usual. Poor Bunny, how is she going to go on from here? It will be terrible for her if she loses him."

Michael said, "He might live, we don't know."

"With a head injury like that?" his friend reminded. "I doubt it." He looked to see if a dose of reality had changed Michael's thinking. He wasn't sure.

"Vinnie, can you hear me, honey?" asked Bunny.

The ambulance siren blared down the highway toward children's hospital. It would take them about thirty minutes to get there. The attendants told her she could talk to him but not ask him to respond. He needed to stay as still as possible. They continued to hook him to monitors and check his vital signs. At least they had the external bleeding under control.

Bunny had no time to think about anything but the immediate moment. She thought, I may never be able to hear his voice again. He hadn't regained consciousness. His breathing was labored as he forced the air out with a groan. His face was terribly contorted due to his disjointed jaw. Bunny ran her hand along his cheek, trying to comfort him. The attendant warned her, "Don't touch it. Maybe the doctors can put it back in place without breaking it."

Vincent had one hand that hadn't been injured, and Bunny held on to it, refusing to let go for anything; it was her lifeline. She felt that if he could borrow her strength like a conduit from her hand to his, maybe he would make it. She held his hand up to her forehead and shut her eyes. "God," she prayed. "Vinnie can't pray for himself, so I'm doing it for him. You might not have a reason to listen to me, but this is for Vinnie. I know he would want me to pray for him, since he can't do it himself. Please don't let Vinnie die. He's too young, and is too full of goodness for this world to lose. Please, God, don't let my little boy die."

She leaned her head on his chest and wept. "Please don't let him die," she repeated.

The attendant reminded her. "I know this is hard for you ma'am, but please don't lean against him. There may be internal injuries or broken ribs. It's hard for him to breathe."

He didn't need to give an explanation. Bunny's head shot up at once. She began again, "Vinnie sweetie, Mommy loves you. Keep on trying to breathe. We are almost to the hospital, baby. Keep on breathing, baby," she cried.

Vinnie's body stiffened. His good hand began to quake. Then his head began to quake in the same twitching tremor. His back began to arch. "What's going on?" she yelled to the EMT.

"Step back," he said. The two began to work frantically while Bunny waited on the side of the ambulance half out of her mind. "Hand me the manitrol," ordered the paramedic, "and morphine." Equipment jangled, tubing was inserted, medications were administered while she waited helplessly, worrying that she was watching Vinnie die.

"Why is he shaking like that!?" she asked.

"Head trauma. If we can keep the brain from swelling that will be the one thing that can save him. It's good that he's not fully conscious. We can keep him quiet without doping him up too much with morphine. It's risky for his heart. Does he have any heart problems?"

"No," Bunny replied.

"M-ma," groaned Vincent.

Bunny leaned over the attendant's shoulder, "Hey, guy. Lay still there sweetie. We'll get you to the hospital and everything will be fine."

"Is he awake?" She caught a glimpse of Vinnie trying to open his eyes. He couldn't focus. As soon as he had both eyes open, they rolled back in his head, and he was out again.

"That's good, isn't it?" Bunny urged.

"Yes Ma'am," he answered. He thought, why dash her hopes so soon?

Vincent's tremors continued as they rushed the rest of the way to the hospital.

Once at the hospital, Vincent was wheeled into the emergency operating room. Bunny was directed to sit in the waiting room while they tried to save Vincent. She paced and watched the clock, one hour, two hours, three hours. While she waited she tried to ward off thoughts of blaming herself for what had happened. Had she left Vinnie with the Amish, he would probably live a perfectly happy life until he was an old man. She thought to herself, I should have kicked Michael out the minute he started hedging about being Vinnie's father. She was plagued by thoughts that God was punishing her for lying about Vinnie being kidnapped. She had done a terrible thing to God's holy people. Maybe since she had messed up God's plan for Vinnie's life, God was just going to call it off, and bring him back to heaven. She argued, but I didn't know he was with holy people; I didn't know where he was. For all I knew he was in an orphanage somewhere. I could have done a lot of things with that money of my dad's, but I used it to save my kid from being lost. If God didn't want me to have him, that social worker never would have found him. Who am I kidding? I don't deserve him. He's too good to be mine.

On Earth as It Is in Heaven

Finally, an exhausted doctor approached her with the news.

"We have been able to put him back together again, Mrs. Muldare. The rest is up to the good Lord. He has not regained consciousness, which is not to be expected, at least not yet. When that time comes we will be able to determine the extent of the damage to his brain."

"Damage to his brain?" asked Bunny.

"Our main task at this point is to keep the swelling to a minimum, which we will do by keeping him under close observation until the critical period is over. We discovered a clot which we successfully removed, but now the danger lies in the way his body responds to the manitrol and the antibiotics. Hopefully we can keep the swelling to a minimum in these first forty-eight hours. He will be sedated, which is why he won't regain consciousness right away. The best thing for him is to lie quietly. In fact, one of the dangers we are trying to avoid is further injury from any sudden, violent movement. As far as pain goes, he won't feel a thing until he wakes up. Even then, we can keep the pain to a minimum. However, if he slips into a coma we may be in trouble. This could happen over the next few days. We'll just have to wait and see what happens. You should begin to prepare yourself now, however. If your son does come out of it, the chances of him living an unrestricted life are pretty slim."

"What do you mean, restricted?"

"In cases like this, it is not unusual for the patients to need nursing care for the rest of their lives. The extent of the damage is impossible to predict. It may be that he will never be able to feed himself or control his bodily functions, or possibly, but less likely, he may simply experience some short-term memory loss. We don't know. But let's take it one day at a time. Hopefully, the CAT scan tomorrow will

260

show the brain swelling to be minimal, and we can begin to slowly decrease the amount of sedative within twenty-four hours. The sooner we can safely reduce the sedative, the less likely it will be that he will slip into an irreversible coma."

"What about the rest of him?" asked Bunny.

"We set his jaw, but unfortunately it had to be wired shut. He lost a finger; we sewed it back on," he said, matter-of-factly.

"Ah, no," Bunny moaned. "He is a pianist."

"Is that right?" said the doctor with interest. Well, fortunately, children have a considerably better chance of regaining the use of their fingers than adults do. And the best news is, there was no damage to his internal organs. They are all working perfectly."

"Good," Bunny said.

"They stitched up his ear and face. I think the plastic surgeon was able to do a pretty good job of making his face look normal. His hip is another problem spot for him. We will have to wait to see if there was damage to his spinal cord. He may or may not have feeling in his legs."

This was getting to be too much for Bunny to handle. Was Vincent going to be an invalid in a wheelchair for the rest of his life? Is this the punishment that God was meting out to Vincent for having such a lousy mother? Then Vincent's words came back to her. God does not punish the children. God does not like it when bad things happen to anybody. He likes us all the same. But how could Vincent go from being perfectly normal this morning to possibly being paralyzed and brain damaged by the afternoon? She remembered, again, giving Vinnie the bum rush before she left for work. A little thing like taking some time to listen had become such a huge mistake by the afternoon. That hurried conversation may well have been their last.

"Mrs. Muldare?"

"Yes, oh I'm sorry, I'm listening."

"I realize this has been a lot for you to take in, but really, if Vincent has a good healthy will to survive, my experience with children is that they can demonstrate tremendous courage and determination. My suggestion to you is to stay with your child through the next few days, and if all goes well, his body and mind will make a remarkable recovery by Christmas."

"What is the real likelihood of that, a complete recovery?" asked Bunny.

"Like I said, we won't know until he regains consciousness, could be tomorrow, could be months."

"Or it could be never?" asked Bunny.

"Yes. I'm sorry. We've done what we can. The rest is in God's hands."

"Can I see him?"

"Yes. But don't be shocked by the tremors he is experiencing. It's a normal symptom of the trauma to his brain.

"Tremors."

"If you recall, he had a seizure in the ambulance."

"Yes," Bunny answered, hanging on the doctor's words.

"Because of the damage to his nervous system caused by the trauma to his brain, he will experience jerking tremors in his hands and neck. It should be a temporary aberration, but it's shocking if you're not used to it."

The doctor added, "When you speak to him, there have been some studies done that indicate the patients can hear what is being said, even though they may not be able to respond. He will most probably have to put the pieces of his memory back together gradually. Any positive stimulus you can offer him now, like a family pet, or a grandmother or siblings that miss him, can trigger a response in his brain that will help him to reboot, as it were. Let your comments be supportive and confident. You can definitely make a difference in his struggle to survive. As difficult as it may be for you, put your own feelings of helplessness and fear aside, and allow him to lean on your strength."

"I understand."

"And remember, don't try to move him or hold him. If you sit quietly by his side, that will be the best."

"Thank you, so much. Tell the other doctors and nurses too, thank you."

"Hey, it's what we do," he smiled.

"Where is he?"

"This way."

They walked the long hallway to intensive care. There was a nurses' station in the middle of the large room, monitoring about a dozen other patients. Bunny passed by them, wondering about their situations. She had never been through anything like this before, and wondered if their children were as sick as Vincent. The nurse touched Bunny's arm and pointed, to show her where Vincent was lying. The doctor began to walk toward the elevator. Bunny waved good-bye, and whispered, "Thank you."

Bunny and the nurse walked to Vincent's bed. His head was completely covered with bandages. She could only see his eyes, and they were both blackened and swollen. His leg was in a cast up to the waist and suspended by a rope. One of his arms was in another cast. His exposed arm was attached to IVs and monitors. There was a drainage tube coming from underneath the bandages on his head that lead to a bag beside the bed. The amber goo dripping into the bag turned Bunny's stomach into a knot. The whole scene frightened her so much that she was afraid she would run out of the room. The nurse grabbed her by the hand. "He needs you," she said.

Bunny's fear was mixed with sadness. Her heart was breaking for Vincent. He was such a sick little boy.

"You have a very courageous little boy, Mrs. Muldare. He's doing very well."

Bunny pressed in toward Vincent in spite of the wires and tubes. "Mommy's here now, Vinnie. Don't worry. We'll get through this, you'll see."

Vincent didn't respond. His hand and neck jerked involuntarily in his sleep. Bunny was reminded of Vinnie as a newborn, and how he jerked as he was recovering from the heroin. She thought, well my poor baby, seems like your mother has done it to you again.

Bunny looked up at the nurse with tears in her eyes. Her expression said, I don't think I have the courage to handle this.

"Twenty minutes, Mrs. Muldare, then we need to let our patient get his rest."

"Yes," Bunny answered. She looked back toward Vincent, determined to do her best for him. She began to wonder what she could say to him, some positive memories she might use to feed his brain. She realized how few good memories she had to choose from.

Bunny took Vincent's weak, and jerking hand. She recalled what the doctor said: "Let him rely on your strength." Bunny took a deep breath and let out a sigh of relief. She thought, at least he's alive, and then said out loud. "Thank you, God. Thank you for Vinnie."

Psalm 13:1–2. How long wilt thou forget me, O Lord? for ever? How long wilt thou hide thy face from me? How long shall I take counsel in my soul, having sorrow in my heart daily? How long shall mine enemy be exalted over me?

Chapter 19

And Now for the News

"Good morning, boys and girls," said Miss Purdy.

"Good morning, Miss Purdy," they replied in unison.

"Everyone stand, please," she said. "And Rebecca, would you please start us off?"

"O beautiful for spacious skies, for amber waves of grain, for purple mountain majesties above the fruited plain.

America, America, God shed his grace on thee, and crown thy good with brotherhood from sea to shining sea.

O beautiful for pilgrim feet, whose stern, impassioned stress, a thoroughfare for freedom beat across the wilderness.

America, America, God mend thine every flaw, confirm thy soul in self control, thy liberty in law.

O beautiful for heroes proved in liberating strife, who more than self their country loved and mercy more than life.

America, America, may God thy gold refine till all success be nobleness and every gain divine.

O beautiful for patriot dream that sees beyond the years

thine alabaster cities gleam, undimmed by human tears. America, America, God shed his grace on thee and crown thy good with brotherhood from sea to shining sea."

"Thank you, children."

"Do you have a question, Mary Kemp?"

"Are there really alabaster cities in America?"

Miss Purdy answered, "That iss a good question Mary. Can someone answer that question?"

No one raised their hand, so Miss Purdy took a chance on Marshall Mueller. "Marshall, can you tell us where the alabaster cities are?"

"Umm, in California?"

"No, that wass de California gold rush."

Becky Perl raised her hand, "That iss de new heaven when Jesus comes back and sets up his kingdom on earth, like in Revelation."

"Yah," Miss Purdy answered. "And what other clue do we have that it iss in de new heaven?"

Marshall waved his hand wildly. This was his chance to save face. "Because nobody will be crying anymore."

"That iss exactly right, 'undimmed by human tears.'"

Miss Purdy asked, "What does this mean: 'O beautiful for patriot dream that sees beyond de years'?"

"Rachel," Miss Purdy pointed.

"It means that de people, de patriots, who built our country, had dreams that this could be made into a Godly country some day like in de new heaven. That iss why they 'endured stern, impassioned stress,' and why de founding fathers wrote de laws like they did, and they were willing to do anything to make it happen, because they had a dream to make America like God would want."

"It must have meant a lot to them, right children?" She surveyed the faces of her students and found it was one of those rare moments when she had the full attention of every child. "Let's turn on de news to see how well their dream iss holding up," Miss Purdy said.

"While we are listening, take out your tablets and get started on your arithmetic. Eighth graders, you will find your problems on de sixth grade board; yours are on de right. Sixth graders, yours are on de left. Eighth graders, we'll be continuing to diagram sentences as we were doing yesterday. When you are finished with your arithmetic problems, it will help you to look over de sentences I have written ahead of time."

Groans swelled from the older boys.

"No one asked your opinion," she said. "How can you write de laws of this Godly land, if you can not even diagram a sentence?" She turned to the old radio sitting high on a shelf against the wall and turned it on.

Gradually the volume came up. The deep voice of the announcer said, "And now for the local news." Miss Purdy adjusted the volume.

"There was a near fatal accident in Carlisle on Saturday. Nine-year-old Vincent Muldare was hit by a tractor trailer as he was crossing the street near his home. He is in critical condition at Good Samaritan Children's Hospital, in Harrisburg. There is a police investigation in progress, as there are allegations being made by an eyewitness who claims that the boy was pushed by his mother's live-in boyfriend."

All heads rose up from their school work. Gradually the whispers and gasps became uncontrollable. Miss Purdy tried for several minutes to quiet them down.

"Did they say our Vincent?" one of the students asked her neighbors.

"Yah! He wass hit by a truck!" they answered.

Marshall said breathlessly, "His new pappa pushed him, they said. Vincent iss not a bad boy. His pappa should never have done that."

"Iss he going to die?"

"He iss critical."

"What does critical mean?"

"That means he might die."

"Oh my goodness!"

"Children, children! Quiet." She clapped her hands to get their attention. "Children, look up here." Many of the children had begun to cry as the news sank in. "I am going to make a phone call. Shh. I am going to make a phone call so we can find out if this has been exaggerated. When I come back, I will tell you exactly what happened. Please, keep your talking down."

Miss Purdy ran into the hallway toward the kitchen. She picked up the receiver and cranked the handle. Sister Anna answered, "Hello."

"Hello, Sister Anna. Have you heard anything about Vincent's accident?" Miss Purdy asked frantically.

"No! Wass he in an accident?" asked Anna.

"That iss what they said on de radio this morning. Saturday it happened."

Anna asked, "Do you want me to call Sister Freida?"

"I think it would be a good idea," said Miss Purdy.

"Sister Freida iss still not talking to me."

"Well, maybe I should talk to Freida," suggested Miss Purdy. "After we are finished, you can call de other sisters to prayer?"

"Good idea," said Anna. "Let's do this. I will ring her, but I will not speak. You start talking as soon as she says hello, and tell her it iss about Vincent."

"Yah, will do."

Ring, ring. Ring, ring.

"Hello," answered Freida, in a trembling voice.

"Hello, Sister Freida, this is Miss Purdy and I'm c—"

"Miss Purdy? Oh Miss Purdy," Freida cried. "Vincent hass been in an accident, he wass hit by a truck and he iss in critical condition, and maybe her boyfriend pushed him into de road." Martin was standing beside her, his arms folded in front of him, as he rocked back and forth with worry; they had both listened to the same report.

"I know, Freida. De children and I heard it on de radio."

"That iss where we heard it too," said Freida, both hands clutching the phone.

"So you do not know any more than we do?" asked Miss Purdy.

"No, I am going to go to de hospital to see him though," said Freida. "They can not stop me. I surely can not just stand here wringing my hands, not knowing what iss happening. She grabbed Martin's hand."

"Sister Anna iss going to call everyone to prayer, Freida."

"Tell her thank you," Freida replied with genuine gratitude.

"I think it iss best that you are trying to see him," said Miss Purdy. "According to de radio he iss in critical condition."

"Yah, thank you for saying so, Miss Purdy. I must go, I have to get ready," Freida said. "Ask de children to pray too, Miss Purdy, would you?"

"Of course. Will you let us know, Freida? De children need to know how he iss as soon as possible. I will probably have to cancel class for today; they are terribly upset."

"I will call you tonight, that iss a promise," she replied and hung up the phone.

Freida faced off with Martin.

"Martin, if you are not going to take me, I will ride de buggy to de bus station, and you can figure out yourself how to get your horse back home."

"Freida, Vincent iss not ours anymore, whether we like it or not. His mother and de judge said we have no rights to see him anymore."

"What? You think just because a fool judge makes a fool's decision, that my son and I do not love each other anymore? He could die Martin! Do you not understand? I am not afraid of that judge—or his mother. I am going to do what I think Vincent would want, and what God would want. And I do not care what you think, or Miss Muldare thinks, or Judge Lenhart thinks. I am going to visit my critically injured son. If you will not go with me, I will ride horseback if that iss how it must be."

"Listen to yourself. How many people have to tell you, if this wass not God's will, it would not have happened?"

"Yah, well, I have heard plenty enough of opinions lately, and I am finished with other people and their cracked pot opinions. Do you want to hear what God says, 'I will tell you whom you should fear: Fear him who, after de killing of de body, hass power to throw you into hell.' That iss what God says."

Martin looked back into her determined eyes. He could see that words were not going to sway her. Besides, he respected her courage. However, he didn't have any hope that they would actually be allowed to see Vincent, no matter how determined they were.

She added, "Iss it God's will for Vincent to get hit by a truck and die in de hospital without his family and friends there to help him pass? I don't think so. I am going, Martin." She grabbed her coat, her bag, her bonnet.

"I am going," she repeated with absolute resolve. The screen door slammed behind her. She stepped off the porch into the pouring rain. It had been raining all night and into the morning. She tromped through the mud toward the barn as Martin watched from the window. She pulled her skirt hem up around her knees. The puddles were splashing cold against her bare legs. She struggled with harnessing an equally stubborn horse, which didn't care for the idea of heading out into a thunderstorm. Zach refused to hold still long enough for her to tie him to the buggy. "Zach! Hold still!" she ordered. He stomped in the mud in protest, splashing Freida in the face. She grabbed his mane and pulled herself up to ride bareback. She missed the first time sliding back down to the ground; mud went into her boot. She tried again. By this time she was crying in frustration. Martin threw up the window.

"Freida! I'm coming with you. Don't leave without me!"

Martin and a grateful Freida harnessed the buggy together and proceeded at a quick pace down the gravel drive and onto the main road. It was going to take about an hour to get to Carlisle, and another thirty minutes to get to Harrisburg, not including the transferring from one bus to another and then finding their way to the hospital. Martin suggested they stop at the Kemps so that Will could take them to the bus station. They couldn't leave the buggy at the bus station overnight. "Do you have money, in case we should have to stay over night?" asked Martin.

"Yah," Freida said.

When they arrived at the Kemps, the news had already been relayed over the phone. Sara put her arm around Freida. Freida was grateful for friends at a time like this. She had no time to consider petty squabbles. Will suggested, "I will take you in de van to Harrisburg."

Martin said, "You do not need to do that. We will let de bus driver drive us. He iss used to de confusion of de city. And to make matters worse, de weather iss bad."

"Then I will take you to de station."

Sara hurried to pack them a lunch. Just as they were getting ready to drive off, she ran out onto the porch and shouted, "Will!" The three looked in her direction to see her, barefoot, on the wet porch, with her shawl pulled over her head. Martin rolled down his window. She was waving a lunch basket and two umbrellas in the air. "Give them these umbrellas. They are going to need them," she shouted over the pounding rain.

"Bless you, Sara," called Martin. He wasn't sure whether she had heard him. Will ran back to the porch for the umbrellas and basket. Sara hurried back inside the house.

She poked her head back out the door, "God go with you," she shouted.

Sara could see Freida and Martin looking back at her through the steamy van window. Freida wiped the window and waved. She looked worried. Sara prayed, "Lord, how we need you. Vincent needs you, Martin and Freida need you. Heal Vincent's broken little body. Open de way for Martin and Freida to see their boy. We thank you, as we put all things into your loving care."

Will saw them off at the bus station, and Freida and Martin settled in for the ride to Harrisburg.

Martin asked, "What if his mother says we are not to see him?"

"I don't know. We will trust God to work it out," Freida said with resolve. She went back to praying as she stared out the window. She refused to be shaken by her fear that once again, God would fail them.

Martin looked at Freida's black leather boots. Her black cotton socks had stretched out and rolled down around her ankles. Mud had slopped up the sides of her shoes. He took her cold wet hand. It was gritty from the mud. Their wet umbrellas were wedged between the seat and the window. Freida untied her bonnet and set it on the window ledge to dry. "Let me see your hat, sweetheart," Freida said. Martin took it from his lap and handed it to her. She put it on the window ledge next to hers. He leaned his head back against the seat and watched as the rolling Pennsylvania country-side passed by.

As they approached Harrisburg, and the prospect of see-ing Vincent again was ever closer, Martin admitted, "I must say, Mamma, if we do get de chance to see Vincent, it will be good to see him again, no matter what de circumstances. Will it not?"

"More than good, Martin. When people say, 'My heart iss heavy,' now I know what they mean. My heart aches for Vincent every day. De hurt never goes away." Freida fought back the tears, as she had done every day for the past year. She took a deep, sad breath.

"I know, Mamma, we will see him again soon." Martin patted Freida's knee. He bumped the basket Sara had packed for them, which Freida held on her lap.

"What iss in there?" he asked, hoping to distract her from her thoughts.

She opened the basket and began to hand Martin a slice of Muenster cheese and a poppy seed roll. "Do you want butter, Martin?"

"Surely, Freida. Mmm, good cheese. Are you going to have some?"

"Yah, yah, I will," Freida replied. She thought, I will as soon as my stomach settles down.

She offered, "There is also milk, and apple pie. Nap-kin?"

"Thank you. We must thank Sister Sara for this when we get back home," Martin said. He hoped it would en-courage Freida to begin talking to their neighbors again.

"Yah, I will."

"We are lucky to have friends who will be praying for Vincent," reminded Martin.

"Yah, you are right, it iss a comfort," Freida conceded. "I hope I am not hindering their prayers by being unfriendly all these months."

Vincent's doctor ordered a CAT scan to be done on Sunday. It showed that they had managed to keep down the swelling in his brain. They began to ease off on the sedatives, but as of Monday evening, there had been no response from Vincent. The nurses comforted Bunny by saying, "These things take time. It is difficult to wait, but that is all we can do, for now. The tremors were still present on Monday, but not as frequent. The concern of the nurses was that if he didn't begin to come around by Tuesday, he would continue to deteriorate, and slip into a coma. Bunny had spent the entire weekend at the hospital. She was staying in a hospice, a block away. It wasn't great, but all Bunny needed was a shower and a place to sleep. Then she was back up first thing in the morning to sit by Vincent's bed. By Monday evening the nurse urged Bunny to take a break. She asked, "Are you taking the day off from work tomorrow, too, Mrs. Muldare?"

"Yes, why?" Bunny asked.

"Why don't you treat yourself to a nice dinner, hon, or an evening at home? I'll be here all night, and I promise I'll call you myself if there are any changes. The reason I'm saying this is because you are looking pretty tired. We don't want you to come down with something yourself. We need you to stay healthy."

"I could get a change of clothes while I'm at home," admitted Bunny.

"Honestly, I don't think you are going to miss anything, but I promise I'll call. You go ahead, honey. I'll take good care of him."

"Okay, I surrender," she sighed, looking up at the clock. It was only eight o'clock. If she left now, she would have time to wash her hair and pack several days' worth of clothing. "But call me," Bunny warned.

"I promise." said the nurse, raising her large hand up to her heart and making a cross. "Cross my heart," she reassured.

After arriving at the main bus terminal in Harrisburg, Freida and Martin still had to take two more buses to the hospital. It never occurred to them that people were staring at them. There was far too much on their minds to worry about the people passing them on the street. They took a wrong bus and got lost for several hours. Luckily, they found a compassionate bus driver who rode them around until they were back to where he picked them up. He told them, "Wait here for twenty minutes and get on C55. It'll say 'Prospect' right up on top of the window. If you watch you'll be able to see the hospital on your way in."

The streets had finally begun to dry out after the rain, along with Freida's shoes and socks. By the time they arrived at the hospital it was eight o'clock at night. It took some time for them to figure out the revolving door. Once that problem was solved, they read a sign on the wall: "Visiting hours end at 9:00 P.M." A gray- haired lady sitting at a desk under the sign told them to take the elevator to intensive care, fifth floor. The carpeted floors, chrome furniture, and fluorescent lights were entirely foreign to their everyday lives. Freida and Martin were beginning to feel their stomachs and knees tense as the elevator began its slow ascent. When the stainless steel doors finally opened, they stepped into an area that looked like something out of a science fiction movie, as if they were entering a spaceship. The nurses' station was directly in front of them. As they approached, a nurse said, "Can I help you?"

"We came to visit our boy, Vincent Muldare," said Freida.

Martin looked around the room, noticing it was round.
The beds surrounded the nurses' station so that they were
able to see every bed from where they stood.

"Vincent Muldare?" she asked.

"Yah." she affirmed. Freida blinked.

"His mother has already been here several times, and
you don't look anything like her," the nurse said.

Freida tapped her umbrella on the tile floor and protested, "Iss his mother de only one allowed to visit?"

"No, but you said you were his parents, and I know you
are not. We can't let just anyone in here. You'll have to go
now, before I call security."

"We are not just anybody," Freida protested again. "We
took care of him for seven years!"

Down the row of patients about five or six beds away,
there was a child screaming as if he had something over his
mouth. All three looked in that direction. A second nurse
flew to his bedside as the screams continued.

"That iss Vincent!" said Martin.

The nurse called excitedly to the head nurse, "Mrs. B.,
come down here, stat."

The three of them started running toward Vincent's bed.
"Hold them here!" yelled the nurse to the two male orderlies. The men intercepted Martin and Freida as they
struggled to pass.

"Let me go!" screamed Freida, but he persisted in holding her wrist and refused let go.

Martin struggled to see what was happening to Vincent.
He watched as Vincent tossed himself from side to side.

Vincent kept groaning, "Mamma, Pappa, Mamma,
Pappa. Over here, over here!" Bed rails and hospital equipment clattered as he rolled from side to side.

"I can't contain him! He's going to hurt himself; we must keep him still," said the nurse's aide. "You better let those people come down here quick; look at his diastolic rate."

"Let them go," yelled the head nurse to the orderlies. Martin and Freida ran directly to Vincent's side.

Vincent settled down as soon as they came into view, but Martin and Freida stopped short when they got a look at him. The nurse checked all of the places his tubes and monitors were attached. She said apologetically, "You two must be just what the doctor ordered. It sometimes takes some jarring, a pleasant memory, an old friend or something of that nature to bring them around. This was one of the most enthusiastic re-entries I've ever seen. Martin and Freida stood in disbelief. They were shocked by the number of bandages. His head was completely covered except for his eyes, his forehead, and a little bit of hair on top. They had removed the drainage tube from his skull, but the intravenous feeding tubes, antibiotic drip, heart monitor wires and catheter bag draped the bed. Martin fingered the pulley at the foot of the cast, which was suspended from a bar over his bed as he stared down at the unrecognizable figure. Vincent paid no attention to any of that. He could only look at his parents with a smile, a smile that no one could appreciate under all of his bandages. All Vincent knew was that before him stood the two people he wanted to wake up and see again more than anyone else in the world. Vincent looked at them through his two blackened eyes. "It's me, Pappa!" His sweet familiar voice broke softly through the silence. "What are we doing in here?" he asked.

Vincent had never seen his father break down into sobs before. Martin held on to Vincent's good hand. Kneeling by his bed, he rubbed the little hand back and forth against his hairy cheek. Martin said, "Vincent, we are so glad to see you again. I am so sorry for what hass happened, son. I wass afraid I wass never going to see you again."

Vincent didn't like to see his parents crying anytime, but it was especially hard to see his pappa cry. Martin wiped his nose on his sleeve. Vincent didn't understand. "Wass I in an accident or something?"

Freida said, "Yah, my dear one, you were. We were so worried about you." Then Freida asked, "Iss there anywhere you don't hurt?"

The nurse stood eavesdropping from the nurses' station.

He answered, "I don't hurt too much."

Freida exclaimed, "It iss such a relief for Mamma to know you are going to be all right."

Martin got up to let Freida get closer. "Can I put my head on your chest?" asked Freida.

Vincent reached with his good arm to pull her close. "Mamma, I have been missing you for so long. I wass dreaming that I wass trying and trying to get home, but de people were keeping me kidnapped and not letting me go. Have I been asleep for a very long time?"

She was puzzled by the question, but answered, "It seems like a very long time, yah." She laid her head on his chest, savoring the moment. He patted her head. As he lay on his back his tears started getting into his bandages.

When Freida rose up, she realized his bandages were getting damp. She took her hanky from her skirt pocket and handed it to Vincent. "Here, wipe your eyes," she said. "You are getting your bandages wet."

"You did not use this already, did you?" Vincent asked.

"No!" said Freida.

"Just checking," he said smiling through his tears. He raised his shaky hand slowly and awkwardly toward his face.

"Here," said Freida, "let me help you."

Vincent looked over at his father. "I want to go home, Pappa," he said through his broken jaw. "I can't stay here one more day. I have a feeling like something bad will happen."

"We will see what we can do," offered Martin, his voice quivering. He remembered what he had heard on the radio, about the eyewitness seeing Bunny's boyfriend push him. He whispered, "We will take it one day at a time." Martin knew it was just a matter of time before Bunny would put a stop to their visits. They stayed for what was left of the hour. They tried to ask him more about the accident, though he didn't remember much. They asked about Bunny's apartment, Vincent's new school, but Vincent told them he couldn't remember very much about it, that it seemed like a dream, and he only wanted to listen to them talk. In reality he didn't know what they were talking about. He asked about Miss Purdy, about Marshall, about his duck, his horse, the farm, Grandmamma and Grandpappa Dunkin, Grandmamma Mueller and all his cousins, everything he could think of.

Freida called Miss Purdy that night from the hotel room. "He iss going to be all right!"

"You got to see him then?" asked Miss Purdy excitedly.

"Yah. He iss one big bandage like a big round snowman, but they were able to put him back together again. De nurses told us that they had been waiting for days for him to come out of his unconsciousness, and when he heard our voices, it wass de very thing to wake him up again! They are not sure if he will be able to walk without a limp. He broke his hip. They must wait and see. But his brain seems to be working fine. That wass de most serious problem for him. He iss having trouble remembering new things, but he remembers all de old things. He asked about you, Miss Purdy."

"Sister Freida, this iss such good news. I'll tell de church to continue to pray, you can be sure." Then Miss Purdy asked, "Do you want to tell Vincent we are coming to visit, or shall we keep it a secret?"

"When are you coming? I can not keep something like that a surprise for too long." Freida sounded excited.

Miss Purdy asked, "Do you think de hospital will have a problem with us coming?"

"Well, this iss what de nurse told us before we were leaving: Her main interest iss in her patient, and she said it wass clear that Vincent wanted us there. And she said we can visit as often as we want provided his mamma does not stop us. But she said she would explain to his mamma that seeing us would help his memory."

"Does that include de children and me?" asked Miss Purdy.

"De nurse told us that since he iss awake now, they will be moving him to his own room. Then it probably will not matter if de children come. But, yah, she said anybody who can keep Vincent out of de dumps iss welcome to visit."

Miss Purdy said, "If I know Vincent, it will be de other way around. Vincent will not let any visitors leave de hospital feeling in de dumps."

Freida forgot herself and laughed out loud. "It wass so very good to see him again, I can not even say it in words. Do you know that little pushstik told us we smelled funny?"

"He did?" said Miss Purdy.

"Yah, he said we smelled like de barn. But then he told us it smells good to him. He even said de smell wass what woke him up!"

Miss Purdy laughed. "He always did have a good sniffer. Remember? I wonder why you would smell like de barn?" asked Miss Purdy.

Freida answered, "Probably because when it wass raining this morning I got a bucket load of horse schtinkum in my boot."

Martin added, "If it woke Vincent up out of a coma, imagine what it wass doing to everyone else?"

Miss Purdy laughed. "That sounds like our Vincent to tell you about it. Now if there iss anything you need, Sister Freida, you must let us know. De deacons told me to tell you two that hotel rooms are expensive, and de church will gladly help you out if you need it."

"Thank you, Miss Purdy. I will tell Martin."

"Oh, and shall we keep our visit a secret?" Miss Purdy asked again.

"I will try," said Freida.

"Iss there a limit on de number of visitors he can have at one time?"

"I think de sign said five. But there are so many questions I am unsure of. I promise you, I will find out everything tomorrow, and call you then."

"All right, Sister Freida. This iss very good news—very good news. I will tell de children that our Vincent iss going to be good as new. Glory to God! God bless you, Freida."

"God bless you, Miss Purdy."

Suddenly Freida let out a short little yelp.

"What iss de matter?" asked Miss Purdy at the other end of the line.

Freida said, "Martin, what iss happening to de bed?"

Martin said, "I put a quarter in it. Huck, yuk."

"You put a quarter in de bed?"

"In this hole, see it there." He pointed to a coin box at the end of the bed.

"I hope it iss not going to be jiggling like this forever. How can we sleep?"

Martin mumbled something, then Miss Purdy could hear Freida giggling. "You two have a nice trip in de big city."

"Yah, we will probably survive it," said Freida.

"Love you, Freida," Miss Purdy said.

"We love you too. Thank you for all your praying for us," said Freida over the vibrating bed.

"Night," said Miss Purdy.

"Night."

The next day, the doctors were with Vincent in the morning. Nurse B. told Martin and Freida to wait in the waiting room until they could go in. It was a small room separated just to the right of the elevator doors. When Bunny got off the elevator she could see the Muellers through the open waiting room door. They never saw Bunny, but she recognized them immediately.

Bunny didn't realize that Vincent had regained consciousness while the Muellers were visiting, and nor did she know that Vinnie didn't remember who she was. The head nurse made a decision during the night, after witnessing how successful the Muellers' visit was, that she would do some investigating of her own on her computer. She searched until she came up with the newspaper's account of the arrest and subsequent custody hearing. What she discovered convinced her that the Muellers had gotten a raw deal. There was no doubt in her mind that it was the Muellers who jarred Vincent into consciousness, and it was possible, that had they not shown up Vincent could have lost his will to live and never regained consciousness. Vincent's nurse also knew that it wasn't clear to Bunny how important it was that he was finally conscious again, and they should all be grateful to the Muellers for bringing him out. She wished she had not let the time get away from her before Miss Muldare left the house. She had tried to call, but Bunny had already left. The nurse's original intent was to let Bunny sleep as long as she could, and then call. If only she had been able to reach her in time, things would probably unfold more smoothly this morning. She considered what would have happened had the Muellers arrived before Bunny left for the evening, and was glad she told Miss Muldare to go home when she did. Who knows what would have happened if Vincent had thrashed around in his bed as his custody battle was reenacted in the middle of the intensive care unit.

Suddenly Bunny stormed the nurses' station. "What are those people doing in the waiting room!? You didn't let them in here last night, did you?"

"Miss Muldare, would you please lower your voice? You are disturbing the patients," said the head nurse. "Now settle yourself down and we will discuss this calmly. Are you referring to his adoptive parents?" asked Nurse B., looking up from her paper and coffee, tucking her chin to see over her half glasses. She had the husky, confident voice of a large middle-aged black woman.

"The Amish people," Bunny replied indignantly, but whispering.

"His adoptive mother and father?" she asked in the same calm tone.

"Yes! They are not supposed to have anything to do with him anymore. He needs to get adjusted to his new life. How can he do that if you let them in here? For all we know, they came to take him back home."

"They aren't trying to take him anywhere. They are just visiting. I'm sorry you had to be surprised by this, but when I tried to call you this morning, evidently you had already left your apartment."

"But I'm his mother—not them! And you, nurse," Bunny squinted at the name plate on her uniform, Bart—, Barti—, you are butting in where you don't belong."

The nurse stood, realizing this was going to require her full attention. She planted her feet firmly on her turf and folded her formidable arms. "And I am his nurse! Getting him well is my first priority. There is one extremely important factor that will determine whether my patient gets better, and that is the boy's happiness—not your happiness, Miss Muldare. If we want him to heal, we're going to have to keep him from being depressed. His brain needs to fire up some pleasant memories to get it working again. Letting him visit with his old family seems to be the perfect solution. 'A cheerful heart is good medicine, but a crushed spirit dries the bones.' And I didn't learn that from the Mennonites, Ms. Muldare. I read it in the Bible."

"I'm going to talk to your supervisor," threatened Bunny. Bunny pushed the button to the elevator.

The nurse took advantage of the time she had before the elevator doors opened. "Unless you want your boy to hate you," she quietly warned Bunny, "you are going to have to consent to them visiting. And, for another thing, I have been told there is a possibility that his little Mennonite friends are going to be visiting this weekend. Shall we tell him the hospital staff was all for it, but you refused?" she whispered. "Don't you care whether your boy gets better, Ms. Muldare?"

Bunny stepped into the elevator and disappeared behind the elevator doors. On her way up to the administrative offices Bunny wondered, how did the nurse know they were Mennonite? Everybody thinks they're Amish. I should probably read what the stinkin' newspaper is spreading around. And how does she know how Vinnie feels? He's unconscious, for heaven's sakes. Somebody's gossiping, as usual. She and her nurse buddies are making their own assumptions over coffee. I wonder how happy he'll be when he has to go back home without his Mennonite family. Maybe I should take that nurse home with me, and she can try to "cheer him up" then. Some people think they are so damned important just because they have a job with a little authority. She likes power, I'll show her power. I'll show her you don't mess with Mom!

Freida turned to Martin as they waited in the waiting room, "Too bad we had to get lost yesterday. We had such a nice visit, but it wass so short."

"We will see him soon. The doctors will be finished before you know it, Mamma."

"Praise to Jesus, he iss alive."

"Yah, praise you, Lord Jesus."

Revelation 21:1–6. And I saw a new heaven and a new earth: for the first earth were passed away; and there was no more sea.

And I John saw the holy city, new Jerusalem, coming down from God out of heaven, prepared as a bride adorned for her husband.

And I heard a great voice out of heaven saying, Behold, the tabernacle of God is with men, and he will dwell with them, and they shall be his people, and God himself shall be with them, and be their God.

And God shall wipe away all tears from their eyes; and there shall be no more death, neither shall there be any more pain: for the former things are passed away. And he that sat upon the throne said, Behold, I make all things new. And he said unto me, Write: for these words are true and faithful.

And he said unto me, It is done. I am the Alpha and Omega, the beginning and the end. I will give unto him that is athirst of the fountain of the water of life freely.

Chapter 20

Good Samaritan

$\mathcal{F}$ive days seemed like an eternity, but finally the children arrived at the hospital. Their 1800s apparel looked terribly out of place in the high-tech surroundings of the hospital lobby, the girls in their colored frocks and bonnets, the boys in their hats and homemade jackets. The towering lobby windows faced the street, where bulldozers and city buses competed for space. Inside, the walls were faced with shining black granite. "Look at de walls," one of the children said. "It looks like Alabaster." The carpets had an abstract twirling pattern that some of the children were following with their footsteps, the pattern leading them inside spiraling circles to nowhere. A few of the children were carrying baskets of food. Each face was freshly scrubbed, their cheeks still rosy from being outside.

The tussling and giggling were beginning to disturb Miss Purdy. She turned to them and said, "This iss a hospital. We cannot act like a bunch of wild monkeys. We are going to walk single file into de elevator, and slowly, we will walk single file out of de elevator. Understood?"

She waited until every child had nodded.

She added, "Until we reach Vincent's room, do not speak. It was very difficult for them to keep quiet when the elevator started to move. Nevertheless, all that was heard were a few children rushing to hold their breath as if a rollercoaster ride were about to begin.

When the doors opened they crept out cautiously, wide-eyed. It was like nothing they had ever seen before. But where was Vincent? They soon found out he had been transferred from intensive care to a room of his own. Miss Purdy pulled a piece of paper from her apron pocket and checked the room number written on it against the numbers on the wall. She pointed in the direction that they would be walking. They followed a long, wide hallway, until they came to a corner with a window. When they passed the window and looked down, it was dizzying. A barn loft was as high as they had ever been, and this was much higher than that; they were on the fifth floor. They noticed the perfectly clean and shining tile floors, and the smell of chemicals in the air, like floor polish mixed with alcohol. There were machines beeping and equipment dangling in every room. A very sick boy was wheeled past them in a wheelchair. Most of his hair was gone and his skin had a yellow cast. The children stared, as did the sick child. "Single file," reminded Miss Purdy, hoping to distract. There was one little girl, the youngest, who couldn't resist waving at him as she passed.

The nurses stopped what they were doing to watch with amazement at their orderly procession. By this time the girls had pushed their bonnets back onto their shoulders, and the boys were carrying their hats in their hands. The nurses waved in unison, some calling, "Hi, there," some smiling, some staring in curiosity. Martin and Freida met them in the hallway. There were plenty of hugs and kisses for Freida and Martin. Only one child had to be reminded not to speak.

"Shh. You'll ruin de surprise," whispered Miss Purdy.

Martin led them to the entrance of Vincent's room. He signaled them to wait there quietly.

Martin and Freida looked down on their sleeping little boy. The same eyes that had been black and blue only a few days ago were now a rosy purple, and the tremors were all but gone. Though his head was still in bandages, enough of them had been removed that he was at least recognizable. Vincent had been in the hospital for nearly a week, and was beginning to put together the pieces of his most recent memories—Bunny, Michael, his new school, the accident. He remembered almost everything prior to arriving at Bunny's apartment, but the most recent memories were harder to recall. The doctor had explained to Bunny that she shouldn't take it personally. It didn't reflect on her as a mother; it was a common phenomenon among brain trauma patients to be unable to recall the most recent memories. Bunny was convinced by Nurse B. that allowing his Mennonite friends to visit would help in his full recovery. And yet, Bunny could not help but stew about the fact that Vincent was reuniting with his Mennonite friends today. She had planned to stay home until evening visiting hours, but it was too difficult to stay away. She was on her way.

Martin spoke into Vincent's ear, "Are you going to wake up? You have visitors today." Vincent lifted his head slightly.

"Miss Purdy!" exclaimed Vincent, bleary-eyed.

"Hello, Vincent. My, it iss so good to see you again. We brought you some visitors."

"Hi, Vincent," said some of the children tentatively. Most were too intimidated by his bandages to get too close.

Freida suggested, "Martin and I will sit out here, to make more room." She and Martin sat in the hallway, directly across from the doorway where they could still see what was going on.

Vincent grabbed for his new glasses so he could see who was there. He stuck one arm of his glasses under his bandage. The other arm he had to ease over his bad ear outside the bandages. He winced. The children winced. That was the expression he caught on their faces when they came into focus. He smiled, a broad happy smile, though they couldn't see it through his bandages.

"Hi, Vincent," they all repeated.

"Am I dreaming? Is this real?" He was so excited he tried to sit up, but the cast around his hip caused him to fall back again. "Can you stand over on that side," he asked, "so I can see you better?" They obediently shuffled to the side of the room. The nurse elevated the bed slightly.

"We have missed you, Vincent," one girl said.

"Yah," said another boy Vincent's age. The boy looked a little frightened like he was talking to a ghost.

Vincent began to point to each child, recalling their names. "Samuel, Nathan, Joseph, Abigail, Holly, and Mary Louise," he said, jaw clenched. The children were pleased to be able to be there for their classmate and friend—no matter how intimidating the hospital was.

Miss Purdy asked, "Why are you talking like that? Why can't you open your mouth all de way?"

Vincent explained, "Because they wired my jaw shut."

"What did you hurt?" asked Mary Louise.

"We want to hear how it happened," said Nathan.

"Yah," said Joseph.

"Well ya see," started Vincent boldly, "my stepfather, I mean, my mom's boyfriend, wass chasing me around de house."

Nurse B. stopped short. It was the first time the nurse or his parents heard about that.

"Then I ran out of de house. It iss an apartment building really, not a house," he explained. "And Michael wass right behind me, so I flew down de steps as fast as I could. And then, I ran between two cars parked on de side of de road, only I did not see de truck that was coming, and—" Vincent seemed to go into a daydream. He paused. At that moment Vincent remembered Michael's arm shoving his back. It startled him. He decided to try to forget it.

"What kind of truck?"

"Peterbilt, eighteen wheeler."

"Ugh," the boys gasped. "Those things are big monsters!" said Nathan.

"How do you know it wass a Peterbilt?" Joseph asked.

"Cause it wass de last thing I saw just before it hit me!" They laughed. Then feeling it might not be appropriate, they began to squirm.

Vincent was beginning to get wound up with excitement. He loved the audience. "It wass huge!" he said. "I am seeing this thing coming right for me. De breaks were squealing, RRRRRR! He wass blowing his horn, but by de time I got turned around to get back, he smacked me real hard, Boom, going about sixty-five miles an hour."

Martin, who now stood in the doorway, cleared his throat.

"Okay, twenty miles an hour," revised Vincent.

"Do you remember anything after that?" Mary Louise asked.

"Yah, I remember my ear and my finger got stuck up inside de grill that goes across de front. You know."

"Yah?" they replied in chorus.

And then de truck driver stopped dead, right in de middle of de road, but I went flying, except for my ear and my finger. They were still stuck in de grate and got yanked right off."

"Ugh!" they all gasped. Most of the girls were holding their stomachs.

Vincent thoroughly enjoyed their squirms and decided to see if he could make it happen again.

"I could feel my ear pulling away, but there wass nothing I could do about it. I just keep sailing through de air without my ear or my finger. I wass not so worried about my finger at that time as I wass worried about de parked car that I was about to smash into."

"Did they sew it back on?"

"They sewed on my ear, at least most of it, but we will not be going into that." Vincent looked at his Dad, embarrassed, half expecting him to tell the secret.

"Go on, son. Tell them how de doctors fixed it," he urged.

Vincent sighed, "They took a piece of skin off my buttoushky and stuck it on where my ear wass."

"Really," they said in amazement and laughter.

"From your buttoushky?" laughed Samuel. He wanted to hear Vincent admit it one more time.

Martin teased, "Yah. You have seen de old men with hair growing out of their ears, haven't you?"

"Yah," they replied.

"That iss how it got there," Martin said straight-faced. To his amazement, most of them believed him.

"That wass not funny, Pappa."

Martin didn't recant.

Vincent said, "If it iss true, Pappa, where did you get those two hairs sticking out of your ear?"

"My ear?" asked Martin.

"Yah, your ear. No one else around here hass hair sticking out of their ears," said Vincent.

Martin stuck his finger in his ear. "Well would you look at that. You are right. Must be from scratching."

"Scratching?" someone asked.

"Yah. Didn't your mother ever tell you to stop scratching? You must be very careful when you scratch your head not to scratch somewhere else, because you can spread de hair seeds around, and when you grow up you will find hair has begun to sprout all over in unexpected places, like out of your ears, or off de end of your nose. See, you scratch your head like this, and then you scratch your nose like that, then someday, de hair seeds will begin to sprout. No, you must never scratch."

One of the little girls gasped.

"Pappa stop that," Vincent laughed.

Miss Purdy said, "Brother Martin, must I put you in de corner?"

Martin chuckled.

"How did they wire your jaw shut?" asked Holly.

"Well, they took a piece of wire, and they jammed it through my jaw, and they wound it around my bottom jaw, and then they pulled on it reallll tight, sort of like a fish hook. You know how you can get it in, but you can't get it out?" he asked.

"Yah."

"Oh my goodness," the little girl said.

This wass de best time Vincent had since he left home. "Then they cranked it around and around, and around and around, reallll tight, so now I cannot open my mouth. It iss hooked on like a fish hook."

"I bet Becky Perl will be glad to hear this," said Joseph.

Vincent said, "Aww, she says, but I know she loves me." He was sure she would protest when they told her what he said.

"How do you eat?" asked the girl holding her stomach.

"Through a straw," he said matter-of-factly. He picked up a glass with goopy white liquid in it.

"What iss that?" she asked.

"Cream of wheat. That iss about de best thing they have to eat in this place. They have ice cream, but something iss not right with it. It tastes like it isss not real milk, and all of that sugar gets to be sickening. No offense."

"None taken," said the nurse. She was amazed by how well he was working this crowd. She had seen Vincent when he was with Bunny, but this was a whole new side of him she had never seen.

The doctor appeared in the doorway with his clipboard in hand. "Hello, Vincent. Wow, look at all the friends you have visiting today."

"Yah! And my teacher iss here too, Miss Purdy." Vincent pointed right at her. The doctor looked to see.

She looked down at the floor, hoping the moment would pass quickly. The doctor noticed she was blushing. He was flattered.

"Nice to meet you," said the doctor.

Miss Purdy lifted her hand, gesturing a quick hello. "And you, as well," she replied, then went back to staring at the floor.

He announced, "I hate to interrupt, but this should take only a minute. We need to check wonder boy's progress."

"Wonder boy!?" asked Samuel a little indignant at such a noble title.

The doctor explained, "That's what the staff has named him. We weren't convinced that Vincent would make it. But he's proved everybody wrong."

"Ohh," Samuel replied, uncomfortable that his friend was so close to death.

All the children backed up, certain that they were in the way. The nurse pulled the privacy curtain around Vincent's bed. The children waited in silence while they were left wondering what was going on behind the white curtain.

The nurse took Vincent's temperature, while the doctor inspected his wounds. The nurse cranked down the bed so the doctor could get a better look at his leg. The bed went down slowly, click, click, click with each rotation of the handle. Every time the bed clicked Vincent yelled, "Ow." Click, "Ow", click, "Ow!" The children grimaced.

"Vincent, you tell those poor children you are kidding," said the nurse.

"Just kidding, just kidding," he admitted.

"You are a rat, wonder boy," someone complained.

Vincent only laughed at them.

The curtain swung open in just a few minutes, as predicted. "Looks good, Vincent," said the doctor. "Excellent, in fact. See you tomorrow." He waved at everyone as he was leaving the room. He poked his head back through the door, "No one in here needs a shot, do they?" he asked.

They all shook their heads no.

"Oh well, just thought I'd ask," he smiled. "You sure?" he asked again.

"No," they answered, out loud this time.

"Okay, okay, just asking, just asking."

"That wass Doctor Waits. He said if I had not broken my jaw, I probably would have died from smashing my head. He iss a good doctor. I like him a lot," said Vincent. He took a deep breath.

There was a pause in the conversation.

"So, anybody want to hear what happened next?" he asked.

"Yah," they agreed.

"Well, after I went sailing through de air, I smashed into de back of de parked car. My chin smashed through de back of de window, and that iss when my jaw broke. It popped out of de socket. My mom, my new mom, told me it wass sticking out crooked on one side, kind of like a gorilla with a bad attitude. That iss what she said anyway. They are not sure when I broke my back. I think it wass when de truck hit me. One of de vertebrates in my back—"

"You mean vertebrae?" said Nurse B.

"Yah, vertebrae. It broke, so they hammered this steel rod through there about a foot long. They just kept hammering and hammering, tink, tink, tink, until they got it all de way up my back."

"Vincent!" said the nurse. "You didn't even break your back!"

The girls were starting to look a little sick, and so were the boys for that matter. Some of the bigger boys were starting to laugh as they looked down the row of horrified faces.

"I wass just kidding about hammering de rod," he laughed, "my back iss not really broken."

They looked relieved. "Ugh, that makes my stomach go weird inside," said one of the girls. "Don't do that!"

Vincent laughed again. "I am sorry, well a little sorry."

"Does it still hurt, Vincent?" the littlest one said.

"Nah." He clanked the cast on his arm against the one on his leg. "They got it all covered up so nothing can hurt it again until it heals. If it starts to hurt, I push this button, and it gives me some medicine to make it better. Mostly, though, it puts me to sleep."

"How long do you have to be in de hospital?" asked Nathan Kemp, one of Sara and Will's children.

"They think I will be leaving about Christmas."

"That iss about two months then," said the boy.

"Yes, it is," said an unfamiliar voice, a young feminine voice.

"Hi, Mom. These are my friends!"

"I see that. Hello," she sang, friendly but reserved. "I just popped in for a short minute to see how the party was going."

"It iss de best thing that ever happened," said Vincent. She leaned over and Vincent gave her a hug. "Thanks, Mom."

Bunny said, "I knew you would really like that." She kissed Vincent on the forehead.

"Yah, thanks Mom."

"You're welcome. I don't want to hold things up though, so I'll just leave you kids to your party, and I'll be back tonight." Bunny looked at Mr. and Mrs. Mueller. They were looking awkwardly at her, as if they wanted to somehow become invisible. Bunny thought to herself, that makes three of us. But instead she chirped, cheerfully, "See you later."

Nurse B. watched her with her eyes as she left the room.

After they could hear her footsteps disappearing down the hallway Mary Louise asked, "Do you like your new mom, Vincent?"

"I love my new mom," he said. "A lot."

Miss Purdy was surprised. She looked at Freida, who was puckering her mouth and playing with the corner of her apron. Martin patted her on the shoulder. Everyone looked a little uncomfortable.

Vincent explained, "When I first woke up there wass a lot of things that I could not remember. It wass like when you stand at de bottom of de steps scratching your head and saying to yourself, what am I doing here? There must be some reason I wanted to go up de steps. It iss like that. You know it should make sense but it doesn't. It makes you kind of embarrassed, like maybe you are going crazy and will not admit it. When my mom came in for de first time and said hello, I said, 'Hello, who are you?' I hurt her feelings, and it made her cry. I felt so sorry, but I did not know her, at least not at first. But now I do."

No one knew what to say.

Vincent wanted to change the subject. "Do you want to see something?" He took the remote for the TV from his nightstand. He started flicking through the channels on the TV. The children sounded like foot soldiers as they turned around to look.

"Are you changing de picture with that thing in your hand?" they asked.

"Yah! There are different stations, or channels, they call them. Every time that you hit de channel button it switches to a new picture."

"Ooooh."

"Hey, look at that one."

Vincent paused on the channel. An advertisement came on for chewing gum, and a young couple in swimming suits started kissing under a waterfall. Miss Purdy grabbed the remote and tried to turn it off, but couldn't figure it out. Vincent turned it off for her. She said, "That will be enough of that."

Vincent replied, "But, I can turn on some music for them? There iss a Christian channel I can turn on. It iss all hymns," he suggested.

Miss Purdy took the remote back from Vincent. "What do I do?"

Martin said, "Already she iss curious."

Miss Purdy explained, "If somebody iss going to control this ungodly thing, I want it to be me."

"Push FM."

"Done. What iss next?"

"Push number 4."

She pushed number five by mistake. The radio blared. It was Aretha Franklin singing "R-E-S-P-E-C-T." She sang: "Wahhhh! When I get home. Sock it to me, sock it to me, sock it to me, sock it to me. Wahhhh!" The children started giggling and jumping up and down with excitement. Two of the boys started boxing to the rhythm. Miss Purdy handed the remote to Vincent to turn off, but it fell between the bed rails and the mattress. Miss Purdy reached for it, but it slipped to the floor. "Wahhhh! Sock it to me, sock it to me, sock it to me, sock it to me." Miss Purdy dove underneath the bed. Finally the music stopped. Silence fell. All giggling and fooling around stopped. When they looked down at the floor, all that they could see of Miss Purdy were her black stockings and black oxford shoes. She slid out from underneath the bed with as much dignity as she could under the circumstances. "Enough with de TV re-motor." She tossed it into the drawer of the nightstand. The children didn't dare move or speak. It was very quiet in the room. Some of them were sucking in their cheeks for fear their smiles would be discovered.

Vincent said, "I'm sorry, Miss Purdy. It wass all an accident. Number four iss always hymns," he explained.

"I know it wass an accident, Vincent. I wass de one who pushed de wrong number. It iss just another example of why we do not bother with such things. It iss something we do not need in our lives." She straightened her hair and brushed off her long skirt. She gave a quick side glance at the only adult in the room, Martin.

"Yah, Miss Purdy," said Vincent. "It wass kind of a silly song. I wonder why anybody would want to get socked when they get home." He couldn't help himself. He started giggling. They all started giggling, even Martin and Freida.

Martin was no help. He added, "Hey sweetheart, come to Pappa so I can give you a good sock in de head."

Everyone howled with laughter—except Miss Purdy.

Finally, Vincent started to recover and tried to apologize. "I'm sorry, Miss Purdy."

"I know you are, Vincent. Let us go on with our visit as before." She glared at Martin.

"Here iss my old glasses." He pulled the mangled mess of metal out of the drawer, and handed it to Miss Purdy as a kind of peace offering. She held them up for the children to see.

"De truck driver gave me this too." He held up a Peterbilt emblem about the size of a large belt buckle from the front of the truck. "He iss a really nice man. His handle iss 'Rollover.'"

"What iss a handle?" they asked.

"It iss what he calls himself on his CB radio. De truck drivers talk to each other on it. I asked him if he ever rolled over and he said no, only for his wife. He said he learned it from his old dog, Easy. I think she might be a little bit bossy, his wife that is. He wass asking me again and again if he could buy me something, so I asked him for a piece from his truck, for like a souvenir. That iss when he gave me this name piece thing." They began to pass it around carefully as if they were handling an antique.

"Where iss Marshall?" asked Vincent with concern.

"He could not come because he did not get picked," admitted the youngest girl sadly.

Vincent looked at Miss Purdy.

Miss Purdy explained, "We had to pick names out of a hat because everyone wanted to come, but we were only allowed to bring six. The hospital said only five, but your mamma, Freida, begged for one more, so we were allowed to bring six."

"Marshall wass real sad, Vincent. He started crying in front of everybody," said the youngest girl.

"You didn't have to tell that," said the older Kemp boy.

"Everybody already knows," she replied defensively. "I tried to tell him, yesterday, he could have my ticket, but he said it would not be fair. I know he wanted it, but he wouldn't take it."

Vincent said, "Tell him he can have my snake."

"I already have your snake, said the older Kemp boy, but when spring comes I can give it to Marshall if you want.

"Hey, what are you doing with my snake?" asked Vincent.

"Your mamma, see, well, my mamma iss always finding reasons for us to go over to your house and bother your mamma." He forgot Freida was sitting in the hallway behind him. "She says your mamma iss spending too much time in de house. So anyway, my mamma told me to go over and tell your mamma she needed to borrow your mamma's broom. See?"

"Yah?" said Vincent, still disturbed that his snake was gone.

"And my mamma says to me: 'If she asks you why I need her broom, just tell her my broom broke.' I told her if she wanted to lie, she ought to do it herself, not make me do it. She gave me her real mean look. Then she laid her broom against a chair and stomped on it. It wass broke, all right, real broke," he laughed. "So I go over there, to your house, and she gave me de broom without asking any questions; I did not even need to explain after all. Pappa made her a new broom though, so it iss okay. And then your mamma says to me: 'Joseph, will you pitch this snake somewhere far, far away?' and she pointed at the aquarium. I said, 'Can I have de aquarium too?' And she said: 'If you are going to pitch it, what do you need with de aquarium?' I couldn't think of anything, so I got de snake out, and I pitched it under my house. It got bigger, Vincent. A lot bigger."

"How much bigger?" asked Vincent.

"It wass maybe about three feet, and I would say last time I saw it, he wass about maybe five feet."

"You pitched it under your house?" Vincent protested, worried the snake would get lost.

"Well, that iss throwing him kind of far away. It iss far away for a snake," Joseph said in defense.

Vincent explained, "But, what if it gets lost?"

"Don't worry, it iss still there. Every once in a while I see it hanging around in de sun, so I just pitch it back under there before my mamma sees it. He iss not hurting anything except maybe a mouse or two now and then. He likes it under there." His adolescent voice cracked. "Or else why would he stay? And I am thinking, by how much he grew, he hass plenty to eat."

"I guess," said Vincent.

Freida was mortified. She made up her mind to call Sister Sara as soon as the visit was over. But then, she thought, it is probably hibernating by now, and if I tell Sara there is a snake under her house now, she will probably worry about it till spring. I guess I will wait until spring and hope it does not find Sister Sara before the boys find it. Suddenly she remembered how badly Sara felt about forgetting to remind her to file the adoption papers.

Martin said, "Marshall fixed Petey's foot."

Vincent replied, "Petey's sore foot? He did?"

"Yah. He came over everyday after school. I'm guessing it wass his way of feeling close to you. He said you would want somebody to take care of Petey for you."

"He iss right."

"I told him I wass going to put Petey down if his foot did not heal soon. He asked me to give him a chance, and after that he came over every day. He took care of de infection. He wrapped it up in a house shoe with foam on the bottom. He harnessed him up off de floor to take the weight off it and to keep it clean. After that he gave him a block to rest his foot on in different positions. Once Petey could stand on it again, he started walking him around de barn everyday, bit by bit. It took him six months, but now, Petey iss ready for de races. We could tape his ankles and run him in de Kentucky derby."

Vincent said, "Marshall hass a lot of patience."

"Yah, he does," agreed Martin. "He iss a good boy."

"Tell him thanks for me."

"Yah. I will."

"And tell Marshall I miss him too. Maybe he could come visit me by himself," said Vincent. Do not tell him though; I have to ask my mom first. I do not want him to be disappointed if he can not come." Vincent heaved a sigh.

"We brought you some food, but I guess we are going to have to eat it ourselves," teased the girl with the picnic basket.

"What do you have?" asked Vincent. He could feel his mouth begin to water.

"Everybody here brought something. There iss strawberry preserves, and rolls and butter, peach cobbler, cheese, German potato salad, and milk."

"Aw," said Vincent. "Give me some milk!"

Miss Purdy suggested, "I could stick your straw into de potato salad, and you can suck out what gets stuck in de straw."

"Yah, yah, yah," replied Vincent with anticipation.

They passed around the basket, shared the bread, cheese, milk, strawberries, peach cobbler, and potato salad, and Miss Purdy said grace. "Our precious Lord, we thank you for healing our friend, Vincent. We have had a wonderful time in fellowship today. We pray you will continue to heal his body, and we pray that someday he can rejoin us at Promise. Amen."

"Amen," they all agreed.

Vincent drank the milk through the straw down to the last drop, making sure to make the most noise possible with the last slurp. He said, "This iss de best milk in de world! You want to know how they thank de cook in China?"

"I am sorry, visiting hours are over," said the nurse's aide.

"Aww," they all complained.

"You may finish your picnic," she insisted. "Just wrap up your visit as soon as you're done."

"We will," said Miss Purdy. "We will clean up our mess, and then we will be going."

Nurse B. passed by the doorway. She called in, "Did you folks have a nice visit?"

"Yah!" they all agreed.

Vincent had a great afternoon. When Bunny came back to visit that evening he told her how glad he was that his friends hadn't forgotten him. The more he thanked her for letting them come, the guiltier she felt for taking the credit. Still, Vincent was uncertain about asking if Marshall could come to visit. He tried, but decided the timing wasn't right.

As Bunny was leaving the hospital that evening, Nurse B. called, "Miss Muldare, could you come here for a moment?"

Bunny cringed, but stopped and turned in her direction.

The nurse said, "I have a memo from my supervisor that says: 'All visitation from the Mennonite community will be halted until further notice.' I assume that would be your doing?"

"That's right," said Bunny, trying not to gloat.

"Well congratulations," she said. "But there is another matter I'd like to bring to your attention, if you don't mind."

"What is that?"

"Did you know that your 'significant other,'" said Nurse B. sarcastically, "chased Vincent out of your apartment and into the street, and that's why he ran in front of a truck?"

"No," she replied, still defensive.

"Are you sure?" Nurse B. asked, concerned.

"I'm positive," replied Bunny.

"I'm surprised Vincent hasn't confided in you already. It makes me wonder if there are other things that are being hidden from you."

"What makes you say that?" said Bunny.

"It's pretty obvious if Vincent couldn't bring himself to tell you about this, he could be hiding the fact that your boyfriend pushed him into the street."

"That's a pretty big leap, isn't it, from chasing to pushing?"

"I don't know," said Nurse B. pensively, "It was the way he paused when he got to that part of the story. He kind of went into his own thoughts there, like he was holding something back, or maybe he was remembering something he didn't like. But after all these years of working with children, I can tell you, if a child keeps a secret, he's liable to be keeping more than just one. Who knows what other things have been going on that you haven't been told."

Bunny's feelings toward Michael turned to anger. She was remembering the way Vinnie covered for Michael when he had a brush burn on his arm. She was so angry with Michael she could barely keep from screaming. It only made it worse coming from this woman. "Believe me, Nurse Bandeller—"

"Bandellerogni," pronounced the nurse. She considered offering the nickname, Nurse B., but decided against it. She preferred keeping the pressure on by not appearing too friendly.

"Yes. Thank you for letting me know. Believe me, I'm going to get to the bottom of this, one way or another. If what you said is true, Michael will be lucky if I don't strangle him right on the spot."

"I'm glad to see you're finally putting that attitude of yours to good use," said Nurse B. Wasn't there a police investigation about this very thing?" asked the nurse.

"Yes, I talked to the police about it, or rather, they talked to me. They said there was a retarded man, a friend of mine, who said he saw Michael push him, but they said he wasn't a reliable witness, and nobody else saw it. Michael said he tried to catch Vincent but it was too late. But nobody said anything about arguing or chasing, or anything like that. And his friend, Perry, who was with him, said the same thing. Except, he didn't know anything about Michael trying to catch him. He said he was upstairs."

Nurse Bandellerogni said, the way only a black woman can, "Uh-huh. I realize none of this is any of my business, honey, but we have something in common here, you and me. I love this boy, and I care what happens to him, as I'm sure you do." She qualified, "A little too possessively, but hey, like you said, he is your child."

Bunny stood rigidly, "So what's your point?"

"We can patch him up this time, but we don't know what might happen next time. And I don't want this boy to have to suffer through anything like this ever again. Are you hearing me with this?"

Bunny stared back at her without answering. She wasn't sure she wanted to listen to this woman's sideline commentary on her life.

Nurse B. continued, "You need to think about whether this Michael character deserves the benefit of the doubt. It struck me as odd that your boyfriend has never come to visit. But now, considering what Vincent told his friends, I'm not surprised a bit."

"Yes, thank you again, Nurse Bandellerogni. I'm going to do something about this, believe me," Bunny fumed.

"Call me Nurse B. Everybody else does."

Bunny punched the elevator button at least six times before the doors finally opened.

Before Vincent went to sleep, he said a special prayer for his friend. "Jesus, could you make it so Marshall does not get lonely? And I wish that maybe he could come and visit me sometime. God bless Marshall, God bless Petey, and God bless all my friends. Thank you. Amen."

Proverbs 17:22. A merry heart doeth good like a medicine: but a broken spirit drieth the bones.

Chapter 21

Michael!

*B*unny drove home from the hospital at record speed. The longer it took her to fight her way through traffic, the angrier she became. She sifted through the information she had learned, so far. As she put the pieces together, it was beginning to look more and more like Nurse B. was right. She had made up her mind she was going to squeeze the information out of Michael, if it killed her. She swung open the door. "Michael!" she shouted. "Where are you!?"

"What, what, what? I'm in here."

Bunny threw her purse and coat on the couch and exploded through the bedroom door. Michael was studying at his desk. Michael's friend, Perry, was lying on the bed watching TV. She lit into Michael. "The nurse told me you chased Vincent out of the house and chased him right into the street!"

"What are you talking about? What does she know about anything?"

"During Vincent's visit with the Mennonites, Vincent told them that you were chasing him around the house, he got scared, he ran down the steps and into the street. And the nurse, who overheard all this, she said, you were right behind him. Sound familiar? Don't tell me you don't remember."

"She doesn't know what she's talking about. Why don't you ask Vincent yourself?"

"Because if he weren't afraid to tell me, he would have told me already. What about the time I came home and found rug burns on his arm? Don't deny that you did it."

Michael answered defiantly, "Read my lips. I did not do it."

Bunny said, "You're denying what exactly? That you pushed him? That you chased him? That you scared him?"

"Look, I never meant for Vincent to get run over by a truck. I admit, he gets on my nerves a lot of times."

"All the time," she corrected.

"But do you think I woke up in the morning and said, 'Gee whilikers, today looks like a good day to throw Vincent in front of a truck?'" Michael mocked.

Bunny charged again, "I'll tell you what I think is the truth. The cops came around and started asking questions. You were going to deny everything, but when the police threatened you with what Robert said about pushing Vincent, and the neighbors said they saw you out there, you had to explain what you were doing in the street. So you figured the only thing that might make a little sense is that you were trying to prevent it. That is such shit, Michael. What were you doing out there—taking Vinnie for a walk, while Perry sat waiting for you upstairs? I doubt it. He pissed you off, you chased him around, he ran out of the house terrified, Robert is coming down the street at the same time, just in time to see you catch up to Vincent and give him a good hard shove into the path of a truck."

"Gee, how long did it take you to dream up this theory of yours? It's fiction, Bunny. All fiction."

"It's only a matter of time, Michael, and I'll prove it. But for now, there's one thing I don't need to prove, and that is this: you don't want to be his father, you never wanted to be his father, and you never will. I was dumb enough to think it would get better, and now look what's happened."

"What's the big surprise?" replied Michael, "I told you I didn't want him from the beginning, before he even got here. It's not like I had any choice in the matter; it all happened so fast, we never even discussed it. What makes you think I should want to play daddy to your old lover's kid? Why don't I bring my old girlfriend's kid over here, and we can have one big happy family? I would never ask you to do that, but you don't give me any choice in the matter. Why don't you decide who you want more, me or your kid?"

"You want me to choose? All right, I'll choose, I'll choose, no problem. I choose Vinnie. And as for your question about your girlfriend's 'kid,' it's not just hers, it's yours too!"

Michael sat quietly. He knew he was the one who led the conversation in this direction, and now he didn't know how to get out of it.

Bunny said, "Well, I guess that settles it. You're not going to get another chance at him. You're not even going to get another chance to insult him. Vinnie and I don't want you around here anymore." Bunny opened the closet door and began throwing Michael's clothes out onto the floor. "It doesn't matter whether you threw him in front of a truck, pushed him in front of the truck, or you chased him in front of a truck, I don't care. He is scared of you, and that is definitely your fault, and that's enough. So we're done putting up with you. Get your stuff and get out of here. Pronto!" She threw his jacket at him.

Michael calmly folded the jacket on his lap but didn't budge.

"Now!" she screamed.

Michael wasn't going to be told by some female what to do, besides, he had paid the rent. "Look, Bunny! Vinnie was just being a pain, as usual, and so I came out into the living room and tried to make him stop. And yeah, I admit, I got a little carried away, but he's the idiot that ran out into the street."

"I think I better be leaving," said Perry. He swung his legs around to the side of the bed, and sat up.

Bunny pushed him back onto the bed. "And you!" accused Bunny. "Why did you tell the police you didn't see anything? You were here; why didn't you tell them Michael was chasing Vinnie around? I know you saw that much. How could you miss it; he chased him clear into the street! Vinnie said so."

"Because Michael was afraid that if the police knew he was chasing Vincent, then the next step would be to accuse him of shoving him. I didn't see anything like that. All I saw was: Michael and Vincent were running down the steps to the front door, there were screeching brakes, and when I got there, Michael told me to call an ambulance." Perry's eyes shifted from Bunny's when he recalled Michael's disturbing smile after the accident.

His shifting glance didn't escape Bunny. She poked him in the shoulder with her index finger and sneered into his face, "You are a weasel, a sniveling weasel. Get out of my house—my house—not your house! How can I believe anything you say when you don't have the guts, for Vinnie's sake, to tell the truth—all of it. You might have thought that everything was back to being nice and cozy again. I'm telling you, right here and now, that you are in a world of trouble. I'm telling the cops you knew they were fighting and you hid it from them. If it turns out Robert is telling the truth, what Michael did was attempted murder, and you, you little coward, you helped him!"

Perry grabbed his jacket and left without another word.

"Well, Michael, darling, now that we're alone," she glared, "why don't you tell me how you shoved my son in front of a truck and tried to kill him?" Bunny crossed her arms in front of her and waited.

"I told you. He's the idiot that ran in front of the truck. I never laid a hand on him. Why don't you ask him?"

"Stop calling him an idiot! If there's anybody that's an idiot around here, it's you! And we're not going to put up with you anymore. I've heard enough already." She waved him off as if to get him out of her sight, adding finally, "As far as criminal charges go, I will get to the bottom of this. You can bank on it."

Michael had to think of another strategy, and he knew it. Vincent was already getting brave enough to tell people he and Vinnie were fighting. It would only be a matter of time, with enough encouragement from Bunny, that he would start telling them everything. Michael knew if he could soften Bunny up now, she wouldn't press so hard about this thing.

Michael stood up and began moving closer to Bunny. "Come on, Bunny, honey. I know you're upset about Vinnie's accident. Any good mother would be. I'm so sorry this happened, especially while I was responsible for him. I've been feeling guilty about it myself, and I never wanted you to be upset. You know how much I love you." He put his hands on her shoulders and slid his hands down her arms.

She flung his arms away from her. "Stop it! Don't touch me, Michael! You make me sick. I never, never, ever want you to touch me again!" Bunny gritted her teeth at his touch.

Michael pressed his body against hers, trapping her against the wall. "You can't mean that, sweetheart. You are going to get so lonely for a man when I'm gone."

She tried to squirm away from him but he held her against the wall. She got right in his face and spit on him. "Do you get it? I—don't—want—you! I don't want you to touch me, and I don't want to look at your face ever again! Ever!"

He touched her hair.

Bunny smacked his hand away, pushed on his chest, raised her knee and kicked him between the legs, then shoved him into the closet. He caught himself just before he went into the hamper.

"Now, are you going to get your stuff out of here, or do I have to start throwing it out the window?"

When Michael stood up he was very angry. "Come, here!" he ordered. Michael's voice had changed. It sounded deeper, and angrier, almost unrecognizable. The look in his eyes turned to utter hatred, "I said come 'ere," he repeated. Bunny knew to fear for her life.

She started to run out of the bedroom, but Michael caught her by the back of her shirt. She struggled to get away, but he threw her on the bed. Bunny started screaming, "I hate you. Leave me alone."

By this time, Mr. Gibbs had begun pacing outside Bunny's apartment. He knew she might be in terrible trouble, but didn't want to butt in where it wasn't his business. Then he decided he couldn't take a chance on Bunny's life, just to save himself a little embarrassment. He thought, so what if I am mistaken, I'm calling the police anyway.

Michael slapped her across the face. Bunny screamed. Michael put his hand over her mouth and with his other hand, held her wrists over her head. "You know you don't mean that. How many times have you loved being in bed with me," he taunted, glad to be able to make her mad. He clinched his teeth. His elbow was pulling her hair, and as she tried to turn her head away, he bit her on the neck.

She screamed again, this time through his hand. She tried with all her might to escape, but she couldn't move anything; he had her trapped. But then, Bunny remembered the gun. She knew if she could scoot herself up a little higher on the bed she could reach it. It was in a holster between the headboard and the wall directly over her head.

Michael ordered, "Kiss me, and tell me you love me!"

"No!" she screamed through his hand. "I hate you!"

She warned. "I can't breathe!"

He took his hand from her mouth and struck her again across the face. This time she didn't scream. She used her feet to scramble backwards, getting her closer to the gun above her head.

Michael repeated calmly, "I said, kiss me, and tell me you love me. Do it!"

"No!" she screamed, knowing he was going to hit her again. He hit her in the mouth this time. She rolled over before he could grab her mouth again. She got up on all fours to get a good grip on the gun. He knocked her down with his knee on her back.

She felt the bandanna that was tied to the bedpost and supporting the holster. She was careful to keep from disturbing the pillow that concealed her hands. Finally, she felt the cold metal of the handle. It was a small pistol that she could lift out easily with two fingers. She tried to wrap her finger around the trigger, but Michael was lying on top of her, and punching her in the side. He was bouncing the bed so violently it made it impossible for her to grab the gun. In spite of the pain, she knew she had to reach her index finger around the trigger. Every blow brought her closer to that trigger. She shut her eyes to help her visualize how to retrieve it. Her lip was beginning to swell, pressing into the sheet each time he delivered another blow. She turned her head to the other side. Michael grabbed her by the hair and pulled her head back. Then he let it bounce back down onto the mattress. At last, she had hold of it! But she knew she had to choose her moment carefully.

Bunny screamed, "Michael, get off of me, please. Don't hurt me anymore," she said in a pathetic tone. "I'm sorry."

He rolled her over triumphantly. She was careful to leave her hands under the pillow above her head. He sat on her stomach. "I knew the old Michael magic would get to you sooner or later," he said sarcastically. "You're so sexy when you're mad."

She yanked the gun out of the holster and pointed it at Michael. "Get off me," she said in a slow growl.

He looked up to see the gun pointed at his forehead. He started to move for the gun. Bunny pulled the trigger, but by then Michael had shoved it to the side. The bullet went into the wall. Michael jumped to his feet. Bunny pointed the gun back at him. He ducked behind the foot of the bed. He started swearing, "What's the matter with you. You almost killed me, you crazy b—"

Bunny answered, "Almost isn't good enough." She shot again. It hit the doorknob and ricocheted back toward the bed, barely missing Michael. He ran for the bedroom door and into the living room. Bunny ran after him. When she got to the living room she saw him crouching behind the recliner. "Maybe I ought to chase you around and see how you like it, Daddy," she taunted. Bunny ran her hand through her hair, brushing it back behind her shoulders.

She started toward the recliner. It rocked slightly. "Now get your stuff and get out." Michael didn't move. Michael, I know you're behind the recliner, now come on out."

She tiptoed toward the corner of the recliner. "I'm not going to hurt you; I just want you to leave." Michael lunged for her ankles. She screamed as she hit the floor with her chin. The gun went off again. Michael pinned the gun to the floor. "Let go of the gun, Bunny," he ordered.

"No!" she screamed.

He twisted her wrist then began pulling her thumb back. Finally, her grip gave way, and she had to release it.

Michael grabbed the gun and knocked Bunny back down on the ground. He had it at the back of her head. "Now we'll see who's giving the orders." Bunny could see out of the corner of her eye that he was taking aim and getting ready to pull the trigger.

Knock, knock, knock. "Police, open up in there!"

Bunny rolled then scrambled for the door. She opened it as Michael tossed the gun behind the couch. The policeman drew his gun, pointing it at Michael. "Put your hands in the air."

Michael obeyed.

"She's the one with the gun," Michael protested. He put his hands down. Two officers stormed the living room and wrestled Michael to the ground. Mr. Gibbs stood out in the hallway in his bathrobe with his mouth open.

They handcuffed Michael, and stood him up in front of Bunny. There were red bite marks on her neck. Her face was beginning to get puffy under her left eye. Her lip was obviously swollen and bleeding.

The policeman said, "How did you get those bite marks on your neck, ma'am?"

Bunny replied in total exhaustion, "He did it."

"Would you like to press charges Ma'am? If you want, we can put a restraining order on him. He won't be able to come near you again."

"She drew the gun on me!" Michael bucked.

"Shut up, tough guy," said the officer, tightening his grip on Michael's arms, which he had pulled behind his back. "We didn't see any gun on her. Where's this gun?"

No one spoke. Michael realized that the only one who could have hidden the gun behind the couch was him. Otherwise, how would he know it was there? And how did Bunny answer the door and hide the gun at the same time? Bunny and Mr. Gibbs said nothing.

"What are you going to do with him?" asked Bunny.

"He's going to the station for a little overnight with the boys. That is, if that's what you want."

"That's what I want," said Bunny. She looked down at the floor. "I want him to get his stuff out of here, though. I don't want him living here anymore."

"We'll draw up the paper work right now if you want. And while he's at the station you can get his stuff out and either give it to the landlord, or take it to the station, or you can always throw it out."

"I'll take it to the station," said Norman Gibbs. "And don't you be coming back here," he wagged his finger at Michael. "I'm changing the locks, and you won't ever be able to get in here again."

Bunny smiled at Mr. Gibbs for being a good friend.

"Ma'am, if he does try to get in your apartment, you call us, even if you see him hanging around in the parking lot. We'll come and arrest him on the spot."

"Don't I get a trial? This is America." Michael protested.

"We got an eyeful of proof when she opened the door, tough guy. Sorry, you're done, your rights end here."

"Yeah," said Bunny. "I want to sign up for that restraining order." She took a deep breath.

"O'Dell, you wanna take care of the restraining order?"

"Sure thing. I'll stay here and write it up. Meet you in the car."

"Yep." He clamped the handcuffs on Michael.

"Ow," said Michael.

He called back to Bunny as the policeman lead him away. "You're gonna be sorry you did this to me, Bunny."

The officer shoved him out of the door. "Let's go, get moving, and save the speeches."

Mr. Gibbs rushed to Bunny's side. "Are you all right? Are you hurt, Bunny?"

"I'm all right, I'm all right."

"All the same, I'll take you to emergency just to make sure."

Officer O'Dell said, "Make sure they get pictures."

Bunny shook her head in agreement.

After the policeman had taken the information, Bunny and Mr. Gibbs walked him to the landing. "Thank you so much, Officer O'Dell." said Mr. Gibbs. "And thanks for getting here so fast."

"Glad to help," he said.

Bunny and Mr. Gibbs stood at the top of the stairs as Officer O'Dell left the building.

"Thanks, Mr. Gibbs," said Bunny. "You saved my life."

"Now I couldn't very well stand around here while you two shot up the place, could I?" he joked. I wish they had seen him with the gun in his hand, and they could have put him away for ever. I waited as long as I could stand it, and then I got too worried about you. I couldn't let anything happen to my little Miss Bunny. Bunny hadn't heard anybody call her that since her father moved to Florida. You deserve better than him. You're pretty, and smart, and nice. You don't need to settle for just anybody. And don't you worry about him coming back. I'll keep that bum out of here. You can count on it." He patted her hand that rested on the stair rail.

The adrenaline in Bunny's body melted into tears that dripped off her swollen, beaten face and landed on Mr. Gibbs hand. It broke his heart. "You're a good girl, Bunny. Don't you worry, everything is going to be all right."

Bunny thought, why does everything in my life turn to crap?

After a time, Mr. Gibbs added, "I'm sorry for eavesdropping, but you were right, you know—Michael did chase Vinnie into the street. I saw him. I can't say he pushed him, but he was giving that boy heck for something or other. They passed me on the steps, and it looked to me like Vinnie was scared half out of his wits. Vinnie knew Michael might hurt him, and he was trying to get away from him."

Bunny wiped her nose. "Where was Perry, that friend of Michael's?"

"He was standing around up on the landing. He didn't see Michael push him, either. But, he'd have to be blind and deaf not to know Michael was giving Vinnie heck, and chasing him out of the building."

"Did you tell the police what you saw?" asked Bunny.

"Yeah, I told 'em. But they were looking for somebody besides Robert to tell them about Vinnie getting pushed. Vinnie and Michael are the only ones who know the real truth."

Bunny said, "Don't forget Robert."

"Do you think he would make that up?"

"No, I don't think so. He's afraid of the police, and he'd probably be afraid of the police catching him in a lie. I'd bet he's telling the truth."

Revelation 22:14–15. Blessed are they that do his commandments, that they may have the right to the tree of life, and may enter in through the gates into the city. For without are dogs, and sorcerers, and whoremongers, and murderers, and idolaters, and whosoever loveth and maketh a lie.

Chapter 22

Richard? Bunny?

$\mathcal{B}$unny found herself, once again, studying the cracks in the all-too-familiar sidewalk on her way from the bus stop to the front doors of Children's Hospital. Michael had come back after his arrest and taken Bunny's car. The police said they couldn't do anything about it; Michael's name was on the title. In Michael's mind, he paid the original $800 for it, so it was his, never mind that she had registered it every year, insured it every six months, and put gas in it. The fact was, as the police explained, she and Michael weren't married, so she had no rights to ownership. It wasn't so bad walking to work, but getting to the hospital had become very difficult. The bus ride was a good forty-five minutes not counting the wait at the bus stop and the walk to the hospital. Bunny spent much of her time dwelling on Vincent and on whether she could ever get him adjusted to normal life. She said to herself, "I can't even adjust to normal life myself, how am I supposed to get him adjusted to it? Maybe if I had neighbors that wanted to be friends with us, that would help. Vincent likes Mr. and Mrs. Gibbs, and so do I, but we need some friends our own age. I feel like a fugitive on a wanted poster when I meet people, like they're going to discover I'm the heroin addict from down the street, the street bum nobody wanted. And then they would say, 'Ah, and this must be your bastard son. And where is his father? Oh, did you say he's in jail? Isn't that nice. But you have another husband now, right?' I could tell them, 'of course, I have a wonderful man, a charming man, a pilot, and a live-in boyfriend who hates my son so much he pushed him in front of a truck. Yes, that's right, and now my son is in the hospital with a fractured skull. Where is my son's new father-to-be, you ask? Well, you see, we got into a little lover's quarrel, and he beat the hell out of me, and so I kicked him out of the house, with a gun. Yes, ma'am, you heard that right, not that I wanted to kill him or anything, but luckily the police got there just in time before he shot me in the back of the head. Maybe your child and my child could begin to play together after school. Not that I am ever there. I work till five. Oh, you heard my son is weird?'"

"Oops. Pardon me."

Bunny looked up from the sidewalk to find she had bumped into her brother. "Richard? Hey, what are you doing here?"

"Bunny? Bunny! Still don't watch where you're going, I see," he flashed his strikingly beautiful smile. He wore a camel cashmere overcoat, with an emerald green scarf and an oxford blue shirt. Bunny noticed his hair was beginning to thin slightly on top, and it looked as if it had been colored to a more chestnut color. It was barely noticeable, except that she remembered how it used to look, wavier and less controlled. He was freshly shaven and smelled of expensive cologne. Still good-looking, she thought; he looks more like Dad than he used to.

"Still know how to be irritating," she volleyed.

A gust of wind whooshed passed them. It took Bunny's breath away, and flipped her hair up off of her shoulder. "Let's get inside," Richard suggested. They ducked into a corner deli, making their way through the breakfast crowd to a barrel table with a checkered tablecloth. They sat across from each other in two old wrought-iron ice-cream chairs.

"What can I do for you folks today?"

"Just hot tea for me," said Bunny, loud enough to be heard over the clattering dishes and noisy Saturday morning crowd.

"Coffee, black," said Richard. He could smell it brewing; the aroma filled the room.

"How can you drink that gut rot," said Bunny.

"Brother have guts of iron," he said attempting a Russian accent.

Bunny said, "I never thought I'd say this, but it's good to see you."

"Ditto," he said.

"Ditto?"

"Yes, as in I agree."

"I know what it means," Bunny groaned. "Ditto," she repeated rolling her eyes.

"Hey, haven't you heard, it's hip to be square these days?"

"Hey, but you were square even before it was hip," she teased.

Richard unbuttoned his coat. Bunny noticed his stomach was starting to pooch. Bunny decided not to mention it. She just looked back into her brother's face, smiling at him. "It's good to see an old familiar and friendly face," she said.

"Ditto," he repeated, smiling, then asked, "So what brings you to Harrisburg?"

"Vinnie is in the hospital. He got hit by a truck," said Bunny.

"No. Oh my gosh. Did he really?" His expression turned serious.

"I was stupid enough to leave him with Michael."

"Michael?" asked Richard.

"You know, the pilot wannabe. You met him at your Christmas party a couple of years ago."

"Oh, him, he's just a kid himself," said Richard.

"Yeah, well, Michael got mad at him for something or other, and Vinnie ran out of the apartment, down the steps, and right in front of a truck. I'm still trying to get to the bottom of it." Bunny began to explain, "Ya know retarded old Robert?"

"Retarded old Robert? I think so, maybe," said Richard.

"You know, he lived downtown Carlisle, he hung out in the park. He's black."

Richard looked back at her with a blank expression.

"Oh well, anyway, retarded old Robert says he saw it happen, and he told the police Michael pushed him. But nobody else can verify that. And the police think old retarded Robert's making it up for my sake. The problem is, even if they believed him, he's classified as an unreliable witness, because he's retarded."

"So what does Vinnie say happened?"

"Well, he says he's not sure. It may be a memory block, or it's possible that he doesn't really know what happened. Or maybe he doesn't want to tell—that's my guess. He's probably afraid of what Michael would do to him if he told. I'm going to keep asking though. Maybe he'll tell me eventually. As for me, if I find out Michael did this to Vinnie, I'm going to make him suffer. I'd like to make him pay, right down to the last penny and then some." Bunny began to relish the thought of revenge. "I want to watch while they tie him down in a parking lot somewhere, and then run over him with a steamroller, flattening his sorry ass right into the pavement so deep, you won't even notice he's there. Then I'd like to make a personal trip to the parking lot to run over him again every day for the rest of my life. I just know he did it, and he's not getting away with it." Bunny could feel her heart begin to race with excitement over the thought of getting even with Michael.

"Do we know the driver? Maybe he knows what happened."

"The truck driver? No, it was a big truck, like a tractor trailer truck. I don't know who he was. He didn't say too much after it happened. To tell you the truth, I was so worried about Vinnie I wasn't thinking about the driver. Vinnie says he's a nice guy and came to visit him in the hospital. It must have been while I was at work. But if he knew something he would have already told the police, don't you think?"

"Oh man. I didn't realize it was a big truck, ouch. I wonder if the guy lost his job because of this. If that's the case, I'm guessing, if he could blame it on Michael, he would. Is Vinnie going to make it?"

"He was in pretty bad shape, he broke a lot of bones, but miraculously, he didn't break anything that they couldn't fix. He should be out of the hospital by Christmas, they said."

"Huh, well that's good, at least. Anything else going on?"

Bunny blurted, "I kicked Michael out, of course. I had to use a gun and three policemen to get rid of him, but he left. I was so mad after I figured out what happened, he's lucky I didn't kill him. I told him Vinnie and I didn't want him living with us anymore, and I guess he figured he'd show me a thing or two, and so he beat me up! The police came and arrested him before anything really serious happened, I mean real serious, like one of us murdering the other one. By the time they busted through the door, Michael had taken the gun off me and had it pointed right at the back of my head. But then when I opened the door Michael ditched the gun. I still haven't found it. But at least they got him for domestic abuse, and if he comes anywhere near me I can have him arrested.

"Who called the police?" asked Richard.

"The landlord, Norman Gibbs."

"Oh yeah? I remember him," said Richard.

Bunny added, "He's real old now. Didn't he used to be your coach?"

"Home plate ump," replied Richard.

"I guess I should feel relieved Michael's gone; he was such a jerk. But I'm still feeling a little lost, like I don't know where I belong. I go home and Vinnie's not there, Michael's not there; it's pretty lonely."

"Bunny, you know, your life reads like a cheap novel."

There was an awkward pause. She knew what he said was true, but at least it didn't wound her to the core like it would have if her mother had said it.

"Just a cheap girl, I guess." Bunny replied.

"That's not what I meant," said Richard. "It's these guys you get hooked up with."

"I know. Just kidding."

"You'll find somebody, Bunny. Just have a little patience and wait for a good one this time. I'm so glad I found Cynthia; she's great," said Richard.

"Well, thank you for that. I feel much better now. Someday, with a little luck, I'll be just like you. Isn't that the story of my life?"

Richard knew that comment was meant for their mother.

"Mother is in the hospital too, Bunny," said Richard quietly. "In fact, that's where I was going."

"What's the matter with her?" asked Bunny with surprise.

"She has bone cancer," he said in a soft voice, almost tripping on the word.

Bunny was shocked, speechless. She never thought of her mother as being vulnerable to anything. Her mother always took good care of herself. Bunny hadn't talked to her in over five years, but who was counting? Bunny certainly wasn't. And it didn't appear her mother was either. Neither of them had so much as spoken on the phone, and yet they lived just across town from each other. Curiously, Bunny had always taken comfort in her mother's toughness. But now she was disconcerted by the fact that even the tough ones can't save themselves, not even her mother. "Is she going to die?"

"Everybody's going to die eventually, Bunny," Richard said, more for his own benefit than for Bunny's. He was still trying to come to terms with it himself. Though he was a doctor, as an ophthalmologist he never had to deal with death. He said with resignation, as if he were expecting the worst, "She's going through chemotherapy. It's a wait-and-see."

"What do the doctors say is the best to hope for?"

"She'll recover, and the entire incident will be nothing more than a bad memory."

"What's the worst?" Bunny's eyes penetrated Richard's, searching for the real truth.

"Her health will continue to deteriorate, and she will be gone in a year, maybe less." It was hard for Richard to speak it, out loud. It didn't seem possible that his mother could be gone within the year. "You know Bunny, you really need to see her again."

"Did she say she wanted to see me?" asked Bunny, half hoping she had.

"Well, not in so many words, but she mentions you from time to time. No one ever really forgets their children. I think it's probably hard for her to accept that she lost you."

"She knew where I was. Why didn't she ever show any interest before?" Bunny was doing everything to keep from crying in the deli.

"Don't you think it's time to take off the gloves? She's not going to be around forever."

"It's just so hard, Richard. It's different for you. You could never do anything wrong. Everything I ever did, thought, and said, was not only wrong, but despicable."

"You put her through an awful lot, especially when you started moving with that Vinnie character."

"Richard, you know as well as I do, we had problems way before that. I've gone through it a million times in my mind, why Mom and I didn't get along. Even when I did well, it was never good enough. She was always ashamed of me for something or other. If I was pretty, I was conceited. If I got good grades, I wasn't trying hard enough the rest of the time, and on and on and on. I talk too much, I don't talk enough, I'm too forward, I'm too backward, you name it. You, on the other hand, could have hocked her diamond tiara for an ice cream cone, and it would become part of her collection of amusing Richard stories. But, I don't know, when Daddy left, I didn't have anyone to stick up for me anymore, and I just gave up. I got sick of her criticism grinding me up day after day until I just wanted out of the house, and the sooner the better. The older I got, the smarter I got about how she really felt. When you're little, you think your mom is probably right, and that you are all those bad things she's telling you that you are. But then when you get older you realize it's not going to matter what you do, she's not going to like you regardless, because it's just plain personal. I get through life by escaping my past. Why would I want to walk back into the fire?" The lump in her throat was getting harder to ignore.

Richard said, "Mom was jealous."

Bunny rolled her eyes. "Oh, please. Nice try, Richard."

Bunny sighed as she remembered what it was like living with her mother. She explained, "It's such a hopeless depressing feeling, especially if you're doing everything you can to be good. You'd think you'd grow out of that kind of rejection, but it never goes away, does it?"

"Not really," admitted Richard. He was relieved to see the waitress approaching the table. He didn't want to talk about his father and himself.

"More coffee?" she asked.

Richard nodded, "Yes thanks."

Bunny put her elbow on the table and hid her face behind her hand. "How about you, dear? Can I get you anything?"

Bunny shook her head, no, without lifting her hand.

"So," Richard asked, "You want to go with me to see Mom?"

"I can't. Don't ask me to go there."

Richard suggested sympathetically, "It seems to me, burning bridges hasn't worked for you so far. Maybe you should consider doing some mending before it's too late. Wouldn't it be wonderful if you and Mother could finally become friends? You're not the same person you were all those years ago, and neither is she."

"Do you really think that's going to matter? You just finished saying how my life reads like a cheap novel. What do you think Mom is going to say about it? Besides, even if I were perfect—which I am trying my very best to be, by the way, but it's just not working out—even if I were perfect and she couldn't find anything to rip on me for; she would remind me how awful I used to be."

By this time Bunny was sobbing into her hands.

She was trying to say something from behind her hands, but Richard couldn't understand what she was saying. He pulled her hands away from her face.

"What?" he said. "I couldn't hear you."

"I can't do it," she said. "She never liked me, and you know it. I don't want to be hurt again, especially now. I'm too weak," she sobbed.

"Bunny, I never knew you to be weak."

She couldn't talk out loud over her crying without drawing attention to herself, so she scratched out a note on her napkin as she hid behind her hand, "Well, surprise, I am. I'm all alone, and there's nobody to comfort me after Mom is done chewing me up."

Richard read her note then said, "I'll be there, Bunny. Besides, you don't have to resolve old conflicts, just be polite, that's all. A little polite conversation is all that's expected."

She wrote, "You don't think I'd start a fight with a dying woman, do you? How insensitive do you think I am?"

"I thought that's what was stopping you. You didn't want to get into another argument."

"No," she wrote, "I'd have to stand there and let her take potshots at me. It hurts Richard. She's my mother, and she hates me." She turned the tattered napkin toward him.

As Richard read, Bunny covered her face with both hands. He could see this was going nowhere, and really, though he didn't want to admit it to Bunny, everything she said was true. He knew how cruel his mother could be to Bunny, and if he were in Bunny's shoes, he probably wouldn't want to go face her either. His mother had always favored him, and he knew it. And how could he judge Bunny, when he couldn't even attend his father's funeral. He thought he'd give it one last shot and then leave it alone. "All I know is, mother is all alone too. I'm the only visitor she's had since she got sick."

Bunny answered, "She has plenty of friends."

"Those kind of friends don't hang around when you're down. They're climbers." He paused, hoping for an answer. He sighed, "Anyway, I know she would really appreciate it if you came to see her. You don't have to say a word, just sit there."

Bunny could hear in Richard's voice that he was getting close to conceding. "Let me think about it," she said.

"I'm going over right now," said Richard. "You could come with me," he suggested.

"NO! I can't go right now," Bunny said, panicked. She blew her nose on her napkin.

"I know Mom would love to see you. It's been such a long time, maybe her feelings have changed," he said, trying to sound convincing.

Bunny shook her head no. "No, they haven't" she said, resigned to the truth.

"Why don't you think about it till tomorrow? If you decide to go, you can meet me here. I'll go with you."

"I have to work."

"Tomorrow's Sunday," he reminded her.

"Oh, you're right." Bunny took a deep breath, relieved she was getting close to walking away from this conversation without really confronting it.

Richard waited for an answer.

"What time is it?" asked Bunny. She took out her compact and swiped the powder across her tear-stained cheeks.

"Ten," said Richard.

"I've gotta go," she said.

"I'll be here at nine o'clock tomorrow," he said.

"I'm not promising anything," said Bunny.

"Okay, okay. But I'll be waiting,"
"No promises," she warned.
"No promises," he agreed.

Ephesians 5:33. Nevertheless let every one of you in particular so love his wife even as himself; and the wife see that she reverence her husband.

Ephesians 6:1–4. Children, obey your parents in the Lord: for this is right. Honor thy father and mother; which is the first commandment with promise; that it may be well with thee, and thou mayest live long on the earth. And, ye fathers, provoke not your children to wrath: but bring them up in the nurture and admonition of the Lord.

Chapter 23

I Knew It

"Vinnie, hi. How's my guy doing today?"

"Okay, I guess."

"Not very enthusiastic for a guy who's getting a visit from Santa pretty soon."

"I know."

"Sorry I'm late. I ran into my brother, Richard, on the way in here. Ran right into him, for real, as in ka-boom."

"Iss he de one that called on your birthday?"

"Yes, that's the one."

"Does he live in Carlisle?"

"No, he lives closer to Harrisburg. He is the ophthalmologist at the Vision Center in the Northridge Mall."

"What iss a oftolomogist?" he asked.

"I don't know. Some kind of eye doctor. I can't even spell it."

"Why do we never see him?"

"I guess we are both busy doing other things."

Vincent stared back at Bunny, wondering how she could think so little of staying close to her family. Vincent noticed she had been crying.

Bunny said, "I should probably make a point of staying in touch," and then thought, if we could manage to see each other without Mom, for once. "Did Santa Claus stop into your room yet?"

"No. But I am a little old for Santa Claus."

"I guess you are." Bunny sighed. "I wish there was something I could do to cheer you up."

Vincent took a deep breath and announced, "I can't live with Michael anymore."

"I know all about it," said Bunny nonchalantly.

"What do you know?"

"The nurse told me Michael chased you into the street and that's why you got hit."

Vincent said excitedly, "She should not have said that! You did not say that to Michael did you?"

"Yes, we had a . . ."

"No! He will kill me! Take it back! Tell him I said I just made it up."

"Now, why would you want me to tell a fib like that?"

"Because, he will kill me!" Vincent screamed. "He hates me!"

"Vinnie, you don't have to be afraid of him."

"Yes I do, you don't understand," Vincent said frantically. "Just tell him it wass not his fault." Bunny could see that Vinnie was so frightened he could barely catch his breath.

"Vinnie, calm down. Michael is history. He moved out."

"He moved out?" Vincent said, surprised.

"Well, not exactly, I booted him out," she said with false bravado. "I would have told you sooner but I wanted to make sure he was good and gone."

"How do you know he iss not coming back?" he asked suspiciously.

"Because if he does, the police said they will come and arrest him. That's why. He's not even allowed in our neighborhood anymore. And Mr. Gibbs changed our locks and won't let him in the building."

"Really?"

"Yep. They took him away, handcuffs and all."

"Really!? But what if he tries to get in here?"

"Nope, everybody knows he's not allowed," she declared.

Vincent thought back to the day she came to visit with bruises on her face. "Mom, you didn't really fall down the steps when you got hurt did you?"

Bunny hesitated. "No," she admitted softly. "Michael did it."

Vincent recognized the look of embarrassment mixed with humility. He remembered how his pappa looked as he entered the court room. And he remembered how he felt after being forced into submission by Michael.

Bunny added, "I'm sorry, Vinnie. I should have done it a long time ago. I guess I was a bit of a chicken. You didn't deserve to be treated so badly."

"He wass your boyfriend before I got there. If it wass not for me you would still be friends."

"None of this was your fault; don't even think like that. Michael is a jerk, because he was born a jerk. And I'm a jerk for trying to put up with him. I should never have let him act that way toward you, or me."

Vincent confessed, "He tied me up and put me in de closet," blurted Vincent. He looked at her wide-eyed. He had held his secret for so long, he was half expecting Michael to jump out from around the corner and beat him within an inch of his life, or worse. But then, nothing happened. Finally, he realized that Michael would probably never be able to get at him again. Vincent began to feel safe again for the first time since Michael put him in the closet. He took a deep breath and sighed with relief.

"Is that why you were always so afraid of him?"

"Yah, I wass afraid if I told, he would do it again. I never wanted him to get even a little bit mad at me, because I never wanted to go in de closet again. Even now, when I am all by myself, I get things out of de closet real fast. It makes me feel jumpy just thinking about it. It wass like I got buried alive in de dark. I was very scared." Bunny cradled his head and rocked him gently. She waited patiently for her moment to find out if Michael pushed Vinnie.

"Vinnie, did Michael push you in front of the truck?"

"Yah," Vincent sniffed back tears of relief.

"I'm so sorry, my baby, so, so sorry. This is all my fault, not yours."

Vincent explained, "I wass running down de steps and I could hear Michael behind me. I ran in between de cars and just when I got to de street, I stopped real fast cause there wass a truck coming. He already screeched on his brakes because he thought I wass going to run into de street. I think maybe he couldn't see if I stopped because de cars were covering me up. But I just got myself stopped, and Michael wass running up behind me. He wass still mad, and he pushed me into de street. I know it because he smashed his arm into my back like a football player, not like it wass an accident. But maybe nobody could see him 'cause he wass stooped down too low. I got up, but de truck hit me before I had time to get back to de curb."

"I knew it!" Bunny declared with satisfaction. She knew she was going to be able to make Michael pay for this.

"There was another time," Vincent admitted, "he turned on de burner on de stove. Then he held my hand over de heat. He made me promise not to tell you about his friend."

"Perry?"

"Yah. They took naps while he wass supposed to be taking care of me," Vincent sobbed.

"Did he burn you?" Bunny asked, feeling the anger rising within her once again.

"No, he just scared me. I told him right away that I would not tell, and I begged him to believe me, so he let me go. I tried very hard to be a good boy, always."

Bunny continued to rock Vincent. He had never felt so close to his mother. He was so grateful that she freed him from the terror of living with Michael. He realized his mother had experienced Michael's wrath. He finally said, "He never wanted to be my pappa." He paused, then added, "And you know what else?"

"What?" asked Bunny looking into Vincent's innocent face.

"Now you can find a happier man."

"You think so, do you?" Bunny answered unconvinced.

"Yah, like my pappa."

"That seems to be the general consensus," said Bunny. "That's what my brother said too. But to tell you the truth, I don't think there are any good ones left." She added, "Michael took the car."

"How are you getting to work?"

"Hoofing it," she smiled halfheartedly.

"Sorry," repeated Vincent.

"Three blocks isn't that far to walk. It'll keep me in shape."

Vincent sat quietly for several minutes. Then he said, "The judge wass right, you know. You should have made Michael marry you before he moved into our house."

"Oh, is that right. Anything else, smarty pants?"

"Um, are you sure he iss not coming back?"

"Absolutely no chance, zip, zero, nada. Now that probably takes a load off your mind. Feeling any better?"

"Yah, well, but, also, I don't want to leave de hospital."

"Why on earth would you want to stay here?" asked Bunny.

"Because then I will have to go back to that school I don't like."

"Everybody has to go to school, Vinnie. You know that."

"Yah, I know. But I'm afraid to go back."

Bunny said, "Now that doesn't sound like the brave boy I know. You can't let your fears rule you. First it will be a little fear, and then it will be a smaller fear, and smaller, till you're afraid of everything, even a little tiny thing, like, doing things you really like, like going to the music store. Now, I don't want to hear any more about that. I have to send you to school. It's the law."

Vincent turned from his mother and stared out the window.

"Are you sure that's all that's bothering you?" asked Bunny, trying to dismiss it.

After another long pause Vincent took a chance and said, "Mom, ever since I saw my pappa again, and my mamma, I kept hoping my pappa would come back here and pick me up and take me home, but he never did. I guess I am going to have to face it, I am never going back home, even to visit, am I?"

Bunny didn't answer, but Vincent already knew the answer. She thought, thank you very much, Nurse B.

"It iss worse now though, because it iss almost Christmas and that wass de very best time of all. I am lonely, and also disappointed they did not come back. We did not even say good-bye, not a real good-bye. I never even knew it wass our last visit."

"Hey, what am I chopped liver? We have each other, don't we? We'll have a nice Christmas. You'll see." She tried to smile. She couldn't let Vincent get away; he was all she had. I knew this would happen, she thought. She argued with her conscience: since when is it selfish to want to spend Christmas with your child? Even if I let him go for a few days, what good would that do? He would still come back moping around the apartment wishing he were back there with them. If I let him go at all I might as well leave him there. He'll never want to come back to me.

"Our house will never be like at my old house," said Vincent.

"What do you mean?" she asked reluctantly.

"Well see, we don't have Santa, and we don't buy lots of presents. What we do iss think up things we can do for each other. We write notes to people we like, and everybody tries extra hard to get along. Both my grandmammas get their houses all shined up. We fill up de windows with things de children have made, sometimes new things, sometimes old ones. Even my pappa's pictures are in de windows from when he wass a little boy. There iss lots of kids. I have twenty-one cousins at one grandmamma's, and five cousins at my other grandmamma's. And they aaaall like me; we all like each other. We spend de whole Christmas day playing at Grandmamma Mueller's.

"How do all those people eat at one house?"

"Well, de table at Grandmamma Dunkin's iss just two boards, two by twelve by twelves sitting on sawhorse legs," he said with authority, like a man who takes pride in showing off his expertise. "You need a sawhorse in de middle, though, or you might put a big fat turkey on there and de whole thing would start sinking down and down until it finally collapsed. KKKepussshh."

Bunny attempted her best Martha Stewart imitation. She shook her blond hair behind her shoulder and said, "That wouldn't be a good thing." Bunny tilted her chin down and smiled politely.

"No, it would be a huge mess of mashed potatoes, and pudding, and gravy everywhere. Sounds like fun!" he laughed through a residue of tears. Gradually Vincent began talking with more and more enthusiasm and animation, as he relived Christmas. "But, at my Grandmamma Mueller's, we have three tables sitting all together. There iss twelve feet here, and twelve feet there, and twelve feet there, on both sides of de table. See, if you were looking down from de ceiling, they would look like a U shape all de way around de room. It fits lots of people. It iss more like a big party than like a dinner. But when we need more space than that, we just get longer boards," he shrugged. "That iss all."

He took a chance, "You could come with me, and we could have Christmas at Grandmamma's house."

Bunny quickly squelched that prospect. "You think you're unpopular. What do you think would happen if I showed up at your grandmother's house?" Bunny tried changing the subject. "You never talk about your Grandfather Mueller."

"That iss because he died before I wass born. He died a long, long time ago."

"Your grandmother had all those kids to take care of by herself?"

"De church helped until they got bigger."

"How can she afford to feed all those people at the holidays?"

"Everybody brings something. She doesn't cook it all by herself. My pappa brings over a big huge side of beef in de morning, and we grill it over de fire."

"Outside?"

"Noooo, silly, in de house, in de fireplace. It would be too big to fit in de stove, and too cold to put it outside. It smells real good by de afternoon. When you go outside and play, and then you come back inside where it iss nice and warm, and smell de food, mmm-mmm."

"That iss at my Grandmamma Mueller's, but my favorite time iss when my Grandpappa Dunkin takes us around in his buggy on Christmas Eve. We start in de afternoon and go till dark. He gets de horses all dressed up. He puts bells on their harnesses, and we go to different houses of poor people around Promise. We sing to them a Christmas carol, and then we bring them bags of fruit, and potatoes, and chickens." Vincent's eyes sparkled with excitement.

"Ugh, do you have to get the feathers out of the chickens and chop their heads off?"

"Usually Mamma does it, or Pappa does it. It iss very fast when you know what you are doing. But, we started bringing them live chickens, so that way, they can get de eggs until they are ready to eat them. We only eat de roosters, so we end up with piles and piles of eggs."

"There iss a black man and woman I like de best when we go visiting. It iss real fun, when de buggy full of children pull up to their house, they are so happy when we come. They can hear de bells ringing from de horses and they start waving at their front door. They always remember our names."

"All twenty one?"

"No, we would never fit in de buggy. There are only five cousins at my Grandpappa Dunkin's."

"Oh. What are their names?"

"My cousins' names?"

"No, the black couple's names," Bunny said.

"Oh, I forgot."

"Even though they remembered yours?"

"No, I forgot we were talking about de black people. Their names are easy, and there are only two to remember."

"What are they?" Bunny asked, rolling her eyes.

"Andy and Candy. On his truck it says Handy Andy Maucandry," Vincent added, "He fixes things."

Bunny said, "Handy Andy and Candy Maucandry?" She was skeptical.

"Yah, it iss de truth; I told you it wass easy to remember. This iss Mr. Maucandry. Vincent lowered his voice and put his chin on his chest. Mr. Maucandry says, 'Aw, looky dere. Is dat Vincent? Look at how he's growed.' Mr. Maucandry made me feel good when he said that, ' cause I never grew, not very much anyway. Then when we give them de food, Mrs. Maucandry says, 'Bless your sweet little hearts.' She's a cheek squeezer. And they have a dog. You know what its name is?"

"Um, let's see. Sandy?"

"No, Duke."

Bunny realized she'd been suckered into that. She gave Vincent a look.

He smiled, knowing. He continued, "Then when we get back to my grandmamma's house, she has all de candles lit for Christmas Eve. She gives us hot cups of wassail, and we sit with Grandpappa by de fire.

"Wassail?"

"Like hot apple cider with orange juice and lemons, and cinnamon and stuff like that. "We give thanks, we clank glasses, and we really mean it, because of all de ones we went to—they are not so lucky. And then we eat all de stuff that my grandmamma and my aunts and my mamma and pappa have made. God loves it at Grandpappa Dunkin's on Christmas Eve. If you were there, you would know what I mean. You can feel it in your heart. It iss love, only it iss not coming out of your own heart, it iss going in—from God—until it feels like you are going to spill over with feeling good. After dinner we all go to sleep. That probably got started because we were all too full and sleepy for de buggy ride home. I am going to miss it all because I won't be there." Vincent looked at his mother, half hoping what he told her had made a difference. "Can we go even for a short visit?"

Bunny insisted, "No, Vinnie. We would just spoil things for everyone else by being there."

Disappointed once again, he turned his face to the window and repeated. "I am going to miss it a lot." He sighed with sad resignation.

"I'll make Christmas special," said Bunny. "I promise. I gotta make a few phone calls. I'll be back. Don't you worry about anything." Bunny reminded, "At least we got rid of the mean old Michael. Right?"

Vinnie looked at his mother with renewed relief. "Thanks, Mom."

"I'll be right back."

After Bunny left, Vincent's thoughts drifted back to Martin and Freida. He was remembering when he and Marshall were six years old. They went with Martin to the watermelon patch. It was late in the summer, and the leaves covered the road with welcome shade from the hot midday sun. They bounced along in the hay wagon down the dry dusty road, sitting side by side with matching clean white T-shirts and straw hats. Martin was to the left, Vincent and Marshall to the right. It would have been easier for Martin to hold the reins from the middle, but Marshall and Vincent insisted on sitting next to each other. They were feeling very important. After all, they were doing man' s work today; they were being real farmers.

"Whoa, Zach. Okay, boys, ready to go watermelon hunting?"

"Are we going to put de wagon up here, Pappa? We should put it down de bank so we don't have so far to carry them up de hill?"

"We don't want our wagon wheels stuck in de mud, do we? Zach iss strong, but not that strong, especially after we get de wagon filled up with all our watermelons."

"Ahh," they said in unison.

The boys began the slippery trek down the five-foot slope. Both slipped and fell on their behinds on the way down. They used the front of their clean T-shirts to wipe the mud off their hands.

"Ah, boys, look at this whopper. That iss a big fellow, isn't he?"

"Yah!!"

"Are you going to carry that one?" asked Marshall.

Martin answered, "I think that would be a good idea, since he probably weighs as much as you, Marshall. Whew, holy canoly, that iss a big boy." Martin wobbled back to the wagon with his prize watermelon.

Marshall asked, "What iss a canoly?"

Martin replied, "I don't know, Marshall. But it must be something holy. But then again, that would mean moley's are holy."

It left Marshall pondering how many things are called holy. He thought, holy Toledo, holy cows, holy rollers, holy Hanna.

"Who iss Hanna?" asked Marshall.

Confused, Martin repeated, "Who iss Hanna?"

"In de Bible. She iss Abraham and Sara's servant girl," answered Vincent.

"Aw," said Marshall, satisfied.

They continued gathering for most of the afternoon, looking under one vine, searching under another, until they were satisfied with their full wagonload. They began a more leisurely, worn-out ride down the road back to the barn. Their faces and T-shirts were smudged with pink watermelon juice and streaks of mud. Martin began to sing, "Ohhhh, sixteen tons, and what do you get?"

The boys joined in, "Another day older and deeper in debt. St. Peter, do not call me 'cause I can not go."

Martin intentionally destroyed the high note, "I ooooowe my sou-ou-ou-ou-oul to de company store."

Vincent started stomping his foot to the beat on the toolbox on the floor under his feet.

"What iss de second verse?" Vincent asked.

No one knew.

Then Martin replied to the rhythm, "Second verse, same as de first."

In unison, "Sixteen tons . . ." This continued as the three tired farmhands rolled back to the barn, each taking their turn at destroying the solo part.

"I have an idea," said Martin. "I will close my eyes and you can tell me if we are staying on de road, and when to turn, like that. It will be like you are steering. I will hold de reins and you will tell me which way to steer."

"Nooo! We will wreck."

"No we won't. Just try it."

Martin shut his right eye, but kept his left eye open, hiding this from the boys. Freida watched from the porch. She was beginning to think something was wrong with Martin. The wagon was weaving from side to side but never going completely off the road. The boys were waving wildly and half-standing in excitement as the wagon crept close to one side of the road or the other. If she didn't know better, she might have thought Martin was drinking. They miraculously turned off the road onto the drive without incident. When they got close enough, she could hear the boys yelling, "No, left, more, more. Yah, now straight. No! Straight."

As they passed by the house, Martin waved to Freida and discretely turned his head, revealing his secret. She put her hand up to her mouth so the boys wouldn't see her smiling. They looked her way too, but were much too busy to wave at her.

The boys excitedly steered Martin in by jumping up and down excitedly and exclaiming, "We're getting closer. We're almost to de barn! Slow, slow. That iss it, Pappa. No right, right! Yah. Straight. Straight! Ahhhhh. Now stop. Stop!! Ahhhh."

They collapsed in their seats in relief. Martin turned to face the boys with one eye open, the other eye shut and said, "Thank you boys. Nice job."

They pounced on him immediately in protest. Vincent started swacking at him with his hat. Martin threw back his head and started laughing.

"I fooled you, I fooled you," he said.

Vincent protested, embarrassed, "You lousy, rotten, useless, good for nothing. You should not have done that. I am telling Mamma what you did."

"Aww," said Marshall, "We are so stupid! No left, no right. Awww, we are going to get you back for sure." Marshall smiled at Martin, his two front teeth missing.

At the same time Vincent was dreaming about the good old days from his hospital bed, Martin searched methodically through the pile of logs stacked at the side of the house. He was searching for a piece of cherry wood, or maybe apple. Freida liked the way they smelled the best. When he found the perfect piece he was looking for, it didn't give him the satisfaction he had hoped for. Vincent had once again crept into his thoughts. If only I knew how to save him. I cannot live with the thought that another man is living with my boy and mistreating him. I know he must be trying hard to do what the man wants. How can I stand by, only a few miles away, and let it happen? I would love to steal him away in the middle of the night and take him somewhere that he will never have to worry. "God help us, God help my boy. I am failing Vincent. I should never have said, 'we will see,' when I knew I wass not able to do anything for him. Please, do not let this go on, Lord Jesus. I know in all things you have a plan, but can you think of another way? It iss much too hard for Freida and me to bear. And Vincent has already suffered so much."

Martin walked several logs noisily through the back door of his unpleasantly quiet house. His boots clomped against the bare pine board floors. He dropped them on the brick floor in front of the cast- iron heat stove. He feared he had waited too long to put them in. He took his stoking tool down from the stone wall behind the stove, and pushed together a pile of the hot coals that were barely glowing on the bottom of the stove. He put the piece of apple wood on top, and could only wait and see, hoping the logs would catch before the fire went out completely.

Freida had rarely gone back to church since she and Zach almost wrecked the buggy. Neither had she been able to begin Bible study again. She knew Christmas was in another week, and she still hadn't been able to get in the spirit. It was difficult enough just getting out of bed and getting dressed in the morning. She tried visiting her mother's house one Sunday afternoon, but she walked away that day feeling as if she had ruined everyone's afternoon.

Mother Dunkin was worried about everyone getting too happy near Freida and Martin. How could they joke and laugh when Martin and Freida were so miserable? Then she would change her mind and think, but why should I make them all subdue their joy for Freida and Martin's sake? There were only two of them, but so many others to consider. Was that fair? She couldn't decide. It was very uncomfortable for everyone.

Deuteronomy 32:35. To me belongeth vengeance, and recompence; their foot shall slide in due time: for the day of their calamity is at hand, and the things that shall come upon them make haste.

Chapter 24

Too Young to Die

$\mathcal{B}$unny walked down the corridor and into the lobby where she found a row of pay phones.

"Hello, may I please speak to the police chief?"

"Who is calling, please?"

"Bunny Muldare. It's about Michael Stern."

"Yes, Miss Muldare?"

"Well, can I speak to the chief."

"Yes, but I need to tell him what it is you are calling about."

"My son, Vinnie Muldare, told me that Michael pushed him into the street, and caused him to be hit by a truck."

"He wants to make a statement?"

"Yes."

"One moment please."

Bunny waited for the chief, impatiently.

"Please deposit thirty-five cents for the next five minutes. Please deposit . . ."

"Okay, okay," said Bunny to the recording.

She put more money in the phone and then, finally, the chief answered, "Miss Muldare. How is everything going?"

"Better, thank you. The reason I called is that I need you to have someone come to the hospital. My son, Vinnie, is in the hospital and he would like to make a statement about Michael Stern, my boyfriend, the one that I have the restraining order on. Michael pushed him in front of a truck. He didn't tell me until today that Michael pushed him. Before this, the story was that Michael tried to catch him before he got hit. But today Vinnie said Michael definitely pushed him on purpose."

"I see."

There was an awkward pause as if the chief were thinking something that would be better going unsaid. Bunny guessed what he was thinking; Vinnie would be better off with the Mennonites.

"Will the two of you be there Monday morning?"

"I'll be here today, tomorrow, whenever you want. Can't you be here sooner?"

"Monday, that's the earliest," he repeated.

"I'll be here."

"Where is your son?"

"Good Samaritan Children's Hospital, Room 545.

"See you then."

"Thank you so much, Chief Holt."

She hung up the phone and began to dial again.

An unfamiliar woman's voice answered, "Hello, Mr. Bigler's office."

"Hello, this is Bunny Muldare, who is this?" asked Bunny.

"Oh, Miss Muldare, this is Connie. Mr. Bigler has asked me to fill in for you till we get caught up. I'm from downstairs, and since I haven't left my other job yet, I told Mr. Bigler I could come in on Saturdays to help out."

"Where is Mr. Bigler?"

"He's right here. Would you like to speak to him?"

"Yes,"

"Hello, Bunny."

"Mr. Bigler, I know this has been hard for you to be patient with me since Vinnie went to the hospital, but he'll be out in a couple of weeks, and then we can go back to normal."

"Yes, Bunny, it has been hard. That's why I am having Connie come in on Saturdays. I can't afford to let our work here get too far behind."

"I know, and I'm sorry. I promise, in just a couple of more weeks everything will be just like it was before. There's just one more favor I need to ask though—can I take Monday off? Vinnie has to talk to the police on Monday, and I need to be there."

"Yes, Bunny, you can have Monday off. But don't bother coming in on Tuesday either. I can't keep making accommodations for you when there are plenty of other girls who are ready and willing to do your job."

"But Mr. Bigler, it will be different after Christmas, I promise."

"I'm sorry, Bunny. I guess we could all see the writing on the wall before this phone call. I'm sure you'll find another job once your life is more settled."

"But, I need this job."

There was silence on the other end of the phone. Then he said, "Thank you for all your hard work, Bunny. It's a shame it had to end this way. You were a very good employee. I'll tell you what: I'll send you an extra two weeks' severance pay, and that should get you through Christmas." He waited. When Bunny had nothing to say he ended with, "Bye now." Click.

Bunny repeated to herself into the phone sadly, "Bye now."

Bunny heaved a heavy sigh. She thought, first my mother, now this. I can't handle any more stress in my life. I have six hundred dollars in a savings account that will last about one month. I have no car, which means I have to be able to find a job in Carlisle, on the bus line, before the end of January. Damn it! I can't believe this is happening!

Bunny gathered her courage and said to herself; well regardless of whether everything goes in the toilet, I have a job to do. I have to get some justice for Vinnie. I'm his mother, and that's what I'm going to do.

Bunny wasted no time. She dialed Perry's apartment. "Hello, Perry."

"Hi, Bunny." He sounded genuinely glad to hear from her. "You know, I never got a chance to apologize for making you so mad."

"Forget it, Perry. You were just doing what you thought was best. The reason I called is to ask you where Michael is?" Bunny rubbed her forehead in frustration.

"I don't know, he just took off and never said. He left you a letter though. Maybe that will tell you where he went."

"Yeah, read it."

"You want me to read it? It's probably personal, don't you think?"

"I don't care, Perry. Just read it. That's what he gets for being too cheap to put a stamp on it."

Perry opened the kitchen drawer where he stashed his mail. "Aw, here it is," he said.

"Perry, did Michael leave you a note or say a proper good-bye?" Bunny asked, sensing that Perry was feeling abandoned.

"No," he whispered sadly.

"Perry, you deserve better. Michael is such a jerk. Don't waist your time pining over him. He's not worth it. You need somebody you can have a real relationship with."

Perry said nothing, but Bunny could hear him breathing into the phone.

"Perry, remember the waitress at King's Korner when we went there a couple months ago."

"Yeah,"

"She asked me about you. I know her. You should ask her out. She's a nice person."

"I couldn't do that, Bunny."

"Why not?"

"I'm too scared."

Bunny understood, and replied "Aren't we all?"

Perry said nothing.

"Read me the letter," Bunny urged.

"Dear Bunny, I am writing to tell you that I am moving far away to start a new life. I know it will be hard for you to be alone, but I need to find a woman who is unencumbered."

Bunny interjected, "My, my. Mighty big word for such a little jerk of a man. Didn't know he knew such big words."

Perry sighed and continued, "I always loved you, Bunny. You are a beautiful woman, but the problem is I never asked to be Vinnie's dad. He was never mine to start out with, and he never will be. It started out nice and simple, just you and me. Then without any warning I gotta be Daddy for your old boyfriend's kid. Since I know you'll never give him up for me, I have to leave. Try to remember the good times, and if you see a jet in the sky leaving a stream over Carlisle, it will be your ever-loving Michael, leaving a bit of his magic behind, just for you. Maybe we will meet again someday, but for now, asta la vista, my darling."

"That is such crap!" Bunny protested. "And he never said anything about where he was going."

"Sounds like he still plans to finish school and be a pilot. Maybe he joined the air force."

"Wherever he went, I'm going to track him down like a dog, and he is going to pay. You watch me!"

"What did he ever do that was so bad, Bunny?"

"You heard about our argument, right?"

"Yeah, and how he barely got out of there with his life," Perry replied.

"Well, remember, there are two sides to every story. And not only that, Vinnie just told me Michael pushed him in front of that truck!"

"Wow! Honestly, Bunny, I never knew that."

Perry turned, covered the phone, and mumbled something.

"Who's there?" Bunny asked. "It's Michael, isn't it?"

"No, it's Danny Burns."

"Burns? Danny Burns! You are kidding."

"You want to talk to him?"

Bunny remembered a skinny teenager about sixteen, who grinned all the time and had little green crescent-shaped slivers for eyes, and teeth to match. He always wore a black felt cowboy hat, a pocket T-shirt, and a huge silver belt buckle that he was especially proud of. It was so big for his skinny waist; it looked more like a cumber bund than a buckle. And who could forget his jeans, the grimiest, holiest blue jeans on earth. She also remembered he was a faithful friend when she was in trouble.

Before Bunny had a chance to reply she heard, "Hey, Bunny, baby, my favorite party princess."

"Well, well, Danny Burns, a blast from the past," said Bunny.

"Don't be mean to me, Bunny, you know how I love you, and how I used to take care of you."

"You saved my life more than once. The only problem is I can't remember much about it. I was too stoned."

"I can't remember much about those days either, or much about these days either, for that matter." He laughed, loud and rapid-fire, like a machine gun. "But who the hell cares as long as we're having fun? We had good times, didn't we, Bunny? Remember old Burns, your best bud, Burns?" he pleaded.

"Of course, Burns. You were a good friend."

"Maybe we could go out tonight, and I'll show you what you're missing in Philly. I moved up from Carlisle—too small-time. I could show you some great places, and get you started with some new buds. Forget Michael. He's nobody."

"Sure Danny. One thing though, I don't go out with anybody that doesn't want to be my kid's dad."

Danny chuckled uncomfortably.

"Still living at home, Danny?"

"Nah, I got a place in Philly, like I said."

"What are you doing with Perry?" Bunny asked.

"Perry and I go out sometimes. He don't do no hooch or nothing, but we get along."

"I'm sure you do. You know, Burns, Perry isn't used to running with the fast crowd. He's straight, Burns. Don't get him messed up. His so-called 'best friend', Michael, just abandoned him, and there's no telling what he'll get himself involved in."

"I know, Bunny. We're just hangin' out, that's all. I ain't pushin' nothing on nobody. What people want to do is their own business. All I do is supply them with what they already need. I'm just sort of like the broker, you know, like always, just me and a bunch of buds, that's all. You sure you don't want to go out tonight, bein' that Michael ain't around no more? I could show you a real good—"

Pangs of loneliness rose up suddenly. Bunny tried to ignore them. "God knows I could use a little relaxation. I've been under a lot of stress lately."

"Sure, Bunny, we could have a good time, like the old days."

"N-no thanks, I have things to take care of. My kid's in the hospital, and so is my mom. Besides, I've moved up from the old buds myself."

"Hey, speaking of the old buds, do you remember Carl Koons?" asked Danny.

"Yeah, how is he?"

"Dead. Heroin finally got him. Same with the McDain brothers, and Cheryl Maloney."

"Wow. Cheryl Maloney was just getting started when Vinnie went to jail. That's really too bad. She was such a good artist, remember?"

"Yeah, she was nineteen when she died. The McDain brothers died on the same night. They were driving home one night and plowed right into a tree, man. Their parents were all messed up after that. They went on TV and started campaigning to get the heroin bosses put away. I'm glad they did. I was losin' a lot of friends to that shit. I hear Vinnie's dead too."

No answer.

"Bunny, you there? Aw man, I'm sorry, Bunny. You know I love you, and I'd never say anything to hurt you. Aw man, I'm so stupid, I thought you knew."

"I didn't," she choked. "What happened?" she asked hesitantly. She wasn't up for more tragedy, not today.

"He got hold of some heroin in jail. Some of them said he did it on purpose. I don't know though, Vinnie always liked to live on the edge. You know how, if he was going to do something, he'd do it all the way. I can't believe he could just fold, and do himself in like that. Vinnie was my hero, man. He wouldn't just fold like that, would he, Bunny?"

"Not the way I remember him, Burns. But who knows what ten years of prison can do to your mind? Maybe he changed. Or maybe he hadn't had any in so long he thought he could handle it, and he couldn't."

Bunny was sad for them all, especially for Vinnie, though it seemed like another world away. All she could say was, "Such a shame, such a shame." They were just kids, she thought. Everything Burns said sounded so remote from her life now. It had been ten years since she had seen any of them. She had been removed from all of them so long ago. She had a sudden realization that she had been mysteriously saved from the tragic fate these other young people had met. She knew if it hadn't been for her baby boy, she would certainly be dead too, right along with the rest of them. The whole sequence of events: Vinnie going to jail, her father dying when he did, not being able to find her baby, and having to stay off drugs for his sake; it just seemed too well-orchestrated to be coincidental. But why? Why her? And why did those other kids have to die? They were no different than me, Bunny thought. And why Cheryl Maloney? She certainly had more talent to offer this world than I did. Maybe Vinnie died like the rest of them, and he was able to keep on doing heroin in jail until it eventually ate him up. "Such a shame," she repeated.

Burns interrupted the awkward silence. "But, hey, this is probably getting to you, all this death talk. Like I said, if you want me to show you around Philly, call me. I got some new buds, and we ain't into heroin too much no more. There's this new shit—"

"You know what Burns, this conversation is going nowhere. I gotta go. But tell Perry I said bye." Bunny started to hang up. "Hey, Burns, you still there?"

"Yeah, baby, what is it?"

"I haven't forgotten how you pulled me out of the barbed wire that night we were running from the cops. You took a big risk, and I appreciate it. If I'm ever in a foxhole, I want to be there with you. And Burns?"

"Yeah baby,"

"One more thing. Maybe God spared us for a reason."

Burns hesitated, "Sure Bunny, maybe he did. I knew you hadn't forgotten. I'll always love you; you were one of my very best friends. Good talking to you again."

"Take good care of yourself, Burns."

"Hey, nobody else will."

"See you," said Bunny.

"Later, baby."

Bunny made her way back to Vinnie's room. She was determined to keep her mind on the task at hand: giving Michael what he deserved. Besides, the prospect of getting even with Michael was a welcome distraction from the pressure of visiting her mother tomorrow. Once again, Vinnie was giving her life purpose. They were going to fight together until they made Michael pay for what he had done to them. She cared about losing her job, but not nearly as much as being there on Monday morning when Vinnie would bust Michael for good.

Bunny walked briskly past Nurse B., who was singing Vincent's song.

"We, we, we got the power of love," she sang.

Bunny paused, "Isn't that Vinnie's song?"

"Yes it is; he taught it to me. Catchy, isn't it? I been trying to get it out of my head ever since, but it's one of those songs that just keeps hangin' 'round, and hangin' 'round, no matter what I try to do, it just keeps poppin' back into my head."

Bunny smiled with approval.

Nurse B. continued, "We, we, we, we got the power of the Lord. We're gonna take that power and sprrread it all over the world."

It sounded different when Nurse B. sang it, but nice, thought Bunny. I wish I could sing low like her, she thought.

"Vinnie," Bunny called. "Mom's back."

"Hi, Mom," sighed Vincent, still unenthusiastic.

"Vinnie, I've got great news," Bunny announced. "I just talked to the police, and they are going to send someone over to your room so you can tell them what Michael did to you."

"Why would they do that?" asked Vinnie with apprehension.

"So that they can arrest him, and put him in jail!"

"Why must we do that?"

"So we can pay him back for what he did, why do you think? There's just one small problem, but I think the police can work it out."

"What?" asked Vincent.

"I called Perry to find out where Michael is, and all we know is, he's out West somewhere. But heck, I know his Social Security number. They'll figure out where he is sooner or later."

"But why must we put him in jail, and how long would he be there?"

"What do we care how long they want to keep him in there? As far as I'm concerned, the longer the better."

"But it would be better if we leave it de way it iss. He iss not coming back, so why must we do anything?" asked Vincent.

The question confused Bunny. She asked, "You're afraid of having to face Michael in court, aren't you?"

"Well, yah, sort of, but we can leave things de way they are and that would be just as good."

"Vinnie, you can't let your fears rule you, remember?"

"It iss not because I am afraid, I am thinking we don't need to get even."

"But he deserves it. What he did to us was very wrong."

"Yah, so."

"So, don't you want justice?"

"No."

"Yes, you do, you just don't know it."

"No, I don't. But you do."

"Well, of course, and I want it for you too."

Vincent replied, "It iss mine to avenge, saith de Lord."

"What's that supposed to mean?" asked Bunny, clearly irritated with Vincent.

"If we only leave it alone, de Lord will take care of him. We should let de Lord take care of it and not get mixed up doing his work for him."

Bunny stood up from the side of Vincent's bed and spun around in exasperation. "I cannot figure you out. Aren't you the kid who, just this morning, was sobbing about how mean Michael was, and how you couldn't go home because you were afraid of him? Don't you get it? We have Michael right where we want him. We have a chance to make him pay for what he did, and you want to let him go!" Bunny ran her hand through her hair.

"I said I couldn't go back home and live with him, I didn't say I wanted to get even. That iss what you want, not me.

"But, Vinnie, the police will gladly put him in jail for us. He deserves it."

"But it iss not going to make things better by paying him back. I would rather just let him go off somewhere far away, and we can all forget about all of de bad things that have happened."

Vincent interrupted the silence. "You can bring all de policemen you want, but I am not talking."

Silence again.

Finally Bunny said, "Merry Christmas."

"Mom, maybe he has already learned it iss better to do things God's way."

Bunny stared at Vincent, and Vincent stared back.

Finally he said, "Michael never wanted to be my pappa, but I don't care; I did not want him to be my pappa, either. We got shoved onto each other whether we liked it or not. When he pushed me into de street, he wass only mad about having to take care of me again, and it wass making him crazy. He got so mad he forgot what he wass doing. Did that ever happen to you? Now that he iss not here, and iss not coming back, everything iss fixed. Don't you see? He needs a second chance to do it God's way, just like you did, Mom. He had a lifelong job of something he didn't want to do, and he wasn't even getting paid. That's not so easy. I wouldn't want to baby sit somebody' s goofy kid my whole life."

"I wish you had told me this before I made all those phone calls. I could have saved myself a lot of trouble."

"Sorry, you never asked me. All I want to do iss forget about it, and maybe someday, somebody else will want to be my pappa. If not, that iss okay, I don't mind 'cause my pappa will always be my pappa. And maybe Michael iss right now thinking that weird kid wass right about doing it God's way, and then he will find somebody to marry him, and they can have a boy of their own. He cannot do that if we put him in jail. And we will be just de same, whether he goes to jail or we give him another chance."

"Unbelievable," said Bunny. "I pity the poor woman who gets hooked up with him." She thought about her conversation with her boss less than an hour ago. If she'd known this was how Vincent was going to act, she would have kept her mouth shut and she'd still have her job. She ran her hands through her hair again and plopped down into the vinyl hospital chair. She added, "I can't remember ever having such a bad day. I can't believe this."

"We don't have to get even, don't you see? Bless them that curse you, and do good to them that hate you."

"I don't know. Why don't you sleep on it, and we'll talk about it tomorrow?"

"I already know for sure. I do not want to put Michael in jail. I just want him to live somewhere else until he gets himself straightened out with God."

Bunny insisted, "Okay, okay, you made your point. As for me, no revenge would ever be enough."

"Yah. I know. You would like more punishment and more punishment and more punishment until de poor guy wass chopped into teenie-tiny pieces."

"You got that right."

"You think it will make you feel better, but it won't. Let's just forget about it."

Bunny didn't answer, but sat in the chair rubbing her forehead to help her think. At this point she didn't know who was upsetting her more, Michael or Vinnie.

Nurse B. came in with a clean bandage for Vincent's hand. "Hey, Vinnie, sweetie, we gotta put a new bandage on that hand of yours. We're going to go with a smaller bandage today."

"Yeh! Are my fingers going to be able to stick out this time?"

"I think we can let your thumb and second finger poke out of there."

"Yeh!"

He sat up in the bed and stuck his arm out. She began to unroll the gauze from his wrist and loosen his old bandage. She hummed, "We got the power of love. We, we, we, we got the power of the Lord, we're gonna take that power and spread it all over the world."

Vincent started, "Take it to the East, take it to the West, take to Gibraltar, take it to Tibet, take it to St. Petersburg, take it to Beijing, but take it, take it, take it, that's the most important thing,"

Nurse B. said, "Woo, yeah, Vinnie, how I love to hear you sing."

Vincent smiled and started rocking side to side to the beat.

"Hold still, hold still. We gotta get this old dirty bandage off."

"Sorry."

Nurse B. said, "Look how good your finger looks, Vinnie."

Then she directed her attention toward Bunny. "Isn't it somethin' how this child has been able to bounce back so fast, God love him."

He put his arm around Nurse B. and watched intently as they studied the progress of his finger, and then slowly wrapped his hand back up again.

Bunny's thoughts were somewhere else, but no matter where her thoughts landed, there was no peace.

Matthew 5:44–45. Love your enemies, bless them that curse you, do good to them that hate you, and pray for them which despitefully use you, and persecute you; That ye may be the children of your Father which is in heaven: for he maketh his sun to rise on the evil and on the good, and sendeth rain on the just and on the unjust.

Chapter 25

Enter Thou into the
Joy of the Lord

$\mathcal{B}$unny sat engrossed in her thoughts as the hum of the bus lulled its passengers to sleep. The Pennsylvania countryside glided past as the bus gently rolled along the turnpike. Outside the day was cold and gray, as if it were going to snow at any moment, though the cows didn't seem to mind. They congregated in small groups randomly gathering along the hillside. Bunny reviewed her horrific day, from Brother Richard's disturbing news, to her phone call with Mr. Bigler, to Vincent's insistent refusal to speak to the police about Michael, to her conversation with Burns about the deaths of her old friends. Bunny had dealt with the fact that her old boyfriend was going to be in jail for life, but she never considered the day when she would find out he was dead. It didn't seem real. So young, she thought. People aren't supposed to die this young. I wish I knew how it happened. With all these emotions coming at me all at once, I'll never be able to handle seeing Mom tomorrow, but I know she needs someone to be with her. But not me, why me? She doesn't even like me. I'll just have to blow Richard off. It's one thing to argue with Mom over the phone; that I can do. If things get too bad I can just hang up, but how am I going to be with her and show any kind of compassion as she beats me up emotionally? I wonder how sick she really is. I wish Richard could have given me more information. Maybe she's so sick she won't be able to hurt me. Maybe I can go in there, and we'll just acknowledge each other, and we can sit quietly without saying anything. But what if she tells me, again, I make a lousy mother? I know one thing, no matter what we talk about, if she can get her mouth open, she'll accuse me of something or other, and God knows, I certainly have some good material for her to chew me up with. Maybe that's what I should do. Maybe I should tell her all the sordid details of my sordid life, and she can have a blast. I'll even embellish it, and make it worse, so she can really get steamed. Bunny began to daydream.

"Hi, Mom. How are you doing?"

"How does it look? What kind of comment was that?"

"I was just asking you how you are, Mom."

"How does it look like I'm doing? Not that you care."

"I'm here, am I not?"

"Well, Bunny dear, are you working?"

"No, lost my job."

"Oh, Bunny. Life gives you a chance and you just keep blowing it."

"Yeah, Mom. I just keep blowing it. Did I tell you I was chasing Michael—"

"Who?"

"You know, the boyfriend I've been sleeping with for the past two years. I was chasing him around the apartment with a gun, and the cops busted in on us."

"Bunny. I don't even know who you are. Richard, dear, get Bunny out of here before she kills me. She's going to break my heart. How can she speak that way to a dying woman?"

Richard would say, "Because maybe, Mother, Bunny needs to protect herself from you. You never have a nice thing to say about her. Bunny, why don't you tell Mother why you lost your job?"

"Nah,"

"Mother, she lost her job because she was spending too much time at the hospital."

"She did not. She never came to visit me once."

"Not with you, Mother, with Vinnie. He got hit by a truck."

"Who, that drug dealer, or his bastard son?"

"Her son."

"Well she should have left him where he was. He was better off. I told her she could never raise that boy. It's obvious she makes a lousy mother."

Bunny's daydream began to incorporate her conversation with Richard in the restaurant, and Richard's words came back to her. "Burning bridges hasn't worked for you so far. Maybe you should consider mending those bridges before it's too late. Wouldn't it be wonderful if you and Mother could finally become friends?"

"You know as well as I do, she never liked me, and she never will."

Suddenly someone tapped on Bunny's shoulder. She jumped.

"Look!" said a voice over Bunny's shoulder. She tried to swallow away the lump in her throat.

"Look, a deer!" he repeated.

She looked out her window. "Two deer," she answered.

"Oh, yeah. No, three!" he said.

Bunny and the man stared at the deer through the window. The animals were walking cautiously beside the highway about twenty feet away.

Bunny said, "Look, there's a fawn poking out from between the bushes."

"How about that," said the man. "It's amazing how well they're camouflaged." The deer were a wintry gray, a perfect match to the bushes nearby.

"Do you think that's an accident—that they match so well, I mean—or is it intentional?" asked the man.

"I used to think it was an accident, but now I'm not so sure. It takes a lot of accidents to make a world, and make it all work," answered Bunny.

"It takes a lot of accidents to make a world," he repeated. "That's pretty good. I'll have to remember that. I hope you'll forgive me for being so bold, but I noticed we've been getting off the bus at the same time for weeks, but we've never spoken."

"Really? I hadn't noticed." Bunny turned around to look into his face. He had a full but muscular face and a strong neck, like a Midwest farm boy. He had dark hair, fair skin, and the whites of his eyes were so clear they were almost blue. He seemed much too wholesome to be hitting on her."

"I think we're neighbors," he said. "I go to the hospital to visit patients about three times a week."

"Are you a doctor or something?" asked Bunny.

"Not in the traditional sense," he said evasively. He looked out the window.

Bunny was beginning to feel uncomfortable. This guy was much smarter than she was. But he seemed harmless enough, and a little lonely.

He turned his attention back to her. "You look troubled today," he said.

"Compared to what?" She wasn't quite ready to spill her guts to a stranger on the bus.

"Is there someone you love in the hospital?" he asked.

"Yes, but he's getting better. My son was hit by a truck, but he should be out before Christmas."

"Oh, was that your son? Vincent Muldare I think his name is."

"Yes."

"I remember him from the newspaper."

Bunny thought, how nice, everybody knows us.

"Wasn't he kidnapped by the Amish?"

"Well, yes, sort of," Bunny answered, hoping they weren't going to dwell on that subject.

"Our church prayed for him after the accident. I'm glad to hear he's going to be all right. I'll be able to relay the good news to the congregation."

She was surprised anyone cared enough to pray for Vinnie. "His ring finger is still stiff, and he may walk with a limp," Bunny qualified, "but I'm just glad he survived it at all. He was very lucky."

"I remember that day," he said. "We watched from the sidewalk as they put him into the ambulance. The prevailing sentiment of our prayer group was that life is precious; we never know when it will be taken from us. It can happen to a little boy like your son, or ninety-year-old, we just never know, do we?"

Bunny didn't answer. Or a young man in his twenties, thought Bunny, sadly.

"When it happened, we decided to live every day we have on this earth as fully as possible, a kind of collective carpe diem experience.

"A what?"

"Carpe diem, seize the day, make the most of life. I guess that fullness means different things to different people."

"Are you a like a pastor or something?" asked Bunny.

"If I say yes, will you start censoring your answers and looking for a way to escape?" He smiled self-consciously.

"I'll try not to." She smiled. "So you are a pastor?"

"Afraid so."

"Are you like a regular pastor or a youth pastor?"

"I'm 'the' pastor." He tried not to take it as an insult. He knew he was young, and looked it. It was one of the obstacles he faced in leading his own congregation. "Most of my congregation is older than I am, and I'm a little sensitive about it. So before I started my first sermon, I confronted the issue by making a joke, 'Please pray for the kid behind the podium.' I'm twenty-eight," he explained. "And a half," he added, smiling.

"I'm sorry if I hurt your feelings," said Bunny. "I just meant that being a pastor with a church and everything is a pretty big job for a young man. Well, not that you're all that young; I mean, you're not really that old either. You look nice; I mean, not handsome, nice."

The pastor looked away, not knowing how to respond.

"I mean, you are handsome, not just nice." Bunny felt like crawling under the seat. Had she just told a pastor she thought he was handsome? Never mind that he was. It's just that she knew she didn't want to sound like she was flirting, and worse, she didn't want to sound like a babbling idiot.

"Oh, never mind," he offered. Both began to feel embarrassed. "This kind of thing happens every time I tell someone I'm a pastor. Naturally it makes people uncomfortable, and immediately they begin to backpedal, but I'm getting used to it. Now that I understand the problem, I can work on how to overcome it. It interferes with what God wants me to do."

"And what's that?" Bunny asked, making conversation.

"Counsel people about their problems. It's hard enough bringing them out under normal circumstances, but you should see what happens when I'm wearing 'the collar.'"

"The collar?" asked Bunny.

"Oh," he said, "this collar." He opened his briefcase and withdrew a stiff piece of cotton that resembled the material in an old-fashioned nurse's cap.

Bunny understood immediately that he was probably right, and it probably did make people feel uncomfortable. She tried to help by offering him a piece of her problems: "I used to think all I needed was a second chance with my son, and I would be the very best mother in the world. I am trying, but I'm not doing very well."

"Raising a child takes a father and a mother, grandparents, aunts and uncles, teachers, church groups, neighbors. It all works together."

"That's part of the problem. My son had that when he lived with the Mennonites, but not with me."

"Who does he have now?"

"Me."

"That's it?"

"'Fraid so," she admitted.

"Where is your family?"

Without answering, Bunny turned forward again in her seat. Then she did the very thing she promised herself she was not going to do. She started crying in public, again.

He pulled a napkin from his lunch bag. "I'm sorry," he said. "Upsetting people seems to be what I do best." He began to feel panicky. If there was one thing that could discombobulate him, it was a weeping female. He shook the napkin nervously over her shoulder until she took it. He could feel his eyes misting up. "Lord, help me," he prayed within himself.

Then he asked Bunny, sounding a little helpless himself, "If I sit beside you, no one will be able to see you crying. Do you want me to do that?"

Bunny nodded her head yes. He moved into the seat
next to hers and waited for her to explain.

"I ran into my brother this morning, and he wants me
to go to my mother's hospital room. She has cancer, and I
don't think I can."

"Are you and your mother close?"

She shook her head no.

He waited for Bunny to tell him more. Finally she was
able to say, "She still thinks of me as the drugged-out, smart-
mouth runaway that I was ten years ago."

"She's never forgiven you then?"

"No. It's worse than that. She doesn't even like me. I've
only talked to her a handful of times since I left home. Every time we talk she loves to be able to remind me of how
I'm the bad one, 'the black sheep.' To her I'm just an awful
person, and I always will be, no matter what I do. Honestly,
it was easier to be bad. At least then I knew there was a good
reason for her not liking me. Or then, maybe I am bad. I
have plenty of stuff going on to give her ammunition."

"There's three more deer," he pointed.

She looked up. "Yeah," she whispered through her tears.
She sighed as she continued to stare out the window. She
managed to gather her composure somewhat.

The pastor said, "If we live for other people's approval,
they're bound to let us down."

"But she's my mother. If she doesn't like me, that's pretty
bad. I mean, I may not be the most likable person in the
world, but everybody's mother likes them."

"Not everybody's. Mine doesn't."

Bunny looked at him with surprise through her red puffy
eyes. "But you're a pastor. How good can you get?"

"Not everybody thinks that's a good thing. Some people would say it's a coward's life."

"Is that what your mother says?"

"Yes," he admitted. Bunny could see the pain on his face.

"But," he added, "as Jesus says: 'Behold my mother and my brethren! For whosoever shall do the will of my Father which is in heaven, the same is my brother, and sister—and mother.' What gets me through the day is that I try to live a decent life, according to God's opinion, and hopefully, when this life is over, God will say, 'well done, good and faithful servant.' That is what I need to live for, not my mother's approval. In the end, it will be God who sorts it all out anyway; no one else."

"That's fine for you; God might say 'well done' to you, but he'll never say 'well done' to me." Bunny looked him straight in the eye and said, "I'll get up there someday, and he'll say: 'Screwed up royal'. Then the ground will come out from under me, and I'll go flying straight to hell."

The pastor laughed out loud.

"It's not that funny," she said. "Especially since it's the truth." But his laughter was contagious, and it made her smile.

"Yes, it is," he said.

"Ahhh," he said in falsetto, trying to recover. "I'm sorry, it just reminded me of a joke I heard,"

"What's your name?" he asked, rubbing his eyes.

"Bunny, well really it's Bonnie, but I go by Bunny," she answered.

"Bunny, I'm Pastor Dan." Then he said smiling, and with all honesty, "Don't you realize that's where all of us find ourselves at some time in our lives. In fact, most of us find ourselves there on a regular basis. There is no solution for it, except one."

"What?"

"You ask for forgiveness, you start over, you leave your sin behind, and go on from there. Simple as that. The hardest part seems to be accepting God's forgiveness, because we think we don't deserve it. We get stuck in our hopelessness, and steep in our regrets. It makes it especially difficult when everyone insists on telling us we don't deserve it. But the Bible says all we have to do is ask and mean it, and it's done; signed, sealed, and delivered, so to speak. Just remember, Jesus is the best friend you'll ever have, better than your own mother. No matter how often you disappoint him, he never holds a grudge. 'He will never leave you or forsake you'. You can bank on it."

"Gee, if it's that easy, why don't I go rob a bank and after I go out on a spending spree, I'll just say, 'oops, sorry, God. I made a little boo-boo.'"

"Because he looks at your heart, not your words. What most people do, when they are really sorry, is to try and fix it if they can, and tell whoever they wronged that they're sorry. And finally, they will try never to do it again. That is true repentance. After that, it's up to the offended party to forgive."

"That would be nice if I believed in God like you do, but I don't. I don't know too much about it."

"You can come to my church; I'll teach you."

Oh great, here it comes, thought Bunny. But when she looked into his face, he looked like he was inviting her to his birthday party, and hoping she wouldn't turn him down. God, he's good-looking, she thought, hoping it didn't show.

He added, "Maybe that's where you can find a family for your son, Vincent."

Bunny thought, wow, he called him by his name. "Maybe, no promises."

"No promises," he agreed.

"That's the same thing my brother and I said to each other this morning. He told me to meet him tomorrow and he would go with me to visit Mom."

"It might be worth a shot, who knows. I don't know if anything I said will help."

"I think so. 'The Lord is my light and my salvation; whom shall I fear?'" Oh, brother, thought Bunny. Did that ever sound phony.

"Good one," said the pastor. "Where did you hear that?"

"My son taught me to let the Bible fall open and see what it says. That verse popped up recently."

"Maybe this meeting tomorrow is clandestine; 'maybe you were born for such a time as this.'"

"Book of Esther," said Bunny, surprised that she even knew what he was talking about.

"Very good. You're getting pretty good at this."

Bunny thought, good at remembering the words, clueless when it comes to living them. Bunny's mind went back to the scene with Michael and the police. Wonder what he would think of me if he saw me swearing and swinging that gun around the living room. A regular Annie Oakley, I am. Pistol packin', scripture totin' Annie Oakley, she thought. I guess it doesn't matter what the pastor thinks, either. There was an unfamiliar feeling of peacefulness, like comfortable love, welling up within her. She thought, I wonder if that's God showing his stamp of approval on our conversation. No sooner had she thought it, and it happened again.

Do you want me to pray for you?" he asked.

"Sure, I guess."

"Shall I pray that you become a child of God?"

"Sure, I guess."

"I can pray the words, but the sincerity of the prayer has to come from your heart."

"Okay."

Pastor Dan began, "Lord Jesus, Bunny wants to be able to overcome her sinfulness and become your child. Holy Lord Jesus, be the Lord of her life, forgive her sins, and give her eternal life. Amen."

Bunny opened her eyes and looked at the pastor. "Are you sure it took?" she asked.

"Did you agree with what we prayed?"

"Yeah."

"Then it took."

"How will I know?"

"You'll know. Give it time."

They both sat quietly as they contemplated what had just taken place. Finally Pastor Dan asked, "You want to hear a joke?"

"A joke?" Bunny asked, "Sure, why not." She held her finger up, signaling him to wait a second. She blew her nose into the napkin.

"Okay, there was this man . . ."

"Uh, do you have another napkin?" she asked, leaving the first napkin up to her nose.

Quickly he scrambled for another.

She blew again, harder this time. As Bunny collected herself he began again.

"Okay. There was a man who went on vacation in the Bahamas. When he got there he e-mailed his wife. Unfortunately it went to the wrong address. It went to a pastor's wife who had recently lost her husband. When the widowed pastor's wife read the message, she screamed and ran out of the house." Pastor Dan paused, smiling at Bunny.

Bunny asked, "So what did the note say?"

"Hello dear. Thought you'd like to know I'm settling in down here. Glad you will be joining me soon. By the way, it's really hot down here."

Bunny laughed. "That's funny."

"I don't want to be a pest," he smiled. "I'm going back to my seat. From now on if you want to talk, let's make it a rule that you have to initiate it."

"It was nice talking to you," said Bunny. "Thanks a lot, P-Pastor Dan," she added awkwardly.

He smiled.

Bunny reviewed what they had talked about until she felt overcome with fatigue. The cares of the day were replaced by a deep sleep that she didn't wake up from until the bus stopped in front of her apartment.

"Bunny, wake up, we're here."

She looked up to see the pastor standing above her in his starched white collar, brown leather jacket, and gloves.

"We're here," he repeated.

Without a word she stumbled off the bus, bleary-eyed. It had grown dark and snowed while she was sleeping, but she managed to stumble her way to her front door and wave good-bye as she opened the front door.

The pastor waved back and began his walk back to the church, the snow crunching under his feet. It had collected on the sidewalk to about an inch deep while he was away. The streetlights threw huge shadows on the snow covered sidewalk. He stopped at the corner and bought a newspaper out of the machine. Seeing his reflection in the store window, he noticed that the snow was collecting in his hair and on his eyebrows. He smiled as he remembered his conversation with Bunny about being so young. The snow looked like he was turning gray on top. He put the newspaper under his arm and drew it in close to stay warm. As he continued on his way, he prayed, "Lord, thank you for bringing Bunny into the family today, and thank you that you would use me to bring her in. And Lord, give Bunny the courage to face her mother tomorrow. I hope they can have a good relationship, but if that's not possible, give her an awareness that you are there for her, and that you love her. And thank you for bringing her son through the accident. I pray you will continue to heal his finger and his hip. Above all else, thank you for putting your love in my heart. I'm so glad this was a productive day today. Thank you, Jesus. You are truly amazing."

Matthew 25:21. His Lord said unto him, Well done, thou good and faithful servant: thou hast been faithful over a few things, I will make thee ruler over many things: enter thou into the joy of thy lord.

Chapter 26

Behold thy Mother and thy Brother

"*B*unny, hold up."

"Hi, Richard," Bunny cringed. "I thought you were going to wait for me at the cafe."

Richard took a few quick steps to catch up. His trench coat flapped open in the winter breeze. He managed to dodge a man carrying a Christmas tree.

"I've been running late all morning," he explained.

"You? You're such an 'on time' kind of guy."

"You remember Spot?"

"How could I forget Spot, the king of bad breath."

"That's him. Threw up in my shoe."

"In your shoe? Nice." Bunny laughed.

"That was only the beginning. There's no hot water. We need a new hot-water tank. I froze my peetidinks off. Then, wouldn't you know, I finally get here, and there's no place to park. I'm parked illegally."

"No room in the inn? Not even for that big fancy car of yours? Somehow, hearing this just warms my heart," Bunny beamed.

"At least one of us is warm," he complained.

Bunny said, "And I always thought you were perfect."

"You can't always go by appearances. Sometimes perfection is only skin-deep."

"Yeah right, Richard. A regular Mr. America you are."

Richard asked cautiously, "What did you decide to do about Mother?"

Bunny hadn't decided anything. She blurted, "Okay, I'll go, but I don't know how long I'll stay. I guess I can put on a good game face for a little while."

"Good girl. I was afraid you'd say no. Don't worry, though, I'll be right there with you."

"I can't believe I said yes. It's like jumping in a cold shower."

Richard shivered, "Ugh, don't say cold shower."

Bunny tucked her neck into her turtleneck sweater to stay warm as they rounded the corner to the hospital. "I had a nice talk with a man on the bus yesterday. He gave me a lot to think about. Maybe that helped." Bunny remembered the pastor's face and could hear him saying: "If you live for other people's approval you're bound to be disappointed." Panic almost seized Bunny as she and her brother started up the elevator, but she brushed it off.

"Mom's ward is different than Vinnie's."

"How so?" asked Richard.

"It's so quiet over here."

"Most of them are dying, Bunny."

"I'm getting scared, Richard," said Bunny.

"Of Mother, you mean?"

"Yeah. It's like asking to be punched in the stomach."

"I don't know why you have to make such a big deal of this. She's your mother."

"That's the point. If she weren't my mother, I wouldn't care."

They didn't say anything for a long time. It seemed as if they were walking forever. "This is it," said Richard.

Bunny's hands had already started to sweat. She let Richard go in first.

"Mother, I brought a surprise for you today." He stepped aside, giving Bunny no choice but to step inside.

Bunny put on a big smile, "Hi! Surprise," she sang.

Mrs. Muldare was not nearly so energetic, but she looked genuinely pleased that Bunny had come. Bunny noticed her mother's hair was nearly gone. All she had left of her beautiful golden hair were wisps at random spots around her head. Her face was so thin that the veins were visible around her temples. She brought out her hand from under the sheet to gesture Bunny to come over. Her arms were sagging and wrinkled from losing so much weight. Mrs. Muldare's ring fell off her finger and rolled onto the floor, resting at Bunny's feet. Bunny reached down to pick it up. "Thank you, dear," she said weakly. Bunny kissed her mother on her forehead, and put the ring into her hand.

"Bunny, your hands are perspiring. Are you warm? You can put your coat in the closet if you like. It's nice to see you after all this time."

Richard reached for Bunny's coat and hung it up. Mrs. Muldare added, "Thank you, Richard darling."

Bunny didn't know what to say. She was shocked by how small and vulnerable her mother looked.

"How is your boy doing?" she asked.

"He was in an accident," said Bunny. "He was hit by a truck."

"That's what Richard told me. Is the boy going to be all right?"

"Vinnie," Bunny reminded. "Yes, he was very lucky. It could have been a lot worse. But he's going to be home in time for Christmas."

"He must be excited about that."

"Well, sort of."

"How old is he now?"

"Nine."

"A nine-year-old who is only slightly excited about Christmas? That's a new one. You do have enough money to celebrate, don't you?"

"Yes," Bunny hesitated. She almost told her mother that she lost her job, then changed her mind. "But he's still homesick. Christmas time is especially hard for him."

"Oh, Bunny. Let that boy go home for Christmas. If he hasn't gotten over those people by now, he never will. I've been telling you since before he was born you would never be able to provide a decent home for that boy.

Bunny felt like she got her first punch in the stomach. The one noble cause she had put her heart and soul into, and this is what her mother had to say for all her efforts. "I think I'm a pretty good mother," she answered, trying not to sound argumentative. "We're not rich or anything, but Vinnie knows I love him, and I'm pretty sure he loves me."

"Of course, dear. I meant financially speaking."

Bunny wished she had kept her mouth shut. She looked down at her lap, then decided to change the subject. "I kicked Michael out."

"Richard told me about that too."

Bunny gave Richard a look.

"Well actually, I read it in the paper first. Richard just filled in the details."

Bunny said with surprise, "I didn't even know it was in the papers. Richard, why didn't you tell me?"

"I didn't think it would make you feel any better, and I wanted to hear it from you."

"What did they say?"

Richard answered, "Oh something like, 'there was a domestic dispute between Bonnie Muldare and her common law husband, Michael Stern. Mr. Stern was arrested and given a restraining order."

"Man, that makes me mad," said Bunny. "They never asked me if they could print my business in the newspaper. What right do they have telling the whole world my business, anyway?" She wondered if Pastor Dan had read it.

Mrs. Muldare said, "Well Bunny, if you live your life in a way in which there is juicy gossip to be had, somebody's going to take it and run with it, especially since you are a Muldare. It's the way of the world."

Bunny knew she shouldn't have come. This time she was able to keep quiet.

"So how did the accident happen? Weren't you there? Did you know where he was?"

"No, I was working. Michael was supposed to be watching him," Bunny explained. She tried not to feel guilty for not being there when it happened. "Michael got mad at him for something or other, and Vinnie was running away from him—"

"So, really, the whole thing was an accident."

"The reason Vinnie was running so blindly into the street was because Michael was always scaring Vinnie. He could never do anything right, and Michael would blow up at him. I could never figure out why Vinnie was so scared of Michael until—"

"Bunny, a boy needs a father's hand to keep him in line. We mothers have a tendency to coddle the children too much."

"No, Mom, Michael was nothing but a big jerk." Bunny could feel her pulse begin to race out of control. "Even when I was so angry at him for what happened, he threw me on the bed and wouldn't let me up. He had the nerve to tell me he thinks I'm sexy when I'm mad. I had to pull a gun on him to get him off me and get him out of there!"

"That was a little drastic, don't you think?" asked Mrs. Muldare. "At my age, you'll take that little comment as a compliment." She tried to laugh but then began to cough.

"I give up." Bunny looked at Richard as if to say, get me out of here.

"I don't know what you want from me, Bunny. I have to say what I think."

Bunny stared into Richard's face, pleading with her eyes for Richard to save her. Richard imagined what she must be thinking about their mother.

Mrs. Muldare added defensively, "After all, you are my daughter, and I think I know a little bit about you from living with you." She turned her head away to stare out the window.

"Mom, that was ten years ago!" Bunny blurted.

"Was it that long ago?" she answered without turning around. "I didn't realize. We really should stay in touch. When you get old, time goes by so much faster."

"Boy, don't I know it," interrupted Richard loudly, rubbing his belly nervously. "It seems like yesterday that Bunny and I were back in grade school. Remember when we went to the lake and I caught that turtle on my fishing pole? We took that thing everywhere. Remember that kid who was terrified of it, and we kept chasing him around with the stupid turtle? That poor turtle took a real beating that week, didn't he?"

"But we did let him go before we went home," Bunny reminded, thankful to change the subject. She tried not to let her mother know how upset she was.

Richard added, "That turtle was probably thanking his lucky stars that day. Don't you think?"

Her mother smiled. "That was the Fourth of July wasn't it?" she asked Bunny.

"Yeah, it was," Bunny answered, coughing to cover up the tightness in her throat.

Richard said, "And every time we shot off another firecracker he'd clam up tight as a drum. We put those sparkler things all around him, in his legs, in his neck hole, or whatever you call that. Remember?"

The lump in Bunny's throat was getting bigger. She hoped no one was looking at her face; she could feel her cheeks getting hot.

Richard added, "The SPCA would put us in jail for something like that today."

Mrs. Muldare smiled admiringly, "Oh, Richard, you didn't really hurt him. Just scared him a little tiny bit," she said with a note of sarcasm. They both laughed.

Bunny smiled, "We just dropped him a few dozen or so times."

"Almost set him on fire once," chuckled Richard.

Mrs. Muldare laughed, "You two are terrible."

"Speaking of jail," Mrs. Muldare asked, "do you still speak—"

"No," Bunny interrupted. "He died. I just found out about it myself yesterday. I don't even know how it happened."

"Oh, I'm sorry, dear. I didn't realize. Well," she paused, "That's two prospects down. Vinnie wasn't much of a catch, but Michael, he was on his way to becoming a pilot, wasn't he?"

Bunny didn't answer. Once again she looked down at her lap.

"Oh well, easy come, easy go," her mother said. There's plenty of other fish in the sea. Got any other prospects?"

Mrs. Muldare looked at Bunny, hoping she might have some good news to tell her, for a change.

"No, not really. Richard, what time is it?" asked Bunny.

"10:30."

"Yikes," said Bunny, springing up to get her coat out of the closet. "I gotta go. Vinnie's probably wondering where I am."

"Aww, so soon," said Mrs. Muldare.

"Shall I walk you out?" asked Richard.

"No, no. I remember the way," said Bunny.

Bunny bent down and kissed her mother on the forehead. She smiled a big smile, hoping it would cover the fact that she was holding back the tears. She noticed there was a clump of her mother's hair beside her on the bed. Bunny grabbed the clump before her mother found it. She dropped it on the floor and then kicked it under the bed.

"Tell the boy his grandmother says hello, and please come back soon, Bunny. I don't know how much longer we can do this."

"Don't talk like that," said Bunny. "You're going to be just fine. Before you know it, you'll be out of here and on your way. See you again real soon. Bye, Richard. Make sure you get a shower tomorrow," she called as she was leaving the room. "Don't want to start smelling like Spot." The last thing they saw was Bunny's pretend smile, and her hand-waving good-bye.

Silence set in once again in Mrs. Muldare's room. Richard looked sideways at his mother, self consciously playing with his fingers. "Don't blame yourself, Mother."

Mrs. Muldare didn't respond.

Bunny spied the sign down the hallway that read 'Ladies Room.' She ran to it. She threw open the door, opened the stall, locked the door, and sobbed long and hard.

After a time she realized she had to pull herself together, one way or an other, for Vinnie's sake. There was something about the tile floor, the cramped quarters inside the bathroom stall, even the mothball scent of the air freshener that was forcing an old memory, a bad memory into the present. Have I been here before? she asked herself. This place feels too familiar. The tile floor, the bathroom walls, the sink. The sink, she thought. It was the sink of that horrible abortion. The emotion of that terrible day flooded her memory. She was repulsed by the scene of the baby struggling for its life and then rolling over in the sink full of water. She shivered and thought, how lucky I am that Vinnie didn't get aborted. He would be dead right now, if things hadn't gone the way they did. The smell of moth balls was leaving her sick to her stomach.

She washed her face and began covering up her tears with makeup. She remembered the old lady with the baby in the jar knocking on the phone booth saying, "The Bible tells us that the sins of the parents will be visited on the children to the third and fourth generation."

Bunny remembered saying: "Oh that's real fair! They sin and I pay?"

"It's not what God wants for your life. This is a warning to all parents to be watchful of what they do, because their sins will inevitably hurt their children. My question for you is this: Are you strong enough to turn this downward cycle around, or will your child have to suffer as you have?"

Bunny remembered hanging over the toilet crying out to God in frustration, "Oh, God, if you're real, I need help." Then she remembered thinking, there's no one to listen to me and my problems. I'm gonna leave this world for good. I've had it."

"Ten years ago, it's like a lifetime," she said to herself as she looked at herself in the mirror. She studied the fine lines that were beginning to develop around her eyes. She took two aspirins for her headache. Her conversation with her mother began to haunt her. She could feel the tears wanting to grip her again. She looked away from the mirror before they took hold of her. She could hear her mother saying, "I told you, you could never provide a decent home for that boy. Michael, now there's a catch. A gun, that was a little drastic wasn't it? I know what you're like; I lived with you."

Bunny wished she had the pastor's phone number so she could tell him what happened. She knew he would understand. She imagined his face and tried repeating what he had told her: "If we live for other people's approval, we're bound to be disappointed." She remembered him saying, "What gets me through the day is to live for God's approval. We all need forgiveness for what we have done in the past. We just have to ask for it, and the Bible says it will be done, simple as that. It's especially hard to accept forgiveness, though, when people keep telling us we don't deserve it. Just ask, and it's done, simple as that."

Bunny prayed timidly, "God, I'm sorry for what I've done in the past. I know it was stupid now, and if I could change it I would, but it's too late. I'm sorry."

She took a deep breath and took another look at her face in the mirror. She looked like a crying person with powder on her face. She tried smoothing on more powder around her red nose.

One of her mother's comments continued to haunt. "I told you, you could never provide a decent home for that boy. I told you. I told you."

Bunny whispered out loud, "Oh God, don't make me give him up. I can't."

When she arrived at the children's ward, there were children's voices singing. The voices got stronger as she approached Vinnie's room. Once inside, she could see six children, a Sunday school group, squeezed into his room. The kindergartners were making the rounds, caroling for Christmas. Bunny tiptoed into Vinnie's room and sat on the bed beside him to see the show. Vincent hugged his mother. They were singing, "Jesus loves me this I know, for the Bible tells me so. Little ones to him belong. They are weak but he is strong. Yes, Jesus loves me; yes, Jesus loves me; yes, Jesus loves me. The Bible tells me so. Bunny's thoughts went back to: "Behold my mother and brethren . . . What gets me through the day is to live a decent life, according to God's opinion; and hopefully, when this life is over, God will say 'well done.'" Bunny felt the same unfamiliar love in her heart that seemed to appear out of nowhere on the bus the day before. Once again it seemed to be affirming her thoughts.

The children curtsied and bowed several times while they gratefully accepted Vincent and Bunny's applause. "Thank you very much," Bunny said. "That was just beautiful."

"Yah, Merry Christmas everybody," said Vincent.

The Sunday school teacher motioned the little girl carrying a bag full of tiny boxes to give Vincent his present. The little girl beamed as she handed the little red box to Vincent. "Merry Christmas," said the tiny voice. She had so many ruffles in her organza skirt that her arms got lost in them. Her mother had dressed her in red satin shoes with big gold lame bows, and the bows in her pigtails matched her shoes. She smiled.

"Merry Christmas," he repeated, gratefully.

"Merry Christmas," they all called back as they filed out of the room. The little girl in the gold lame bows was the last to leave. She smiled again waving good-bye. Bunny waved back and smiled.

"Wasn't she just the cutest thing you ever saw?"

Vincent opened the little package. He held up what looked like a tiny spinning top.

"A top," said Vinnie.

"No, not just a top; that's a gyroscope," explained Bunny.

"What iss a gyroscope?"

Bunny placed it on the end of her index finger and pulled the string. Vincent was amazed at how she got it to spin around on the end of her finger without falling off.

"Wow. I never saw anything like that."

Bunny was delighted to be able to show him something new. "It's easy, try it."

In the background they could hear the children singing, "Yes, Jesus loves me. Yes, Jesus loves me . . ."

Bunny squeezed Vincent as they watched the gyroscope spinning round and round on Vincent's finger. Peacefulness finally surrounded her. What a great kid I have.

"I love being here with you, Vinnie. Merry Christmas."

"I love you too, Mom."

Matthew 12:46–50. While he yet talked to the people, behold, his mother and his brethren stood without, desiring to speak with him. Then one said unto him, Behold, thy mother and thy brethren stand without, desiring to speak with thee. But he answered and said unto him that told him, Who is my mother? And who are my brethren? And he stretched forth his hand toward his disciples and said, Behold my mother and my brethren! For whosoever shall do the will of my Father which is in heaven, the same is my brother, and sister, and mother.

Chapter 27

You Always Hurt the One You Love

"Hello, Mrs. Gibbs?"

"Yes."

"Hi. It's me, Bunny."

"Well hello, Bunny. Nice to hear your voice. How is Vinnie?"

"He's fine. He'll be coming home for Christmas."

"Oh, how nice, home for Christmas."

"That's what I called about, Mrs. Gibbs. Would you and Mr. Gibbs like to spend Christmas with Vinnie and me? I could make—"

"Oh I'm sorry Bunny, dear. Charlie, you know, our son Charlie?"

"Yes." Bunny was already beginning to feel foolish.

"He is flying us to Phoenix to have Christmas with him and his family."

"Oh," said Bunny, disappointed.

"Mr. Gibbs and I were just discussing how we were going to get to the airport. Norman's eyes are getting so bad, you know. And since my knee operation, I can't work the pedals. We are a sorry team."

"I could take you," offered Bunny, covering her embarrassment and disappointment.

"You mean in our car! That would be wonderful. Are you sure you don't mind?"

"No, I don't mind."

Mrs. Gibbs covered the phone for a moment then said, "Bunny, Norman said if you'll take us to the airport, he'll lend you our car while we're gone."

"Sure, that would be great, Mrs. Gibbs," said Bunny unenthused.

"What's the matter, dear? Are you feeling a little down?"

"Oh, I'm trying to figure out how to keep Vinnie from being homesick over Christmas, and I'm running out of ideas."

"Oh, I see. Vinnie still wants to go back home, does he?"

"Yeah," whispered Bunny, next to tears.

"It's a sad situation, maybe one that we can't undo."

"I can turn this around, Mrs. Gibbs, even if it kills me."

Mrs. Gibbs measured her words carefully. "Bunny, you're not going to want to hear this, but I feel it needs to be said. Perhaps it's time to let him go."

"Really, we'll be just fine."

"We? How is Vinnie benefiting through all this. You made a valiant effort, but it's just not working."

Bunny didn't answer.

"You're his mother, Bunny. You are supposed to be the one giving him what he needs, not the other way around. But you know that. I know you do."

"What?" asked Bunny, by reflex, as if her brain refused to accept it the first time?

"Our children weren't put on this earth for us. It's supposed to be the other way around."

The words rang through Bunny like a shot. She remembered saying those very words to her mother before Vinnie was born. Could she really be that selfish? She said, "No, Mrs. Gibbs. I'm his mother, not that Mueller woman, me."

Mrs. Gibbs decided not to push. She changed the subject. "I'm sorry we won't be able to get together for Christmas. You know how much Norman and I enjoy visiting with you and Vinnie. Maybe we could get together after we get back. How does that sound? We could bring you and Vinnie a little something from Arizona."

"Yes, Mrs. Gibbs. That would be nice." Bunny sighed.

"I'll let you know when we will need to leave for the airport. Are you sure that will be okay?"

"Yes, you can count on me. Talk to you later, Mrs. Gibbs."

Mrs. Muldare gathered her courage from her hospital room. She set the tape recorder, took a deep breath, and rang Bunny's phone. Bunny jumped when she heard it ring. She had been sitting by the phone recovering from her conversation with Mrs. Gibbs. She decided to let the answering machine pick it up. Bunny's message announced. "Hello, this is Bunny, but I can't come to the phone right now. Leave a message and I'll get back with you later."

Mrs. Muldare's anticipation sank when she heard the message. She let the tape recorder leave her message for her. It sang an old tune, "You always hurt the one you love, the one you shouldn't hurt at all. You always take the sweetest rose and crush it till the pedals fall. You always break the kindest heart with a hasty word you can't recall. So if I broke your heart . . . ."

Bunny was sure it was a busy body telling her she should give Vincent back. She was sure it was someone who had been reading about her in the newspaper. She looked to see if she recognized the number. She didn't. It was a Harrisburg number confirming her suspicions. She picked up the phone and roared, "Mind your own business!!" She slammed down the phone.

Mrs. Muldare sighed and resigned herself to staring at the wall and steeping in her regrets.

Chapter 28

Freida, Wake Up

ONE WEEK LATER

"Freida, wake up." Martin pulled back the covers. Freida barely moved. He opened the shutters. Freida's white cotton nightshirt shone brightly as the morning light rested on her sleeve. She looked at Martin through sleepy eyes. She knew what he was going to say next.

"It iss time for worship."

"Oh Martin, please, leave me alone. You don't know how hard it iss for me."

"That does not mean we should not try," Martin urged.

"It iss barely possible for me to get through de day without dwelling on our problems. I am getting better at it, but when I try to go to church, every time we start to sing songs about how wonderful God iss, I must struggle so hard against my heart."

"He iss wonderful."

"If he iss really so kind and so wonderful, why has he chosen to turn a deaf ear to us. I always thought he was our friend." Once again the tears welled up in Freida's eyes. "See what happens? It iss better if I stay here and keep busy in de kitchen, then I do not have to think about it so much."

"You are running from de very one who can help us through this. Trust him. Let his spirit comfort you. He knows how you are suffering."

"Please, Martin. I went with you last week. Do not make me go again. My heart has been broken enough already; I am tired of fighting back de tears."

"But Freida, isn't God so good and merciful most times, so that we should not also bless him in the bad times? Worship iss a time to set aside our troubles. And in the doing we can get a measure of peace for ourselves, at least enough to hold us for a short while."

Freida didn't answer.

He thought, then offered, "I will leave de carriage here. If you change your mind, I will have it ready for you."

"Thank you, Martin. I love you." Freida turned on her side in relief, wiped her tears on the patchwork quilt and pulled it over her shoulder.

"I know you do, Freida." said Martin. "I know you do," he repeated. Martin felt lonely. It was as if he not only lost Vincent, but Freida as well. He thought, how hass my happy home turned to this? He brushed his hands across the soft flannel squares of their quilt. "In your keeping busy, could you say a small prayer for me? I am hurting too."

"Yah, Martin. I am sorry. I sometimes forget that you also love Vincent."

He urged, "Let me see how much you love me and my stomach when I get home with a nice dinner. Yah? Unless, maybe, you want to go to my mamma's house for dinner?"

"I will make something special, Martin," Freida promised.

"Vinnie, wake up," Bunny said.

"Huh?"

"Wake up sweetheart," she repeated.

"What, what's going on?" He rubbed his eyes.

"I got a Christmas surprise for you, but first you gotta get up and get dressed."

"Am I going home today?"

"Yep, now get up so we can go."

"So de doctor said I can go?" asked Vincent.

"Yes, he did. He said you're good to go. You'll just have to come back to get your cast off in a couple of weeks. Here, I brought your pillowcase." She held it open. "We can throw all your stuff in here."

"There iss a Christmas present I made for you in de drawer," said Vincent. "Don't look. It iss not wrapped."

"When did you have time to do that?" she asked.

Vincent slipped his glasses on. "I had lots of time, lots and lots and lots of time. Well, it iss already sort of wrapped."

"Do you want to give it to me now?"

"Well," said Vincent, scrunching his mouth to one side as he thought. "Since you are giving me my present today, I guess you can have yours too."

He opened the drawer and handed Bunny a shoe box. The lid and box had been wrapped separately in red tissue paper. Vincent had drawn stars across the lid with a silver pen. He thought to himself how disappointingly homemade it looked. He knew how his mother loved beautiful things.

"How cute!" said Bunny. She was honored that he had put so much time and effort on a present meant for her.

There was a mysterious hole in the lid about the size of a quarter. He had covered the hole from the inside by taping on several layers of clear plastic wrap.

"There's nothing living in here, is there?"

"I hope not," he laughed.

At the end of the box he had screwed in a brass peephole, usually found in a front door.

"Where did you get the little peephole?" asked Bunny.

"Nurse B. bought it for me. I asked her to. She asked me what I wanted for Christmas, and that iss what I told her. She thought it wass kind of strange, but she bought it. Look through there, and see what iss inside."

Bunny closed one eye and squinted through the peephole. Inside the box, the light from the plastic wrap in the lid shown down over a manger scene. It transformed the fluorescent lights of the hospital room into moonlight shining down inside the stable. As she moved the box around the room the light shown down from different angles, revealing the figures of Mary Joseph and the baby, the shepherd boy, the wise men, even a cow and a camel. Every time a new figure was revealed, Bunny would exclaim, "Oh, look at the shepherd boy. Oh look at the wise men. Oh look, the camel is even eating grass!"

Vincent beamed, "That iss a green twist-tie. I peeled off de paper till it looked like grass, and then I glued it on his mouth."

"Where did you get the people?"

"The salvation army lady visited me, and gave them to me. They are a little bit chipped up but you can only tell when you see them with de lid off. She helped me make it. She got de shoe box and de glue and stuff we needed. De peephole, I added later. Before, it wass just a hole. We had fun making it."

"This is beautiful, Vinnie, absolutely beautiful. I don't see any chips at all." Oh, look at that, you even poked holes in the back of the box so you can see the stars in the background."

Vinnie was smiling. "So you like it?"

"I love it," she said. "I'll keep this forever. Thank you." She gave Vincent a big hug.

"Where are we going for de surprise?" asked Vincent.

"Home," she said. "Can you fit your pants over your cast?"

"I can wear my old pants over it but not de new ones."

"Okay, okay, wear your old pants."

"Yeh!" said Vincent.

Vincent finished getting dressed while Bunny filled his pillowcase. "You don't want these old broken glasses anymore do you?"

"Yah! It iss not every day a guy gets hit by a tractor trailer and lives through it. It iss my proof!"

Eventually the two made their way down the hallway, the pillowcase slung over Bunny's shoulder, Vincent hobbling along with his crutches. "Is that Vincent I see walking out of here?" asked the head nurse.

"Yippee!" said Vincent, grinning at Nurse B.

"Well, you don't have to be so glad about it," said Nurse B.

"If you want to know de truth, I would stay here forever, but my mom says they are kicking me out. Here Nurse B., I made something for you." He pulled a piece of cardboard out of his pillowcase. It had band aids taped to it in a message.

"Now what could this say?" She took the card and put on her glasses. She read the homemade card: "WORLD'S BEST NURSE. MERRY CHRISTMAS. Aww, isn't that nice?"

Vincent said. "Don't show de other nurses. They might get jealous."

"I'm sure they would, especially since it's from you."

"Do you want to see what he made with the peephole you bought him?" asked Bunny.

"Yeah, I've been wondering about that."

Bunny held up the shoe box and told her to stand under the light.

"Oh my goodness, would you look at that? I never would have guessed that was what it was for. Did you make that for your mom?" she asked.

"Yah," replied Vincent proudly.

Bunny and the head nurse glanced at each other, still embarrassed about their rough start. Bunny said, "You have a very Merry Christmas, Nurse B. And thank you so much for taking such good care of Vinnie."

"It was my pleasure," she said. "He's a very good patient, you know. She looked into Bunny's eyes. She seemed different, somehow, more grown-up, settled. "You all have a Merry Christmas too."

"Thank you," they answered.

"But who is going to sing us a song when you're gone?" she asked.

"We got de power of de Lord," Vincent sang.

"Oh no. Don't get me started on that song. I'll be singin' it all week," she laughed.

Vincent smiled and shifted his weight onto his good leg.

"Miss Muldare, here is his appointment card. Just bring him to outpatient care in two weeks, and they'll take the cast off."

Vincent hopped on his good leg toward Nurse B. for a hug. She whispered in his ear, "Now you be good for your momma, and don't worry about that old Michael anymore."

"I'm not worried," said Vincent. "All he needs iss to have Jesus in his heart like I got."

"Aren't you something. You sure are. I'll see you, baby doll. She gave him one last squeeze.

"Bye Nurse B.," he called from down the hall.

"Bye-bye sweetheart. And keep that finger moving, it'll be all right," she reassured.

"How are we getting home?"

"Mr. Gibbs lent us his car."

"That wass nice of him. It iss a good thing; it iss kind of hard to walk with this klunking-along old cast."

"You didn't think we were going to walk home, did you?" Bunny asked.

"I wass not sure. I wass thinking we were taking the bus home like you do." Vincent looked out the lobby window to get one last look at the city. "I am still not used to de big city. Harrisburg is much bigger than Carlisle."

"Yes, it is." said Bunny. "And certainly bigger than Promise."

"Promise iss big, but the buildings are small."

"I guess that's true."

Soon they were driving down the highway that passed the exit to Carlisle.

Vincent said, "De clouds are looking like snow. Can I turn on de radio to see what de Indian iss saying about it?"

"What Indian?" asked Bunny.

"De one that tells us de weather."

Bunny chuckled, "That's not an Indian, silly. That's a computer."

"A computer? I always thought he wass an Indian. Huh." Vincent smiled a crooked smile, embarrassed.

"I guess he does kind of sound like an Indian." she smiled. "Go ahead, let's see what he says."

"Okay Mr. Indian, put your finger in de air, and tell us de weather," chuckled Vincent.

The mechanical chant began: "For the areas of York, Harrisburg, Carlisle, and Blue Mountain; Sunday will be clou-dy in the morning, turning to snow showers by afternoon diminishing to flurries by evening. Accumulation will be six to eight inches, ten to twelve inches in the higher elevations."

Bunny exclaimed, "Cowabunga!"

"Yeh!" applauded Vincent.

She was looking for the exit at an overpass that read Creek Road. Ah, there it is, she thought. The reality of the moment was pressing in on her. I must think of Vincent, she thought, not myself. She took a deep breath. Soon they were driving up the Muellers' driveway.

"Hey, this iss de way to my old house?"

"That's right. I have something I want you to read." She took a large manila envelope from underneath the seat. "Open it up," she urged.

"It hass my mamma's name on it."

"I know. It's all right. You can read it. I wrote it." said Bunny.

"There iss some business papers in there, or something," he said.

"Those are adoption papers. I have already signed them. All your parents have to do is put their signatures on there and mail it back in the envelope, and it will be official. You will belong to them. Now read the letter."

Vincent's heart pounded in his chest. He began to read slowly, "Dear Mr. and Mrs. Mueller, I am writing this letter to ask your forgiveness for all I have put you through." Vincent looked up at his mother who was looking straight ahead at the road. He couldn't tell how she was feeling. Vincent was puzzled. "I am afraid that I have made a mess of things once again. I am returning Vincent to you, because I realize I am depriving him of the family and friends that he cherishes—"

When Vincent looked up from the letter, Bunny asked, "How far back is the house?" Her heart was pounding as well.

"Am I dreaming?" he asked.

"You're not dreaming. We're really here." Bunny tried to smile.

Vincent's house unfolded just past the covered bridge exactly as he left it.

"I am not visiting? You are leaving me here!?"

"Merry Christmas," she said, trying to keep her voice from quivering. She knew her bravery was beginning to crumble.

"Don't you want me anymore?" asked Vincent.

Startled, she stopped the car just short of the house. She took Vincent's hand. "How can you think that, Vinnie? That is ridiculous."

"It iss because you are mad at me, because I did not want to put Michael in jail."

"No, Vinnie, that's not it at all! I thought this is what you wanted."

"Well, yah, but I don't want you to give me away and never see me again."

"Vinnie, sweetheart. This is not easy for me. I love you, don't you know that?"

"I think. But you gave me away before. Are you sure you are not mad at me? Why else would you do this?"

"Vinnie, come here." She scooted over to him and looked him square in the eyes. "I have been doing a lot of soul searching lately, and I realize I have been very selfish. And what I have had to come to grips with is this: I shouldn't force you to give up everything and everybody you love for me. And as much as I'd like to keep you all to myself, everybody knows it's for the best, especially me. I just refused to accept it." Bunny locked eyes with Vincent. "I love you more than you will ever know, but I have no job, no money, no father, not even a grandfather or a grandmother. All the things I wish I could give you while you are growing up, like a good school, and good friends, are already right here waiting for you. How can I ask you to give it all up for me? Do you understand? Do you know how much I'd like to be able to keep you with me?"

Vincent gave his mother a hug. "Thank you, Mom. I love you."

Bunny wiped the tears from her cheeks. "Now you better get going before I change my mind."

Vincent got out of the car. He hobbled over to Bunny's window with his crutches, pillow case, and letters in hand. "You are going to come see me sometimes, aren't you?"

"If you want," she replied, grateful for his invitation.

"I do want. I want you to come with me right now!"

Bunny dodged his request. Another time. Give me a hug, angel baby.

Vincent set his things on the ground and wrapped his arms around Bunny's neck. Bunny savored her last hug.

"Go on, get going, kiddo. I don't want them to see me out here." She watched as he hobbled down the stone pathway to the front porch. The knot in her throat was getting unbearable. He must have waved five times before he finally arrived at the front step.

Vincent stood at the bottom of the porch step. He couldn't get his pillowcase, his cast and his crutch up the steps by himself. Bunny got out of the car to help him onto the front porch. Vincent yelled, "Hey, Mamma, Pappa, iss anybody home? I am out here."

The shutters from inside Freida's bedroom flashed open. Vincent started waving with the same hand that carried the adoption papers. Freida's voice carried all the way outside. Vincent could hear her screaming, "I am coming, Vincent! I am coming! Mamma iss coming."

She swung open the door and ran out on the front porch barefooted and in her nightgown. She sat on the steps and hugged Vincent around his chest. "I have missed you so much," she cried. "Are you all right?" Bunny thought how beautiful Freida looked in her own element with her long shiny brown hair hanging loosely over her nightgown.

"Yah, Mamma."

Freida said, "I have been so worried about you since I saw you in de hospital. You were covered from head to toe with bandages. Let me look at you." She held Vincent up in front of her.

"And they said I wass a dead man. They will be soon calling me Lazarus, raised from de dead." Vincent beamed.

Bunny stood awkwardly on the front pathway a few feet away.

Vincent, not knowing where to begin said, "I come with papers this time." He waved the envelope at Freida. She took it and briefly looked inside. Vincent looked at Bunny. Can you help me with my stuff, Mom?"

Bunny obliged. She and Freida helped Vincent up the steps and into the living room.

Freida began to read. Vincent interrupted her and said, "Iss today Sunday?"

She shook her head yes and continued to gobble up the words on the page.

"Well, why are you not in church?"

She put her finger in the air signaling him to wait, as her eyes flashed across the page.

"Are you sick or something?" he asked.

Freida looked up at Bunny, then at Vincent. "Oh, Vincent sweet one, I have made a big mistake. God forgive me. We must go to de church and explain!"

Bunny interrupted. "Well, I guess it's time for me to be going." She turned.

Freida caught Bunny's arm. "No, wait," she said. "Vincent, did you have a chance to give your mother a proper good-bye?"

Bunny answered for him. "Yes, Mrs. Mueller. We said our good-byes in the car."

Freida could see that Bunny's heart was breaking though she was doing her best to stay composed. She said, "I would like to give you a present, if I can."

"Oh, no. That won't be necessary," Bunny answered.

Freida said, "Really, I would like to be able to give you something, if it iss all right."

Bunny looked at Vincent, uncertain whether she should accept. Vincent was wide-eyed for having both his mothers talking to each other in the same room, a day he never thought he would live to see.

Freida said, "We are all brothers and sisters in de Lord, Sister Bunny, no matter where we come from. Please, I know my husband and I have not much of anything of importance, but I would like to give you the thing that means de most to me. I mean, after all, it iss de least I can do. You have given me your most precious possession, your son."

Bunny answered, "Well, yes, that's true. But I'm giving him to you, because this is where he will be the happiest. I should have brought him back sooner." She glanced at Vincent to see if he was listening. He was.

Freida took her Bible from the shelf. "Do you have a Bible?"

Bunny shook her head no.

"This iss my most cherished Bible. It belonged to my grandmother. She gave it to me before she died. I want you to have it. It will help you on your way. It would mean a lot to me if you would take it and use it to learn of our Lord."

She was awed by Freida's generosity. Bunny put the leather cover to her nose. It had a unique smell that reminded her of Vinnie. When the cover opened she saw Freida's hand-writing in the margin. Or was it her grandmother's writing? "It's like handling a fine antique passed down through the family. Thank you. Maybe someday I'll be able to pass it on to Vinnie's family." Bunny stood stiffly, not knowing what the next move should be.

Freida put out her arms as an offering of friendship.

Bunny did not resist. The two women embraced in friendship.

Freida said in Bunny's ear, "You are always welcome here, Sister Bunny. Please come back whenever you like. Vincent hass told us he loves you very much."

"Thank you, maybe I will." Bunny looked at the well-worn Bible with the yellowing tissue pages.

Freida added, "Thank you for your sacrifice. You must be very courageous to be able to give him back to us." Then she patted Vincent on the back, Vincent, give your mother a hug."

Vincent gladly obliged. Bunny's heart was breaking though she knew she was doing what God wanted. Suddenly the tears broke like a river spilling over its banks. She held tightly to Vincent, not sure she would ever see him again. Finally she stood, determined to walk away courageously.

Freida asked, "Would you like to come to church with us?"

"Oh, no, thank you. I can't do that, but thank you for asking." She wiped her tears away.

"Don't cry, Mom. We will see each other again, I promise."

"Yes, I promise too. I'll be seeing you real soon." She turned, to go. Freida followed her to the front door.

Freida asked, "Would it be unkind to ask if I may read your letter to de church? They have been praying for so long."

"Yes, it's written to all of them. And thank you again, Freida, for the Bible."

Bunny and Freida looked at each other, two immeasurably different women leading two immeasurably different lives. But at this moment, they could not see each other's differences. Both understood the deep pain and sacrifice that the other had experienced, and it bonded them forever. They shook hands knowing that God had very specifically entwined the destinies of these two very different women.

"Friends?" asked Freida sniffing back her tears.

"Friends," answered Bunny.

Bunny looked back at Vincent as she walked down the front walk. He waved to her from the old stone front porch while holding Freida's hand. They watched as Bunny drove slowly down the drive and disappeared into the tall pines.

Freida's bare feet carried her quickly up the steps to get dressed. Her shoes were dirty, and so were her stockings, but she didn't care. She threw on the first dress she saw.

"Where iss Pappa?" Vincent yelled to his mother from downstairs. He fingered the handrail as he recalled every scratch in the paint.

"He iss already at de church," she called back. "I will meet you in de barn. I will only be one minute."

"Yah, okay, Mamma."

Vincent headed for the barn. He saw Petey, his pony, waiting for him at the gate.

"Petey!" exclaimed Vincent.

Petey was too excited to stand still. He ran around the barn not once, not twice, but four times. Each time he passed Vincent, he would stop for a second, take another look, and then take off again. When he finally came to a stop he lifted his injured foot. Vincent brushed off the dirt and straw. The hoof was completely healed with no signs of an injury.

"That's good, Petey, real good." Petey rested his chin on Vincent's shoulder. Vincent rubbed his neck. "Good to see you again, Petey, my old friend." Vincent heaved a grateful sigh of relief.

When Freida got to the front door, she saw that Vincent had driven the carriage to the front door to pick her up. "Look at you, de big man driving de buggy."

"Yah, look at me. And my feet are touching de floor."

"How did you get in the buggy with your cast?"

"Zach gave me a boost. He remembers me. I wass surprised; all de animals remember me. You should have seen Petey. He took off running. He wass running around and around de barn four times!"

"Well of course they remember you. Who could ever forget about you?"

Vincent smiled.

"Scooch over, Mr. Man. We are going to church, yah?"

"Yah," said a relieved little boy. He handed the reins to Freida.

When they arrived at the church, Pastor Dunkin had already begun his message. Freida and Vincent tried to enter without disturbing anyone, but the front doors creaked. Vincent noticed that someone had replaced the board that had the bullet hole in it. "My goodness gracious in heaven!" said Pastor Dunkin, "It appears we have a visitor!"

Vincent's heart sang. For the first time, he felt truly at home again. He was overwhelmed by the building full of familiar faces, who all turned at once with gasps of surprise and smiles for him and his mamma. Vincent stood where he was and put his crutch up in the air in excitement and victory. Everyone stood and clapped. They didn't stop until Freida and Vincent made their way to the front. Martin joined them.

"Come up here and talk to us, Vincent," beckoned Pastor Dunkin. Freida and Martin helped him up onto the old wooden platform. "Are you here to visit?" asked Pastor Dunkin.

"No, I am staying!" he proclaimed, raising his crutch in victory once again. Martin bent down and picked him up, cast and all, for everyone to see. The congregation roared with approval. Vincent caught sight of Marshall sitting with his mother, bouncing up and down in his seat.

"God answers prayer, does he not, Vincent?" Pastor Dunkin said.

"Uh huh. Hi, Marshall." Vincent beamed a smile at his friend.

Freida stepped forward and said, "If it iss all right, I have something I need to say." She held on to Bunny's letter in her pocket.

"Surely, sweet girl," Pastor Dunkin said.

"As you know, I have been very angry with de Lord for taking our Vincent away from us. All I could understand in my tiny pea-brain wass how unfair it wass. I have been thinking I could never trust Him again for allowing such a thing to happen, and I am afraid I have taken it out on some of you who refused to agree with me, including my pappa. Please forgive me." Pastor Dunkin had his arm around her and patted her on the shoulder, telling her she already had his forgiveness. She licked her lips and gathered her thoughts. "All along, God had a plan. He had a reason for everything that happened. Pappa would say, 'Jesus loves you,' and I could not believe it. He would say, 'We can not always understand what God iss doing, so until we understand it, we have to exercise our faith.' But I had no faith. I thought I did until it wass put to de test. And now, let me read to you this letter, and we will all be able to understand what God wass doing."

The folded letter crinkled as she withdrew it from her apron pocket. She cleared her throat, took a couple of quick breaths, and smiled. "Dear Mr. and Mrs. Mueller, I am writing this letter to ask your forgiveness for all I have put you through. I am afraid I have made a mess of things again. I am returning Vincent to you, because I love him too much to deprive him of the family and friends that he cherishes so much." Freida looked up at them and smiled. "That would be all of you, my wonderful brothers and sisters in de Lord."

She continued with Bunny's letter, "A wise old woman said to me while I was carrying Vinnie, 'The sins of the father and mother are visited on the children to the third and fourth generation.' Then the woman said: 'Do you have the courage to turn it around?' Well, I guess this is my defining moment. The only way I can figure out to turn around the mistakes of my past, and my parent's past, so they don't also hurt my Vinnie, is to give him back to you.

"While Vinnie was in the hospital, I spent a lot of time thinking about what would be best for him, and at every turn, you were the best choice, even though I didn't want to admit it. With you, he has a mother who will be there for him when he gets home from school, and a father who will teach him moral responsibility and integrity. You have a close family, and a supportive community, you have financial security, and best of all, you are showing him how to live a wholesome Christian life.

"I know I am not ready for a family yet, but because of your example, at least I have a road map to follow. I am only twenty-seven, so there is still plenty of time for me to start a family—the right way, God's way. Pray that He will give me a second chance.

"As I said before, I am truly sorry for what I put you through. I feel as if I know you all because of everything Vinnie has told me. Freida and Martin, Pastor Dunkin and

Grandmamma Dunkin, Mr. and Mrs. Perl, and Becky, Grandmamma Mueller, Marshall, Miss Purdy, and too many aunts, uncles, and cousins to count. Thank you for being a good Christian example for my son and me. And as I embark on a new beginning in my life, I will always be grateful to all of you for showing me the way. Sincerely yours, Bunny Muldare."

No one moved as they considered the import of Vincent's mother's letter. Freida said, "You know, I gave up on God, but he stayed faithful to me. Freida almost broke down again. She took a deep breath. "Let it be known, here and now, I am making God a promise. From now on, when things go wrong, even if I never understand until de day I die, I am going to trust him always; he knows best. What I have learned iss, eventually, 'all things work together for good for those who are called according to his purpose.' God iss good, and he knows what he iss doing." said Freida emphatically.

The congregation applauded in recognition that what she was saying was true.

Pastor Dunkin said, "Can you repeat that last part?"

Freida repeated with even more emphasis and with her great friendly smile, "God iss good, and he knows what he iss doing!"

They applauded again.

"But now," she added, barely able to contain her excitement. "The Lord iss finished with Vincent, and he iss back to stay!" she exclaimed. Freida was so excited she started jumping up and down in small circles on the platform. Vincent started laughing to see his mamma so happy.

Martin stepped forward and whispered something in Pastor Dunkin's ear. Pastor Dunkin went over to Freida, put his hands on her shoulders, and whispered in her ear. She shook her head in agreement.

Marshall ran up to the platform and took Vincent's crutch. They stood with their arms around each other. "Well, Vincent," said Pastor Dunkin, "we are all sorry about your accident. Are you going to be all right now?"

"Yah, Grandpappa. I get my cast off in two weeks, and then I will be good as new.

"Ah, glory to God." Then Pastor Dunkin asked, "Vincent, your mamma has told us what she has learned from this trial. Can you think of something you have learned?"

"Well, I learned that if someone iss different from you, you should talk to them, because maybe they are not so weird as you think, and maybe they can be your friend."

Marshall gave Vincent a hug to let him know he was truly with friends again.

Bunny drove very slowly toward Carlisle. She wished the sun would shine, as if that would make a difference in how empty and alone she felt. Instead, a thick snow began to accumulate on her windshield, melting down in large drops until she finally conceded and turned on the windshield wipers. They beat back and forth on the window relentlessly, while doing nothing to clear the windshield. Two cars lined up behind her, the drivers waiting impatiently for their opportunity to pass. Bunny found a place to pull off the road. One of the detained cars looked in her window and honked rudely as he passed.

Bunny rested her head on the steering wheel. "Lord Jesus, can you hear me? I would have to be a fool not to see that this past year was all your doing. But now that I've given Vinnie back, now what? I know it was the right thing to do, or else I never would have done it. But how can I bear this terrible loneliness? Everyone is celebrating, and here I am, left totally alone." Bunny was beginning to feel like she was talking to herself. "I'm still planning to start over and

do it your way, like I said, but it's hard starting out all alone."
She pictured Vinnie celebrating with his family, not giving
her a thought. She envisioned the church cheering at his
return. She imagined they would be having a celebration
this afternoon. In her loneliness she threw herself onto the
steering wheel and wept as the thick wet snow covered the
windshield. The car became more and more quiet as the
snow slowly insulated it from outside. "I guess you don't
want anything to do with someone like me." Bunny continued to cry until eventually emotional exhaustion took over,
and she drifted into a deep sleep.

About an hour later, she stirred. She looked out the window, but could see nothing but a snow-covered windshield.
She was quietly insulated from the snow storm outside.
Then, as quietly as her dream came into her sleep, the echoes of her dream came into her consciousness. When she
realized what had happened, gratitude swept over her. She
remembered the words that had been spoken to her over
and over again as she slept. She slipped back into her dream
where she was lifted off of the ground in a rising helicopter.
A man stood on the ground under them as Bunny and her
pilot hovered above the ground. The noise of the helicopter
made it difficult for her to hear, but she could read his lips.
It was easy; she had heard him repeat the same phrase over
and over again in her dream. He was calling, his hands
cupped around his mouth, "Tell them you have been forgiven. Tell them all, you have been forgiven."
Bunny waved back enthusiastically, grateful for his acceptance. She stirred again in a twilight sleep.
Bunny called to him in her dream over the sound of the
helicopter blades, "Thank you. What can I do for you?"
He said nothing, but blew her a kiss and continued to
wave good-bye. It was as if the stranger in her dream had

become a good friend—a friend that was difficult to leave. She was grateful for the time they spent together but wished it didn't have to end. She pressed her hands against the glass to watch him as long as she could, until the helicopter was lifted above the clouds, and he was out of sight.

Bunny breathed a sigh of relief as she began to awake. The air was cool, and the clouds smelled like moist clean snow. She felt completely rested. Her dream echoed to her, "Tell them you have been forgiven. Tell them all, you have been forgiven." She opened her eyes again to the snow-covered windshield. "Thank you," she repeated gratefully. The now-familiar peace enveloped her, and she realized her good friend had not really left her after all.

"Thank you," she whispered.

Bunny went to the little church down the street that Sunday morning. By the time she arrived she was thirty minutes late, her hair was wind blown, her lipstick had worn off, and her shoes and socks were cold and wet. But Bunny didn't care. God had dropped something into her heart, something that no one could take away. On her way through the front door the message bulletin read: There is therefore now no condemnation to them which are in Christ Jesus, who walk not after the flesh, but after the Spirit.

Pastor Dan stood at the front behind a wooden platform. He was wearing his collar. Bunny quickly surveyed the crowd.

Pastor Dan was beginning his summation. "Blessed are the poor in spirit. Blessed are they that mourn, the meek, those who hunger after righteousness, the merciful. Doesn't exactly sound like an upwardly mobile, sky's the limit bunch. Sounds more like a group therapy session." The small congregation chuckled. "But it says here in Matthew 5 that they are blessed. Blessed! I don't doubt that most of you here have not come to the Lord because you won the lottery. You didn't decide that you had a desperate need for God in your life because you were born rich and beautiful. No, more likely, you came via a long and winding road of tribulation, of sickness, sin, or sorrow. Maybe it was a terrible loss, or heartache. But at the end of that long and winding road of tribulation was Jesus. Halleluiah! It made it all worth it, didn't it? Given the alternative of a life without Christ living in our hearts, we would do it all again. Of course we would. And why? Because we are blessed—blessed with a blessed assurance.

Pastor Dan began to sing as the congregation followed:

"Blessed assurance, Jesus is mine.
Oh what a foretaste of glory divine.
Heir of salvation, purchase of God,
Born of his spirit, washed in his blood.

This is my story, this is my song, praising my savior all the day long.
This is my story, this is my song, praising my savior all the day long.

Perfect submission, perfect delight,
Visions of rapture now burst on my sight.
Angels descending, bring from above,
Echoes of mercy, whispers of love.

Perfect submission, all is at rest,
I in my savior am happy and blessed
Watching and waiting, looking above,
Filled with his goodness, lost in his love.

This is my story, this is my song, praising my savior all the day long.

This is my story, this is my song, praising my savior all the day long."

Romans 8:1–2. There is therefore now no condemnation to them which are in Christ Jesus, who walk not after the flesh, but after the Spirit. For the law of the Spirit of life in Christ Jesus hath made me free from the law of sin and death.

Chapter 29

My Soul Doth Magnify the Lord

Four years later:

"Hello, anybody home?" called Bunny from Mother Dunkin's front hallway. She hung her coat and scarf on one of the iron hooks. Pastor Dan closed the door behind them.

Bunny heard shrieks coming from the kitchen answering, "They are here!"

"Well, go, go, get de door, quickly."

A small herd of children rushed Bunny and Pastor Dan at Mother Dunkin's front door.

"Hi, everybody," called Bunny and her husband.

Vincent, now fifteen and as tall as Bunny, grabbed his mother's arm and pulled her into the living room to sit by the fire. "Sit by me," he urged in an unfamiliar voice.

Bunny said, "Vinnie, is that you in there? You're so tall, and your voice is changing."

"Yah, soon I will be taller than Pastor Dan."

"Not a chance," Pastor Dan teased.

Vincent said, "I have a job at de Christian radio station."

"Really," said Bunny.

"Yah, I get to pick de songs for de programs. I asked them when they are going to give me a microphone. They said when my voice stops cracking."

"Wow, that's terrific, Vinnie," Bunny said. "Guess where Dan and I went this year?"

"Where?" asked Vincent.

"Beijing."

Vincent sang, "Take it, take it, take it, that's the most important thing." He smiled. His old song embarrassed him, like looking at an old photograph.

Pastor Dunkin arrived in the living room to greet the couple, "It iss so good to see you safely home again. Did you have a difficult trip?" He shook Pastor Dan's hand vigorously.

Dan and Bunny looked at each other and sighed in exasperation. "We'll tell you about it later," they moaned.

"Where is the wassail?" asked Bunny.

Freida and Mother Dunkin overheard from the kitchen. "It iss coming. We are coming."

Mother Dunkin entered the room carrying a huge tray of cups all different shapes and sizes. "No, no, Sister Bunny, sit down. I have everything ready." She stretched the tray toward her guests, suggesting that they choose a cup. Bunny chose a navy blue cup with gold lettering. She read, "Kutztown State College, Kutztown, Pennsylvania."

Freida warned, "Careful, that one has a chip on de lip. Why not choose another?"

Bunny answered. "This will be good. I like it because it says Pennsylvania."

Pastor Dunkin said, "So you were missing us in Pennsylvania while you were across de ocean?"

"That's an understatement," said Pastor Dan. "There are months when it rains for days and days, and we find ourselves tromping through the mud with an infant under our raincoats for miles."

Freida said, "God sometimes must be sending you de rain to give a place for de child to hide."

"Yes, Sister Freida, I'm sure you're right," answered Pastor Dan. "I guess we should be grateful to God that he has allowed us to rescue another child, rain or no rain."

Martin teased, "Freida, please, let de people grumble a little bit."

Vincent explained, "Mamma has no mercy when it comes to questioning why things happen de way they do, no matter how miserable you are. It iss no use grumbling to her. You will never get any sympathy; de woman hass no heart, noooo heart, none."

Freida laughed, embarrassed. She tried to balance her cup in the midst of the laughter saying, "I am sorry. I know you are right."

Mother Dunkin asked, "Have you seen your family yet, Sister Bunny?"

"We're going to a party at my brother's house for New Year's Eve."

"Will your mother be there?"

"I'm sure she wouldn't miss it. Everybody who's anybody will be there."

Pastor Dan added, "Even us."

"By default," Bunny said, rolling her eyes. "No, honestly, she is doing very well. We are still praying."

"How many children have you smuggled out of de country this year?" asked one of Vincent's cousins.

Bunny answered, "Three hundred and forty-two."

"How can you save so many when there are only de two of you?" asked Pastor Dunkin.

Pastor Dan answered, "The missionary alliance has sent us reinforcements. There are six of us."

Freida said, "We are very fortunate to live in this country. It iss good you are home now, safe and sound.

Mother Dunkin said, "Everyone has their cup, yah? Shall we say a prayer of thanksgiving, dear?"

Pastor Dunkin answered, "Are you children ready? Freida, could you hold your little Liza's cup for her while she bows her head?"

Freida whispered, "Liza, let Mamma hold your cup. We do not want to spill. Thank you, sweet girl."

"Ah, praise you Jesus," prayed Pastor Dunkin. "There iss so much to be grateful for."

> Luke 1:46–50. My soul doth magnify the Lord, and my spirit hath rejoiced in God my Savior. For he hath regarded the low estate of his handmaiden: for, behold, from henceforth all generations shall call me blessed. For he that is mighty hath done to me great things; and holy is his name. And his mercy is on them that fear him from generation to generation.

Sources

Mrs. Carol Everett
Abortionist Turns Pro-Life
Tape CS429/118
Focus on the Family Ministry
Colorado Springs, Colorado
1994

Adrian Rogers
Countdown in the Holy Land
Daniel 9:24
Tape S-HO5-P RA-1512
Love Worth Finding Ministries
Memphis, Tennessee

Doctor D. James Kennedy
Something from Nothing: Shattering Existing Myths
Evolution's Bloopers and Blunders
Coral Ridge Ministries
Fort Lauderdale, Florida

Published by Wolgemuth and Hyatt

Merle and Phyllis Good
Twenty Most Asked Questions about the Amish and
Mennonites
People's Place Book No. 1
Published by Good Books
Intercourse, Pennsylvania
1995

Songs:

America the Beautiful
Lyrics by Katherine L. Bates
Composed by Samuel A. Ward

Blessed Assurance
Lyrics by Fanny Crosby
Composed by Phoebe Knapp

Jesus Loves Me
Lyrics by Susan Warner
Composed by William B. Bradbury

O Little Town of Bethlehem
Lyrics by Philips Brooks
Composed by Lewis H. Redner

Respect
Composed by Anthony Roberson
Performed by Aretha Franklin
Aretha's Best
Rhino Records
2001

Sources

Twelve Days of Christmas
Eighteenth Century Folk Song

You'll Never Find Another Love Like Mine
Composed by Kenny Gambles and Leon Huff
Performed by Lou Rawls
Lou Rawls Greatest Hits
Capital Records

You've Got a Friend
Composed by Carole King
Performed by James Taylor
Mud Slide Slim
Warner Brothers
1971

You Always Hurt the One You Love
Composed by Allen Roberts and Doris Fisher

To order additional copies of

ON EARTH AS IT IS IN HEAVEN

Have your credit card ready and call:

1-877-421-READ (7323)

or please visit our web site at
www.pleasantword.com

Also available at: www.amazon.com